William Stephens Hayward

The Black Flag

A romance

William Stephens Hayward

The Black Flag
A romance

ISBN/EAN: 9783337102845

Printed in Europe, USA, Canada, Australia, Japan

Cover: Foto ©Andreas Hilbeck / pixelio.de

More available books at **www.hansebooks.com**

THE
BLACK FLAG

A Romance

BY

W. S. HAYWARD

AUTHOR OF 'HUNTED TO DEATH,' 'LOVE AGAINST THE WORLD,'
'STOLEN WILL,' ETC., ETC.

LONDON:

JOHN AND ROBERT MAXWELL

MILTON HOUSE, 35, ST. BRIDE STREET, LUDGATE CIRCUS,

AND

14 AND 15, SHOE LANE, FLEET STREET, E.C.

CONTENTS.

CHAP.		PAGE
I.—THE SEA-EAGLE IN A CAGE		7
II.—THE STRANGER GUEST		9
III.—THE VOLUNTEER AID		16
IV.—SNATCHED FROM THE SEA		19
V.—THE SPANISH BEAUTY		24
VI.—LOVE'S AURORA		30
VII.—THE LOVER'S PLIGHT		34
VIII.—A MARVELLOUS HORSE TRADE		42
IX.—WHEN WOMAN COMES IN AT THE WINDOW MONEY FLIES OUT AT THE DOOR		51
X.—THE FRIEND IN NEED AGAIN		66
XI.—FINE FEATHERS		70
XII.—A HIGHWAYMAN FROM BENEVOLENCE		74
XIII.—BENDING A BUTTERFLY AND BREAKING A BAR		86
XIV.—A CURIOUS LOVE-TRYST		103
XV.—A CROSSING OF SWORDS AND WITS		111
XVI.—QUEEN AND FONDLING		121
XVII.—KING AND CORSAIR		124
XVIII.—THE REVELATION		131
XIX.—ANOTHER EVENING OUT		134
XX.—THE DOUBLE ARREST		140
XXI.—THE TRAP		148
XXII.—THE ESCAPE		155
XXIII.—THE NEW LIFE COMMENCES		160
XXIV.—THE FREEBOOTERS AT HOME		165
XXV.—WILLDFLOWER		169
XXVI.—SAVED FROM THE SPANIARDS		173
XXVII.—THE DUEL COMES TO AN UNEXPECTED END		180

CHAP.		PAGE
XXVIII.—A DAREDEVIL PROJECT		185
XXIX.—THE UNSOUGHT PASSENGER		191
XXX.—THE GUILELESS MAIDEN		193
XXXI.—THE WOMAN SCORNED		199
XXXII.—THE TWO AGAINST THE TOWN		206
XXXIII.—THE COPE COVERS MANY SINNERS		212
XXXIV.—DOVE AND RAVEN		218
XXXV.—THE LONG CHASE		226
XXXVI.—THE WASP AND THE BULL		233
XXXVII.—THE TORNADO		239
XXXVIII.—THE SINKING SHIP		244
XXXIX.—THE RESCUE		248
XL.—THE CAVERN-HARBOUR		251
XLI.—THE REVOLT		255
XLII.—THE CRITICAL MOMENT		260
XLIII.—THE REMEDY		262
XLIV.—WILDFLOWER'S DEPARTURE		265
XLV.—WILD MEN AND WILD CATTLE		270
XLVI.—WILDFLOWER AT HOME		279
XLVII.—THE SPUR TO THE WAR-HORSE		282
XLVIII.—EVERY MAN HAS HIS PRICE		286
XLIX.—THE SEA-EAGLES ASSEMBLE		289
L.—THE COUNCIL OF WAR		297
LI.—THE INCONVENIENCE OF SHORT SIGHT IN GENERALS		302
LII.—TAKING THE FORT		306
LIII.—THE AVENGER		317
LIV.—THE JACOBITE PLOT		323
LV.—THE FIRST BLOW		328
LVI.—THE SECOND BLOW		337
LVII.—NATIVA REAPPEARS		340
LVIII.—TAKEN UNAWARES		345
LIX.—NATIVA'S REVENGE		349
LX.—IN THE COILS		352
LXI.—THE RESCUE		356
LXII.—FALLEN FROM HIS HIGH ESTATE		368
LXIII.—WHICH WAS THE GRANDER?		373
LXIV.—THE END		381

THE BLACK FLAG:

A ROMANCE OF THE GOLDEN INDIES.

CHAPTER I.

THE SEA-EAGLE IN A CAGE.

In the year 1694 there stood, a mile from the village of Penmark, in Cornwall, and near the sea, a small house roughly built of clay and fragments of rock. It was a dull, solitary place, unlikely to attract the notice of travellers.

A weather-cock, surmounted by a coronet, proudly adorned one end of the roof. The stable was of recent construction, with an elegance and stability which suited the belongings of a castle rather than the odd mass of buildings to which it was annexed.

Penmark, in the year 1694—since when the state of things has greatly altered—was, on account of the evil reputation of its inhabitants, visited by few strangers, to say nothing of its inaccessibility.

Of a fierce and sanguinary character, greedy of gain, proof to pity, always ready for theft, or even murder, the wreckers of Penmark, unlike other Englishmen, only gave shelter to strangers with the intention of killing them. The means of living which this wretched people had in the seventeenth century were extremely limited. The only pursuits known to them were fishing and smuggling ; and, indeed, so famous were their want of honour and their ungovernable violence that their bad repute nearly deprived them of the latter resources, for people inland feared to have any business transactions with such a set of sea-ruffians.

The principal—almost their only—resource concording with their habits, was the right of collecting the spoils cast on shore from vessels lost at sea. By an extension of the custom the wreckers considered whole vessels as equally their jetsam ; and as the tempest-beaten and dangerous coast was fruitful in wrecks the inhabitants of Penmark did not fail to gather an abundant

harvest by their infamous industry. We need not dwell upon
details universally known with regard to the shameful deceits
practised to aid the ravages of the winds and waves ; how on
the approach of a storm the wreckers never failed to drive cows
along the shore with lights fixed to their horns and their forelegs
tied, a device which at a distance gives an exact imitation of the
motion of a labouring vessel. The luckless seamen deceived by
the resemblance believed they had the open sea before them, and
ran on the rocks. We omit as well the hideous details of their
barbarity ; how misfortune claimed in vain their pity ; and how
they threw back into the sea the unconscious victims who had
escaped a watery grave. The aspect of the coast is in character
with these ancient inhabitants. The imagination could scarcely
conceive a more gloomy and inhospitable landscape.

Seaward, the eye beholds only rocks, a barren coast, and
foaming waves ; on land, dreary and deserted wastes of barren
heath.

The ground-floor of the small dwelling mentioned consisted
of two rooms only—a kitchen and a larder ; above were a sitting
and a bedroom.

In the first, meanly and scantily furnished, sat a young man
of some five-and-twenty, before a table covered with maps. His
face, square rather than oval, denoted considerable energy ; his
thick black hair fell over a broad forehead tanned with exposure
to the weather ; his dark eyes looked as if they dared face either
foe or danger undaunted. A slender moustache covered the
young man's upper lip, and his teeth were remarkably small and
close together. His figure, which was a little above the middle
height, was strong, active, and well developed. Notwithstanding
his round shoulders and slight stoop, his appearance was distinguished and even graceful. Such was our hero, Sir Lewis
Morgan.

It was at the beginning of June, about five in the afternoon.
The day had been very hot, and the air was heavy with the
electricity that always precedes a storm. Soon a loud clap of
thunder, repeated by a hundred echoes, sounded like a park of
artillery as it rolled from rock to rock.

Morgan, starting impatiently as if he wished to chase away
some importunate idea, rose from his chair and walked to a
window looking out on to the sea. As he leant forward on the
balustrade an extraordinary sound which resembled the distant
roar of an infuriated lion rose above the harsh murmur of the
waves.

The young man turned pale, and, biting his lip, walked up
and down the apartment. Every time that he passed a pair of
richly-ornamented pistols hanging against the wall, he stopped
and looked at them, and then continued his walk. It was easy

to see by his contracted brows that deeds of violence were in his thoughts. Appearing at length to have made up his mind upon some question which he had been debating, he opened the door of the room, and in a tone of command called "Allan." Twice he repeated the summons. Almost instantly the noise of heavy shoes was heard upon the stairs, and a short and negligently-dressed young man presented himself. He slightly touched his cap and awaited the orders of his master.

'Is the brig ready to sail?' asked Morgan.

'If you wish so she can stand out in an hour,' answered Allan, scratching his ear; 'but I hope you will not risk her ribs.'

'And wherefore should I not, sirrah?' returned the knight.

'Because it would be a fool's trick to put to sea when the Friar Rock howls so that you can hear him twenty miles round. It would be a sheer tempting of Providence! Lend an ear to 't, sir!'

The strange roar was heard again louder than before.

The master and servant gazed at each other a moment in silence.

'What do you say to that?' asked Allan.

'I answer that if I delay one hour, the Cornish coast by day-break to-morrow will be heaped with wreckage.'

A smile of satisfaction, not unmarked by Morgan, passed over Allan's face.

CHAPTER II.

THE STRANGER GUEST.

'By George! if I did not know you, Allan,' said the knight, 'to be an honest knave, that smile of yours would have cost you a thrashing. Are you not ashamed to be more pitiless than the sea, and rob and murder the poor wretches that are cast on shore? Can you be such a monster? Come, let us hear what excuse you can urge for such revolting cruelty!'

Allan listened to this rough speech in respectful silence.

'You won't thrash me, master,' he answered quietly; 'you are too honourable to take advantage of your superior strength. It would be vain to give you my reasons, for they would only make you angry.'

The rustic's bluntness disarmed the gentleman's anger.

'Well, Allan, tell me, and I promise not to be wroth.'

'Oh, sir, since it is your command, I desire nothing better than to tell you my mind,' answered the servant, rubbing his hands; 'but, first, you must know that there is not a man in all Penmark but hates and detests you.'

'Me?' cried Morgan hastily; 'pray what have I done to win their hatred?'

'You have never respected our old customs! you have always set your face against Godsends and windfalls! All along the coast that's the name for everything thrown up from the open sea.'

'But this custom is atrocious, Allan.'

'How can that be,' answered the man, 'since it is heavenly doing? To return to what concerns you, folk pretend that at Oxford College you learnt all sorts of foreign customs, though at fourteen you were the best at single-stick in the whole duchy, and could wing a duck with your musketoon at a hundred paces, and now, forsooth, you never use anything but a pistol. Pistols, indeed, are good playthings enough for those town gallants, but are unworthy of a man who can shoulder a ducking-gun. But I am only making you warm.'

'Go on, Allan, don't hide anything from me.'

'Then they insist that you don't fear Friday as a sailing day, and only make sport of pixies and goblins that wander of a night about the heaths and marshes.'

'Well, it is a fact; I don't believe in goblins,' answered Morgan gravely, 'but I am too sound a churchgoer not to mind Fridays. Why, have you not observed, Allan, that when the weather is stormy I never put to sea on a Friday, or on the thirteenth of the month?'

'Why, that is true enow; but as regards pixies?'

'Well, Allan man, what can I do if I *can't* believe in them?'

'Oh, but it shows a sad sort of religion! Still, I believe the neighbours would overlook that if you only respected the law of the coast, and did not fly to the aid of shipwrecks as you do.'

'I am sorry to be out of favour with the good people of Penmark; still, they must put up with me as I am constituted; for never will I consent by a shameful connivance to be an accomplice in their murders. If they don't like my conduct let them come and complain to me. The Morgans know how to answer cavillers fist to fist.'

'Oh, there is no fear that they'll blame you to your face. They know too well that when you say to a man, "You are guilty, and shall be punished," that the fellow is in luck if he only gets a broken limb; but you will see one of these days they will do you a mischief! so be on your guard.'

'I do distrust them, Allan. For a long time I have noticed the black looks the rogues give us when you and I put to sea at the approach of a storm. In future we will go armed. Take your cutlass, and I will carry my pistols.'

'Then you won't give up tempting fate on the sea?' asked Allan, in a vexed tone.

'Less than ever. I am now going to the cliff to spy for a sail in the offing. Let the brig be ready on my return.'

' What a misfortune it is,' groaned Allan in a despairing tone, ' that you, who are so clever, cannot understand that old Ocean's gifts are sacred !'

' Do you refuse to go with me ? Then I sail alone.'

' Oh, master !' cried Allan mournfully, ' what have I done to be treated thus ? Have I not always faithfully earned my wages ? But since you have lived among those city people even plain truth angers you. I am ready to go with you, but if the fishers should try to stop our going—which would not astonish me if you see Tregallac among them—what can we do ? That rascal would raise the whole village against you ?'

' Have you never tried to silence him ?'

' Indeed but I have, master mine ! I have grappled fins with him half-a-dozen tries ; but unluckily, as we are about level in strength and skill, I have not been able to floor him. But when I say we are equal, I don't do myself justice—the odds are in my favour, for though he has smashed three of my teeth, I have broken four of his—so I have good hope of mastering him in the last tussle.'

' Let us waste no more time in words,' interrupted Morgan. ' Hie you to the boat, while I scan the horizon. The storm will be upon us in less than an hour.'

In spite of this dismissal Allan remained stationary.

' Don't you hear me ?' said his master impatiently.

' Yes ; but before we push off I have a duty to fulfil, and I beg you to spare me a short time.'

' What is it, Allan ?'

' I want to set up a candle in the church for our success to-night.'

' Is that all ?'

' I'll swear it if you like.'

' Take you half-an-hour ; and here is half-a-crown to help on your pious work. Make haste.'

The man greedily snatched the piece of money which his master offered him, in two bounds cleared the staircase, and set off with all speed towards the village. Although the distance was nearly a mile Allan reached it in ten minutes, and entering the church bought an end of wax-taper and fell to praying.

Scarcely had he finished his prayer before the taper was burned out. Allan then desired the sacristan to light two double candles, for which he paid. This prayer was that the Good Lady of Penmark would prevent his master's embarking that night.

Allan watched the candles burning brightly, and added a petition that the storm might bring many wrecks to that shore, and that he might break Tregallac's ribs the next time they fought.

When the candles were burnt out Allan rose joyfully, and rushed out of the church with the same impetuosity with which he had entered.

At the turn of the road, half-way between the village and his master's house, Allan made a sudden stop to avoid falling under the feet of a horse coming towards him, but not soon enough to avoid contact with the animal which, being startled, swerved on one side, nearly unseating his rider.

'Stupid ass!' cried the rider.

'Thou tailor!' shouted Allan, simultaneously, both considering themselves aggrieved.

'What does the knave mutter?' continued the horseman, feeling for his pistols.

Allan had that prudent courage which only fights when backed by a strong chance of success. This was not the case now, so he smothered his resentment for the present, knowing he should find it still green and fresh when an opportunity for revenge offered. Seeing the bright barrels of the stranger's pistols, Allan knew that his iron-knobbed stick stood a poor chance, so quenching the fury of his gaze under an idiotic stare, he looked at his adversary as if not understanding what he said.

'Come, varlet!' cried the horseman, smiling and changing his tone, ' you are a true peasant, and no mistake ; but that fool's look does not go down with me ; I am awake to such tricks. Let us rather have a friendly chat ; I want to ask you a few questions.'

Allan, although inwardly disconcerted by this speech, pretended not to understand, and put on even a more vacant look.

At this the horseman burst out laughing, and feeling in his pocket drew forth a crown, leant forward and presented it to Allan, who after a slight hesitation seized it quickly.

'Come, I am glad to see your senses are coming back,' said the rider gaily.

'What do you want now?' asked Allan, anxious to be off.

'I only want you to answer a few unimportant questions.'

'And for that you give me a crown? Well, if that be your fashion, say what you want to know.'

' You belong, no doubt, to you village of Penmark, and know Sir Lewis Morgan?'

Allan was not a little astonished at hearing his master's name, but he answered carelessly, ' Yes, I know the knight ; as every one knows him,' he added, after a slight hesitation.

'What sort of a man is he?'

'Oh, a man like others.'

'With such answers you run no risk of committing yourself.'

'In sooth, I answer what you ask me. I am a poor ignorant fellow ; I only understand what is told me. But I am in a hurry to be off.'

'More fool you,' said the other quietly; 'I was about to give you another crown.'

'Oh, I have time enough to take that.'

'Nay, on second thoughts I shall keep it, and hand it to the next knave I meet who will give me better information about the gentleman than you can do.'

Allan hesitated a moment before he said, 'No one can tell you as much about the knight as I can, for I am his servant; only, make haste, for I am in a great hurry.'

'Ah! the knight's servant; and never told me, you knave.'

'You did not ask me!'

'You are right, there. Now, what is your master's disposition?'

'He is a devout gentleman.'

The horseman knit his brows, and said in a stern, sharp tone, 'Explain! What do you mean by that?'

'I call things by their right names. I say the knight is a pious noble, for he is kind and generous to the poor, as gentle as a lamb with children, and as terrible as an enraged wolf with the wicked.'

This answer apparently gave much satisfaction to the stranger, who smiled as he said,—

'Then your master, it seems, is not a man to trifle with.'

'If you have come to Penmark to pick a quarrel with him, my advice is, "Be off!" It is well worth a couple of crowns, and you will never lay out your money better.'

'Your master, then, is a hard nut to deal with?'

'Hard, forsooth! why, there is not his equal for twenty miles round. Tregallac and I are the two stoutest in Penmark; but one day, at his bidding, I had a wrestle with the knight, and he squeezed me so tight that all my bones cracked, and if it had not been out of respect for him and the education I have had, I should have screamed like a scalded cat.'

'Tell me if the chevalier has many flames?'

At this question Allan coloured and looked angrily at his questioner.

'If you think for the sake of a crown you can insult my master before my face, you are mistaken. I have only my cudgel against your pistols, but, zounds! don't try it again, or I'll try the odds.'

Allan's anger must have been very great thus to master his caution. But the questioner, instead of taking his threats in bad part, only seemed gratified with what he had heard.

'Here, good lad, is the crown I promised you. Go your road; I will not keep you any longer. By the way, which is the best inn at Penmark?'

'There is no inn.'

'And where does your master live?'

'In that house by itself that you see close to the shore.'

'Well, good-bye for the present. As there is no inn, I must find a lodging in one of the cottages.'

'If you will take the advice of an honest man you will not seek a lodging or stay one night in Penmark. A gentleman who is as free of his money as you are ought never to have come here.'

'Oh, I am acquainted with the hospitable habits of the Penmarkers,' answered the stranger, on whom Allan's advice produced no alarm; 'I shall be upon my guard.'

A violent clap of thunder interrupted the conversation; the two men separated, the stranger no doubt to obtain shelter, Allan to rejoin his master.

As Allan placed immense faith in the efficacy of candles, he was not very much surprised on reaching the shore to meet his master, who told him that no sail being visible they were not going to put to sea. The servant, therefore, rejoicing at his first wish having been so promptly fulfilled, took for granted that his second would be so likewise, and, consequently, the night would not pass over without bringing numerous wrecks on shore.

So he hastened back to his master's house to be out of the way of the storm, as heavy drops already began to fall; in truth, scarcely had the knight and his servant reached home when the storm burst in fury. It was then six o'clock. Sir Lewis stood at the window of the sitting-room facing the sea, looking on with a mournful gaze at the sublime, yet awful spectacle of the fury of the elements; his thoughts meanwhile were sad.

'That ocean,' he murmured to himself, 'is the image of my heart: it is stirred by the tempest, as my heart is by passions. Mad dreams, bold projects, fierce passions, unbounded ambition, all by turns have inspired, then shattered me. Have you not also wrecked my soul? How much have I hoped, how much endured! But the ocean, when unchained, leaves at least marks of its anger; whilst I, crushed beneath my humble lot, have not the power of influencing the fate of the least of my fellow-men. In the world of men I am like a grain of sand—an atom! What human being cares for my life or would mourn my death? Not one. Yet I can love and hate with fervour! I feel within myself that undaunted strength which lifts a man out of the unknown herd to power and influence. Only I want a starting point—encouragement, advice! And who takes any interest in me? No one.'

As the Knight of Penmark murmured these last words a violent knocking at the door made him start. Superstitious, like most half-read men of his period, he thought that Heaven had heard his prayer and sent him the friend he wished for, therefore it was with some slight emotion he saw Allan approach.

Master,' said the servant, 'a stranger asks for shelter for himself and his horse.'

'Put the horse in the stable, and tell the stranger that I shall be happy to receive him; but no, stop! I had better go myself.'

'You need not trouble, sir; he is coming up.'

The servant had scarcely uttered the words before the new-comer entered the room. He threw a rapid glance around, and slightly bowing to the host whilst pointing to his wet clothes, said,—

'I fancied, sir, that my deplorable condition would be my best letter of introduction to you.'

It was the same person whom Allan had met.

The stranger's rough manner of introducing himself rather surprised Morgan, but he answered with cool politeness,—

'There is no need of introduction; I count it a duty and an honour to open my doors to whoever asks for hospitality.'

'A duty it may be, but an honour is another thing,' said the horseman, unceremoniously shaking the water from his hat. 'You may thus run the risk of receiving very indifferent company. But, after all, the shore of Penmark is so little frequented by strangers that your generosity may not be greatly taxed. What dreadful weather! Hark! What is that loud moaning heard even above the roar of the waves and wind?'

'It comes from Friar Rock,' said Morgan, with a shade of sullenness, for the easy, vulgar manners of his guest vexed him.

'What is the Friar Rock?'

'A natural well between two rocks close to the entrance of the village is filled every tide. Tradition relates that a monk fell into the chasm chasing a village maiden, and since then it always moans at the approach of a storm. The truth is, that at that place there are vast subterranean caves, and that roaring is caused by the sea entering and finding no issue.'

'I am astonished that a Cornishman should ascribe a natural cause for such a phenomenon,' answered the stranger, laughing loudly, 'for you must allow that your neighbours are absurdly credulous.'

On hearing this speech the knight was obliged to remember his position as host, but he could not help regarding with more attention than he had hitherto done the man who so ill-requited his hospitality.

About fifty years of age, and dressed in the style usually adopted by farmers and tradespeople of the seventeenth century, this individual had nothing remarkable in his person. His complexion was, however, deeply sunburnt; his insignificant countenance denoted little intelligence; his large, rather square-shaped head was fixed on a bull-neck; his stout figure—at least so it seemed in his thick great-coat—was scarcely over five feet four ; he wore no beard. In regard to his expression, it was rather gentle and jovial instead of rough and impertinent as might have been judged by his previous conversation.

'He is a good heart who has not seen polite society,' thought Morgan ; 'it would be folly to take umbrage at his want of tact.'

In the meanwhile the stranger, unaware of the scrutiny to which he was subject, left his chair, and walking up and down the room amused himself with inventorying everything it contained.

'Odsfish ?' he cried, stopping suddenly before a long gun hanging against the wall, 'here is an odd fire-iron ; I have never seen its like. What can its use be ? Perhaps to shoot wild-fowl. Allow me.' Without finishing his sentence he took down the long gun and began to examine it with the eye of a marksman.

'That gun was made by Gideon, of Sheffield,' answered Morgan complacently ; 'it is of very great range, and is not now used in Europe.'

'Why not in Europe ? Prithee, where then ?'

'Five thousand miles from here ; in the Western Isles.'

'Oh, yes, I know ; a fine country where the land needs no tilling, and harvests of gold and rubies come without labour— save of the sword-arm.'

CHAPTER III.

THE VOLUNTEER AID.

'Have you been to the Indies then ?' asked Morgan in great astonishment.

'I ! what an idea ! I am a horsedealer. Ireland and the south coast are the only parts of the world I know ; but a kinsman of mine spent ten years over the seas, and he told me all about the country. It seems a man may make a good living there if he have a strong arm, a quick eye, and is not too squeamish.'

'Ah, you have a kinsman ten years in the West,' repeated Morgan slowly, as if he were pondering deeply ; 'tell me,' he went on, fixing his eyes eagerly on the stranger, 'did your cousin succeed ?'

'I should rather think he did ! Indeed, when he went away he had only a penny in his pocket and scarcely shoes to his feet, and now he possesses a hundred thousand crowns and rides in his glass coach.'

'He has been very fortunate,' said Morgan, sighing.

'So he has ; but then, it seems, every one is lucky there. If

I were young I should not hesitate to set off even if I had to work
my passage out. Zookers !' continued the horsedealer after a
short silence, 'why should not you who are in the prime of life
try your fortune there ? I don't know you, it is true, but judging
from appearances fortune has not overwhelmed you with her
gifts. Quite the contrary; but why need you blush and turn
angry ? I don't say so with any wish to hurt your feelings. I
am a plain dealer, and say what I think. The life that you must
lead here does not suit the activity of youth. At five-and-twenty
one does not mew one's self up like an owl in an old rusty mansion.
Why, in your place I would rather be a hermit ; at all events,
that would be a trade of some sort.'

'I am a gentleman, sir,' said the knight haughtily, thinking
to cut short his companion's observations and advice, but it had
not the desired effect.· The stranger only laughed and said,—

'Oh, you would have astonished me much if you had said the
contrary ! is not every one in Cornwall a noble ? Your ba-
ronial residence is splendid : four cracked walls and a tumble-
down roof. If your castle imposes much over your vassals,
those good soft fellows must ——'

'I beg, sir, you will cease this conversation,' interrupted the
knight, imperiously rising, his face and lips pale with the effort
he made to control his passion. 'As your host, I have endured
enough from your want of good manners to have a right to desire
you to be silent. What is your name, sir ?'

'Matthewson,' said the horsedealer, not in the least affected
by the outbreak of the young man.·

'Well, Master Matthewson, have the kindness to go downstairs,
where my servant will give you what you need. I wish to be alone.'

The horsedealer obeyed this rough dismissal, without showing
in his countenance shame or anger.

His quiet manner made the host ashamed of his harshness,
and he considered that he had no right to be angry with a man
for his ignorance of good conduct ; so he determined by special
politeness and attention to make amends for his misbehaviour.
When, an hour later, Allan went to tell him supper was ready,
Morgan entering the kitchen, which also served as a dining-
room, went up to Matthewson, and, holding out his hand, said,

'I claim your indulgence for the poor repast set before you,
as you took me unawares.'

The horsedealer accepted the proffered hand in a friendly
manner, and sat down to table without observations, whilst
Allan, according to old usage, seated himself at the lower end.

The first part of the supper passed in silence. In vain Sir
Lewis made various efforts to excite conversation. Matthewson
always received what he said with an approving nod and a pleasant smile, but answered not a word.

Out of humour that his advances were not responded to, the noble was hastening to finish the slice of cold meat on his plate, that he might leave the table. when Allan, busy in despatching an enormous basin of broth, suddenly stopped, and looking aghast at his master, cried,—

'Did you hear that, sir ?'

'What, that last thunderclap ; of course ! What makes you ask ?'

'Oh, nothing,' responded Allan, applying himself again to his basin.

'Do you think that thunderclap threatens a yet greater storm ?'

'Oh, no, sir, I only spoke for the sake of talking.'

A minute later the knight thrust his plate from him and listened attentively.

'Why, that is not thunder,' he exclaimed, leaving his seat and hastening to the door ; 'it is a heavy gun !'

'Aye, I knew that,' muttered Allan, 'my candles have brought that about, thank thee, our dear lady !'

'Allan,' cried Morgan, 'quick, to the oars, it is a vessel in distress !'

'Set out !' responded the servant in dismay ; 'one might as well leap head foremost down into the Friar's Cell as put to sea in such a storm.'

'What, you're afraid, Allan ! then stay on shore.'

'Yes, I am afeard.'

'Yes, you are afraid of being drowned, and still more of Tregallac opposing our putting off.'

'What, me afeard on Tregallac ! have I not already broken his jaw?' and full of passion, Allan caught up a pair of long oars standing against the wall, and laying them on his shoulders, said, 'I am ready, master.'

'I must fetch my cloak and pistols,' observed Sir Lewis Morgan, hastily mounting the stairs ; but returning almost instautly, he added, 'Come along.'

The horsedealer, who had not moved, now rose, and said very gravely to his host : 'Sir knight, as you desired me not to speak unless spoken to, I've obeyed you. Now, though, will you allow me to accompany you ? I am no seaman, it is true, but any one can use an oar, and in such a storm as this, in an open boat, another pair of hands is not to be despised.'

This unexpected request made an impression on the young gentleman which he sought not to conceal.

'I accept your offer, sir,' he answered ; 'you have a noble heart, which I have misunderstood. I crave you to forgive my foolish anger.'

'Tut, men never think of the past. But time is precious, come on,' said the horsedealer.

CHAPTER IV.

SNATCHED FROM THE SEA.

WHEN the three sailed forth to succour the ship in distress the coast of Penmark presented a strange and mournful sight. A cow with a lantern was hobbling along, followed by a hideous crowd of women with dishevelled hair and clothes in disorder, whose vile greediness made them insensible to the raging of the pitiless storm. Men armed with knives and long boathooks wandered like ghosts along the shore.

Here and there was to be seen a Penmarker, kneeling on the sand, praying that heaven might send them many shipwrecks. It seemed a whole population of cannibals or murderers.

Although the night was dark, the approach of Morgan and his two companions was quickly perceived by the villagers, and they had scarcely reached their boat before they were surrounded.

Morgan, as the wisest thing he could do, pretended not to be aware of this, and, with Allan's aid, began quietly to bring out his boat. Whilst he put forth all his strength to do this, he yet managed to keep a vigilant eye on the crowd; some had got so near as even to hustle him. He jumped on board his boat, and taking out his pistols, cried: 'My good men, you mind what you are about! stick to your own craft, and leave me to mine. You know me well enough to trust my word, and I swear by St. Bridget that I will fire at the first man who stops me.'

At these threatening words the beachcombers drew back, grumbling.

'Sir Lewis,' said one voice from the crowd, 'a gentleman born should have a little more respect for our privileges if you want us to respect yours. Heaven's gifts belong to us; so beware yourself!'

'Sir,' whispered Allan to his master, 'that's Tregallac! be on your guard, for he is a tricky rogue.'

Morgan might have replied, but three guns fired rapidly by the vessel in distress made him prefer acts to words, and he pushed his boat off the shingle.

Judging by the threats of the mob that a contest was imminent, Allan looked around to see if he had any chance in a fight with Tregallac, but finding him surrounded by partisans he hastened after his master into the boat, which was floating twenty feet off shore.

His flight made the Penmarkers still more daring. When the horsedealer Matthewson was about to follow, he was surrounded by the furious mob. Hitherto he had remained quiet and unconcerned, as if, either from bravery or stupidity, quite unconscious of the hostile attitude of the bystanders.

'This stranger at all events shall not spoil sport,' cried Tregallac, seizing Matthewson by the collar, 'we won't be deprived of our rights by him.'

'Friend,' responded the horsedealer, 'if you have the right to stop me, you have none to tear my clothes. I will remain quietly, but if you maul-handle me it is another matter ; and so I warn you, "paws off ! " '

'Come, Master Matthewson,' cried Morgan, not aware of the critical position of his guest, and keeping the boat within wading distance.

'Good friend,' said the horsedealer, facing Tregallac, 'you hear ? I am called. I have no time to lose ; so tell me straightway what right you have to keep me, or let me go.'

'The right of the strongest rules here !' answered Tregallac, raising his cutlass.

'Then it follows by the same right that I should free myself,' answered the peaceable stranger, suddenly snatching the other's cutlass, and laying about him vigorously with the flat of its broad blade.

In less time than it takes to write it, three smugglers lay half dead at his feet ; it is needless to add that the threatening crowd had dispersed as if by magic.

'I am very sorry I got wroth,' remarked Matthewson to the fugitives, 'my nature is gentleness itself when let alone ! but I gave you warning.' Still armed with Tregallac's cutlass, he waded quietly into the sea, and clambered on board the boat.

'Shall I steer ?' he asked the gentleman.

'Do you know how ?'

'Not too well ; it is out of my line.'

'Then take an oar and pull with Allan, while I hold the helm.'

Without a word about the danger he had just escaped, Matthewson took an oar.

He certainly made up for his want of politeness, by knowing when to act and when to be silent.

The worst dangers of the little crew only began when the boat had passed out of the creek into the boiling eddies of the raging waters. The oldest seafarer would have shrunk appalled. The wind stood so furiously towards shore, that the efforts of the three could scarcely bear up against it, and their progress was very slow.

'Take care, master,' shouted Allan, 'I see some one on the rocks with a musketoon.'

'There is no fear ! the night is too dark, even if he has a gun, for him to take aim,' answered the master carelessly.

'Boat ahoy !' roared a voice from the rocks, 'good luck to you ! but if anything happens, remember you sailed on a Friday !'

These words made so strong an impression on both Morgan and his servant, that the first let go the tiller, and the latter caught a crab.

'If that's the way you manage boats,' commented Matthewson very coolly, 'it's useless to try and aid others, and we had better turn back.'

'Oh, Lor'! it is too true! this is Friday!' moaned Allan, overwhelmed with the fatal discovery.

'Fool,' cried Matthewson; 'what, have you fifty-two misfortunes befall ye in a year?'

'No!'

'Well, then, why do you specialize Friday?'

'Oh, I am an ass,' returned Allan eagerly; 'I forgot that I wear a medal of our Lady round my neck, so I need fear no danger.'

Reassured by this thought, Allan returned to his oar, and Morgan steadied the helm, ashamed of giving way before one who had no superstition.

Guided only by the guns that at uncertain intervals were fired from the bark in distress, the adventurers pursued their way at a venture. The night was so dark and the sea so tempestuous, that nothing was visible half a cable's length. Sir Lewis, steering with considerable skill and consummate coolness, was well seconded by Allan and Matthewson; the latter, especially, though he had said rowing was not in his line, showing great address with the oar.

Twenty times they were in peril of foundering, and as often their united energy, intrepidity, and skill saved them from impending danger.

Chance seemed at last to second their heroic efforts. Towards three in the morning, after striving six hours against the storm, the wind slightly lowered, and the sea became rather calmer. Morgan profited by this truce of the elements to consult his companions, for they had not spoken a word the live-long night.

'I regret, mates,' he said, for nothing puts men so much on a par as imminent danger,—'I regret that you cannot take my place at the helm, for you must be overcome with fatigue. Lie a moment on your oars, while I look out.'

'I don't understand rowing, and I dare say I am awkward enough at it,' apologized Matthewson, 'but I am not at all tired; but I should be glad of a mouthful of brandy.'

'That is easily got at,' remarked the helmsman, unrolling his great coat in which he had taken the precaution to wrap his pistols, 'I have a bottle in my pocket!'

'Your brandy is not over strong, but it will do very well,' observed Matthewson, passing the half-empty flask to Allan. 'Where do you take us to be? I fancy we cannot be more

than a mile and a half west of Penmark, and not more than five
hundred feet from shore.'

'You are right.'

'Come, come, I shall think myself a regular tar before long !
and this encourages me, Sir Lewis, to ask you a question.   Pray
what was your motive in setting out ?'

'Why, you know as well as I do it was to help the poor
creatures who implore our aid and count on our courage.'

'Oh, I know that !   What I want to learn is, in what way
you hope to be of use ?'

'Simply by being their pilot ; preventing their being deceived
by the lights, and in consequence falling into the hands of the
Penmarkers.'

'Do you know how to steer great ships, then ?'

'I have gone two voyages to Ireland, and I am well acquainted
with this coast.   If I can only reach the vessel before she strikes
on the rocks, and while she still obeys the helm, I will engage to
bring her safe into harbour.'

Whilst he was still speaking, a loud report made the boat rock ;
it was the last appeal for help of the labouring vessel, scarcely a
cable's length from them.

Morgan headed towards the sound ; his companions plied their
oars vigorously, and in less than five minutes they were along side
a large three-master.

'God o' mercy,' groaned the gentleman, 'the ship is lost ! she
has foundered on the Devil's Head.'

The wrecked ship lay on her side, in danger every moment of
being engulfed in the waves, while cries of distress arose from
all on board.

'I think,' said Matthewson, 'that the best thing for us to do
would be to go back.   There is not the slightest chance of saving
the ship ; we had better take advantage of this lull to get back !
who knows if an hour later we may be able to reach the shore
ourselves ?'

'Oh, pray, master, let us go back !' said Allan, eager for his
share of wreckage.

'Silence,' thundered his master, ' I know as well as you that to
save the ship would be impossible ; but we may snatch a few from
a watery grave.'

'You know, sir, the boat will not be manageable at all with
more than seven on board,' said Allan timidly.

'Well, we are but three ! do you count four men's lives
nothing ?'

'Not much,' said Matthewson drily ; 'but, not to return empty-
handed, we may as well load up with a couple of brace.'

A few more strokes of the oars and the boat was close to the
ship's bows.

The people on board seeing unexpected help, rushed in a crowd towards the boat to take refuge on board.

'Sheer off,' cried Matthewson, 'those lubbers will rush on board and swamp us.'

The advice was good, and Morgan followed it.

Then happened one of those fearful yet sublime catastrophes which are but too common in a sailor's life.

A man of low stature and far from muscular frame now threw himself, cutlass in hand, among the sailors, and in an imperious voice commanded them to stand back. 'Wretches,' he cried, 'is it for sailors to be whitelivered and like cowards escape, and leave women and passengers to perish, who have trusted to their honour? Deuce take your safety until the earl and his daughter are safe! By the beard of Charles the Fifth I will cleave the skull of the first who tries to get into the boat. Come, young mistress,'continued the sturdy fellow, turning towards the deck, 'there is no time to lose, come.'

From the speaker's manner, Morgan and Allan judged him to be the captain, though they lost the sense of what he said, as he spoke in Spanish.

Had the Cornish gentleman and his servant been less absorbed by what was passing on the vessel, they would have been startled at the sudden change that came over their companion. An expression of intense hate made his good-humoured face scarcely recognisable. At the captain's threat the sailors gave way, and when Morgan, who had again neared the ship, saw the captain approach, he was accompanied by a young lady.

Morgan divined at once what was required of him, and taking advantage of the boat rising on the crest of a wave, he caught a line and sprang on board the ship.

The captain spoke to him eagerly in Spanish, which he did not understand, when a gentleman of haughty appearance, clad in black, drew near, and said in a calm voice, and in English : 'The captain begs you to save my daughter first and to send us help as soon as you reach land.'

The knight felt that time was too precious to be lost in words of explanation. His simple reply was,—

'Help me yourself, my lord, to save your daughter.'

Passing his left arm round the young lady's waist, and holding by the ratlins with his right, Morgan waited till a wave brought the boat within reach.

'Father,' cried the generous girl, trying to release herself, 'I will not be saved without you. I will abide beside you.'

'I am coming, too, Nativa, fear not,' answered her father; 'but in your mother's name I charge you not to resist the offer of this generous stranger.'

The father was still speaking when Morgan, seizing a fit moment, sprang into the boat with his precious burden.

For a moment the sailors forgot their fearful peril to watch the Cornishman's bravery and the young lady's danger. A cry of alarm and then of joy arose spontaneously from the thirty men as the noble reached the boat in safety with Nativa.

'Father,' cried the latter, holding out her arms, 'come, oh, come to me.'

Like Morgan had done, the Spanish earl clung to the ratlins, and then sprang when the boat was lifted within reach.

Whether by accident or from evil intent, Matthewson shoved the boat off, and the luckless noble fell into the sea. A piercing shriek arose, and Nativa fell fainting to the bottom of the boat. There was an awful pause. For an instant Morgan hesitated; then, before Matthewson or Allan could stop him, he plunged into the billows.

'A thousand thunder-bolts!' cried Matthewson, for the first time losing his coolness; 'this is not devotion, but pure madness!'

The horsedealer had already taken off his coat with the intention probably of following Sir Lewis's example, when he saw the latter approach the boat holding the Spaniard by the hair and seize hold of a rope dangling from the gunnel.

'Courage, my boy,' he cried, holding out the oar to the Englishman, who seized it; 'you are all right now.'

A minute later and both Morgan and his prize were safe in the boat, the latter insensible.

'Come,' cried the horsedealer, 'let us try for land before the storm comes on again!'

All this passed so rapidly that Morgan had not once observed the face of the young lady, but now when he saw her lying senseless at his feet he uttered an exclamation of surprise and admiration which made Matthewson grind his teeth with anger, and give so strong a pull as almost to break his oar.

CHAPTER V.

THE SPANISH BEAUTY.

NATIVA was seventeen. Born under a tropical sun her beauty even at that age was fully developed.

Never had Sir Lewis Morgan in the ecstacies of his brightest dreams imagined such exquisite, adorable loveliness. Scarcely had his eye rested on the beautiful features and form of the young girl than a new horizon of delights arose, and he grieved deeply to have wasted so many years in foggy England.

A West Indian beauty is not, as credulous romancers who have never travelled describe them, a Messalina glorying in her shame, who stimulates the waning love of her admirer with the point of a dagger, or a pitiless coquette triumphing over and mocking the sufferings of her victims, making her pedestal their despair. Far otherwise. The true Creole is especially kind and pitiful, credulous and artless as a child. She leads the deepest psychologists astray by a candour and simplicity incomprehensible to them. They try to explain it as 'theatrical.' True as steel in spite of the graceful freedom of her manners, the Creole's love is her religion, and she joins the submission of a slave to the intelligent devotion of a wife. She can love a fool and never find out how much she is his superior, and this illusion she carries to the grave. Now reverse the picture. Suppose a Creole in her early youth betrayed, and her feelings outraged. She ceases to be a mere woman and becomes a tigress. Once throw out of her gentle, easy nature, she no longer knows good from evil; her vengeance stops at nothing; straight she pursues her way, trampling under her tiny feet family, religion, and honour.

But to return to our heroine, whose resemblance or diversity from her race will be made manifest. The luxuriant tresses of her lustrous dark hair fell in picturesque disorder round her oval face. Her large, deep blue eyes beamed with intelligence, gentleness, and energy. Her Grecian nose had none of those delicate ridges which, by their harshness, disfigure the prettiest faces, giving them a resolute, determined character at variance with feminine weakness and timidity, those two irresistible charms which captivate the eyes through the heart. As to her mouth it was child-like, save for full ruby lips of exquisite shape, a ripeness not found in infancy.

When Morgan first saw Nativa she was not as beautiful as we have endeavoured to describe her, for her horror at seeing her father engulfed in the sea had lent a death-like pallor and rigidity to the incomparable features. But if her beauty were less triumphant it was only the more touching.

The Cornish gentleman's first thought was to abandon the helm and succour the young lady, but a mighty wave soon warned him of the danger of so doing.

'A thousand thunders,' swore Matthewson, who seemed aware of the young man's intention; 'take care, man, there is a time for all things.'

Morgan blushed and remained silent. Almost at the same moment Nativa recovered consciousness.

'My father, my dear father,' she appealed, placing on her lap the head of the elderly stranger; 'it is Nativa who is near you, why do you not answer?' Then turning to Morgan and speaking in French, she added, 'I entreat you to help me. Oh, you shall be well rewarded! my father is as rich as generous.'

At these words the Englishman reddened with anger.

'Put your life in jeopardy for such a reward,' sneered Matthewson. 'These cursed Spaniards understand neither honour, kindness, nor devotion! their god is gold. Oh, when will their hated race perish from the face of the earth?'

'Lady,' said Morgan, suppressing his emotion, 'you little know the character or motives of those who have risked their lives in the hope of saving yours. I am of gentle birth, and the two persons with me accompanied me out of humanity.'

'I beg your pardon, sir,' answered the lady; 'I thought from your dress——'

'Probably in dress, manners, and appearance, I differ little from those who would thankfully accept your charity,' said Morgan, interrupting her; 'therefore you need make no excuses.'

Nativa perceived from the bitterness of his tone how much she had wounded him, and would have renewed her excuses had not an enormous wave nearly overturned the boat. This sudden shock restored Nativa's father to consciousness. He muttered a few incoherent words, smiled at his daughter, and rested his head on her lap, murmuring, 'Am I not lost to you, then, dear one?'

Easy about her father, the Spanish girl raised her large blue eyes towards Morgan, and asked in a soft voice:

'Do you think that success will crown your efforts? Is there still some hope of our being saved?'

'The tide is in our favour, and if the wind keeps in the same quarter in half-an-hour we shall land.'

'What gratitude I shall owe you!' said Nativa, musing.

'None at all,' answered Sir Lewis coldly. 'It was not because you were in danger that I came to help you, for I knew you not. I simply obeyed the voice of humanity and conscience. What I did for you I would have done for any one. We live— but others yonder perish!'

'But, my father, my poor father! without your heroic daring he would have died.'

'I would have thrown myself into the sea just the same to save a common ship-boy.'

Morgan's cold, dry replies produced a different effect on two of his hearers, for a cloud gathered over the features of the young lady, while a pleased, approving smile lighted up Matthewson's visage.

Morgan was right. After twenty minutes' silence they were scarcely more than a hundred paces from shore. In a few minutes more their feet would again touch land, when the steersman suddenly turned the boat.

'Have you a fancy for another trip?' asked Matthewson, in that calm sneering tone habitual to him.

'No,' answered the other ; 'but I have no fancy for being killed. Just mark the reception awaiting us.'

'Indeed !' exclaimed Matthewson, 'how persevering those wreckers are ! How good of them to have waited patiently ten hours for our return ! If they were only intelligent what might they not do ? What a store of harpoons and cutlasses ! Enough to cut up a dozen whales.'

'We are lost,' murmured Nativa, turning pale.

'Fear nothing,' answered Morgan ; 'thank Heaven I came armed !'

He drew forth his pistols from his cloak, and having seen that they were primed, cocked them.

At that moment a man lying on a rock scarcely fifteen paces from them pointed a gun at the helmsman.

'Tregallac,' shouted Allan, throwing himself before his master.

He was too late, for the man had fired.

'Hit?' queried Matthewson laconically.

Before answering, Morgan took aim and fired ; the assassin staggered and fell, with his head in the water.

'In the shoulder,' he said ; 'no harm done ; but what had we better do ?'

'If we were alone, I should vote for our making our way ashore,' answered the horsedealer, 'but this young lady and her half-drowned father would hamper our movements. Had we not better coast round until we come to refuge ?'

'Six miles farther is the castle of the Lord of the Manor,' said Allan.

'Just the thing. What do you say, sir ?'

Morgan cast one glance at the lovely Creole, and sighed.

'Well, then, let us go to Pemrose Castle, if you have still strength to row ; but you must be dreadfully fagged.'

'As for me,' said the horsedealer, 'it is so amusing to learn rowing, that, were I not afraid that your wound is more serious than you think, I could pass all night at sea.'

'I was dead beat just now,' said Allan, 'but Tregallac's fall has made me as strong as an ox, and as brisk as a curlew.'

Sir Lewis took the tiller in his left hand, his right being hidden in his cloak.

For the first half-hour not a word was spoken. Several times Morgan's glance wandered to the young girl. Each time her eyes met his with a grave thoughtful expression, which made him turn away. Brave as was the young Cornishman in the face of danger, he felt timid and confused, and trembled before the beautiful Spanish girl. He feared he was ridiculous, and would willingly have given ten years for the happy assurance of Whitehall courtiers, or even for the impudence of the silly fops at Truro, whom he had so often despised.

Allan first broke silence.

'Master,' he said, 'I think I see flames coming from your house.

He waited in vain for an answer.

'Sir, the fishermen are amusing themselves with burning your house.'

'All the better,' answered Morgan carelessly.

'How, sir, so much the better! I say, I fear your house is on fire.'

'I understand you well enough. I repeat, all the better.'

'Eh!' ejaculated Allan with wonder, for he thought his master must have lost his senses. 'Such a fine house! worth at least thirty pounds. And then where can we live now?'

'Such a hovel is not worth regretting,' rejoined Morgan, looking furtively at Nativa; 'it was no fit abode for a gentleman. I don't understand how I could have remained there so long.'

'It kept out rain and cold, nevertheless,' grumbled Allan, 'and thirty pounds to go up in smoke is enough to make one cry one's eyes out.'

'If this fire really has taken place,' continued Sir Lewis, 'I shall take it as a warning from Heaven to quit the place. I have remained too long idle. A gentleman is not like a churl, attached to the land. His blood is the king's and his country's. I will fight our foemen on sea.'

'Good Heavens!' murmured Nativa, hesitating at each word, 'if your house be on fire, we no doubt are the cause of the misfortune! If, instead of saving us, you had——'

'Been a robber and murderer?' interrupted the Englishman, coldly and proudly. 'Pray, go on. You are silent. Is it not easy to say to a man: "You are a poor wretch, and a few handfuls of crowns will reward your devotion and the losses you have incurred through us. Take them, friend, and may they prosper with you. We are now quits. We don't need you any more?" It is so easy to say this, I wonder you should hesitate.'

Morgan, aroused to anger by his own taunts, threw back with a gesture of proud scorn his hair, which the wind had blown over his face, and Nativa could not help admiring his noble features.

'That's what I call speaking with a vengeance,' cried Matthewson delightedly. 'It's only unlucky such words should be wasted on a woman. Now, spoken to a hidalgo, two swords would have leapt out of their scabbards at the instant, and that would have pleased me vastly; Spain would have had a swordsman the less.'

This odd and quite inexplicable sentiment recalled Morgan to himself, and he felt deep regret that he had allowed himself to be carried away by anger towards a young lady, and pretending to be very busy with the helm, he turned his head aloof, and remained silent.

An hour later the boat was opposite Pemrose Castle, and the party landed without further mishap.

'I am happy,' said Sir Lewis to Nativa, 'that accident prevented my offering you the shelter of my humble house, where you would have come in contact with privation and poverty; whereas at Pemrose Castle you will receive a sumptuous welcome, well-dressed servants to attend you, and rich and gallant young gentlemen ready to blindly execute your orders, or sacrifice themselves to do your pleasure.'

'But nowhere shall I find,' answered Nativa, 'courage and generosity equal to yours. But,' she added quickly, seeing Morgan about to return to the boat, 'will you not accompany us?'

'No,' replied the knight in a hollow voice, and turning pale, 'I have not the honour of knowing the Lord of Pemrose, and I prefer remaining a stranger to him.'

'Saint Maria! what is the matter?' cried Nativa, bending towards him.

'Nothing, thank you! only that bullet in my shoulder—some loss of blood—but it is nothing.'

'You are seriously wounded, and for two hours you have stayed bravely at your post, without a complaint or a single betrayal of your suffering! Oh! if all English gentlemen are like you, your nation is the greatest in the world!'

Morgan tried to answer, but, overcome with weariness, he would have fallen, had not Allan supported him in his arms.

The servant laid him gently on the sands.

'Take care of your master while I run to the castle for help,' said Matthewson, but Allan caught him back by the arm.

'First, tell me who you are,' he said, looking earnestly at him, 'how can I be sure of your coming back, or that I shall ever see you again if I let you go? Your conduct is not frank, and you may be an accomplice of Tregallac for aught I know. You shared our dangers, I grant, but that might be only a deep trick; for why should you give me money to tell you about my master, and then beguile him from his house? What did you want with the knight?'

'To offer him my services in selling him a horse.'

'Make me believe that if you can. Do you think because I have no learning I am an ass? You a horsedealer! that's a sham. Why, there is not a seafarer in Bristol who could row as you do. I never saw such a stout oarsman, and you pretend to be a horsecoper! That is too much of a joke; but, come, what are you?'

'I am rather in a hurry' answered Matthewson, smiling; and taking the Cornishman round the waist, he fairly lifted him up as if he had been a child, and sent him rolling on the sands.

Whilst Allan, more astounded than hurt, slowly regained his feet, his victor hastened away.

A paint-brush, not a pen, would be needed to portray the look of implacable hatred that the horsedealer cast on Nativa's father lying on the shore.

'What a most strange meeting!' he muttered, his hands clenched, biting his lips fiercely. 'And strange too that Lewis should have served him. Ah, Sandoval, Earl of Monterey, since fate has again thrown you in my way, look well to yourself!'

CHAPTER VI.

LOVE'S AURORA.

In a large-curtained bed, in a richly-furnished chamber, lay a young man, pale and reduced by illness. This was Sir Lewis Morgan, who, taken to Pemrose Castle, has passed a fortnight in fever and delirium. His wound had been most serious; it had required the strongest will, after having received it, to keep at the helm. But his duty once done, and Nativa in safety, he had fallen as described in the last chapter. Taken charge of by the domestics of the Baron of Pemrose, Morgan for a whole fortnight had not recovered his senses. It was one of those mysterious phenomena which we, in our ignorance, call interposition of Providence, that he had not died under the operation when the surgeon extracted the ball deeply embedded in his shoulder.

On the morning we recur to him, the doctor for the first time, to Allan's great joy, pronounced all danger over, and that he could answer for his cure.

Leaning over his master's bed, Allan watched his sleeping master with a solicitude foreign to his rough nature.

'If the doctor is in fault I could break his bones with my club for giving such false hopes; but what good would that do my poor master? How unlucky that he killed Tregallac! I should have found such pleasure in pounding him to a mummy. Hark! he speaks! Oh, dear master mine, it is your servant, Allan! don't you know me? There he is again calling Nativa! How can any one be so stupid as to care about a young thing like that whom one could break with a finger? How my master will laugh when I tell him that all through his illness he worried himself about that pale-faced chit! What a strange thing delirium is!'

Whilst muttering these words, the door opened and Nativa entered.

The young lady, dressed in black, after the Spanish fashion, was no longer the same as when first presented to the reader; she had recovered her sovereign imperious beauty. Nothing could exceed the graceful composure of her manners, her deep enchanting gaze, and the delicious smile that occasionally played over her ruby lips.

Her complexion, which was pale, but not of that sickly hue that a sedentary yet exciting life gives to town ladies, had quite recovered its brilliant tone. A poet contemplating Nativa would have despaired of doing justice to her charms.

But Allan was no poet, and his only thought in seeing the young lady was that she might take his place by the knight's bedside, while he ran to the church to set some tapers a burning.

He therefore advanced eagerly towards her, and pulling his forelock by way of a salute, said :

' Pray, mistress, take great care of my master whilst I am away. If he wishes to get up, his clothes are on the chair. You will find the broth ready on the table. Pray do not forget, if my master questions you about my absence, that I have watched him faithfully all through his illness, and that I am away now on his account.' Fearing a refusal he hastened away.

Allan's forcing her to a *tête-à-tête* with Sir Lewis, did not seem in the least to annoy Nativa. She moved softly towards the bed, and seating herself, examined with earnest attention the pale features of the invalid.

It was strange that during the whole time she was looking at him no expression of pity or of gratitude appeared on her own face. On the contrary, the pencilled brows were three or four times contracted, and a ray of joy darted from her eyes.

Half an hour had passed since Allan's flight, when Morgan having thrown about his arms, and muttered some unintelligible words, opened his eyes.

Nativa was the first object that encountered their gaze.

' Always the same face ! always Nativa,' he murmured without manifesting any surprise, and thus revealing to the young lady how her likeness had haunted his delirium.

Now, for the first time, Nativa gave way to a feeling of compassion. 'Poor young man,' she whispered. After a short silence raising her voice, she added :

' You feel quite yourself again, my lord, do you not ? '

The wounded man started, and the colour came back to his cheeks.

' Do you not know me ?' continued Nativa, ' do you not remember that I owe my life to your bravery and devotion ?'

Morgan wished to answer, but the words died on his lips. After a strong effort he managed to breathe :

' Oh, I prithee, leave me not again.'

The Spanish girl seemed not to notice the emotion. She rose and prepared a cooling draught, and presenting it to him, said :

'You are still very weak, I fear you will fatigue yourself too much by talking.'

'Indeed you are mistaken, I never felt stronger, and I have so many things to tell you.'

'To tell me!' said Nativa coldly, but not surprised; 'then speak.'

'Is it not natural,' said the wounded knight in a faltering voice, 'that I should wish to know if your father is out of danger; and if the other persons on board the vessel were saved?' He added with hesitation, 'If you have received from the Lord of Pemrose the attentions and considerations which are your due?'

'My father, except that the violent shock that he received has left him very weak, has recovered; our unfortunate shipmates, whose boats were all stove in by the storm, have been pitilessly murdered by the wreckers. As for the gentlemen here, I can tell you nothing, as I have scarcely seen them.'

These last words appeared to give much pleasure to the convalescent, who sighed in relief.

He was about to speak again, when Nativa laid her finger upon her beautiful lips, smiling reproval.

'If you are determined,' she said, 'to delay your recovery, I warn you I will not share the responsibility of your imprudence. I shall leave you.'

'Oh, pray do not go,' cried the gentleman, with emotion.

'Then try to sleep,' said Nativa, with gentle command.

Morgan, as obedient as a child, closed his eyes, but it was easy to guess by his irregular breathing that if he yielded in appearance, he did not in fact, but was never wider awake in his life.

Nearly an hour passed, when suddenly Morgan started up and cried:

'I think I hear footsteps approaching; perhaps you would be vexed to be found here?'

'Why so, pray?' she asked haughtily; 'do you think Nativa de Sandoval can be compromised by her compassion?'

'Oh, you are very cruel to a poor suffering fellow,' rejoined Sir Lewis, letting his head fall back sadly on his pillow.

Whilst he was speaking Allan came back, showing no sign of surprise at finding his master restored to consciousness. He merely remarked, 'I hope, fair mistress, that my master has no reason to complain of your not taking good care of him.'

'I have done my best,' she answered, smiling.

'That is, the best that you can do for him; but as you have not left my lord, tell me when he came to himself?'

'Directly after you left.'

'Well, how odd!' cried Allan regretfully, 'I might have saved the candles.'

Nativa, who was amused with Allan's blunt manners,

motioned Sir Lewis to be silent, who was vexed at his servant's want of respect.

'Good-bye,' she said, 'for the present; and do not scold Allan, who seems much attached to you, and whom I take under my protection. I will return to-morrow to hear how you are. Good-bye.'

The grateful look that was Morgan's answer to these words said much; a mute eloquence of the heart which could not escape Nativa's penetration.

'What! that foreign lady take me under her protection,' cried Allan, as the beautiful Spaniard left the chamber. 'Rather a good joke that!'

'Be silent,' cried Morgan angrily.

'By my faith, sir, if you fly in a passion it is a good sign! you must be quite well again.'

'Come here, Allan,' proceeded his master, 'and tell me all that has passed during my illness. How long have I been ill?'

'A fortnight, sir. I don't want to flatter you, but you must have an iron constitution not to be dead before this. For days you were at death's door. As for news, master, two hours ago I could have given you none, for I had not left you a moment; but I have just returned from Penmark.'

'And what is the news there?'

'I don't know the news, but I know that your house is burnt to the ground—not a stone left standing.'

The confirmation of this misfortune, already expected, caused the homeless knight no regret.

'And what has become of the horsedealer Matthewson?' asked the young gentleman.

'Ah, that is strange enough! he is gone, and nobody knows where; but I have my own thoughts about that.'

'Well, what do you think?'

'I think, master, that he was the devil himself, and every day I expect those two crowns he gave me to change into dead leaves. A Godfearing man never vanishes in that style.'

'In truth, his conduct is odd; but tell me,' continued Sir Lewis with some slight hesitation, 'has not our Spanish lady sometimes inquired after my health?'

'Oh, yes, indeed.'

'But she never came to see me, did she?'

'On the contrary, there never passed a day that she did not stay at least two hours in your room. Oh, she is a queer young lady. She looked at you with those great dreamy eyes of hers so long that she fidgeted me. But I cry your pardon, sir. Will you be so good as to tell me what is to become of us now your house is burnt down? I am rather uneasy on that score.'

'What will become of us!' Morgan exclaimed in so gay a tone that Allan feared he was again delirious, 'we shall go to the wars

gain riches and honours—great riches, do you hear, Allan, and have
as much power as the Lord High Constable.'

'What, in very truth!' cried the servant. 'Then you will give
me higher wages, eh? But how are we to become so rich and
powerful, sir?'

'Oh, I don't know exactly, but I swear on my honour that
if I escape death, I'll do it.'

'And I will follow you with all my heart.'

The young gentleman, overcome by the effort he had made,
let his head fall back on his pillow, and was soon locked in a
quiet beneficial slumber; his last words were:

'Oh, heavens, how I love her, and how happy I am!'

CHAPTER VII.

THE LOVERS' PLIGHT.

A WEEK had scarcely passed since the interview between
Nativa and the Cornish gentleman, when the latter was quite
restored.

The lovely Spanish girl, faithful to her promise, came daily
to inquire after her preserver's health. After each visit an extraordinary amendment was observable, much to the doctor's
surprise; the leech being probably not aware that happiness is
the panacea for all diseases. Morgan was now so happy, that his
heart overflowed with joy.

The appearance of Nativa was, we repeat, the revelation of a
new world to the rustic squire.

It was not surprising that he passed by easy transition from
the deepest admiration to the most engrossing love.

Endowed with an ardent imagination, rendered still more im-
pressionable by the austere loneliness in which the greater part
of his youth had been spent, the young knight laid at Nativa's
shrine the hazy yet enrapturing dreams, the passionate aspi-
rations of his whole life, the deepest yearnings of his heart; his
whole being centred in her.

Since he had met Nativa, he had not once considered her
strange wilfulness: if she smiled on him he almost trembled at
so great a happiness; if she regarded him haughtily, he was in
despair, and confused thoughts of suicide passed through his mind.

Had he not loved her with all the violence of a first love,
Morgan would have been often shocked by the young lady's
fitful humour; she was all contradiction, spontaneity, and
mystery. Sometimes she fell into deep reveries, which seemed
to betray a past life of sad events and memories; then all at

once she gave herself up to a mad and causeless gaiety. Sir Lewis contented himself with sympathizing alike with her joy and sorrow, though the source of both being unknown to him.

One morning, after a night of delicious wakefulness, the young gallant, in order to calm his thoughts, went down into the park, and perceived Nativa seated on a bench, absorbed in deep thought.

'Ah, it is you, my lord,' she said, after he had gazed at her long unperceived ; 'I am glad that we have met, for I wanted to speak to you.'

The knight wished to answer, but his heart beat so violently that he could only bow in silence and seat himself by her side, as she had graciously beckoned him to do.

'Last night my father told me,' continued the young lady, ' that he felt strong enough to set out, and it is likely that to-day or to-morrow we shall continue our journey. Until now, Sir Lewis, I feared to cast a cloud over our sudden intimacy by expressing my gratitude, but I cannot part from you for ever without telling you how deeply I feel indebted to you ; my father and I will never forget your noble devotion, and each day your name shall be remembered in our prayers.'

'We part,' echoed Morgan, after a moment's silence, in a stifled voice. 'Impossible ! Oh, Nativa, what can I do without you ?'

His emotion was so real, his pallor so deathlike, and his suffering so great, that Nativa could not reprove the outburst.

'Nativa,' continued he, in a husky voice, 'since you think me entitled to your gratitude, listen to me, I entreat you, and be not angry with my presumption ; this will reward me a thousand times for the little I have been so happy as to do for you.'

'We part to-morrow, sir, so do as you will to-day.'

With the mysterious changeableness of the human heart, Morgan instantly repented his boldness, and would have given ten years of his life to retard an explanation, which he yet so ardently desired ; but to draw back now was impossible, and with a trembling voice he continued :

'Oh ! do not fear that my boldness should rise to mad presumption. You have told me that you are rich. I know that your name ranks with the highest and most illustrious in Spain, while I am only a poor obscure young man, without fortune, patronage, or future. You see how mad it would be for me to seek to unite our destinies. But what I long to tell you is, that I love you so intensely that my love approaches adoration, and that if you refuse to accept my devotion my future life will be a blank. What I entreat of you, Nativa, is to allow me to follow your steps at a distance, ready to receive your orders. Oh, fear not you will ever have cause to blush at my devotion. Your dear name, enshrined in my heart, shall never pass my lips. I will be your slave. Merely a look from you shall command me!'

Too much moved to proceed, Morgan's voice sank. Nativa was perfectly calm and collected, but pensive.

After a short pause, she replied, 'I accept your friendship, but I repudiate the strong expressions with which you offer it, and which I attribute partly to momentary weakness after your serious illness. Besides the exaggeration of your language, I also blame the distance which you place between us on the score of fortune. You are a gentleman of good family; therefore, equal in rank. You have a sword, and have a right to defend with it your country's glory and your own honour. Perhaps,' continued Nativa in a different tone, 'I speak in a manner that would seem strange in one of your own countrywomen, but you must forgive me. Spanish girls, unused to trivial compliments, take things seriously, and answer, not with our wit, but with our hearts and consciences.'

Vague as was Nativa's rejoinder, it overwhelmed the hearer with joy, but he endeavoured to control his emotion. Love had already taught him circumspection.

A disinterested observer might have detected in her fixed gaze, pensive brow, and abstracted air that some serious thought weighed on her mind and controlled her will.

Suddenly the beautiful girl roused herself from her meditation, which the observer fondly hoped was caused by his avowal, and turning to Morgan said:

'Sir Lewis, are you superstitious?'

This question not a little surprised Morgan, who answered smiling,—

'We men of Cornwall believe in all things that we cannot understand.'

'They are right.'

'May I ask you,' went on the gentleman, 'what makes you wish to know?'

'Oh, I believe that our meeting proves that you were born under a fortunate star. No foolish protestations. You misunderstand me, sir knight,' continued Nativa, solemnly. 'You long for glory and wealth! Well, if you will aid me in what I wish, and success crowns your efforts, not a man in all Christendom shall yield to you in wealth and influence.'

'Wealth and influence, did you say?' cried the other, in surprise; 'pray explain.'

'I may not reveal to you a secret not mine. You have promised me obedience, and you will oblige me by not insisting on this point. Besides, who knows,' pursued Nativa, passively, 'whether this project which fills my dreams at night, my thoughts

by day, can ever be realised ? We women are so apt to take our
fondest hopes for certainties. But when the time comes, you
will go forward without hesitation, without fear, like a true
gentleman, will you not, to redeem your promise with your life ?'

'Too happy,' cried the knight in ecstasy, 'to lay down my life
in your service.'

'I believe you !'

The lovely Spanish girl remained a few moments thoughtful,
then with that charming archness which was natural to her, said :
'Do you know that for the last fortnight you have greatly
excited my curiosity ?'

'I have? pray, in what ?'

'Why, in everything ; your whole existence seems a riddle.
How is it that at your age you shut yourself up in the dreadful
solitude of a fishing village? you, with wit and courage, to pass
your youth in the midst of such rough, cruel boors, and at the
threshold of life mewed up from the world? I fancied that
some great grief might weigh over you, and darken your life.'

'You are mistaken,' replied Sir Lewis sadly ; 'no one has
hitherto taken sufficient interest in my existence. I have been
entirely abandoned to my fate.'

'But your parents and relations?'

'I have no near tie but my father, and for seventeen years I
know not what has become of him. As for my relations they
are all too rich and powerful for me to seek their friendship ;
they would think I was asking their charity.'

'And your mother?'

'I have never known her ; she died at my birth.'

'Forgive me,' continued Nativa, in so gentle and tender a
tone that it touched the young man's heart, 'if I go on with my
questions. The least I can do, if we are to be true friends, is to
mourn over your griefs and share your unhappiness.'

'You wish to learn my history? Heaven knows it is simple
enough, and scarcely merits your attention. My father, Sir
Ralph Morgan, who was justly esteemed in our province, had the
misfortune to be mixed up with the last rebellion that took place
in the Western Marches ; a price was put on his head, his lands
were confiscated, and he was forced to fly. Since then I have
never heard of him. A relation, the Marquess of St. Pol, took
charge of me and had me educated, but it seems I bring ill-
fortune on those who love me—he died also. When my education was finished I wished to turn what I had learnt to profit,
but the gentlemanly accomplishments in which I was thought
not deficient would not help me to a livelihood, as on the other
side my name, obnoxious at court, forbade me to hope for any
situation there. I was about to enlist as a private soldier when
I received a letter from a noted banker and ship-merchant at

Bristol, Master Compton, desiring me to go to him. Judge of my surprise when this banker, having satisfied himself as to my identity, gave me fifty gold crowns, saying, " Sir Lewis Morgan, this money has been sent to me for you from the West Indies, I am desired to pay you every month a sum of twenty pounds, and as the person who instructs me to do this is well known to me, and I perfectly depend on his honour, you may rely on having this sum paid regularly to you wherever you please to appoint."

'This mysterious affair did not please me, and I demurred. "I give you my word, sir," the shipmaster said, " that you can accept this money without fear. This allowance comes to you from a kinsfolk, and there is nothing humiliating in accepting it."

'In vain I entreated Mr. Compton to name my relation, but he constantly refused to do so. Perhaps I ought to have still rejected the money, but I was so desolate and so unhappy, and the fair fame of Mr. Compton inspired me with confidence; so I gave way. With my fifty livres I bought a small lonely cottage, within musket-shot of Penmark. I resolved to keep my hermitage without making advances to society, which seemed to disdain me. Since which time, except making two voyages to Ireland, as a volunteer under a brave merchant captain, a friend of mine, I have remained in the dreary solitude in which you found me.'

Nativa, although she had herself asked for the story, had paid little heed to it until he came to the providential assistance that had reached the hero from the West Indian Islands. The face of the Spanish girl then lighted up, her large eyes shone with a strange lustre, and she laid her hands across her heart to still its tumultuous beatings. Morgan, plunged in sad memories, had not noticed this agitation, and when she spoke her voice had regained its calmness.

' My curiosity,' she said, ' thanks to your frankness, has enabled me to learn all the nobleness of your character. You forgot, in speaking of your solitude, to allude to the noble revenge you have taken of the world's disdain, by exposing your life to save the unfortunates shipwrecked on this shore. I learnt from the Lord of Pemrose your bravery and devotion in saving castaways.

'I have ess merit than you think in doing this,' answered the gentleman mournfully, ' for I count my life as a straw, though I detest the cowardice of suicide.'

'And now, sir, what do you intend to do?'

'Now,' he said, with an accent which paraded what ties bound him to his fair companion, 'I await your orders.'

'But if I wished you to succeed to gain riches and power, what would you do?'

I would put into execution a plan which has for a long time

haunted my imagination and troubled my repose. I will leave
England, and seek in foreign lands the patrimony my country
refuses me.'

'You will go to foreign lands ; but whither ? The world is
wide ; towards what country have your dreams led you ? '

'Towards the Island of Hispaniola, which you call Saint
Domingo.'

This answer produced a wonderful effect on Nativa ; a
shudder which she could not control agitated her frame ; her
lips became pale, and for an instant Morgan thought she would
have fainted.

'In Heaven's name,' he exclaimed, seizing her hand,which he
pressed without her heeding it, ' what is the ill ? shall I call
for help ? '

' No, thanks ; it is nothing ; only a momentary weakness. I
am better,' answered Nativa faintly. Continuing the conversation, she added, ' So you think of going to Hispaniola ? '

' I do.'

'How strange is fate ! ' ejaculated the girl, with such joy as
greatly surprised her hearer. 'How impossible not to see the
designs of Providence, when such extraordinary circumstances
concord with my most secret thoughts ! Shipwreck drives me
away from port, and throws me on the deserted Cornish coast. I
murmur at the delay this event causes in the accomplishment of
my designs, and here, on this lone shore, I find what I might
have sought in vain elsewhere. Oh, Chevalier of Morgan, I
believe now that our destinies have a mutual tie, and that we
shall meet again.'

'May Heaven grant it ! ' cried the knight devoutly ; 'but pray
explain how my words can have moved you so deeply ? '

'My lord, devotion obeys blindly and never questions,'
replied Nativa, tempering with a delicious smile the harshness
of her censure.

' You are right,' answered the young man simply.

A short silence followed, which Nativa was the first to break
by saying : ' If you had to set out to-morrow on a long voyage,
would not you be impeded by want of money ? '

'I have a little,' answered Morgan, blushing.

'That is to say a few hundred crowns ? '

' Much less.'

' Then you must permit me——'

' Not another word, prithee ! ' interrupted Sir Lewis, in spite
of his love turning pale with shame and anger. 'We gentlemen
may *give* our bodies, and *risk* our very souls for woman ! but
never do we sell our honour !'

'I honour your sentiments, they are truly Castilian,' said
Nativa with a tender glance. 'I own myself in fault, but now

let us hie back to the difficulty.   If your savings will not cover
the expenses of the voyage, what will you do ?'
    ' I will borrow.'
    ' How can you borrow who know no one ?
    ' You are determined to make me drain the cup of humili-
ation to the dregs,' said Morgan sadly ; ' but fear not ! to obey
your orders, I will entreat Mr. Compton to advance me my year's
allowance ; I feel sure he will listen to my prayer.'
    Morgan expected that Nativa would thank him for his sub-
mission with a few kind words, but he was deceived.
    Entirely engrossed with her own plans, she answered coldly :
' Well, this arrangement appears feasible, and if you are resolved
to try it, you must set off for Bristol to-morrow, at the latest.
Time is precious.'
    ' In that case, I will leave to-night.'
    ' Truth to say, that would be better.'
    The young lady rose as she spoke.   Morgan detained her
with an imploring look.
    ' You also,' he observed with emotion, 'will leave to-morrow,
and you forget to tell me when I may hope for the pleasure of
again seeing you.'
    ' I might leave that to chance, sure as I feel that fate will
shortly re-unite us,' answered Nativa, 'but not to leave you in
error, I must on that subject consult my father.   On your arrival
at Bristol, you will find a letter from me.'
    ' A last question, I entreat you,' said Morgan, anxious to de-
lay the moment of separation, ' tell me, I implore, for everything
about you fills me with wonder, how it is that you speak English so well and French no doubt with a purer accent ?'
    ' I was born, it is true, in America, where my nurse taught me
English ; but until I was twelve years of age I was educated at
the Court of Spain.   It is to my excellent and august godmother,
Queen Maria Sousa, who was very fond of me, and often kept me
with her, that I owe my knowledge of French.'
    Morgan bowed, and Nativa was pursuing her way towards the
castle, when the former, who was gazing after her, perceived a
red ribbon fall from her hair, which he ran to pick up.   As he
raised it to his lips, Nativa turned suddenly, bestowed on him a
parting smile, and disappeared.
    This precious keepsake, sanctioned by the tender smile, seemed
to the young lover a gift and a confession.   A joy greater than he
had ever experienced before plunged his soul in ecstasy.   How
absurd and ridiculous such ardent devotion and love would have
been considered at St. James's !   Poor young man, he had much
to learn.   Half an hour later, Sir Lewis Morgan, faithful to his
word, gave Allan orders to prepare for their immediate departure,
which caused the latter no small astonishment.

'What is the meaning of all those grimaces?' asked his master, perceiving at last Allan's pantomimed chagrin.

'Oh, master, I try my best to understand you, but it is no use. Now, you are going to be angry; it is strange how your temper is changed. What do you wish me to get ready? You have not a single thing left! It is no fault of mine if the good folk of Penmark burnt your house, even if you had killed Tregallac. I might have had my revenge out of *him*, but now he is dead what can I do?'

'You are right, Allan,' remarked his master sadly. 'I wished to assist the distressed, and my kind intentions have been rewarded by the loss of everything I possessed. All is gone.'

'With all respect to you, sir,' continued Allan, 'you did very wrong to deprive the people of driftage, and harm came of it, of course. But tush upon spilt milk, let us say no more about it. The only thing you have left is your horse Jewel, which Garvey saved.'

'My horse saved!' cried Morgan joyfully.

'With saddle, bridle, and all complete.'

'Well, that is good news! Go and take these two crowns to Master Garvey, and bring me my horse.'

'But, sir, I am told he did not save Jewel for you so much as for himself.'

'Hark ye, first go offer these two crowns to him, and, if he is willing to come to terms, you will add another crown and bring away the horse; but, if he refuses point blank, you will give him a thorough thumping, and bring away the horse just the same.'

'All right so far, but that is not all.'

'Why is not that all?'

'Oh, I mean, what am I to do with the crowns if Garvey will not take them and forces me to fisticuff payment?'

'You may keep them for your trouble.'

'Oh, then, master,' cried Allan joyfully, 'I can answer for it what will happen! Garvey is as stubborn as a donkey. I know he will choose blows, so the crowns will stay in my pocket.'

'It matters not to me, that is your affair; do as you please.'

'In two hours dear Jewel shall be here,' said Allan, running off.

Before the time specified the servant had returned, leading the horse triumphantly.

'What news?' asked his master as soon as he saw him.

'Garvey preferred a beating,' answered Allan, whose face was covered with bumps and bruises. 'It has rather spoiled my looks, but that is over; so no more about it.'

CHAPTER VIII.

A MARVELLOUS HORSE TRADE.

Sir Lewis passed the rest of the day endeavouring by ingenious stratagems to see Nativa again, but they proved abortive.

Evening had closed in when, true to his promise, the young noble took leave of the Lord of Pemrose, thanking him for the hospitality he had received ; he then sought for Allan, but could not find him. Going to his chamber, he loaded his pistols carefully, wrapped himself in his cloak, and left the castle as quietly as possible. Once beyond the walls, his first care was to observe the sky. Masses of dark clouds covered the landscape like a heavy dome, Morgan smiled and set off rapidly in the direction of Penmark.

An hour later, for the distance was only half as long by lana as by sea, he reached the blackened remains of what three weeks before had been his home. Having listened eagerly and reconnoitred all round, he advanced towards a heap of stones to the right, close to the shore. There he stopped and listened attentively, but hearing nothing but the low moaning of the sea along the sands, he knelt down, and groping about until he found a large scallop shell, he set to work to scoop up the sand.

Morgan had scarcely begun his task when he stopped at the sound of a low stifled groan.

The youth was brave enough, but too much of a rustic not to be superstitious. This moaning, which he took for that of a disembodied soul, frightened him and paralyzed his efforts.

However, the first alarm over, and the moaning having ceased, Morgan was ashamed of his fright and resumed his work.

Almost at the same moment, a blow aimed at the rocks close at hand, accompanied by a rough oath, made him aware that his adversary was human, and his courage returned.

Morgan pulled out one of his pistols, and, advancing towards the spot whence the sounds proceeded, cried out :

‘ If you budge, I fire,’ at the same time taking aim at a dark figure, just discernible against the rocks.

Scarcely had he uttered this threat, before a sudden breeze rolled away the masses of clouds and shed a gleam of moonlight over the scene. A double cry arose of—

‘ My master !’ ‘ What, my man, Allan !’

‘ What are you doing here at this hour ?’ asked the former.

‘ You see sir, I am digging,’ answered Allan, slightly enr barrassed.

‘ Well, that is droll enough ; yet why should not the same thought occur to two persons at the same time ?’ said the chevalier, laughing. ‘ Shall I tell you, Allan, what brought you here ?’

'There is no need, master,' said the other discontentedly, 'I know my own affairs, and that is enough.'

'You came to dig up a treasure!'

'Treasure, indeed!' cried the man, in a vexed tone.

'You need not be angry; I also came to dig something out of sand : so we are a pair at that game.'

'Well, sir, I am right pleased to hear it, for I thought you gave all you could spare to the poor, and I am very glad you have had the prudence to lay by.'

'Why so, Allan?'

'Oh, sir, because a young gentleman who is not saving never comes to good, however hard he may try.'

'And doubtless you want me to make a fortune?'

'Certainly, sir, as I am in your service.'

'Just lend me your spade, then, for I am in a hurry.'

The knight set to work, and soon dug a hole two feet deep. Stooping down he took out of it a small canvas bag containing twenty-five pounds, his whole fortune.

'It is your turn now, Allan,' he said, returning the spade to the servant.   But Allan did not set to work.

'Don't you hear me, sirrah?'

'Ay, master, but I cannot do anything while you look on.'

'What, can't you trust me, fellow?'

'Oh, how can you say such a thing!' reproached Allan, in tears; 'you know that if I had all the gold in Christendom, and all the Turks to boot, I would let you have it with my eyes shut, and not ask you for your hand and seal to the receipt.'

'Then why this concealment now?'

'Oh, this is another thing; I don't like any one to know my affairs.'

Morgan, aware of the eccentricities of the peasant, and not perhaps quite exempt from them himself, let his servant have his own way and left him.

No sooner was Allan alone, than instead of digging he broke open a strong cairn of stone formed with considerable skill, out of which he took, not a bag but an old boot, containing a few silver crowns, his savings during three years.

The master and servant regained Pemrose Castle with their hoards.   Jewel was ready saddled awaiting his master; and the latter, having tossed a crown, which he could ill spare, to the groom who held his stirrup, set forth.   Allan, an awkward valet, but zealous and faithful follower, strode after him.   As soon as they were a musket-shot from the castle, the young knight looked back and wafted a passionate farewell to his lady love.

It was one hundred and forty odd miles from Penmark to Bristol. It took Morgan over four days' riding to accomplish that distance ; the roads were bad, and in some places almost impassable.

His horse was overcome with fatigue, but his servant was as fresh as ever.

Nativa's image, is it necessary to say, occupied the youth's mind during his three days' journey. The lover pondered fondly over the slightest circumstances of their mutual intercourse, recalled to his imagination her various charms, and, as if she could hear his words, made a thousand vows of eternal love and constancy. After he had given full course to his passion, he began at last to reflect. He was shocked at the poverty of the return that had been made him ; for, though he would fain have persuaded himself that the charming Creole had given him her whole soul, he could not but allow that the only favour—and that he owed to accident—she had vouchsafed him was the ribbon that had fallen from her hair, and which he had since worn next his heart. There had been no question between them of promises, engagements, or even distant hopes, and Morgan owned sadly that, though she had accepted his devotion, she had kept herself entirely free.

When he once began to reflect calmly over matters, the young adventurer tried in vain to fathom the contradictions which he could not help observing in the young lady's words and actions, and he felt that there was somewhere a mystery which his sagacity could not penetrate. The last question he put to himself was whether Nativa had really a generous nature, or whether she was cold-hearted, and this, deeply in love as he was, he dared not decide. However, the conclusion of all his reflections was, that nothing in the whole world could be as divine, enchantingly perfect as Nativa, and that he ought to be only too happy to be her slave and consecrate his life to her.

Lovers may sometimes argue justly, but, unluckily, they always come to a false conclusion.

Morgan's first care on reaching Bristol was to buy a sword, his own having been lost when his house was burnt, and he wished to present himself as a gentleman to the person from whom he wished to borrow money. It was two o'clock when he arrived at the substantial dwelling and business-place in one, of the shipmaster, Compton. His heart beat fast ; it was the first time he had ever asked monetary aid, but thoughts of Nativa soon calmed his emotion, and he felt happy that he could offer up his pride at the shrine of Nativa. Having made his way through a mob of sailors, clerks, and porters who filled the court-yard, Morgan mounted a stone staircase and reached the office.

'Master Compton,' he called to a clerk who was zealously making out the papers of several merchant captains.

The clerk gave a slight glance towards him, and evidently seeing nothing in the young gentleman to deserve attention, continued his employment without answering.

Thrice did Morgan, with a patience and politeness inspired by the image of Nativa, repeat the same question with equal unsuccess, except that at the third demand the clerk gave a sort of inward growl, which proved at least that he had at last become aware of his presence.

Though the knight was patient, yet the rudeness of the Jack-in-office nettled him not a little ; but considering that it would ill-become a man who came to borrow money to begin by getting in a passion he strove to conquer his feelings, and for a fourth time asked most politely for the ship merchant.

' Deuce take this chattering hobbledehoy !' burst out the clerk in an insulting tone.

This outrage was so unexpected that, for a moment, Morgan stood aghast. But the next instant he seized the clerk in an iron grasp, lifted him from his seat, and hurled him with violence against the wall.

' By Heavens !' he cried, pale with rage, ' wretch ! you shall pay for this.'

This had taken place so quickly that the number of persons crowding the office had no time to prevent it. It was only when Morgan put his hand to his sword that they thought of inter-posing between him and his victim.

It is probable that in other circumstances the youth would have little heeded their intervention, but now he felt himself in so false a position that, ashamed of his anger, he thrust back his sword in its sheath.

' What does the gentleman want ?' asked an elderly man, who seemed to hold a responsible position.

' I wish to speak to your master,' answered the fiery visitor ; ' will you have the goodness to repeat my name : Sir Lewis Morgan ?'

' I would do so with pleasure, but Mr. Compton is away from home at present, and will not be back for a week ; but,' con-tinued the head clerk politely, ' if your business is urgent, you can see the person with whom Mr. Compton has left full authority.'

' Yes, my business is urgent,' answered the other, disconcerted ; ' and pray who is the person to whom I can apply in the place of the principal ?'

' His wife, sir.'

This answer completely nonplussed the caller. He had strong repugnance to address himself as a suitor to the shipbroker, but he had humbled his pride to do so, and now, when he had made the effort and conquered his scruples, an event occurred which enhanced the degradation of his position. With that rapidity of conception given by the approach of danger he saw himself in the presence of an unknown lady, overwhelmed with shame, not daring to utter a word, and when he at last should break silence it would be to ask for money. The thought alone was dreadful.

'Well, sir, do you wish me to usher you to my mistress?' asked the elderly clerk.

Morgan was on the point of refusing. Two considerations prevented him : first he feared that if he left after his punishment of the insolent clerk, his departure might be taken for flight, and besides that Nativa might doubt of the great devotion he had vowed to her if he let himself be stopped by the first obstacle on his path.

It was necessary to decide promptly ; any longer hesitation would have only aggravated the annoyance of his position : so Morgan, as cowards often do, burnt his vessels and rendered retreat impossible.

' Let me see Mistress Compton, by all means,' he said.

The head clerk led the knight through several offices ; then opening a door without knocking, said :

' Mistress mine, here is a young gentleman who wishes to speak with you.'

Morgan, ill at ease and embarrassed, bowed lower to the delegate of the banker than he would have thought necessary under other circumstances.

Mrs. Compton was a stout, short woman of some fifty years, with a meaningless ordinary face and vulgar manners.

Busy, when Morgan entered, in casting up a long column of figures, she merely looked up inquiringly, made him a slight nod, and inquired :

' What is your business, and to whom have I the honour of speaking?'

' I am Sir Lewis Morgan, of Penmark,' answered the gentleman, hoping that Compton had mentioned him to his wife, and therefore his name might be known to her.

' I don't know the name, sir. Pray, what is your business?'

' I am in need of money, and I came to ask your husband to advance me the year's allowance which he is commissioned to pay me monthly : that is to say, £240.'

' I don't know anything of this business. Be so good as to call again in a fortnight, when Compton will be at home.'

' I am about to sail a long voyage, and it would be impossible for me to wait till then.'

' What ! are you so short of money, or so destitute of friends, that you cannot do without a couple of hundred?'

' I am in that position.'

' Then I beg you will say no more about it. You must be aware that one cannot lend even a hundred pounds to a stranger about to make a long voyage, and with neither a friend nor a pound to bless himself with,'

At this ill-bred answer, though uttered without the least in-jurious motive, Morgan was astounded; he repented bitterly that he had not killed the clerk and demolished the house! About to make a most cutting reply, he restrained his indignation, and moved slowly towards the door. It opened suddenly, and Morgan could not repress an exclamation of wonderment at finding himself face to face with the horsedealer, Matthewson. He called out his name.

'The same, young sir. By the rood! I little thought of meeting you in Bristol. You seem quite recovered from your wound.'

The horsedealer advanced towards Mr. Compton's deputy, who rose eagerly to give him as gracious a reception as she could.

'Do you know this young gentleman, then?' she asked un-easily, as if already repenting her ungracious answer.

'Oh, thoroughly,' answered Matthewson. 'The knight only lately treated me to a most delightful outing on the sea.'

'Then why did you tell me just now,' asked the banker's wife, 'that you had no friends? If Master Matthewson will be your surety, I am willing to lend you the £240 or £250 that I have just now refused you.'

This last humiliation alone was wanting to complete the dis-comfiture of the unhappy Cornishman.

Matthewson gazed at him steadfastly, a smile of derision curling his upper lip. The youth only wished he had been an adversary worthy of measuring swords with a Morgan.

'The young gentleman knows well,' said Matthewson, after a short silence, 'that horsedealers are not Crœsuses; still, I have shelved a trifle, and if he will do me the honour to accept a loan, at fair interest, of course, I shall be happy to do him this slight service!'

'Thanks, sir,' answered Morgan drily, who in his anger forgot all his previous humility; 'since the absence of my banker prevents my having the money, of which accidentally I find myself in need, I must fain turn elsewhere.'

'Oh, I remember now,' cried Mrs. Compton, 'did you not say, young sir, that your name was Morgan?'

'Yes, madam, I am Sir Lewis Morgan.'

'Then here is a letter which the postrider brought for you this morning.'

Sir Lewis hastened to open the letter which the banker's wife put into his hands, and read at one glance the following lines:—

'In a fortnight I shall be in London. You will learn my address at our Ambassador's. Come quickly. I require you. Trust in your good star! Come! come!—N.'

'Well?' inquired the horsedealer again, 'do you still refuse my offer?'

‘Even still, sir,’ answered Morgan, annoyed against his will at the marked emphasis Matthewson had given to the word ‘ still.’

The gentleman bowed slightly to the horsedealer and the banker’s wife, and departed slowly, and with seeming indifference, which, alas ! he did not feel.

On Morgan’s arrival at Bristol, from motives of economy he had taken up his abode at a paltry inn, which had for its sign the ‘Golden Wain,’ and thither he betook himself after his unsuccessful attempt at raising funds.

‘Ah,’ moaned he to himself, hastening along, for he fancied all passers-by could read defeat on his brow. ‘Ah,’ he sighed, ‘I never knew before the shame that poverty entails on the influence of riches. That horsecoper is received with open arms, whilst the Knight of Morgan is treated almost with contempt ! And wherefore ? Merely because this knave did not want money, and I did. Nativa is right ; I ought long ago have set about doing something, and not wasted my best years in useless solitude. Ah ! but I am now determined by assiduity and perseverance to make up for lost time. The ambitious longings that have so long slept in my heart are aroused with redoubled force ; I feel I must succeed.’

Having poured the healing balm of hope over his wounded pride, Morgan turned his thoughts again on Nativa. He read ten [times at least the note she had sent him by the light of his own wishes, and consequently came to the gratifying conclusion that the two lines contained an avowal of love.

This assurance was so comforting that on his arrival at the Golden Wain, the uneasiness and discouragement felt on quitting the banker’s was gone.

The first person he saw on entering the inn yard was his servant Allan, busy grooming Jewel. The sight of his master gave great pleasure to the valet, who, bewildered by the many and narrow streets of Bristol, had not dared to venture out.

‘My good Allan,’ said Morgan kindly—for he knew he could blindly trust to the devotion of his follower, and the idea of being loved even by this ignorant lout was at this moment balm to his spirit—‘ my dear rogue, the business which brought me to Bristol is over, and, if you are not too tired, we will start for London to-morrow at daybreak.’

‘ With all my heart, master ; I like long walks far better than large towns.’

‘ What will you say when we get to London, then ?’

‘ Oh ! that is another thing ; as we only travel to make our fortunes, I shall like large towns better than long walks. Money makes all the difference.’

The youth sighed at Allan’s reasoning, and owned there was justice in it.

Having ordered a frugal dinner Morgan retired to his room, where he was surprised by a knock at his door, as he neither expected nor knew a single person in the town. However, he said, 'Come in,' and great was his surprise when he saw the horsedealer enter.

'You here !' he cried, astounded.

'And why, forsooth ? You called out, " Come in," and here I am.'

'In good truth, then, I am glad that accident brought you here.'

'Thanks, only no accident brought me here, I came to talk to· you on business.'

'We will fall to .business presently. But first I want to know what your motive is for calling yourself a horsedealer ; for you will allow me sufficient penetration not to be duped by your pretence.'

'In troth,' answered Matthewson, with a hearty laugh, 'I see that your servant Allan has been setting you against me. And what the deuce then should I be ?—a prince in disguise ? Alas, my dear knight, I am only a shabby horsedealer, in proof of which assertion I am now come for the purpose of offering to buy your horse.'

Matthewson's face looked so honest, his voice was so frank, that the hearer was taken aback ; yet, not willing to give up the point at once, he replied,—

'The uncommon hardihood you showed in accompanying me on the expedition to try to save the vessel. wrecked on the Penmark rocks, ·and then the very odd manner in which you afterwards disappeared, appear to me at variance with the craft you pretend to follow.'

'Deuce take me if I understand your arguments,' answered Matthewson with another laugh, 'though no doubt they are really ingenious. Why should not a horsedealer have bravery and humanity as well as any other man ? "Well," says I to myself, "if a gentleman plays at pitch-and-toss with his life to save the shipwrecked, why should not I do the same ?" As for my sudden departure, you don't expect a horsedealer to stand much on the order of his going. I had pressing business elsewhere.'

'But why when you came to Penmark did you make inquiries about me of my servant ?'

'I questioned your servant because I wanted to make you an offer, and to get your groom on my side—not at all an unusual thing in the way of business.'

'Well, what business is it ?'

'The same that brings me here now. A rich traveller has seen your horse and wishes to buy it—what do you want for it ?'

'My horse is not for sale,' answered the youth coldly, yet rising from the rickety chair on which he sat.

But no doubt the horsedealer did not comprehend this signal for taking leave, for without rising he went on with—

'Well, sir, I don't mind being frank with you. The gentleman who fancies your nag will stand a long price, and I can make money out of him. So don't turn up your nose at the offer. Such crowns don't grow under one's feet, and I know you want money. Only pride or folly would refuse a good dicker. So let us come to terms without more ado. What did you pay for your horse?'

'Some thirty odd pounds,' answered the chevalier, not sorry in truth to find a means of doing without Compton.

'Only over thirty!' cried Matthewson, astonished. 'By my faith, though my business is to cheat, you must be joking! and I won't take advantage of your ignorance. Your horse is worth eighty pounds if it is worth a noble.'

'Will you give me so much for him?' asked Morgan, feigning an indifference which he was far from feeling, for that sum dazzled him.

'Yes, and I will, if you like, hand you twenty-five in cash, and trade you two horses, not very handsome, but quite equal to a long journey.'

'I accept,' answered Morgan.

'Then it is settled? I have your word as a gentleman upon it.'

'Yes, my word and honour.'

'Well, then,' cried Matthewson joyfully, 'I may own to you that Jewel is worth not barely eighty, but a hundred pounds.'

'I am glad, sir, that you have made a good bargain. Your generosity delights me, and, not to be behindhand, I will throw you in a saddle and bridle for the groom's horse.

'Here, my lord, are your five and a score pounds. Will you permit me to take Jewel at once? and to-morrow morning I will send you the two horses. You need not fear; I am well known in Bristol.'

'Take Jewel, sir,' answered Morgan, ' and may he prove one to the new proprietor.'

As soon as the horsedealer had left, the knight gave loose to his gratification at so unexpected and fortunate an occurrence. Allan, whom his master took into his confidence, showed more scepticism in the matter.

'This horsedealer cannot be the devil,' he reasoned, 'as I thought, for the crowns have not turned into dry leaves; but before I rejoice I must see the two horses he is to send—if he does send them!'

The following morning the suspicious lackey, and even his master, were astonished at seeing in the yard a really magnificent charger, and a strong hack well harnessed, which the horsedealer had sent.

'Holloa!' cried the knight, who, after eating a hasty breakfast, mounted his new horse. 'This is a good beginning of our travels.'

Allan proudly bestrode his horse, and the two adventurers took up their road.

As they were leaving the town Morgan was accosted by a man who asked him how long he had had that horse.

'Only since morning,' answered the gentleman, uneasy at what mischance might follow.

'Well, sir, take my word for it, you have got a prize there ; I sold that very horse myself yesterday for seventy pounds, and he is worth even more.'

CHAPTER IX.

WHEN WOMAN COMES IN AT THE WINDOW, MONEY FLIES OUT AT THE DOOR.

DURING the whole of that day the Cornishman and his servant never ceased talking about Matthewson, but, though the conjectures were innumerable, none sufficed to explain his extraordinary conduct.

Allan took it for granted that he was a sorcerer, and, though his less credulous master rejected this notion, still the question remained undecided ; for, whether Matthewson were a sorcerer or no, what could make him interest himself so much in Morgan's affairs ?

The latter determined, should he see him again, not to leave him until he had obtained a clear explanation of his mysterious conduct.

Their journey was joyless. Constantly they met on the high roads whole families, chased from their poor dwellings by the implacable tax-gatherers.

Other unfortunates, less patient, did not accept their dreadful fate without a struggle ; so that the travellers heard of highway robberies and other deeds of violence.

The knight wished to buy a sword and a brace of pistols for Allan, but the latter, notwithstanding his usual obedience to his master, turned restive in this instance.

'What can I do with a sword or pistols ?' he expostulated. 'Thank Heaven, I am a British man, and don't know the use of those things. Now suppose you buy me an axe ! I won't say no to an axe. That's something to lay hold of ; it knocks down a man in good style, and don't snap against a button.'

'But, Allan, your axe is antiquated now that men are not armoured. I should look as if I had hired a woodcutter instead of a serving-man.'

'Well, then, my club must do.'

After much contention—for Allan obstinately maintained his

point—it was finally settled that a musketoon should do duty for the desired axe and the rejected pistols.

'There is one comfort,' muttered Allan, poising the new and ponderous weapon. 'I can always club it and knock a man down with the butt if the bullet does not upset him.'

It is not our intention to recount stage by stage the alarms, troubles, and privations which our travellers passed through ; we must hasten to London. Still we must mention an adventure that they met with at Hill-over-Edgeley, as it is intimately connected with our story.

Towards midday Morgan and Allan met a coach with the blinds down, drawn by two cart-horses, and escorted by two tall lackeys, shabbily dressed, and armed with tremendous rapiers. These latter, on perceiving our travellers, drew their spits, and placed themselves in the middle of the road to intercept their passage.

Morgan perceived at once, by the style in which the pretended gentlemen rode, their manner of handling their swords, and the deplorable state of their horses, that there was not much danger; so he advanced quietly, with his sword in its sheath, and his pistols in his holsters, as if not aware of the hostilities with which he was threatened.

He was not more than ten paces from his opponents when one of them tried to move towards him, but his horse, indignant probably at the absurd swayings of his rider, turned restive and kicked instead of coming forward.

'If you approach one step, sir,' cried the horseman to Morgan, 'I will run my sword through you.'

'I doubt whether your sword cuts as deep as my whip,' answered the knight, setting spurs to his horse, and giving the fellow a lash across the face.

Instead of avenging himself the fellow yelled out with pain, and, throwing away his sword, dropped his hands entreatingly, saying, 'I yield, sir, and own myself conquered ! In Heaven's name don't kill me.'

The other valiant horseman fled incontinently. At the odd figure of the discomfited paladin the Cornishman burst into a hearty laugh.

'Why, fool, did you threaten me ?' he asked.

'Alas, sir ! I knew I had no chance with you, but I only did it in zeal for my master.'

'What good could it do your master, dolt ? Who is he, and what harm have I done him ?'

'My master, sir, is in that glass coach. He has run away with his cousin, who was about to be forced into a convent; and who called him to her aid. Fletcher and I were only escorting the poor things ; we thought you pursued us, so we did our duty.'

'Your master did well to run away with his cousin if she loved him and was persecuted ; only he might have chosen braver champions.'

'Forsooth, sir, in these adventures it is not every one that can be trusted, and me and Fletcher have served master for ten years.'

'And what is your master's name ?'

'The Viscount Charmai and.'

'Well, tell him from me that he has very ill-placed his confidence in you and Fletcher. What ! you don't know who I am, and yet you give at the first bidding your master's name !'

'Oh, sir, indeed you are unjust ! Such a handsome gentleman as you are must be a favourite with the ladies, and no doubt you are in love with one, and, as lovers are always kind and compassionate, I ventured——'

'A truce to this balderdash,' interrupted the youth, blushing. 'Run and tell the viscount and his cousin that if I can do them a service I shall be very happy.'

'Oh, sir, you are nobility itself, as I thought.'

'No more chattering ! Go and execute my order.'

Allan had listened attentively to his master's conversation with the servant, and when they were again alone he smiled slily, and said,—

'If I were you, sir, I would have nothing to do with this romantic couple.'

'Thanks, Allan, for your sage advice,' replied Morgan, laughing.

'In troth, master, I have heard say that sometimes fools give good advice, and wise men do very foolish things.'

'What, then, do you see to blame in this gentleman's conduct ?'

'First and foremost, master, I don't like people who run away with young ladies. They must be shameless. Then it was very odd that the viscount, believing he was pursued, did not shove even his nose out of the coach door ; that does not say much for his courage. Then, though you are a gentleman, there was no need to go slavering as that ill-looking varlet has. I don't think much of flatterers.'

'I see, Allan, that travelling sharpens your wits. What do you think of this viscount ?'

'I think, sir, that his cousin has not run away with him.'

'In all honesty,' cried the chevalier, laughing, 'that is an odd idea. Pray why has not the nobleman run away with his cousin ?'

'I say the young lady has not run away with him, for then one must expect to be pursued.'

'Assuredly ; and did you not see Master Fletcher and his companion's dismay when they saw us ?'

'Then, if they expected to be pursued, how was it there were cart-horses harnessed to the coach? They are as slow as slugs, and could not cover more than nine miles in the day! Why, it is much the same as mounting light horsemen on snails.'

Morgan's clear mind admitted the justice of Allan's observation, and it gave him food for reflection. After a short silence, he said,—

'I vow that there is something mysterious in all this, and I shall be on my guard.'

When five minutes later they passed the viscount's carriage he could not help scrutinizing it. But it was too closely shut for him to discover anything, and Morgan was obliged to proceed on his road with his curiosity ungratified.

The village of Hill-over-Edgeley, where our two travellers were to pass the night, reaching about three, boasted at this period three houses. Two of them were inns on occasion; the third was a blacksmith's forge.

It was at the sign of the 'Wizard Merlin' that they stopped. While Allan, after removing the saddles, walked the horses gently to and fro before taking them to water, his master entered the inn, looked about him, and cast a glance of dismay at the kitchen hearth, in which there was no fire. The interior of the 'Wizard Merlin' contained three rooms,—the kitchen iu the centre, a bed-room on each side.

As these rooms were equally ill-furnished—that is, not furnished at all—Morgan threw his cloak, as a sign of possession, in the one to the left, aud then betook him to inquire about dinner.

After much talking he at last obtained half a fowl and a quarter of a pouud of bacon, and, satisfied on the dinner question, he went according to his daily habit to the stables to see if his horse was properly attended to. Towards five o'clock the knight was seated with Allan at their meagre dinuer, when he saw the mysterious carriage stop before the 'Merlin.'

He hastened to the window, thinking that the young lady could not escape him now, but his curiosity was only partially gratified.

Charmarand's cousin did alight, it is true, but she was so closely veiled that it was impossible to distinguish a feature. He judged, however, by her light, lithesome figure that she must be pretty. Her cousiu watched her with a vigilance that bespoke rather jealousy than love. He held her arm and followed her like her shadow. What especially struck the watcher in the man was the profusion of bright ribbons with which his dress was decorated; but thinking this might be a new fashion, and seeing nothing farther to keep him at the window, he returned to his dinner. At night Allan bade his master 'good night,' and retired to the barn, where he was to sleep,

Morgan threw off his coat, and unclasping a leathern girdle from his waist, which he had bought at Bristol to keep his gold, and having carefully deposited it under his pillow, and his pistols on a chair by his side, he threw himself, clothed, on the bed.

About ten, when the young gentleman had fallen into a sound sleep, a knock at the door awoke him with a start.

'Who is it?' he called out.

'For Heaven's sake open the door!' answered through the keyhole a feeble, stifled voice.

Morgan threw himself off the bed, snatched up one of his pistols, and advanced to the door. As it opened inwards he drew back quickly after having unlocked it, lest he might be thrown down by some one rushing in.

What was the chevalier's astonishment to see a lady, with her clothes and hair in disorder, fall on her knees at the entrance, and in a suffocated voice moan,—

'I trust myself in your honour and your courage! save me! save me!'

As a necessary precaution on going to sleep, Sir Lewis had left his candle burning, but from its long snuff it gave but a feeble light. He was about to question his unknown visitor, when the sound of footsteps approaching from the kitchen was heard.

'Shut the door, pray shut the door, or we are lost,' cried the lady eagerly, in evident terror.

'I don't see, madam, why you need be afraid,' answered the knight, 'as I am here. And you need have no fear for me, for we Cornish gentlemen are noted for having hard skulls and heavy fists. The first who enters here falls a dead man, that's all!

The stranger, without heeding his words, rose suddenly, rushed to the door, and turned the key; then as pale as death she fell forwards on the bed. The knight stood looking at her aghast, for hardly could he persuade himself he was not dreaming.

'Oh, my dear sir,' cried the lady, 'I owe my life to you.'

'At least you owe me an explanation,' answered Morgan, giving the candle a jerk which threw off the superfluous snuff, and making it brighten again.

'Oh, pray spare my modesty and my shame,' said the lady, with timid grace, shading her bosom with her abundant dark hair.

These words, spoken in a feeling voice, drew the champion's attention; he gazed earnestly on the fair face, and could not refrain from an outburst of admiration when he saw such lovely features. Except Nativa he had never seen so beautiful a creature.

'Will you have the kindness to tell me,' he began after a long silence, and in a faltering voice, 'what dangers you have reason to fear, and in what manner I can save you? I am sure of the justice of your cause; I pray you have equal confidence in my honour and my sword.'

'Oh, I can trust in nothing now; I have been so fearfully deceived. I can trust in nothing now,' she repeated.

'Distrust cannot hold good against facts,' said Morgan, quietly. 'Order, and I will obey.'

These words, spoken in a straightforward manner, somewhat allayed the fears and grief of the young lady, who soon ceased to weep, and raised her less tearful eyes, already beaming, towards Morgan.

His honest countenance, and perhaps his respectful attitude, seemed still farther to reassure her, for she presently said :

'You ask for an explanation, which it is only right you should have, from the unhappy person you promise to protect.'

'But I beg you to believe,' interposed Sir Lewis, 'that the offer of my protection is without reserve. I do not wish to gratify any idle curiosity; only I thought that if I knew your past misfortunes and your present position I could more effectually help you.'

'A thousand thanks for your generous forbearance; but, alas ! I am so unhappy that I only long for the solitude of a convent. But I would not have you think ill of me, and I need your help so much.

Whilst the young lady spoke thus in a soft supplicating voice Morgan eyed at her with admiration so respectful that, had she observed it, she could hardly have taken offence.

'My name is Miss Baggot,' she said. 'I am the daughter of Sir Humphrey Baggot, whose name cannot be unknown to you.'

'Excuse my contradicting you,' said the gentleman.

'What ! have you never heard of my father ? There is no one at Court who is not acquainted with his high position in the royal favour. I could be a maid of honour to-morrow if I sought it.'

'I do not belong to the Court, I come fresh from the Land's End.'

'Is it possible, when your manners are so fine ?'

Morgan bowed and blushed at this compliment.

'An only daughter and heiress,' continued the stranger, 'I was surrounded by a host of admirers who contended for my hand, and my father had innumerable offers for me; but a spoilt and idolized child is horrified at the idea of giving herself a master, and I refused all suitors. Two months since the Viscount Charmarand, dismissed from Court for ill-conduct, came to our shire, and solicited my father's protection and influence to regain his

lost office. The viscount comes of a very good family, but he
possesses every fault ; violent, cruel, untruthful, a gambler—he
is incapable of a generous deed ! On the other hand, when his interest or his passions are concerned, he stops at no vileness, no
crime ; he is a perfect monster of villany and hypocrisy.

'The viscount presented himself to us as a victim ; he pretended frankness and virtues, distributed alms in the neighbourhood, and made himself beloved by the simple country folks, till
on all sides he was lauded to the skies. Need I tell you that his
hypocrisy deceived me, and, grateful to him for not having
paid me those silly compliments that others had showered, I now
felt for him at least a sisterly affection. Four days ago I was
walking in my father's park, when I met the viscount, pale, and
careless in toilet, and who seemed a prey to some profound emotion.

'"Hail, mistress !" he cried out as soon as he saw me, "Heaven
sends you to me in my need."

'So great was his bewilderment, he seized me by the arm, and
dragged me on with him crying out the whilst, "Oh, unhappy
girl, may we even now be in time to save her !"

'I questioned him in vain ; his anxiety only seemed to get
stronger and stronger : at last he reached a private door of the
park, that opened on to the main road.

'"Ah," he cried, throwing himself at my feet ; "angel of goodness, you will not let my sister die without help? Oh, unhappy
girl ! this is the consequence of that foolish infatuation which I have
so often deplored. Thou hateful cause of her misery, vile wretch,
thou shalt not escape me ! I will follow thee round the world."

'Speaking thus, the viscount pushed me towards a carriage
that was by the roadside, and added—

'"She is therein ! Oh, I dare not see her, the sight of me would
drive her mad ! Enter the carriage, I beseech you, and assure her
that from my heart I forgive her ! "

'I was so taken by surprise, so bewildered, that I made no
objection, but entered the carriage.

'Vile treachery ! the viscount leaped in after me, and drawing
a dagger, cried, "One word and you die ! " He closed the door,
and bade the coachman drive on at full speed.'

'I presume not with the wretched jades I saw?' interrupted
Morgan.

'Oh no ! We drove at dreadful speed, and only stopped when
the horses could drag us no further. My fear and terror was so
great that I could not cry out or make an effort to extricate myself. Taking advantage of my fainting state, the viscount quickly
bound my arms, feet, and hands ; then placed a handkerchief over
my mouth to prevent my crying out.'

The girl stopped, with sobs stifling her voice,

Morgan ground his teeth with rage.

'And what happened afterwards?' he inquired.

'When I revived from my swoon,' continued the young lady, 'the viscount coolly told me that he had thus compromised my reputation to make me willing to marry him.'

'But such dastardly conduct I shall have signal revenge! Since you have honoured me by trusting your defence to me,' cried Morgan, with honest indignation, 'I hasten to meet this disgrace to the gentry.'

'I entreat you to forbear; a meeting between you could only render my position still more wretched.'

'What!' cried the knight with energy, 'would you remain in the power of this wretch?'

'It is a sacrifice to my honour. If in your generous indignation you killed this vile man in a duel, who could prove that I did not go with him willingly? Nay, he must live for my justification.'

'Then how can I serve you?'

'By watching over my safety. Do but follow us to town, then you will notify the proper authorities, and have the viscount taken to prison.'

'I will obey you, mistress,' answered the gentleman gloomily; 'still it is very painful to know a lady worthy of all respect and admiration has been so shamefully deceived and yet keep my sword undrawn in her defence.'

'Oh, believe me, I fully appreciate your courage and devotion,' cried Miss Baggot, taking his hand and looking at him with eyes that beamed with gratitude even through her tears. 'Oh, how can I ever repay such generosity?' she murmured softly.

A strange thrill passed through Morgan's form; but mastering it with an effort, he gently drew back his hand and replied—

'In the name of the lady I love I offer you my services. Who knows whether she may not one day need also the protection of an honest man?'

At these words the lady raised her eyes to heaven, and, opening the door, bowed her farewell to Morgan.

'Oh, Nativa!' cried the youth when he was alone, 'I have a right to say I love you, and you alone.'

Too much moved by what he had heard to sleep, Morgan paced restlessly up and down his room. So indignant did he feel at the viscount's conduct that it required a strong effort to restrain himself from going to seek a quarrel with him on the instant.

'Perhaps,' he thought to himself, 'I have done wrong to leave Penmark. Scarcely out of sight of its rocks I meet with humiliation and deceit. At Bristol Mr. Compton's reception proved to me how little high birth or good manners are esteemed if not accompanied with riches. Here I see to what deep infamy the love of riches can make a gentleman stoop. Who can tell whether I may not at every step lose some cherished illusion? I may gain experience, but what good will it do me if my heart grows so callous that it becomes dead to every noble feeling, even to love itself? No, I need not fear,' continued he fervently; 'the thought of Nativa will be my safeguard, my salvation there.'

After a time his thoughts grew calmer, and the fatigue of the preceding day at last made him seek his couch, where he instantly fell asleep.

Scarcely had he closed his eyes, however, before piercing cries aroused him, and snatching up his sword and pistols, he rushed out of the room.

This time he perceived what it was, and felt neither surprise nor hesitation: one horrible idea alone made him shudder, it was that he might be too late.

'I am coming!' he vociferated, as he ran through the kitchen to the door of Miss Baggot's chamber; 'fear not—I will save you.'

He burst the door and went in. The room was empty. Morgan was now at a loss which way to turn, when the renewed cries of 'Help! help?—murder!' burst forth louder than ever. They came from outside the house. The young man rushed back through the kitchen, traversed the yard, and as he passed by the stable called aloud to Allan without stopping, and bent his course rapidly in the direction whence the calls had proceeded.

At the same instant a man, hidden in the large kitchen fireplace, glided quickly into the room the knight had just left, returned almost immediately, and cautiously made his way to the stable which Allan had just quitted.

The environs of the village were covered with rushes and brambles, so that, although the moon lighted up the landscape Morgan was some time before he could trace the person he was in search of.

At last he perceived a female figure flying a hundred yards off. It was Miss Baggot. He was up with her in a few moments.

'Pray calm yourself; it is I, Sir Lewis Morgan, your protector; you have nothing to fear.'

The young lady seemed so beside herself with fright that at first she hardly recognised the speaker, but cried out, 'Pity, my lord; do not kill me! I will declare I was your accomplice—I will not betray you.'

It was only after a great deal of trouble and much loss of time that Morgan was able to persuade her that she had fallen into good hands, and was under the protection of a friend.

'Oh, thank Heaven!' she wailed passionately, 'you are my good angel.' Sobs stifled her voice.

'Follow me,' cried Morgan, 'and fear nothing! By Heaven, the viscount shall never persecute you again! He is guilty enough to deserve the death—and by this blade he shall die!'

When Sir Lewis devoted a man to death, it was, as remarked at the beginning of this true story, a sign infallible of deep and terrible rage.

On hearing these words the young lady shuddered and turned pale. However much a woman may have been wronged by a man, however deeply she may feel his injuries, yet she shrinks back appalled by the thought of a violent death. Miss Baggot therefore strove to lessen her befriender's action.

Morgan listened to her unmoved, and answered:

'My obedience to your commands has nearly cost your life. Stern necessities must be grappled with, not shrunk from. You honoured me by confiding your interests to me; allow me now to act as I think best.'

After this reply he gently disengaged himself from the grasp of the young lady, who had seized his arm, and with a resolute step returned to the inn, where he expected to find the Viscount Charmarand.

About twenty paces from it he met Allan, who, holding his gun by the barrel as if it had been a club, was returning from reconnoitring.

'Oh, master,' cried the man eagerly, 'I am glad to see you. When you called me, I thought you had to do with another Tregallac, and I rushed after you, but could not find you. What is the matter?'

'Allan,' answered Morgan, 'a crime deserving death has been committed.'

'Then his fate is decided. I will go with you.'

'No, I forbid it. You must remain with this lady and protect her.'

Allan looked at the lady attentively, and exclaimed—

'With all respect to you, sir, the lady would do better to dress, instead of scampering about the country that fashion.'

There was no time to contest the point: moments were precious. Morgan made no answer, but the lady did.

'I entreat you to leave me here! force me not to witness such a dreadful deed. And then who knows but the viscount, seeing his prey escaped from him, may not turn his rage against me! He is armed.'

'You are right,' said Morgan, 'it is better you should learn in safety the punishment of the guilty man.'

'You mean the issue of the combat; for the viscount, I must do him so much justice, is brave, and will fight.'

'I hope so with all my heart; his cowardice would vex me. Then I shall find you here?'

'Yes, generous protector, I will take shelter in this outhouse, and pray for you,' said the lady, going towards the stable.

Morgan bowed to her; then turning to Allan, commanded him to follow.

'That suits me best,' said Allan.

A few minutes later they came back to the kitchen, where all was in darkness.

'Master,' whispered Allan, 'it strikes me, as the man you seek has pistols, he might put a bullet in your head. Let me get the candle out of your room. When you can see your way you need not fear treachery, and you can punish the rascal finely.'

His master acquiesced in such a reasonable notion.

Allan hastened to seek the light, and returning with it, resolutely entered Charmarand's room first.

Both exclaimed with astonishment,—

'No one here! he is gone!'

'And he has taken his things away with him,' added Allan.

The master and servant looked at each other.

'Confound it!' said Allan, eagerly; 'have you your gold about you, sir?'

'No, but why do you ask?'

'Why, sir, because when I went for the candle I saw two pieces shine on the floor. We have been robbed!'

At this cry, which seemed to come from Allan's very heart, Morgan was thunderstruck. He rushed into his room. Allan had guessed right! The leather belt in which he had placed all his money was gone.

This discovery had such an effect on the young gentleman that he could not utter a word.

At last he cried out,—

'No, it cannot be; I have mislaid it.'

With a trembling hand he turned over his bedding, he sought carefully on the floor, but his misfortune was too true. It would require the brush of a Wilkie to paint Allan's comic dismay.

'Come, man, don't be cast down,' said his master, 'there is still hope that we may catch the villain; we are well mounted, whilst he is on foot. Come, pluck up courage.'

'A thousand devils!' cried the servant, 'that jade shall pay for this.'

'Of whom are you speaking?—not Miss Baggot? Your grief bewilders you: that unfortunate lady is more to be pitied than we are.'

'Pitied! that shameless creature! Well, master, the words choke me. She is a woman! so much the worse for her.'

Allan, choked with passion, rushed out, Morgan following him.

Scarcely had our unlucky travellers quitted the house when they saw coming from one side of the stable the Viscount Charmarand and Miss Baggot, and !from the other Fletcher and his comrade; the first two mounted on Morgan's steed, the other two on Allan's strong hack.

'Heaven speed our next merry meeting, chevalier!' called out the perfidious distressed maiden, in a voice quivering with laughter. 'Charmarand is a rascal, but I love him!'

At this unexpected and unmistakable confirmation of his misfortune, aggravated still more by the loss of his horse, Morgan, notwithstanding all his courage and presence of mind, stood aghast, his head hanging down, his mouth open, as if struck with paralysis.

Not so Allan.

'I can run,' he shouted; 'Heaven grant I catch these rascals!'

The peasant set off with all his might after the fugitives. For a minute the knight remained rooted to the spot, when he heard the report of a gun. Fearing that his faithful Allan might fall a victim to his devotion, he followed with all speed in the direction whence the noise came. Fortunately his fears were unfounded. He soon perceived Allan, who, with his head down and faltering steps, was returning from his unsuccessful chase.

'Well?' inquired Sir Lewis.

'Well, master, I am convinced now that horses run better than men.'

'But that gun I heard?'

'A blight on the gun, I say.' replied Allan, with increasing ill-humour; 'I had good reason to complain that those shortened guns are good for nothing but show.'

'You missed your man?'

'That is to say, I missed two men! or, at least, if I did touch one, balls from these pipe-stems don't hurt, for both my rascals went on all the same though I took good aim.'

'Well, we must give up all hope for the present,' said the knight, making his way back to the inn.

'Why would you meddle with these people's business? I did warn you,' said Allan.

'That is true, in faith! But how can one resist his fate?'

'One can resist his fate; I am sure of that. I would wrestle Master Fate for it any day.'

'But what can we do now, Allan? What is to become of us? How can we proceed on our way without a penny in our pockets?'

At his master's question a smile of satisfaction and triumph passed over Allan's face.

'We are not as luckless and helpless as you fancy, sir,' he answered, with a grin.

'What help do you wot of ?

'Forsooth, I am not as trustful as you. My money and I never part company : I have my savings.'

'But your savings don't belong to me : it would be painful to me, even with your consent, to use them.'

'Why so, sir ? '

'Because,' answered Morgan, with some hesitation, ' you and I are not equal in rank.'

'Very true ; therefore, when you get some money, you shall pay me back double. Your inferior can accept fat interest.'

'Well, be it so ; I agree. Only I fear, Allan, your savings will not take us to London.'

'Your pardon, sir,' answered Allan, stopping to give more effect to what he said, 'I possess five pounds.'

The fellow held back a sixth part of his money, as he thought it best to keep thus much in reserve in case of a new disaster, and not give all to his careless master.

Allan's wonder was great when Morgan, smiling sadly, answered that five pounds would go no way in buying a horse.

'Master,' he proposed, ' the best thing we can do is to go back to Penmark. You can easily get credit to rebuild your house. You must try and forget your hopes of making a fortune abroad, and all about this journey ; and we can jog on with our old life again.'

It may be easily imagined how little this advice pleased the love-sick adventurer. He did not deign even to discuss it, and only answered,—

'You are free, my good fellow, to leave me and take your way back to Penmark. If I should be obliged to walk all the way to the capital barefoot, begging my bread, I will do it, and get there at last.'

'Then, master, we'll get there together,' answered Allan 'What, do you think me such a despicable knave as to leave you in the lurch ? But it is getting late ; you need rest ; go back to your room and try to sleep. To-morrow morning, if you permit it, we can talk over what is best to be done. Night is said to bring counsel.'

In spite of Allan's excellent advice Morgan could not close his eyes all the rest of the night. The misfortune which had overtaken him so suddenly brought with it such fearful consequences, that our hero dared not contemplate them. One thing alone seemed certain ; nothing short of a miracle—and miracles were rare even in those days—could take him to London in time to meet Nativa there.   This thought tortured him and made him almost mad with rage.   Willingly would he have given ten years of his life for a handful of gold.

The deep-laid roguery of the pretended viscount and the abducted maiden confounded him ; he could not conceive such deception and perfidy possible.

'Allan,' he said in dismay, 'have I overrated my strength in striving to carve a position for myself ?   If at first starting I am defrauded by such an arrant hussy, what will become of me when later I have to fight my way among vicious nobles grown grey in deceit and intrigue ?   They will not deign even to think me in earnest.   They will scoff at me as a rural curiosity.   But, by heavens ! not so.   A Morgan may be deceived, but he is not to be scoffed at !   My sword shall answer their gibes.   Bloodshed stops laughing.   Yes, but Nativa is rich, very rich, she told me. I must then get gold, much gold, to be her equal ; if not, some great noble—But never !' cried Morgan, turning pale, 'I would kill her sooner than leave her to become another's bride !'

When, three hours later, the sun rose, the young gentleman, a prey to bitter thoughts, with uncertain, nervous steps, still paced his chamber.

Allan soon appeared.

'Master,' he said as he entered, 'I have come for orders, and also to tell you an idea that has struck me.'

'I have no orders to give.   Tell me your idea.'

'It is very simple.   Our last-night thieves, in making their escape, have left behind them four horses and a carriage. What prevents us from taking each a horse, and selling the two others with the carriage to the innkeeper ?   In that way we may get part of our money back again.'

After a moment's reflection Morgan said,—

'I don't see any objection to that ; it is a fortune of war. Go and call the host.'

'For the last hour I have been seeking him.   It is odd that we have seen nothing of the man since last night, and that he did not show himself when that jade with her clothes half on was howling murder with all her might.   Perhaps he is an accomplice of the thieves.'

Allan had scarcely finished speaking when the inn keeper appeared at the door.

'Good morning, honoured sir,' he said to Morgan, in a cheerful, hearty tone, 'I hope you have slept well.   I come to know whether before setting out you will take a stirrup cup ?'

Although since his sad mischance the young knight had become very suspicious, yet he could not but allow that the innkeeper's countenance expressed neither embarrassment nor annoyance.   Still, after he had in a few words told the trick

that had been played him, he asked the host how it was that at
the screams of the false lady in distress he had not made
his appearance.

'Godamercy!' answered the innkeeper, laughing, 'if I
were to rouse myself every time a shindy is kicked up I should
not sleep one night out of four. Not a week passes without
several robberies in my house. But what is that to me? I am
not a magistrate. Before I go to bed of a night I make every
traveller pay his bill, I lock up my plate and retire to my attic,
leaving them free to rob or to quarrel or to kill each other just
as they please.'

There was nothing to say against this logic. And not to
lose time in vain discussions, Morgan proposed to the innkeeper to sell him the two horses and the carriage. At this proposition the host burst out laughing.

'What the deuce could I do with a coach?' he answered;
'and even supposing I were fool enough to buy one, do you
think me quite such an ass as to pay down good crowns for a
carriage that has most likely been stolen, and might be claimed
any day? Pho! pho!'

These words enlightened the young chevalier to the fact that
if he took possession of the two horses left by the pretended
nobleman, he ran the risk of being implicated in a disgraceful
affair. Therefore, turning to Allan, he said,—

'My good fellow, chance takes from you here what chance
gave you at Bristol. The higher Will be done! When we left
Penmark you followed me on foot; I hope you will not refuse,
now I am unhorsed, to accompany me on foot.'

'You travel on foot?' cried Allan indignantly, 'that's not
possible.'

'So possible, my good fellow, that I set out at once,'
answered Morgan, nodding farewell to the host, and taking his
departure without turning back.

Nearly a mile from the inn Morgan thought he heard groans,
and leaving the road he hastened towards the spot whence they
proceeded. What was his surprise at seeing a man lying on
the ground covered with blood, evidently in a dying state.

'Heaven be praised,' cried Allan joyfully, 'the townsfolk are
not such fools as I thought them. Their musketoons are really
fine things.'

The servant had recognised in the wounded man Fletcher's
companion.

CHAPTER X.

THE FRIEND IN NEED AGAIN.

THE appearance of the traveller caused no emotion to the accomplice of the false viscount. The poor wretch felt death so near that he feared neither vengeance nor punishment.

'For Heaven's sake,' he murmured, in a voice already hoarse with the death-rattle, 'give me water, my throat is on fire! water, water, I entreat you!'

Morgan made a sign to his servant—for Allan always carried at his girdle a bottle of drink—to give some.

The servant knelt down by the wounded man, and held up his head with one hand and the flask in the other.

'I will only give you some,' said Allan, 'if you answer my questions truly.'

'Water! water!' gasped out the dying man.

'Well, I am really too good-natured! come, drink away, on no condition.'

The poor wretch seized the flask eagerly, but scarcely had he tasted its contents when Allan drew it away, saying,—

'That is enough for the present. You can speak now, and if you answer my questions truly you shall have some more. Who is your Viscount Charmarand, and that jade that was with him?'

'Charmarand, Fletcher, and I are deserters from the army. As for Mistress Bessie, she is no better than she should be.'

'Whence got you the carriage and horses?'

'By theft; we stole them the day before from a company of strolling players. But some drink—water!'

'I will give you as much as you like if you will answer me as frankly as you seem to have done hitherto these questions. What are the real names of Charmarand and Fletcher? what road did they take? where can we meet them?'

'Charmarand is named Ratley, and Fletcher is Fletcher. I don't know what road they have taken. We were fleeing we knew not whither when your ball struck me. Now I have told you all I can. Give me drink.'

The deserter did not deserve much pity, still he seemed in such agony that Morgan felt compassion for him.

'Give your flask to the poor fellow, and let him drink without worrying him with more questions. He can have no interest now in deceiving us. He has told us all he knows.'

The servant obeyed. The dying man seized the flask eagerly, but hardly had he put it to his lips before he let it fall; a strong convulsion shook his frame; he stretched his limbs, and with one deep sigh expired.

' Let us depart,' said Morgan.

' You look quite unhappy, master.'

' Is it not enough to make me so to see a man die a miserable death from his love of gold ?'

' Still, gold is a fine thing,' remonstrated Allan, enthusiastically ; ' my ambition always was to possess as much as would load me or any other ass.'

The two left the deserter and went on their way, but they had scarcely gone a hundred steps before the servant stopped short and observed,—

' Be so kind, master, as to wait for me a minute, I have forgotten something very important.'

' What can you have forgotten, Allan ?'

' To render the last duties to the dead,' said Allan. Without waiting his master's consent he ran back. Five minutes after, he returned, looking very pleased.

' Here, sir, is what I found in the dead man's pockets, as the undertaker's wages,' he said, opening his hand and showing about a dozen gold pieces ; ' we have a right to take our own wherever we find it.'

' You see, Allan, we must never doubt Providence,' commented his master, who hesitated not to avail himself of this restitution, which his position did not allow him to reject.

Towards the close of the day our wayfarers, after long fatigue, approached Reading, where they meant to sleep, when they heard the galloping of a horse behind them ; they turned, and at the same moment an exclamation of surprise escaped from both. The horsedealer, Matthewson, mounted on an excellent horse, was a few paces from them.

Whether from preoccupation of mind or indifference, Matthewson did not appear to remark his old acquaintances. He was even riding on, when Morgan called to him, ' Have the kindness to stop a moment, Master Matthewson, I have something to say to you.'

The horsedealer drew rein, and his horse stood motionless.

'What do you want with me, friend ?' he asked. ' What, is it you, my lord ? You on foot, in this sad plight ! In faith, I should have passed you a hundred times without knowing you. What is become of that first-rate horse you had from me at Bristol, through an unlucky mistake ?'

'That horse was stolen from me last night ; but to what unlucky mistake do you allude ?'

' Why, the mistake my man made, which has put me out greatly. The stupid booby mistook two horses which I had just sold for those I was to furnish you with in exchange for Jewel.'

'Then the horse that was stolen last night—— '

: Was not intended for you. As soon as I found out the

mistake I went to your inn, but you had left four hours before, and I could not overtake you. So I am a loser to the tune of forty pounds ! But after all, Sir Knight, I think you are too just and honourable not to make me amends for my loss. Errors are excepted in horsedealing, &c.'

The horsedealer's words demolished as quickly as the child's breath the castle of cards, the whole scaffolding of suppositions which Allan and his master had built on Matthewson's mysteriously benevolent behaviour.

In truth, the groom's stupidity fully explained the horse-dealer's supposed generosity ; the claim made by the latter finished clearing up the matter.

'Friend,' answered Morgan, with embarrassment, ' I will not deny that I was astonished at seeing the beauty of the horse which you sent me, but I give you my word of honour I did not know its value. As to making up to you the loss you have sus-tained through me, it is at present quite out of my power. I was last night, I repeat,'entirely stripped by thieves. I have'scarcely enough left to take me on my journey. I think you do not doubt my honour? Otherwise, my sad plight, to use your own expression, proves more than words. All I can do for you is to promise that if I become more fortunate, I will make you re-compense later for the loss you have sustained.

'That will do, sir, for, legally speaking, you owe me nothing. And look you, I don't know how it is, but I have faith in your future. The first time I saw you I said to myself, "That young man will get on."'

'May your prophecy come true.'

'Still, it must be allowed that hitherto there does not seem much prospect of that coming to pass. You don't get on very fast. From landowner—not that your property was of much account—you have become a wanderer without goods or abode. I fear such a bad beginning must have discouraged you a little.'

Sir Lewis had before remarked the horsedealer's ill-breeding ; therefore these observations, which from any one else would have deeply wounded him, from Matthewson aroused neither feeling nor anger. He even continued the conversation.

'It is true that finding myself so completely cleared out, made me feel down-hearted at first, but only for a time ; now I am resigned to my ill luck.'

'Such courage bodes well ; it proves you have a fine spirit. Well, will you make another bargain with me? Something tells me I shall profit by you after all.'

'What is your bargain, Matthewson ?'

'First of all—for I should not like to appear dishonourable in your eyes,' continued the horsedealer after a short silence,—'let us settle our relative positions. I have no need of you, while you can scarcely do without me ; so the advantage is on my side. If you are willing to promise me a sum of five hundred pounds sterling, I will offhand lend you a tenth of that sum, that is, a clear fifty !"

Morgan thought a moment before answering.

'Well,' continued Matthewson, 'what do you decide ? But observe, I beg, there is no usury here. The usurer is a prudent thief, who only advances money upon good security ; but I am a bold speculator who risk mine on a problematical future. On the other hand, such matters have generally succeeded with me better than safer investments. Well, what will you do ? Decide as soon as you can, for my time is precious.'

' Master Matthewson,' replied Sir Lewis, 'I am obliged for your good opinion, but I will not profit by it. To borrow money without being sure of ever having the means of paying it, seems to me wrong, almost dishonourable. I am sufficiently resigned to bear my poverty proudly, and too much of a gentleman to endanger my honour. I refuse.'

' You have pondered it well—your refusal is final ?'

' Quite so, sir.'

' Then good-bye, my lord, and good luck to you.'

' Fare thee well !'

The horsedealer set spurs to his horse and was quickly lost in the cloud of dust raised by the hoofs.

Allan, who out of respect for his master had taken no part in the conversation, remonstrated strongly with his master on his refusal.

'Indeed, you are very wrong, sir,' he said ; 'you will never get on if you have so proud a stomach. Zounds! money, too! who would refuse that ?'

' Would you barter your soul for gold, then, Allan ?'

' Well, master, perhaps after all you are in the right,' answered the servant. 'A Morgan cannot be under obligation to a horse-coper.'

The two travellers found at the town a piece of very unexpected good fortune; that is to say, they met with some merchants who on their way to town, fearing the dangers of the road, offered to lend them two horses for fifty shillings if they would join their party. This Morgan very willingly agreed to do.

A fortnight later the pair, having arrived safely at the end of their journey, dismounted at the Old White Horse Inn.

Allan had been frightened at the grandeur of Bristol, but the sight of London filled him with the deepest astonishment.

Morgan's first thought on alighting was to inquire the direction of the Spanish Envoy's residence.

CHAPTER XI.

FINE FEATHERS.

As soon as the young gentleman had obtained the information he desired, he asked to be shown to a room where he hastened to arrange his dress, which had become so worn and soiled as to give him the appearance of a vagabond rather than a gentleman.

Impossible to present himself in such rags before the Marquis de Monterey's daughter : a new suit was absolutely necessary. This discovery made Morgan look at his purse, which contained seventeen shillings or so.

'What matters it ?' he said to himself, 'I must make the best of it ; if Nativa loves me she will be too pleased to see me to think whether I am well dressed or not.'

Notwithstanding his pretended unconcern, he felt uncomfortable and vexed. A man may bear gallantly a sword-thrust who yet cries out lustily at the reiterated pricking of a needle.

Trying to hide this little weakness even from himself, the knight walked up and down before the glass. A prolonged inspection of himself proved still less satisfactory. He gave utterance to something very like an oath, and stamped angrily. His appearance was simply disgraceful.

'By George and all the dragons !' he cried, after a moment's thought, 'I am saved ! Why the deuce did I not think of it before ?'

He seized his pistols, inspected them carefully, then putting them under his arm, and wrapping his cloak round his shoulders, he quitted his chamber, and ran quickly downstairs.

In the street he moderated his speed, and assumed the air of a man well used to the wonders of town. For nearly ten minutes he continued this listless walk, until he stopped in the Strand before a gunsmith's shop, and entered. Addressing the master, who was occupied in polishing a sword, he said, with slight hesitation,—

'I have just come off a journey, and I wish to dispose of a pair of capital pistols, of which I have no further need. Will they suit you ?'

'I don't buy second-hand arms,' said the gunsmith, without leaving his work. 'If you want money, apply to a broker.'

This scarcely civil answer made the blood mount in the gentleman's face, but determined to bear everything for Nativa's sake, he was not discouraged. He continued, in tones which he strove to make steady, although he shook with anger,—

'Will you be so good, then, as to direct me to a broker ? As my pistols were made by a famous smith, and are worth a good sum, I wish——’

‘Oh, your pistols are antiques, are they ?’ interrupted the gunsmith, raising his eyes to Morgan, ‘ that makes a difference. Be so good as to show them to me.’

He handed him the weapons.

‘Really,’ said the latter, having examined the pistols minutely and tried their locks, ‘ these are not so bad.   I shall not be able to sell them save as curiosities.   What price do you fix on them ?’

‘These pistols cost fifteen pounds.’

‘Fifteen pounds!’ echoed the shopkeeper ironically, scanning the speaker from head to foot. ‘ It seems, young sir, you don’t set much store on money.’

‘These pistols were sold to me at the same price the ship captain gave at Bristol,’ replied Morgan, who, to keep his temper, had still greater need of invoking Nativa’s image.

‘Oh, that is likely enough ; every one knows sailors are noted for throwing their money out of window ; but you——’

‘I,’ replied Sir Lewis, biting his lips till the blood came, ‘ I am in a hurry, and wish for an answer, yes or no.’

‘Well, I don’t object to purchase ; not, as I say again, that I have any chance of making anything by the bargain, but only to keep the pistols as curiosities in my line.’

‘And what do you offer for them ?’ asked Morgan, who wished to end the matter.

‘Wait till I make sure they are in good condition.’

Just at this moment two richly dressed young men entered the shop and asked to look at some swords ; the shopkeeper laid the pistols on the counter, and without even excusing himself to Morgan, attended to the new-comers.

‘Just as it was at Compton’s,’ muttered the country knight. ‘These courtiers are well dressed and I am in rags, therefore they are my superiors, and I must give way.   Zounds ! I am much in need of clothes, yet I would give my pistols if one of these young dandies would dare to affront me.’

Morgan almost unconsciously frowned fiercely at the young gentlemen, who dared not return his glance.

The former understood by that mysterious instinct which never errs, that had those gentlemen and he had a passage of arms, he would have had the better of them.   This consciousness of his own superiority of right hand calmed his anger.

‘Well,’ he murmured, ‘ it is a good thing to be well-dressed and have money in one’s purse, but there is something better still, a brave loyal heart that knows no fear, and a hand that can wield a sword.   I was wrong to despair.’

The young dandies, disconcerted by Morgan’s fierce looks ordered two swords, gave their addresses, and left the shop.

The gunsmith, after writing a few lines in his ledger and replacing the swords he had taken down, deigned to remember that some one was waiting.

He took up the pistols again, examined them still more minutely, looked at the name of the maker through a magnifying glass, and said :—

'Will you take four pounds for them ? that is the most I can give.'

'But, I repeat, they cost me fifteen.'

'No more words upon it. In my turn I say yes or no ? It is for you to take it or leave it as you please.'

'Well, I accept,' answered Morgan, fearing that if he did not submit to this sacrifice he should not have courage to try anywhere else.

'Now, young gentleman,' said the shopkeeper when he had paid him the money, 'you have only to keep up the street, and to the right, four doors farther on, you will find a dealer in second-hand clothes, who will sell you some very presentable, and almost in the fashion a fortnight before.' This sneer would have elicited a sharp rejoinder if not chastisement, but now Morgan only said,—

'Thanks for your direction. I shall take advantage of it.'

He was evidently profiting by his lessons in life. The cheating of old clothes dealers is too well known to need comment. Suffice it that Morgan, after much haggling, was properly equipped from head to foot for about four pounds. But as the customer's purse was slender the dealer kindly consented to take his old clothes for a portion of the money.

Allan's wonder at seeing his master so elegantly draped was only equal to his delight.

'Mercy o' me !' he exclaimed, clapping his hands, 'how handsome you look !'

This simple compliment of his warm-hearted follower gave Morgan pleasure, for his thoughts reverted to Nativa.

'Well, master,' continued Allan, 'we seem to be getting on. I begin to think that they speak too ill of London down our parts. If in your first walk, and in less than an hour, you get such handsome clothes, I should not wonder if in a month you found a carriage and could afford yourself the pleasure of increasing my wages.'

These hopes did not please his master as well as his compliments had done ; they recalled the poverty to which he was reduced, and the obstacles which he had to overcome, and he could not repress a sigh.

His master's sadness greatly astonished the servant, who drew nigh to him and said with considerable embarrassment,—

'I wish, sir, you would permit me for a moment to forget the respect I owe you.'

'What do you mean, sirrah?' cried Morgan, who thought he must have misunderstood.

'I wish you would allow me for a moment to forget the respect I owe you.'

'Have you gone mad? Explain yourself.'

'I only mean, sir, I wish, as a friend to a friend, just to whisper a piece of advice in your ear.'

'Oh, that is your want of respect, is it? Say what you have got to say. I consent.'

Allan came a little nearer his master, hesitated, reddened, cast down his eyes, and at last found courage to say,—

'Dear master, do not trust in women. Do not look at them, and when they speak to you do not reply. The best among them, look you, is not worth a doit.'

'Fool!' cried Morgan angrily—for at that moment he was thinking of Nativa, of course.

Allan retired, much disconcerted.

Morgan on his arrival had been received with some distrust by mine host of the 'White Horse,' his travelling costume being no letter of recommendation to an innkeeper; but when after a short absence he returned so handsomely apparelled, he sent a servant to learn what he would have for supper.

The poor young gentleman could not vow that he had not a shilling left, nor could he go without eating. He ordered a very simple repast. Emboldened by the deference shown him— for our hero was not wanting in perception, only in knowledge of the world—he asked if a messenger could take a letter for him to the Spanish Ambassador's.

The waiter bowed low at the name, and said that if the gentleman would please to entrust him with the letter he would undertake to deliver it and bring back an answer in an hour.

Morgan asked for writing materials, and wrote these words :—

'I have only just arrived. If, to-morrow, my life can serve you, it is yours.'

This note he signed and gave to the servant, who brought back a speedy answer.

It is easy to guess Morgan's emotion in opening his letter, which contained these words :—

'Thanks : to-morrow I cannot see you ; but the day after be at Carraway's, the pastrycook's, at three, and ask for the foreign lady. I shall be there.'

Overcome with joy, the gentleman put his hand to his pocket to give the messenger a coin, but reflection stopped him.

'Waiter,' he said, in an embarrassed tone—for even this half-falsehood was repugnant to his pride, ' I shall probably want your services again ; we will settle accounts later to your satisfaction.'

At the thought that he should so soon see Nativa, Morgan

could scarcely restrain his delight. His happiness seemed to choke him. He even thought of taking Allan into his confidence.

Suddenly his face grew thoughtful, and he turned pale on reading Nativa's note ; he had perceived that she had not given him Carraway's address.

After a moment's reflection he said to himself, ' No doubt the man is well known, or Nativa would not have omitted it.'

It was now night ; the day had been a busy one ; Morgan retired to rest.

Notwithstanding he was much fatigued he could not sleep. The pastrycook's whereabouts still was in his mind. It was daylight before he dropped asleep.

At ten he awoke, and dressing himself quickly, he hurried downstairs to seek the information he wanted.

On the stairs he met one of the merchants in whose company he had travelled to London.

' Dear sir,' he said to him without preface, ' as you have been frequently in town, can you tell me where I can find a pastrycook of the name of Carraway ? '

' Nothing easier ; why, every one knows him.'

' Oh, indeed,' cried Morgan, delighted ; ' and pray where does he live ? '

' Oh, you will find him at Charing Cross ; and I bet twenty to one, my young friend, you have got a love-tryst there. Ha ! ha ! I wish you joy ; all the ladies go there who belong to the nobility. No others would dare be seen there. But as you do not know Carraway's, allow me to give you a piece of advice, —that is, to put plenty of money in your pocket. Everything there is horribly dear. I could tell you, if I were not in a hurry, some odd stories, but I am waited for. So I will wish you good morning, and a pleasant meeting with the fair one.'

The merchant passed on, leaving Morgan a prey at once to joy and grief. He had learnt what he wished to know, and something besides, which, in the present state of his finances, was alarming. One must own that his position was a little embarrassing.

The chevalier returned to his room, and threw himself on the bed in despair.

CHAPTER XII.

A HIGHWAYMAN FROM BENEVOLENCE.

ALLAN, tormented neither by love nor ambition, had slept soundly ; and as he had risen soon after daybreak, towards ten o'clock, as was to be expected, he felt very hungry ; so that when he saw his master throw himself on the bed without saying a word about breakfast, he heaved a deep sigh.

'What is the matter?' asked Sir Lewis, with that ready sympathy for the troubles of others that superior spirits always feel.

'I am hungry, sir; don't people eat in London?'

'How happy you are to think of such common wants! Well, go tell John Tapster to bring breakfast.'

'I don't know anything about the customs here, but I suppose cockneys can cook eggs and bacon. Shall I tell them to bring you some?'

'No, thanks; I am not hungry. I shall not eat breakfast.'

'No breakfast, sir?' cried Allan in astonishment. 'You must be ill?'

'I don't know.'

'Don't know? Oh, dear master,' continued Allan sadly, 'yours is a noble heart, and you can bear to hear the truth. Will you allow me to tell you I am afraid that yesterday to obtain those fine clothes, you made a compact with the devil, for certainly the devil, or a woman, has thrown a spell over you.'

These final words set Sir Lewis blushing.

'Oh, if I believed in the devil I would call him to my aid now; how willingly would I sell him one year of my unhappy life for twenty pounds!'

'Avaunt, Satan!' cried Allan in consternation; 'pay no heed to what my master says—he has gone mad!'

'Yes, Allan, I am mad,' said Morgan, getting up and pacing the room in violent agitation. 'Heaven pardon the profane words I have just used. I am mad at being young, strong, brave, and clear-headed, and yet to be forced for the sake of a handful of crowns to renounce the greatest happiness in life—a happiness for which one would risk one's head,—is not that enough to drive any fellow mad?'

Morgan scarcely considered he was addressing his servant: it was rather a cry of pain that broke from his lips.

One thing alone was clear to Allan's mind —that the young gentleman wanted twenty crowns, and that it was the impossibility of getting that sum which made him ill and caused him to blaspheme.

Solely from attachment to his master, Allan racked his brain to find a means of procuring the sum which his master so coveted.

The solution of this problem was so difficult, that the Cornishman thought it prudent first to go and get his breakfast.

'Oh, master,' he cried, laughing, when he came back, 'would you believe it? these townsmen, who think themselves so clever, don't even know how to toast pilchards! Every one eats them at Penmark; yet Penmark is not a large town.'

A waiter brought a tolerable repast.

'Well, master,' observed Allan, casting a greedy and curious glance at the meats which he had never seen before, 'is your appetite still asleep? This mess has a delicious smell. After all, there is no great merit in cooking well. Londoners ought to excel in something. They do cook well; that is a fact.'

Allan was much disappointed when his master threw himself again on the bed, and refused to join in his good cheer. Still, his sympathy for this sadness did not take away Allan's appetite, or prevent him making a famous breakfast. In ten minutes the dishes were cleared.

'It was not bad,' he said, wiping his mouth with the back of his hand, 'only the pieces were too small to taste. These new-fangled dishes are not equal to a good basin of barley broth, though I do feel much better than I did a quarter of an hour ago.'

Absorbed in his thoughts Sir Lewis did not answer; and soon Allan, following his master's example, with his elbow on the table and his large hand supporting his head, fell into a brown study.

'Thank goodness, master,' cried he, starting suddenly off his chair, 'an idea has struck me, and you shall have your money!'

'What is your project?' asked Morgan, with indifference, for he thought that the brave rustic, ignorant of city life and its resources, was probably led away with some impracticable dream.

'I would rather not answer your question, sir. To give over one's victory beforehand, I have always found leads to defeat. Could you give me a holiday to-day, and do without me till evening?'

'You have forestalled my intentions, I was going to send you to look at the curiosities. But take care not to lose yourself, and not to forget the name of the street and the inn.'

'Holborn Bars, the White Horse Inn. I have that. As to the curiosities, master,' added Allan, sneeringly, 'one need not trouble about them. What is to be expected from people who can't toast pilchards? So I may go, sir, with your permission?'

'Yes, you may go at once, if you like.'

'It does not please me, sir, but it is necessary.'

Allan pulled his broad-brimmed hat well over his eyes, gave a tug or two at his coat, and ran his fingers through his hair. His toilet being thus finished, he descended the stairs with a confident air, his stick in his hand.

In parading his indifference to City curiosities Allan was in the wrong, for no sooner had he set foot in the street than his amazement was so great that he leant against the wall for support; never had the brave fellow, even in a dream, beheld anything half so wonderful. The gorgeous coaches with six horses, the wretched hackney vehicles covered with mud, the number of foot passengers who crowded the roads, made him think at first that it must be a coronation day.

His admiration was great at sight of the rich dresses; everywhere silk ribbons, feathers, large watches hanging at fobs, and handsome canes, the knobs set in jewels.

Several times Allan remained open-mouthed, and scarcely believing his own senses, before men who stopped in the middle of the street to gloat at themselves complacently in small mirrors they carried, and combed their wigs with the greatest coolness imaginable.

This custom of making their toilet in the public streets deeply impressed the Penmarker. He fancied that those who took such liberties must be great lords at least, whereas most of them are lawyers' clerks, dancing-masters, shopmen, and servants out for a holiday.

Allan found everything delightful.

After half an hour's bewilderment, having somewhat recovered his coolness, he bethought himself of accomplishing some project for getting the twenty crowns that his master wanted.

In his peregrinations chance guided him off the thoroughfare into Lincoln's Inn Fields,—a bad direction, for at that time the Fields were frequented by the most expert thieves and pickpockets, therefore the least likely place wherein to find purses.

On the other hand, the place was the noted resort of mountebanks, adventurers, idlers, vagabonds, beggars, disbanded soldiers, and footmen out for a holiday, full of dangers for the inexperienced countryman.

Engrossed by his thoughts and bewildered by the busy, noisy crowd which elbowed him at every step, Allan at first did not observe the strange living picture it presented. It was only after being boldly mixed in the crowd that he remarked what was passing around him.

'Why, who can that great lord be who is standing up in his carriage, and is about to speechify to the people?' Allan said to himself. 'Let us listen. Good gracious! how he is covered with gold embroidery! and what handsome feathers! He must be a royal prince at least. Now there is silence—he is going to begin.'

The person whom Allan honoured with the title of royal prince was a quacksalver, who began by speaking of his travels in Arabia and China, the extraordinary success he had had at several foreign courts, especially in that of the Grand Turk. After a search of twenty years he had found certain rare plants endowed with the extraordinary virtue of changing in five

minutes a man's features. It was sufficient to rub one's face
with the marvellous tincture extracted from these plants, to
change ugliness into beauty, or at all events into comeliness.
This physician affirmed that, thanks to his precious secret, he
had already brought about ten thousand marriages.

'What a liar!' muttered Allan, about to proceed on his way,
when the quack added,—

'I can understand, gentlemen, your receiving this miraculous
announcement with suspicion. Some things must be seen to be
believed. Well, I will give an incontestible proof of what I
say. I will work this miracle before you. Let the ugliest man
present come forward, and here, under your very eyes, and in
five minutes, I say again, I will improve him so greatly that he
will not be recognisable! Come, I am ready. Who is the
unhappy man among you afflicted with the most frightful, most
ridiculous, the most stupid, most hideous visage? Let him
come forward without fear. I am ready.'

His musicians, three in number, held their peace, as if to
await the upshot of his challenge.

As was to be expected, no one came forward. Allan, however, whose curiosity had been greatly excited, stayed to see if
the experiment was made.

'Well, though no one speaks,' said the man with the beauty
philter, after a short pause, 'I understand this silence. Every
one thinks himself an Adonis. A mistake, gentlemen, a great
mistake. I see, on the contrary, a great many unpleasing
faces.'

Every one looked at his neighbour; and the quack, after
another pause, continued,—

'Since no one, through self-love, dares devote himself for
the happiness of his fellow-creatures, I will myself choose the
ugliest person present.'

The musicians—two blind men and a hang-dog—dressed in
the Spanish costume, began to play while the quack, with his
right hand placed over his eyes as a shade, examined the crowd
around him. Allan, whose suspicious mind saw a trick in all
this delay, was leaving, when a young gentleman very well
dressed, and with a sword by his side, touched him lightly on
the shoulder, and observed,—

'My master sent me to you, sir, to beg you will come and
speak to him. Have the goodness to follow me.'

'You make a mistake, sir, without doubt,' answered Allan,
abashed; 'I know no one in town, and I cannot be the person
your master wants.'

'I assure you, sir, I am not mistaken.'

'But who, then, is your master? and what does he want
with me?'

'My master is the best second-sight seer in Europe ; he wishes, I believe, to return to you a purse-full of crowns that he saw a pickpocket take from your pocket ! See if you have not lost something.'

These words caused at first immense astonishment to Allan, and then equal delight.

'I understand now,' he said ; 'my good star sends me the crowns. I don't mind following you.'

The young gentleman took his way directly behind the plat form where the quack was gesticulating, and pointing to a ladder, said,—

'Be so good as to mount.'

'What did you say ?' asked the peasant.

'Be so good as to go up.'

'What, is your master that man who pretends——'

'The very same,' said the messenger, gently pushing Allan towards the ladder ; but the other stood still, and looked fiercely at his guide, who only remarked, coolly,—

'Then, sir, may my master conscientiously give the twenty odd crowns in your purse to the poor ?'

The words ' twenty crowns,' which corresponded so precisely with the servant's wishes, removed the vague scruples he felt.

'Not so fast !' he interrupted eagerly. 'I want my money myself.'

'Then go, and I hope you may get it,' answered the messenger, with a show of impatience.

Allan mounted two steps, then turning to his conductor, said,—

'I warn you that we Cornishmen strike hard, and don't understand being made fools of.' Then he went up.

The crowd welcomed Allan's appearance on the platform with hoots of joy ; but as the dupe saw a purse in the mountebank's hand, he paid no attention to the jeering, and eagerly strode up to the man with the beauty draught, who seemed to invite him forward.

Alas ! Allan had barely neared him before the perfidious scamp, addressing the crowd in a loud voice, said—

'Behold, gentlemen, the ugliest man present, who comes of his own accord to try the virtue of my elixir ! The monster will not have cause to repent his confidence in me. When he leaves my hands all the women will be in love with him ! Look at his ugly phiz ! in five minutes the change will be effected ! —Musicians, play up !'

The mountebank, aided by his three servants, among whom was the fine gentleman with the sword, seized Allan's head and pulled his ears so sharply that the poor victim uttered a loud scream and made a frightful grimace. The crowd did not hear the cry, which was drowned by the music, but saw the grimace, and gave a shout of laughter.

Overwhelmed by rage, the Cornishman stood a moment motionless. He thought that he had fallen into the devil's clutches and had lost his head. The mock doctor took advantage of his stupefaction to proceed with his sham toilet. He first combed out his long hair and brushed it up off his forehead. Then with carmine and flake-white he so painted his face that in less time than it takes to relate it, the rustic, sunburnt cheeks had acquired a beautiful complexion.

'Now it is effected!' roared the quack, pretending to cork an empty bottle which he had not used. 'What do you think gentlemen, of the metamorphosis? Is it not miraculous? And remark, the difficulty of the undertaking did not stagger me! I chose a very ugly subject.'

The combed and painted servant, from a distance, did not look unnatural, so the crowd, instead of laughing, applauded.

'Now for the next,' continued the charlatan, pushing Allan aside. This push awoke the luckless clown from his lethargy. A redness darker than the carmine covered his face.

'Odzookers!' he yelled in a fury, flourishing his club, 'I never thought a cockney would have dared to make game of me. Ha! you are fond of laughing, are you! Fools! laugh now if you like!'

These words were scarcely out of his mouth before his cudgel circled in the air and fell with irresistible force on the shoulders of the servants, on the head of the quack, and on the phials.

At the first blow the renowned physician fell, bathed in his beautifying draughts; the servants soon followed, and the musicians were banged like big drums. All was confusion and dismay. The spectators, thinking it was part of the farce, laughed more than ever. Luckily the elixir in which the quacksalver's man swam veiled his face, or Allan would have recognised his once antagonist, the pretended Viscount Charmarand.

'Now that's done,' said Allan, coming down the ladder. 'If ever I return home I can tell how I beat the townsmen who made game of me. It will be a good joke all round.'

He was running off at a good pace when some one overtook him and pulled him by the sleeve.

'Friend, friend, a word with you, if you please. If you would be so good as to teach me that trick of yours I will give you a crown. I might frighten my wife by pretending to beat my apprentices and break everything in the shop—it would be profitable fun.'

'I don't understand you,' answered Allan, on his guard, for he thought he had to do with another mystifier.

'I ask you,' repeated the man, 'to teach me the trick of your blows which appear to knock every one down and raise so much dust.'

'It is not difficult : get a thick stick and strike hard.'

'What !' cried the man, 'did you strike in earnest ? '

'If you are in doubt, go and ask the rogue who makes man beautiful for ever.'

'You astonish me. And may I beg, friend, your reason for beating the quack and his assistants ? '

'Did you not see me beautified ? ' answered Allan, covered with shame at having been covered with paint.

'Yes, I witnessed the transmogrification,' answered the other, 'and I think you were the gainer by it ; you look much better than before.'

'Master,' cried Allan, 'as I am not so keen as the cockneys, I answer their jokes with my club. I advise you therefore to let me alone. I am a quiet fellow enough, and don't wish to kill any one.'

'Indeed, friend, you quite mistake me,' said the other, much amused by the rural's eccentricities, 'and in proof thereof, if you will dine with me it will give me pleasure.'

This proposal sounded pleasantly to the countryman.

'I am willing to dine with you,' he answered, 'but I warn you beforehand I will not pay my scot.'

'Oh, that is understood. I came out this morning to recover some bad debts, telling my wife not to wait dinner for me ; and as I have had better luck than I expected, it is only meet— meat and drink, I may say, ha, ha !—that I should take a treat, especially as my wife won't know anything of the expense. Come and dine.'

This explanation was lost upon his hearer, who only understood the last three words, and answered,—

'The sooner the better.'

The new acquaintances passed into the Strand, and soon reached Butchers' Row, where the new law courts now rise. This place, noted for edibles, was still better known for an establishment called 'The Syren and Bag-o'-nails' (Silenus and Bacchanals ?), which was the resort of military men, swindlers, and merry-minded tradesmen. The two new friends entered the tavern.

'My friend,' said the amphitryon to the peasant, 'I am a linen-draper, and my name is Dowlass. What are you ? '

'I am servant to the Knight of Morgan, in Cornwall, and my name is Allan.'

'A Cornishman with a Scotch name, ha, ha ! But now for dinner.'

They seated themselves at a table in the public room, and began their repast.

The draper rarely allowed himself a treat, so wishing to celebrate his day's freedom—for he had the means of hiding his extravagance from his wife—he made a brave onslaught on the wine. An hour had not passed when cordial Master Dowlass's head became so heated that he began to talk with the people at the other tables, and soon the conversation became general. He was kind-hearted, but, like most citizens, talkative and fond of a jest. He therefore did not long resist the temptation of turning his companion into a butt for the company.

He related the painting and the beating in the Fields, and that Allan, being born in Cornwall, fancied himself not an Englishman.

'Ho, friend,' cried a sergeant, wishing also for an oratorical triumph, 'so Cornwall, then, does not belong to the King of England?'

'Certainly not,' said Allan, to whom the question was pointedly addressed; 'do you not make your kings of our Dukes of Cornwall?'

This poser rather damped the impression of the wits that they would have all the arguments their own way. Nevertheless, they pursued the same tenor, and Allan could not help perceiving, by the loud roars which his answers to some absurd questions elicited, that he was being laughed at. Dowlass made this still more evident by getting up repeatedly to clap his shoulder, crying out,—

'My dear fellow, how you make me laugh! I would not have missed this treat for a score of broad pieces.'

Whether from having made up his mind, or the wine had put him in spirits, it even seemed that Allan lent himself willingly to the sacrifice of his vanity, in order to promote the general hilarity.

The draper again chirruped gaily.

'My dear fellow, Tarleton never amused our fathers as much as you do me. Whenever I have spare cash, we must dine together. Hold, here is my address; when my wife is not in the way, come into the shop and we will appoint a place of merry meeting.'

'Are you sure that with that scrap of paper I shall be able to find you?' asked Allan.

'How odd you are! certainly, it is my address.'

'All right,' said the rustic, as he carefully put away the paper.

By eight o'clock Allan had forty addresses. As for Dowlass, he chanted vespers, and talked seriously of sending for his wife to abuse her for her stinginess and assumption of authority in the household.

Every one knows how in the seventeenth century the rich and noble were possessed with a passion for gambling. The example coming from high quarters bore sad fruits. Merchants, petty landlords, artizans, shop-keepers, soldiers, all classes tried their luck at basset ; there was not a house where there were not cards and dice in abundance. It is not therefore surprising that Dowlass wished to finish such a delightful day with a game.

On the other hand, as the good man was in a state bordering on drunkenness, and rattled ostentatiously his shillings and crowns in his pocket, it followed that on hearing ·his wish half a dozen persons got up readily and offered to take a hand with him at anything.

Allan, with his eyes half closed, leaning against the wall, seemed in a delightful state of somnolency and paid little heed to what was going on.

However, as soon as the game commenced and the coin rolled on the table, the countryman roused himself, rubbed his eyes, and gave earnest attention to the game.

As might be expected, the linen-draper began by winning, but fortune soon changed, and in five minutes he lost what he had gained in a quarter of an hour.

'I say, friend,' whispered Allan to him, 'it is my opinion that we had better be off.'

'Leave off in the middle of a game ? never !' cried Dowlass. 'Do you take me for a loon who knows nothing of life ?'

'But I observe something,' continued Allan, 'which is not in your favour, friend, and I fear what may happen.'

'What do you observe, dear cudgel-player of my heart ?'

'That while you are speaking, singing, laughing, and swearing, the others don't say a word, pay the greatest attention to the cards, and only grin every now and anon. Friend, you may hang me this minute if you are not being plucked like a Michaelmas bird.'

'Zounds ! will you leave me alone ? Thou fool ! ' cried the draper, annoyed by an unexpected mischance, which made him lose ten shillings, ' your croakings bring me ill luck ; hold your tongue, or I'll beat you for meddling.'

'I am silent,' answered Allan quietly, on whom the draper's menace had no effect. The event proved the counseller in the right. Very soon Dowlass lost all the money he had before him, and was obliged to take some from his pocket.

'Take care,' said Allan again.

Dowlass's only answer was a blow aimed at the speaker's chest, who received it as coolly as he did the threat. The draper played badly. In five minutes again he had recourse to his pocket.

' How much money have you left ? ' inquired Allan, seizing his arm and holding it so tightly that the other turned pale.

'Take care, or you'll break my bones.'

' How much money have you left ? '

' A score crowns; but leave me alone: you shall see my revenge.'

‘I won’t let you play any more, do you hear?’ cried the Cornishman in a tone of authority, which exasperated the other.

‘You won’t, indeed? why, that is good fun!’

‘If you don’t do as I tell you, I’ll go and fetch your wife.’

This threat produced a great effect on the unhappy gamester.

‘Oh, you are no friend of mine!’ he whimpered, with tears in his eyes.

‘And I will tell her how you have been ridiculing her before everybody, and how you wanted to send for her to abuse her in public.’

‘Hold your tongue, viper that I have warmed in my breast! Speak lower, Sophonisba might hear you, and it would be all up with me : she would never let me go out alone again.’

‘If you want me to hold my tongue, get up, and let us be going.’

‘And are you not afraid, wretched witness of my excesses, that I should kill you when we get into the street?’ roared Dowlass, with tipsy anger.

‘You can kill me, then, if that amuses you : but the most important point now is that you should go with me.’

‘I follow you, rascal ; but you shall see!’

‘All right : I shall see moons and marvels! Come along.’

Dowlass got up unsteadily, and, much against his will, followed Allan.

When the two left the ‘Syren and Bag-o’-nails,’ the night was dark ; a fine rain fell incessantly and increased the gloom.

This rain and the sharp night air, after the close atmosphere of the room they had quitted, greatly augmented the draper’s drunkenness ; he was obliged to lean on Allan to avoid falling.

The latter was very pale, and his eyes looked haggard : the convulsive trembling of his hand and the beating of his heart denoted that a severe conflict was going on within him.

‘I won’t let master fret his noble heart out,’ he muttered, ‘I must have this ass’s money.’

Still supporting the clothier, he went a few steps further, where he stopped, and seized him by the throat, crying out,—

‘Give me your money!’

‘Eh! what do you say?’ faltered Dowlass, whom this attack recalled to his senses.

‘Quick, your money or your life! Have you not said fifty times that you would not lose the day for twenty crowns? I take your crowns, and leave you the pleasure of the day!’

Allan, whilst saying these words, slid his hand into Dowlass’s pocket, and took his purse.

‘Oh, wretch! murderer! thief! But here comes the watch ; I shall call out and you will be hung.’

The measured tread of the patrol was heard in the distance.

'If you utter one word I'll strangle you!' hissed Allan, tightening his grasp on the inebriate's throat.

'Mercy! you are choking me!' gurgled the latter.

The patrol drew near; not a moment was to be lost.

Allan promptly decided to put the stolen purse into his belt, and leaving the luckless clothier half dead with fright, he ran forward at full speed, not knowing whither.

For more than half an hour he continued his flight. At length, overcome with fatigue, out of breath, and his eyes dizzy, he threw himself on the ground. He had descended into Westminster, and was on the river roadside.

'I may as well rest here as elsewhere. I must wait for daylight.'

It was then near midnight, so until four, when the sun rose, Allan lay on the grass, sobbing like a child. He was ashamed of his first attempt to rival Monsieur Duval.

'Nevertheless,' he said in justification, 'I could not let my master damn himself; and Dowlass, who asked me to dine with him, repeated so often he would not have lost his fun for twenty crowns. But if I have made a mistake, after all, Dowlass shall have his crowns again! And, besides, had it not been for me, would he not have lost them at play?'

At daybreak he rose, and proceeded up the rising ground to Charing Cross. Having recovered his usual cool demeanour, he asked his way.

When he reached the inn, he found Morgan a prey to extreme agitation.

'Sir,' he said to him, 'never more despair, and calm yourself now. Here are the twenty crowns that you wanted; I only beg,' added Allan, understanding from the young gentleman's astonishment, that he was likely to be overwhelmed with unanswerable and embarrassing inquiries, 'that you will ask me no questions. I have done nothing wrong to get the money. I have borrowed it, and it can be paid back.'

Notwithstanding Allan's entreaty, Morgan tried to draw out the recital of his adventures, but the Cornishman maintained an obstinate silence.

'Bah,' said Allan to himself, as his master set out joyfully to keep his appointment with Nativa, 'I really was absurdly stupid to make myself so wretched all night. After all, these citizens cheat the countryfolk so often, that to chouse them now and then is no great evil.'

CHAPTER XIII.

BENDING A BUTTERFLY AND BREAKING A BAR.

AT nightfall, on the previous day when Allan met with his adventures in Lincoln's Inn Fields, a well-appointed carriage, though it had no armorial bearings and was driven by a coachman out of livery, stopped at a small house in Charles Street, Soho, situated not far from the mansion inhabited afterwards by Sir William Hamilton. A short, thick-set man jumped out and knocked at the door.

This man, who seemed to be about fifty years of age, was very fashionably dressed. He wore a cocked hat with feathers, an embroidered coat, with large sleeves covering the wrist, a long waistcoat, a sword knot and ribbons, a Hollandish cravat, Spanish breeches, and rolled stockings.

Sir Lewis Morgan would certainly have passed this person a hundred times without thinking of Matthewson; nevertheless, it was no other than our friend the horsedealer.

Barely had Matthewson knocked when a footman in rich livery opened the door.

'Announce to your master the Baron Legaff.'

'*I* should first have been asked if his lordship receives,' answered the footman, with affected politeness, that bordered on impertinence of correction.

Matthewson slightly knit his brow, but without saying a word, took the valet by the collar, and sent him spinning up the passage.

The man certainly did not expect such an attack, but when he rose he hastened away, and returned in less than a minute, saying :

' If my lord will be so good as to follow me, my master waits for him.'

The footman led the way to a room on the first floor, and opening wide two folding-doors covered with velvet, announced Baron Legaff.

The room into which Matthewson, or 'Baron Legaff,' was ushered, was furnished in the most sumptuous manner ; only, thanks to its present disorder, its luxury was not imposing.

In this chamber, before a table covered with papers, sat a man, whose dress was rich, but donned carelessly ; he might be about sixty years of age, and his face wore an expression of mingled acuteness, indifference, good-nature, pride and impudence, which was very striking.

On seeing the visitor he rose, bowed slightly, and opened the conversation.

' My servant has told me, sir, of the rather rough manner in which you made your entry.   Have I the honour of speaking to one of my creditors ? '

' Not at all, my lord,' answered Matthewson, ' unless one of my men of business, which may possibly be, can have bought up some of your bills.   I was in a hurry ; your servant wished to give me the pleasure of his conversation, and I passed through ; that is all.'

' I am delighted, sir, that you are in a hurry, for I also am pressed for time——'

' A thousand excuses for interrupting you, but I must have a long conversation with you, and I very much doubt you will be able to go out this evening, so you had better send your coach away.'

' Oh, indeed !' remarked the Dutch nobleman, laughing. ' This is certainly very droll.   It appears, Baron Legaff, and allow me to observe, by the way, that I never even heard your name before in this or foreign peerages,—it appears, then, that you are accustomed to dispose of people's time whether they will or no.'

' In fact, I have extraordinary earnestness in business.   And after all, if I consulted every one's convenience, there would be no end to it.'

Whilst Matthewson said this, the master of the house looked at him attentively to convince himself that he had not a madman before him.

' Monsieur Legaff,' he said, rising suddenly, ' do you know in whose presence you are ? '

' Perfectly, my lord.   In presence of a man whom many do not appreciate justly, who makes his godmother, our good Queen Mary, tremble, who defies the anger of warrior King William, and who is Lord Menzil here and Mynheer Lusthoos in the Low Countries.'

' Well, then, sir, you, who know so many things, cannot be ignorant——'

' Allow me to interrupt you, my dear lord,' said Matthewson coolly.   ' You are about to threaten, which, in the first place, is in bad taste, and will bring you the mortification of having to make excuses.   Believe me, we had better be friends.   Don't you think, now, that the soil of St. Germain's is available for any kind of cultivation ? '

At this question, which had nothing to do with the conversation, but which the intruder put very pointedly, Lord Menzil turned pale, and, notwithstanding his great impudence, was evidently hit hard.

' In truth, baron,' he answered after a short silence, ' Heaven blesses and protects the efforts of the tiller which are expended conscientiously on the land.'

'The cuckoo, Mynheer, is the most hopeful of birds——'

'And the *fleur-de-lis* the most beautiful of flowers,' added the other, whose pallor increased.

'Your lordship is really the most learned man I know. I cannot express the pleasure that I expect in your conversation. Will you not now be kind enough to send away your carriage?'

'As you please,' answered the nobleman, giving the order accordingly.

'Now,' said Matthewson, 'as we are not in a hurry, will you allow me to begin our interview by a question in no way connected with the interests that will engage our attention presently?'

'Well, your question, baron?' answered Menzil, affecting an ease of manner habitual, but which he was far from feeling at this moment.

'My question may perhaps seem indiscreet, but attribute it, pray, to the strong interest I feel for you; and be persuaded that it is not dictated by curiosity. Every one knows, my dear lord, the shameful and inexplicable illiberality with which the king treats you, remarkable even—allow me—in a Dutchman.'

'Do not mention it, baron,' interrupted the other, with a sigh. 'One would really think that my royal kinsman does nought for the honour of my house. Between ourselves, my godmother has more pretension than he has to birth—he a stadtholder——'

'Ought to be meanness itself when his pride is not concerned.'

'Alas, you only too clearly guess William's character. If discretion had not prevented me, for it is bad policy to make family dissensions public, I should have chid him in a pamphlet. Well, dear baron, what is your question?'

'Your frankness puts me at my ease,' said Matthewson. 'Are you not at this moment rather short of money?'

'Rather short? you are an optimist! say dreadfully, shockingly short, and you will be within the truth.'

'Now I, on the contrary, am possessed of certain sums which I don't know what to do with, and which I want to place out.'

'Ah! if it is about investments—bah!' said Menzil, in a disappointed tone.

'I had an intention at first,' continued the pretended French baron,' of applying to some banker like Childs, but I assure you I have an aversion to the whole race, and I determined to manage this matter like a gentleman and with a gentleman.'

'A good idea,' cried the other, whose disappointed look at once gave place to a joyful smile. 'And pray how can I serve you in this matter?'

'Why, by becoming depositary of this money.'

'Oh, very well,' said the Dutchman. After a short pause he inquired gravely, 'What are your conditions, baron?'

'I repeat, my lord, I wish to arrange this matter as a

gentleman, not as a financier.   First thing, no writings between us.'

'I have a horror of notes of hand ! but, pardon me, you have forgotten to mention the amount of the money.'

'Five thousand pounds, roundly, my lord.'

'Good ! that is a pretty sum,' said Menzil, with affected indifference, belied by the tone of his voice and the animation of his look ; 'go on, if you please.   You said no writings ? '

'What point, then, remains to be settled ? '

'Why, first the time of repayment ; then the interest—do we say eight per cent ? '

'Now, my lord, you will take it in a business light ! fie !   I should not have expected such a thing from you.'

'What, I take a commercial view ! '

'Assuredly ! don't you talk of interest ?   What has your lordship in common to do with Change-alley ?   For shame ! '

'You are right,' agreed Menzil, ' it is the merchants about his majesty that put such things in my head.   Laying aside the interest, it only remains to settle the falling due and repayment.'

'Let us say thirty years, if you will, dear count ? '

'Thirty years,' repeated the spendthrift, with a solemn air, ' that is a long time.   You put on me, my dear baron, an awful responsibility.   No, decidedly, I cannot allow so long a delay '

'Then let us say five-and-twenty years ? '

'Well, be it so ; five-and-twenty years, that is the most I can do for you.'

A moment's silence followed, until the Dutchman asked in a tone of eagerness,

'And when will you put the five thousand in my possession ? '

'Directly, if you will permit me,' answered Legaff, who, taking out his pocket-book, handed a doubled paper to the other.

'Oh, paper ! ' cried Menzil, with comic despair, ' Der Teufel ! What's the use of that to me ? There is not a gull in all London who would cash me even a "Treasury note ! "'

'Is a bill of the Tonnage Bank also valueless ? '

'Oh, that alters the case,' exclaimed my lord joyfully, unfolding the paper and looking at it with much satisfaction.   ' Dear baron, I don't know any one in the world who does business so pleasantly as you do.   Really, I am delighted to have made your acquaintance !   Pray make use of me and of my influence ; it is entirely at your service.   Even if you needed more money invested, I should not be able to refuse you.'

'I will take a note of that ! for this first investment is only a feeler.   I have still much money to place out.'

Lord Menzil looked at Matthewson with intense admiration.

' Are you very rich ? '

' I am overburdened with riches ! But as you have been so good as to offer me your services, may I trouble you for some information that I am in want of ? '

' Speak without reserve, my dear baron ; you know I have sent away my carriage.'

' What I want to know now is not very important. What are the days and hours when the king works with his Navy Minister ? '

' What, that poor fag Barstairs, who is the deputy of Lord Russell, gone to command the Channel Fleet ? '

' A fag, if you will, but it is precisely about him that I seek information.'

' Master Barstairs works every night, sometimes till eleven o'clock with the king. As you know, he pleases him and is quite a character. He amuses himself by creating difficulties, and his secret aim seems to be to destroy the navy, which he detests. His greatest pleasure is to be disagreeable to those who need his influence ; and one must do him the justice to admit that he succeeds admirably in that. He is the harshest minister there ever was to his subordinates.'

' But as to his abilities, my dear lord ? '

' He has just enough ; not quite devoid of intelligence, you understand. But have you business with him ? '

' Unfortunately I have ; and I count on your kindness in obtaining for me an audience with him to-morrow.'

' An audience to-morrow ? ' repeated the queen's godchild, laughing. ' Do you fancy, then, one can do as one pleases with such a bear ? '

' I have nothing to do with the difficulties you meet,' answered Matthewson coldly. ' What I wish and what I require from you is to see him to-morrow.'

' Be it so,' replied Lord Menzil, with a submission that was at variance with his naturally combative and independent character ; ' to-morrow you shall have your ticket of audience.'

Menzil, who from his impudence and continual exactions was a great charge upon her majesty, permitted himself greater liberty of speech than any other courtier, and did not always restrain himself even in the royal presence.

Thanks to the immunity which he enjoyed, and perhaps also to his cynicism, he was, if not much sought after, at least much feared. Ministers of state themselves, though they might not greatly esteem his character, yet paid him deference, and to avoid irritating him affected to listen seriously to his arguments. The docility he had shown in submitting to Matthewson's imperiousness was really such an extraordinary event which, had it been known, would have caused no little surprise and sensation.

'My dear lord,' continued Matthewson, 'it is possible that Mr. Barstairs may not comprehend the greatness of the plans which I lay before him. One has not the good luck every day to meet with a business man like Lord Menzil, therefore I must warn you, that you may be prepared beforehand, that in the case of my plans encountering invincible opposition, you will have to procure me an interview with your patroness the queen.'

'Oh, you wish to see the queen too, do you?' ejaculated Menzil, with an impatience that he could not conceal. 'In faith, I don't disguise that I hate to make my friends common. You will, therefore, greatly oblige me if you will find some one else to present you to her majesty.'

'You suit me too well in several respects for me to think of applying to any one else. *Apropos*, have I received your opinion of the soil around Versailles?'

At this reiterated query Lord Menzil was troubled, but he soon resolved what to do.

'Baron Legaff,' he cried, 'let us not go back to the fertility of France, and whether its lily will bear transplanting! I know perfectly that you are "one of us." Don't let us imitate children who in playing with fire burn themselves. And pray, what advantage does the knowledge of this secret give you over me? Do you fancy you have me in your power?'

'Assuredly,' answered Legaff coolly, 'you are in my power.'

'Not so much as you in mine. Will you be so good as to explain?'

'Why, it is all as clear as crystal. You conspire, if not against the person, at least against the dearest interests of the king. I know your project; one word from me and you are lost.'

'And when you have said that mighty word, shall I be silent? Will gratitude for your generosity prevent me from compromising you, think you? Come, baron,' added the Dutchman in a tone of mocking raillery, ' you are far cleverer in finance than politics. You should keep to the money question.'

Matthewson laughed in his turn.

'Truly, I would never have believed that a man like your lordship, so well versed in court intrigues, should be so purblind. Why, all the shades and tints of the matter escape you. Now let us show our cards. I have just given you a large sum, have I not?'

'You mean to say that you have confided it to me.'

'Excuse me, it is agreed that we show our cards ; therefore I say, "Give." For these five thousand pounds, which fall in the nick, for only last night you lost eight hundred pounds on your honour, and had not a single crown to pay with, what have I asked in return for this five thousand? Nothing. Neither a service nor a receipt. You must admit that a man who is neither a fool nor superior to all vulgar prejudices on the subject of money does not willingly throw away twenty-five thousand silver crowns!'

'Well, baron, I own that your unexplained generosity gives you an advantage over me,' answered the Hollander gravely.

'As I care not to take advantage of you, I will explain the cause of my generosity. Nothing is more simple. I wished to prove to you that I was very rich. Do you understand?'

'Not in the least.'

'What, don't you understand that a man who would sacrifice such a sum to obtain a royal audience would pay down half a million in a matter of importance?'

'Well, I believe you would, baron.'

'And you, judging that I have a million or so at my disposal, think me such a fool as to keep my money and put my head in peril? Really, you must have a shocking opinion of me, and give me credit for no wit at all.'

'Go on,' said Menzil, with as much equanimity as if he were treading on live coals.

'Well, then, my dearest lord, if I took it into my head to-morrow to inform against you, or any of your confederates, not only should I save myself from sharing in your disgrace, but I should be thanked and rewarded for doing the king this service. Therefore, dear lord,' continued Legaff, in a tone that revealed no pride or triumph in the fact, 'I may be permitted to count on your kindly presenting me to her majesty if I obtain not what I want from Barstairs.'

'That question, baron, is a noble proof of your generosity. Thanks for your kindness in requesting what in your position you might have demanded.'

For some time the noble kept silence, as if, contrary to his habits, absorbed in thought.

'Do you know, my lord?' said Matthewson, 'that what you are now meditating proves neither generosity nor gratitude. I am well enough aware that ingratitude is so natural to man, that one could not be blamed for feeling it; still, there should be some limits even to ingratitude; it should not grow to vengeance.'

At these words, spoken in the coolest manner, Menzil lost his composure entirely ; still, he strove to keep up appearances.

'Really, baron,' he cried, with a feigned smile, 'I don't understand you.'

'Believe me, my dear Menzil,' rejoined Matthewson, with perfect good humour, 'you had better keep the five thousand pounds fallen down from heaven into your lap to play with, and not amuse yourself with planning secret assassinations which must fail. A man with a breastplate of thousands cannot be murdered like a Konigsmark.'

'Faith of my fathers!' ejaculated the Dutchman, rising hastily and traversing the chamber like a madman ; 'By George, baron, you must be a wizard ! May the devil, your master, scorch me this moment if I enter the lists with you. I would rather trust to your generosity than brave your power. I own myself vanquished. Command, and I will obey.'

'A thousand thanks, my dear master, for these words of friendship and devotion,' answered Matthewson, who, rising, saluted his host with a slight bow, and retired.

Menzil could not close his eyes all night. In the morning Matthewson received a letter of audience with the Naval Minister for that day.

When Baron Legaff—for so we will continue to call the mock horsedealer—entered the pro-minister's sanctum, Mr. Francis Barstairs was busy reading despatches, and did not appear even aware of the presence of a visitor.

It was only after the lapse of a quarter of an hour that he said in a rough, ungracious manner, 'Who are you ? and what do you want ?'

'The usher announced to you Baron Legaff, and Legaff himself reminds you that you are speaking to a gentleman.'

This bold answer was so contrary to the usual style of petitioners that the hearer was astounded.

'What is your rank in the navy, and what do you wish ?' he inquired, less rudely.

'Thank Heaven, sir, I have no rank in the navy you oversee, and far from soliciting your favour, I have come on the contrary to offer you *my* advice and *my* support.'

The secretary was now so confounded that he could not answer.

'I have at my disposal,' continued Legaff with the same coolness, 'a large naval force, which is powerful enough to encounter your king's, and not to disadvantage.'

'This is really unpardonable of Menzil,' murmured Barstairs. 'I shall complain to the king of his behaviour.'

'I am waiting on your lordship,' observed Legaff.

'You may retire, sir,' answered the secretary, returning to his work.

'Not, my lord, before you have read this letter which I have promised to place in your hands.'

'Leave me, sir ; you disturb me !' cried the official, giving way to his anger.

'This letter is from one of my lieutenants, Bloxam,' continued Matthewson.

'From Captain Bloxam !' exclaimed Barstairs, who took the letter eagerly, broke it open, and read with much interest.

'Baron Legaff,' said he, with a politeness quite at variance with his usual habits, 'the captain tells me that he has served under you, and that he considers you the greatest naval commander of the age, and begs me to listen in all confidence to certain proposals that you have to make me. I will not deny that I hold the captain in great esteem. What do you desire?'

As Barstairs spoke so frankly he was probably aware that Legaff knew the contents of the letter he had put into his hands.

'Sir,' replied Legaff, 'I desire to give you three things of which, at the present moment, you stand much in need: money men, and glory.'

'I cannot conceive how Bloxam can speak of you as the greatest naval commander,' said Barstairs, as if he had not heard Legaff's last words. 'I don't remember ever to have heard your name before.'

'Jean Bart, the Frenchman, who has just taken five *Dutch* ships of war in the Baltic, and the English merchantmen they were conveying, was scarcely known at Versailles court a few years back. Sir Henry Morgan had to pay handsomely before he was knighted by the second Charles. However, I will not conceal from your excellency that Legaff is not my real name.'

'What, have you ventured before me under an assumed name?'

'I have dared many things in my life, sir, and fortune has always favoured my boldness,' replied Matthewson, with a smile; 'so that now I generally act according to my own pleasure or convenience.'

'Well, let "Legaff" pass,' said Barstairs, who could not help regarding his visitor with much curiosity, and looking again at Bloxam's letter. 'The name is of little consequence. You are then, sir, one of those famous buccaneers looked up to so much?'

'Yes, my lord, I am their admiral, heir to Sir Henry Morgan, who was heir to old Mansfield and Pierre the Picardian.'

'Their chief? why, I thought those people had no commander, or rather a hundred.'

'It is true that in their ordinary expeditions buccaneers choose whom they like to command them, but above these there is a permanent and hidden authority which extends all over the seas of the Antillas. By only lifting up my finger, and with the magic of one word, I can, in less than a week, bring together ten thousand sea dogs.'

'Then in transacting business with you I am treating with a power,' said the secretary, half seriously, half in derision.

'Yes, my lord, I propose a treaty between two powers,' answered Legaff, who drew forward a chair and sat down poposite the minister.

A short pause followed.

With his calm air, his determined and brilliant eye, and bold, not to say proud, bearing, Legaff was no longer the same person whom we have known hitherto as the picture of carelessness and good humour.   There was seen in him a strength of will and depth of thought that fitted him to rule mankind.

Accustomed as he was to treat even men high in the service with rudeness, Barstairs did not feel at his ease with Legaff. Something in the latter awed while it annoyed the minister of state.

Legaff was the first to resume the conversation by saying,—

'In this interview which your excellency has kindly granted me, I beg permission to explain my place clearly and without reserve or concealment, put you in possession of the facts.'

'You forestal my wishes, sir,' answered Barstairs ; 'but first pray tell me how long you have known Captain Bloxam ? '

'I repeat, Bloxam has served under me.   We have known each other fifteen years.'

'And since the captain has been in the navy, your acquaintance with him has continued ? '

'We still continue intimate.   I can even say with truth that since that period my advice has occasionally been of great service to him.'

'Your advice ! ' repeated the secretary, with surprise. 'Nevertheless, Bloxam is a very superior man.'

'I am quite of your lordship's opinion ; I recognise in my friend unflinching courage and admirable coolness, joined to great perseverance and experience ; in fact every quality that could fit a man for great deeds.'

'And still in acknowledging in him all these great qualities, you pretend that he conducts himself solely by your advice; that clearly proves that you consider yourself his better in intelligence.'

'Assuredly,' answered the buccaneer quietly.

Barstairs, struck by the cool decision of his answer, eyed his strange visitor with a curiosity bordering on awe.

The minister for the navy was at this juncture much interested in a marriage in contemplation between one of his brothers-in-law and the only daughter of the old buccaneer, but now a very rich and distinguished naval officer.

Therefore a letter from Bloxam was the best possible introduction.

Soon, as if ashamed of the ascendancy that he felt Legaff had over him, he remarked rather tartly,—

'We have lost much time in fruitless talking.   What are your wishes, pray ; explain them briefly and clearly.   More important business than what you have to speak of requires my attention.'

'I doubt that considerably.   What I have to propose is as

vast as it is simple. I can explain it to you in a few words.
Though it is an undeniable fact that England is hard pressed,
drained of men and money, she uselessly imposes cruel sacrifices on herself to maintain the gigantic strife in which she is
engaged with the European Powers. What she requires is gold
—much gold, and it is impossible to obtain more by taxation, as
that has already reached the extreme limits of justice, and greater
taxation would be robbery of the toilers.'

'Sir buccaneer, you forget in whose presence you are.'

'In the presence of a minister of state to whom I promised
the whole truth, and to whom therefore I shall tell it. In the
interests of our country, you have no right to refuse to hear a
man who offers you an annual revenue of ten millions sterling
taken from the enemy.'

'Enough, enough; if you talk of millions,' sneered Barstairs,
'it is useless to enter into any explanations. I don't doubt, sir,
your cleverness in plundering half-armed vessels, but in regard
to matters of business you seem to belong to that category of
persons unfortunately so numerous, who every morning propose
to me a dozen different South Sea Bubbles. If you are writing to
Bloxam, say that from friendship for him I have sacrificed an
hour to you. Good morning, sir.'

'Your excellency,' said Legaff, who, in spite of the dismissal
so formally and ironically enforced, kept his seat, 'what rendered
Torrington a regretted loss to the Navy Board was that he
listened even to the most humble, though he may have winked
at contracts for vile beer and viler bread.'

'Sir, this insolence,' began Barstairs in a rage.

'Is simply the boldness of a man who fears nothing but
heavenly anger, and is too confident of his own strength to bend
before the puerile and uncalled-for pleasantries of a minister
unfaithful to his duty and a traitor to his sovereign.'

'Do you dare to call me traitor?' returned the secretary,
bounding from his seat to confront Legaff, who still remained
impassable.

'Yes, your excellency,' repeated the buccaneer with provoking.
calmness, 'I say this to you, as to-morrow I shall say it to the
queen : you are a traitor to the king.'

While speaking he looked fixedly at Barstairs, no doubt
tainted with Jacobite inclinations, for a slight smile of disdain
curled his lip as if he felt his own strength and superiority to
his adversary.

In truth, terrible as was Barstairs' anger at first it soon
melted away without any apparent reason.

'Do you know, sir,' he said, 'that had it not been for my
friendship for Captain Bloxam you would already have been on
your way to the lock-up?'

'Although, sir, I prize liberty above all things on earth, yet the prospect of four-and-twenty hours in the calaboose would not deter me from doing my duty.'

'Four-and-twenty hours, sir? you certainly know nothing of how hard it is to get out of Newgate or the Tower.'

'That is very possible, sir; but one thing I know, there is no prison door which will not fall into shivers when the battering-ram of Plutus is used against it. You look astounded, but you can never prevent gold from giving supreme power. Believe me, if I took it into my head to waste a million in overturning your superior, even such a sacrifice is not beyond me. A week hence Lord Russell would fall like Delaval.'

Legaff spoke in such a confident manner that his auditor seemed seized with sudden fear, for never had this harsh minister met with such resolute opposition as on the part of the freebooter.

'My especial friendship for Captain Bloxam, Baron Legaff I repeat, has already saved you from harm; and in sight of this friendship I am willing to grant you a few minutes' attention. But I require before we resume our conversation that you retract those offensive words which your want of education, and the company you have kept, make less blameable than they would otherwise be.'

'To what words do you allude, my lord?'

'To the abominable fact which you dared to state that I was a traitor to the king.'

'By habitual command, your excellency, I have acquired the custom of saying what I think, but I never say more than I mean, and therefore cannot recall my words.'

Whether the boldness of the buccaneer awed him, or some other motive influenced him, Barstairs turned the subject with a hollow laugh, and in a good-humoured way, extremely at odds with his usual habits, said,—

'It is really impossible to believe you serious, or to take umbrage at your rough manners. Besides, I had long wished for a personal acquaintance with one of those famous sea-rovers so much talked of. I ought to thank my good stars for sending me in you one of the most unique specimens of the race. You are really to me a study and a curiosity.'

'It is a great honour to me, my lord.'

'And pray,' continued the official, after a moment's hesitation, 'in what am I, according to your notions, a traitor to the king?'

'You are a traitor because you refuse to accept the help of the immense yearly revenue which I offer you to "plump up the exchequer."'

'Really, is it a fact,' cried Barstairs, in the same sneering tone, ' that I deserve the axe? Well, suppose I were to alter my mind; there is mercy for every crime, is there not? Come, teach me in what manner we can get those riches which your munificence offers us.'

'Your excellency seems to jest ; but I would stake my life that you await my answer with anxious impatience. The buccaneer's folly would enhance the favour of the king.'

'More and more delightful !' murmured Barstairs, trying to smile.

'Your excellency is aware that Spain, only our friend for the moment, maintains her power by the resources which she derives from her foreign possessions. The principal ports which unite by commerce America and Europe are ten in number. In each of these ports I have secret friends. Let England only back up us buccaneers, and I swear to you that six months hence the Red Cross of St. George shall float victorious throughout the Spanish Main.'

'It is a fleet of five hundred ships, manned with two hundred thousand men, that you require, baron, eh ?'

'Master Pepys would not have joked in this strain. I want King William's moral support ! I want my sea-devils to fight for once without halters round their necks ! Keep us from being interfered with by your fleet, and we will become masters of the American coast ; then nothing should be easier than to make the forts impregnable. It would be a glorious feat, unrivalled as yet in the history of the world, sufficient alone to make a reign illustrious ; thirty millions of men would be tributary to a handful of dare-devils, and work for the glory and power of their conquerors. Spain alone would ransom herself with ten millions ; and to what greatness might not Britain rise when William the Third, maintained by the gold of his old ancestral enemy, would require only bravery from his subjects !'

Legaff, enthusiastic in his subject, spoke boldly and proudly. Notwithstanding his narrow views, Barstairs caught for a moment the spirit, but it quickly died away, and he answered roughly,—

'Captain, your proposition is absurd. You would rob Spain of her American colonies with an ease and quickness which proves you are utterly ignorant of the grand rules of war. You fancy, no doubt, that a well-fortified seaport can be taken with the same ease as a coal barge. I am convinced that Bloxam, in spite of the deference which he pays to your judgment, won'd laugh to scorn such a plan if you proposed it to him.'

'Mr. Secretary, I was a sea-boy under Sir Henry Mo, when he took Puerto del Principe with but five hundred fighting men. Did not we Brothers of the Coast capture Puerto Bello, too, and Carthagena, and—— but enough, I have seen these Spanish trounced ! Not only does Bloxam know and approve of my plan, but we have concerted together all its details. This work has cost us three years of cares, dangers, and sacrifices. I can conceive, sir, how you cannot understand all our hopes. But permit me to recall Panama, Vera Cruz, Gibraltar, San Pedro, Campechy, and a hundred other ports of less celebrity which have cowered under my carronades ! Wherever the red and yellow flag has floated I have waged war, and either in large or small engagements have come off victorious. The honour of England has been safe in my hands.'

These words breathed more satisfaction than pride, and Barstairs, hardened and narrowed as his mind had become from contact with politics, could not but feel some slight admiration for a man who merged all personal triumph in his country's glory.

'Captain Legaff,' he answered, almost affably, 'if I cannot admit the feasibility of so vast a project, I fully admit your energy, knowledge, and experience, and if you have some less colossal plan than the conquest of the Spanish Indies to propose to me, I will listen to you with pleasure.'

'I never give up my plans, my lord, but I can wait. Now that you are willing to encourage me and take things seriously, I have still to speak to you of an enterprise which would throw millions into the Exchequer. I speak now for Bloxam, as my friendship for him would willingly yield him the honour of the expedition. It would be worth some thousands to him.'

This was a well-concerted move, or a happy thought, on the part of the sea-marauder.

Barstairs' civility became almost friendliness.

'I am so grieved to have to refuse your first proposal,' said the minister of state, 'that I have every wish to entertain your second, providing there is the least chance of its succeeding. Pray explain it.'

'The enterprise which I have to submit to you relates also to conquest in the West Indies. I would recall to your remembrance that Spain possesses ten rich and important ports in the two Oceans, of which Carthagena is the most important and the best situated.'

'That I am aware of, sir,' answered Barstairs.

'Well, then, my lord, my proposal—speaking for our captain, not myself—is for you to take possession of the all-important and exceedingly rich port of Carthagena.'

Barstairs pondered long before he answered.

'The taking of Carthagena, which you speak of as so simple and easy, is, in truth, a very arduous undertaking ; still, as coming from you and from Bloxam, it deserves at least to be discussed.'

'Well, Mr. Secretary, let us discuss the matter.'

'The first serious difficulty which presents itself is the great expense that must be incurred to fit out such an expedition. The finances are, as you said yourself, encumbered. Moreover, our present state of hostility, in regard to the rest of Europe, exacts too great sacrifices to enable us to undertake anything abroad beyond our projects in operation.'

'Many thanks for your excellency's frankness ; but allow me to observe that, if I understood you at first, you have also mis-judged me in taking me for a mere Ishmael of the sea, whose only employment is in attacking vessels ; the immense respon-sibility which I have borne for the last ten years has enlarged my mind and ripened my judgment. In proposing the Car-thagenian expedition, I was fully aware that the Government was not in a position to make the necessary advances.'

'Then who is to do it, pray ? '

'I, sir,' answered Matthewson simply.

The official looked at him with surprise and admiration.

'Have you any idea, sir, of the cost of such an expedition ? '

'Yes, I have calculated it with the most scrupulous exacti-tude. The whole cost will run to a hundred thousand pounds.'

'And can you disburse that enormous sum ? '

'Had I not been able to do so I would not have troubled you in the matter. Let the king sign to-morrow Bloxam's commis-sion to head this expedition, and one hour later I will place that sum in your hands.'

In spite of his unamiable and jealous temper, Barstairs had sufficient penetration to appreciate real worth, and he felt con-vinced that Legaff could and would keep his word. He remem-bered, too, the regret that ministers had felt under Charles II., that they had not recognised the corsairs of the Indies at the Council of the Treaty of Utrecht. He answered slowly,—

'Captain Legaff, you must not take in bad part an obser-vation I have to make. You are too well versed in business not to know that in affairs of importance, one point left doubtful or obscure creates innumerable difficulties.'

'Speak boldly, sir,' answered the buccaneer.

'I should be sorry to be unpolite, but you are aware that you free-seamen, though you have achieved great things, have not in regard to morality a high reputation.'

'It is too true that many persons, jealous of our success and our wealth, have sought to slander us.'

'I have no wish to debate the point ; I only state the fact. Therefore I fear that an expedition set on foot and maintained by the sea-rovers, recognised and directed by the British Government, would have a disastrous effect on the rest of Europe.'

'You are perfectly right ; the same objection struck me.'

'Indeed ; then you are as keen as you are bold. And what plan suggested itself to you ? '

'That it would be well to make the commerce of Jamaica and St. Kitts a pretence for the Carthagenian expedition and apparently at least bear the cost.'

' Your idea is excellent : but in that case what benefit could the Government have from the capture of Carthagena ? '

'The Government can lend its officers and its ships and then reap great advantages. I calculate that the money gained by the Crown would be nearly ten millions.'

' And what advantages would the buccaneers derive from it ? '

'The buccaneers,' answered Legaff bitterly, ' are the hunting dogs who are made use of and then thrust aside. When the expedition reaches St. Domingo, ten of my vessels, manned by twelve hundred men, will join it there. Call them Spy-boats, volunteers, pilots, what you will ! '

' A last objection, sir, or rather a question. What personal interest have you in the capture of Carthagena ? '

' Rather a meagre one, you will think, no doubt, my lord. I hate the influence and power of Spain, and I love my native land ! '

Barstairs rose and, bowing, said,—

' You may depend, sir, on my giving the subject my most serious attention. You will hear from me soon. In the meanwhile I need scarcely recommend the greatest discretion.'

Legaff's only answer was a smile, but that was worth a whole host of protestations. The minister had returned to his work, and the buccaneer had reached the door, when he returned and said,—

' One final word, if you please. Will your lordship allow me to speak to the king about Bloxam ? You need not fear that I would in any way forestal the glory which will accrue to you should this expedition prove successful. I will not even let the king know of the interest you have kindly shown me in this interview.'

' But you talk of speaking to the king as if you had the right for a presentation.'

' Allow me to repeat the observation, sir, which I made at the commencement of our interview. Fortune has always so greatly favoured my boldness that I now act just as I please. If I wish to see the king I shall do so.'

' Be it so,' answered Mr. Barstairs ; ' I offer no opposition, and shall be glad to know if you do not value yourself too highly, and can break down the barriers that encircle the throne.'

On leaving the minister, Legaff called in at Charles Street. He found Lord Menzil's anteroom full of angry tradesmen, and was conducted at once to the master.

‘ Oh, is it you, dear baron ? A hundred welcomes. Have you more money to put out at interest ? ’

‘ Not so, my lord,’ answered Legaff ; ‘ I warned you yesterday that I might desire an interview.’

‘ Very well ; you wish to pay your respects to the queen ? I can refuse you nothing. When do you want to be presented ? ’

‘ As soon as possible ; to-morrow for instance ? ’

‘ To-morrow,’ cried Menzil, ‘are you mad? But what matters?’ he added after a pause. ‘ I need not be over scrupulous with a godmamma who has behaved so shabbily to me. That is settled. I will call to-morrow on this loving lady, and as I shall not ask her for money, I will take advantage of this momentary independence to revenge myself for the innumerable humiliations she has made me suffer. You cannot think how gay I feel at having some money in the exchequer. I am ten years younger than I was yesterday.’

‘ Here is my address, dear lord,’ said Legaff ; ‘ as soon as you have obtained an interview for me be so kind as to let me know.’

‘ What, going so soon ? ’

‘ I fear to be in your way; your anteroom is full of visitors.’

‘ A capital joke !   I would wager anything you could never guess who they are or why I had them brought here,’ cried the Dutchman, with a short burst of laughter. ‘ But not to excite your curiosity too much, you must know they are all my creditors.’

‘ Then I suppose you brought the good people together to pay them.’

‘ Good people, indeed ! vile speculators on my luck at cards. Do you think I would pay them ? ’

‘ Well, I don’t know ; perhaps you intended to reproach them.’

‘ Such flinty hearts would be callous to reproaches. No ; I called them together to show them the five thousand pounds.’

‘ I understand you less than ever.’

‘ Nevertheless, my conduct is most logical. These men have reported everywhere that I am as poor as a church mouse, and now they will declare that I am rolling in riches. My friends will rage, my godmamma will rejoice, and a hundred fresh tradesmen, hearing of my wealth, will offer me credit. I have not felt so light-hearted for years. And to prove that I am not ungrateful, you shall have your interview the day after to-morrow at farthest.’

CHAPTER XIV.

A CURIOUS LOVE-TRYST.

ALTHOUGH Carraway's establishment in the Strand was no longer in high fashion, still it was much frequented by the nobility; but as gravity was now in vogue in court it was visited less openly.

Morgan could scarcely repress the emotion he felt in approaching a place where, as he imagined, must be decided the happiness or misery of his life. He was about to enter when loud bursts of laughter attracted his notice. He saw a woman with a monstrously high head-dress, a laced bodice, and full-flounced dress, who was followed about by a crowd of giddy young men.

Although the lady's face was entirely concealed, from her movements Morgan judged she was young, and concluded she must be beautiful.

The lady showed no embarrassment; indeed seemed hardly aware of the boisterous admiration of her numerous followers.

'Really, my charming girl,' cried one, 'your striking costume and modest silence make you a delicious riddle. Who the deuce can you be? Not a court lady, or you would be too used to these rendezvous to come in such a dress. Not a milliner, or our jokes would long ago have set you laughing. Come, don't keep us long in suspense, my charmer. I am the Marquis of Rothesay; my friends are Brankhouse, Charlesworth, Steinkerque, Daunce, all discreet and honourable men, not to know whom is to argue yourself unknown!'

Whilst he addressed her, the unknown lady walked on without heeding him, but as soon as she saw the Cornish knight, she approached him, and in a voice which thrilled through his frame, said,—

'Give me your arm, sir!'

The voice was Nativa's. He cast a glance of withering scorn at the young noblemen, who fearing that a quarrel could only tell to their disadvantage, moved away quietly. The young man hastened to offer his arm to Nativa, and a waiter showed them into a room.

'Bring us to eat,' said Morgan.

Five minutes later a table was spread with fruits, confectionaries, and wine; and the servants, withdrawing discreetly, left the knight and Nativa to themselves.

'Chevalier,' said Nativa, taking off her veil and disclosing to the enamoured Morgan that dazzling and sovereign beauty always present to his memory, but still surpassed by the reality, 'I must first explain the reason of my being here. I was told that this house was a sure and convenient place to meet you, and have thus exposed myself to the insults of those young fops who fled at your approach.'

'To me it matters little where I see you,' answered Morgan, 'but for your own sake I should have preferred seeing you elsewhere.'

'In my residence it would have been impossible,' replied Nativa eagerly ; 'my father owes his life to you, but never would he consent to let an Englishman enter his doors.'

'And wherefore ?' asked Morgan.

'I regret to appear so discourteous ; still it is better that you should know the truth : my father has the deepest, most inveterate hatred of your countrymen.'

Though her hearer had rarely dared, even in his dreams, to contemplate an union with Nativa, still, happy privilege of youth ! he cherished a hope, and it was very painful to find that a new barrier had arisen between them.   He sadly inquired,—

'How is it, then, that with such feelings, the Earl of Monterey should have come to England ?'

'A project which my father has much at heart has for the time absorbed his hatred.'

Morgan was silent, a prey to painful emotions, ere he said mournfully,—

'You probably think me, a mere stranger to you, unworthy of your confidence ?'

'That is unjust to yourself, and a reproach which I do not deserve,' answered Nativa, 'for I place implicit trust in your honour.'

There was a pause : Nativa, cool and composed, Morgan agitated with strong emotion, which he sought in vain to suppress.

'If I pain you, forgive me, Nativa ! do you love me ?'

'No,' answered Nativa quietly, showing neither anger nor surprise at such a question.

Morgan hid his face in his hands, while Nativa waited with quiet indifference.

'Perhaps,' said he, at length, with tears in his voice, 'you cannot feel for me such love as I feel for you, but surely true regard, friendship——'

'I feel for you neither love nor friendship,' said Nativa coldly.   'You saved my life, I am grateful, that is all.'

'And yet you seemed not displeased ; you accepted my devotion.'

'We Spanish women,' said Nativa, with singular sweetness, 'care little to conceal our feelings ; and I will tell you frankly, that if I cannot love you, it is because I am no longer worthy.'

'You not worthy !' groaned Morgan.

Often had he despaired of gaining Nativa's love, but such a barrier had never presented itself to his mind ; he could not bear the torture it inflicted. Despair and jealousy nearly drove him mad.

'What is your lover's name ?' he asked fiercely.

'Sir Lewis Morgan,' answered Nativa with proud disdain, 'do your countrywomen esteem dishonour only the last stage of degradation and shame ? Do you fancy I could have outlived dishonour ?'

'Oh, then, you are still worthy an honourable man's love,' cried Morgan, with a sudden burst of joy.

'You shall judge for yourself. A year since, on our passage from Carthagena to Saint Domingo, we were attacked by the buccaneers of Tortoise Island. Our vessel was manned with fifty men, under one of the bravest and most skilful of Spanish captains. The buccaneers were only eighteen, in a vessel that leaked excessively. The issue of the attack seemed so little doubtful, that our captain only saw in it a means of ridding the world of a few miscreants. Our first fire foundered their vessel.'

'And all perished ?' cried Morgan.

'Half-an-hour later,' answered Nativa, turning pale, 'the desperadoes had boarded our vessel, massacred two-thirds of our men, and took the rest of us prisoners.'

'But what you tell me seems impossible.'

'Nothing but good is impossible to buccaneers. This which seems so marvellous to you is only an everyday occurrence with them. My father, who during the contest had fought bravely, received a severe wound and fell among the dead. Oh, why had he not rather stayed with me ? for rather than let me fall into their hands he would have stabbed me himself, and I should have escaped this moment's torture,

'The pirate captain who conquered us was indeed an extraordinary man. A finished gentleman and man of the world, he paid me those delicate attentions which proved him accustomed to the highest society. Conquered by his devotion, grateful for his kindness to my father, I responded to his regard ; and as I have promised you a full confession, I must own my imagination was charmed with the extraordinary life of this man. His shrouded early life vividly created my curiosity and engrossed my thoughts.

'What more can I say ? This wretch, from diabolical motives, spoke to me of the purest love and was not repulsed. He told me that, born of an illustrious house, he had been induced by family misfortunes to seek a life of adventure ; that the deep love which he felt for me had opened his eyes and made him bitterly deplore the crimes of the past, and that he should strive by noble efforts and sincere repentance to redeem the errors of his youth. He painted his future in such glowing colours as to make me proud and happy at the conversion I had effected.'

'And this belief led to an engagement on your part, Nativa?' asked Morgan, grinding his teeth.

'Even so, chevalier,' replied Nativa, hanging her head.

'Let me know all,' cried Morgan, whose livid face and compressed lips marked the agony he was suffering.

'The day before the buccaneers put us on shore,' continued Nativa, 'as I must own, without ransom, the villain came to me and said, "Lady, if the buccaneer whom you have saved from perdition should one day return to you an altered being, would you shrink from completing the reformation which you have inspired? would you thrust the poor wretch back into infamy?" "No, I would not repulse him," I answered. "Thanks, you are my good angel," he cried fervently, and pressed my hand to his lips.'

'The next day, as I was mournfully gazing after the vessel that bore him from me, a letter was put into my hand. It contained these words : "Dear Child, I am prouder of the victory that I have gained over you, haughty and noble as you are, than of my victories over all your countrymen together. If I did not hold all women in contempt, I could almost have taken a fancy to you. You are rather engaging, and your simplicity is very laughable. When buccaneers are ill-spoken of in your presence, I hope you will take our part. Don't vex yourself that I decline making you my consort, for I should have tired of you in a day, whilst I now leave you with a pleasant remembrance of the amusement you afforded me! Farewell."'

Nativa's manner of repeating this grossly insulting letter proved too plainly how deeply her pride had been wounded and how it still bled.

Her hearer could not resist a thrill of joy. The pain the confession gave Nativa showed the delicacy of her feelings, and the pity she felt for an adventurer gave him better hope for himself.

'You must now own, sir,' she went on, 'that I have no longer the right to accept the love of an honourable man?'

'Worthy it a thousand times,' he cried, fervently. 'You are not in fault. Who would dare to think you guilty? You were the dupe of your generous feelings ; and this event, which weighs so heavily over you, is, in fact, a matter of little importance, and only deserves to be forgotten.'

'What you have just said proves that you have a deplorable opinion of me and little respect for yourself. Could a gentleman consent to give his unsullied name to a woman who had confessed her love to another man?'

'But, Nativa.'—

'While this man still lives,' continued Nativa, bitterly, ' who has thus insulted me ! Oh, my father is right to despise your countrymen ! As for me, whose feelings are quite different, I have sworn that so long as this man lives, before whom I have cause to blush, I will never consent to listen to any other love, but will bear my shame and grief alone.'

'You are right, Nativa,' answered Morgan, after a pause. ' My joy at finding that the barrier that is between us is not insurmountable blinded me at first to the deepness of the insult you received. I now thank you for recalling me to a proper sense of my own honour. The wife of an English gentleman must not have cause to blush before any man. You need no vengeance, for the behaviour of this buccaneer never touched your honour ; but you must be placed out of reach of insult. Tell me the name of this wretch who has marred your happiness ?'

Nativa paused, in deep thought.

'You who confessed the story,' said Morgan, ' hesitate to give up the name ! When your words have sealed his death does your heart feel pity for him, or do you doubt my honour or courage ?'

'I cannot doubt the courage of one who saved my father's life,' answered Nativa, ' and if I hesitate to accept your aid it is because your devotion deserves gratitude, and not a risk which generous hearts should not impose.'

'It is necessary to repeat, Nativa, what I told you before in the castle of Pemrose, that I am a slave to your will, and shall rest my happiness in my obedience ! Once again, I beg you to tell me this scoundrel's name.'

'But at this moment he is two thousand miles away. Would you cross the seas to seek him ?'

'I would—though they were fire.'

'You are, indeed, generous,' cried Nativa, with more emotion than she had hitherto shown. 'The more I think of our extraordinary meeting the more I am persuaded that Heaven sent you to my aid.'

These words, spoken with deep feeling, thrilled through Morgan's heart.

'Your answer dissipates my doubts,' continued Nativa, ' and I will frankly tell you all. But as the secret which I have to reveal is not mine, I must exact from you a solemn oath not to betray it.'

'On my word as a gentleman, I swear that even to save my life, not one word that could betray your secret shall pass my lips.'

'Thanks ; now I shall speak without fear. Do you remember a few mysterious words which I said to you at Pemrose Castle about your future ?'

‘ Perfectly ; you spoke of an enterprise, the success of which might render me both rich and powerful.’

‘ It is of that enterprise that I wish to speak to you. You cannot imagine the immense injury which the buccaneers that infest the Antilles do to the commerce and prosperity of my country—ay, of all civilized countries. Not only do the bold robbers insult the Spanish flag, but, alas ! success almost invariably crowns their audacity ! Every day their power increases with our humiliation. Our Government has made enormous efforts and sacrifices to destroy these buccaneers. Our gold and our blood have been expended in vain !’

‘ I cannot conceive,’ interrupted the knight, ‘ that a powerful country like Spain should be unable to resist a handful of men without discipline or resources.’

‘ You fall into a common error in fancying that buccaneers are undisciplined sea-robbers. What renders them most formidable is their perfect discipline and fanatical devotion to a chief whose authority is unbounded. The Spanish Government know this to its cost, but has not yet been able to discover what their government is or who is at its head. The buccaneers that have fallen into our hands have been exposed to the most fearful tortures, but whether the poor wretches were themselves ignorant, or that their enthusiasm was superior to their sufferings, they all died with a cry of defiance on their lips.’

‘ How much it is to be regretted,’ cried Morgan involuntarily, ‘ that such men should have been robbers ! What great things they might have accomplished in a good cause ! But I do not exactly understand the interest that you can take in the destruction of these buccaneers.’

‘ Oh, that is the secret still to be confided in you. The unbounded confidence and friendship which our unfortunate queen, Maria Souza, felt for my father made him suspected by the rival dynasty, and after the death of that excellent princess, he was forced to leave the court ; since then, that is to say for the last six years, my father retired to Hispaniola, where he had a good opportunity, which he eagerly followed, of studying minutely the lives and actions of the Brothers of the Coast. He has now come to the thorough conviction that if he could only discover the tie that binds them together, he should be able in less than a year to quench the scandalous power of these robbers, and leave of them only the memory of a terrible retribution. My father only six months ago returned to Spain, and, having hinted his hopes and projects to the king, received from Charles the Second full powers and credentials to carry out his plan; and this is the reason of our coming to the English court.’

‘ Do you think that William the Third will enter into the views of Spain ? why, Spain is Holland’s hereditary foe. The

buccaneers are pirates, but still their depredations by embarrassing Spain add to our security and power. You must therefore
allow me to doubt that the Earl of Monterey will obtain the
support that he expects from the king of Great Britain.'

'Oh, as to William's concurrence,' answered Nativa, smiling,
'my father is secure of that. He has a sure means, if not of
eliciting his sympathy, at least of constraining his will. No, we
lack neither money, courage, nor allies ; all we want to know is
the link that binds these buccaneers together and makes them
irresistible, to our shame and dishonour.'

'Still I cannot understand,' said Sir Lewis, who, however
interesting the subject might be to him, would at this instant
have much preferred talking to the beautiful Spanish girl of his
love than of politics, 'how all these things can concern me.'

'I am coming to that,' interrupted Nativa. 'My father has
full powers from Charles the Second to confer rank and dignity
on whomsoever he thinks proper. An officer's commission signed
by him will be recognised by the king, as also an annual pension
of a hundred thousand dollars : now do you understand ?'

'Perfectly ; but not that that has anything to do with me ?'

'What, do you not understand that, thanks to your being
English, to which nation the bravest and boldest of the sea-
rovers belong, a nobleman, and—what we found out as the
luckiest hazard—a kinsman of the great Sir Henry Morgan, who
was the terror of the West Indies under your King Charles the
Second—you, you, Sir Lewis, are the very standard-bearer we
could have imagined? Who but you can penetrate their lair
and acquire their secrets of state? The better to deceive them and
to have them more completely in your power, you could take part
in their expeditions. You will be one of them. Your pride will
suffer, I know, from this deception, but the thought that you are
serving the world, and that high rank and large fortune, which
you will have so fully deserved, await you will sustain you under
difficulties.'

Nativa pronounced these words with much enthusiasm, but
in proportion as her eagerness increased, Morgan's cooled.

'Nativa,' he answered, noting her enchanting glance, 'I am
grieved to the heart that you have formed so poor an opinion of
me.'

'What can you mean?'

'I mean that were the buccaneers the most ruthless villains
on earth, a man who could sit at their table, partake their dangers
only to sell them afterwards, would be a traitorous dog, and a
spy. And should he by his degradation acquire wealth and rank,
he would only live the more dishonoured.'

A long silence followed, which the gentleman was the first
to break saying in a tone of soft emotion,—

'If I have offended you, forgive me ; but why did you ask me the sacrifice of my love ?'

'I ask you that ?' cried Nativa astonished ; 'I thought I was paving the way to enable you to overcome insuperable obstacles.'

'Is not asking me to become unworthy of you asking me to sacrifice your love ? You can feel neither sympathy nor tender, ness for me, or my honour would be dearer to you.'

'I assure you,' answered Nativa with some emotion, 'that I do not look at these things in the same light that you do ; to ensure so much good to mankind, and punish such villains by a little deceit, seems to me right and just. Still, I understand your scruples, and honour you for them.' Nativa added, with a smile of enchanting grace, 'So now you have escaped the fatigue and danger of a long voyage.'

'Not so,' answered Morgan ; 'it does not follow because I refuse to embrace your father's plan that I should hold myself free from my promise to you. Permit me to ask you again the name of the villain who insulted you.'

'I cannot tell it you yet,' answered Nativa ; 'I wish you first to hear of this man, the most noted of all buccaneers in the theatre of his exploits. When you have learnt how formidable he is, I will tell you his name ; that is, if you still hold your noble resolve. Until then I release you from your promise. But it is getting late, I must leave you.'

'One word before you go,' said Morgan, taking her hand. 'Although I refuse absolutely to play the part of a traitor, yet I never said that I would not join an expedition against the buccaneers ; those ruffians belong to every nation. Making war on them is not taking arms against England. Let the Earl of Monterey take me with him as a simple volunteer, and I will willingly risk my life in so just a cause.'

'No, that cannot be,' answered Nativa, 'you just now reproached me with not being careful of your honour, but never would I allow you to serve in a foreign land in a position unworthy of you. Thanks for your offer, for which I feel deeply grateful.'

The young lady rose, and, taking Morgan's arm, descended to the garden. As they were leaving, the bill of the untouched collation was handed to Morgan ; it amounted to forty shillings which he immediately paid.

Nativa and Morgan had not taken many steps before they again met the young gentlemen who had so insolently accosted the former.

'We are in luck,' cried one, who had evidently been drinking, 'here is our fair riddle again. Let us have a little sport.'

'Sir,' cried Morgan, 'I am averse to have to pass my sword hrough a defenceless man, and in presence of a lady too, but if you will be so good as to wait for me, I shall be back in five mniutes.'

'That will suit me neatly,' said the young rakehell, bowing. 'I should be so sorry to miss the pleasure of your acquaintance, that I will wait your return till night.'

'How foolish of you,' said Nativa, in a whisper, 'thus to risk your life !'

'Thanks for your kind interest,' answered Morgan ; 'but fear nothing. We rustics wear sharper stings than those cockney butterflies.'

'Nevertheless, I shall send in an hour for news of you. Think of me ! for the present, farewell !'

Her coach departed, and Morgan, enchanted at the thought that Nativa feared danger for him, stood gazing after it until it was out of sight.

'Well, now for my spark,' he said with a sigh, as he retraced his steps to the place where he had left his unknown adversary.

CHAPTER XV.

A CROSSING OF SWORDS AND WITS.

THE person who had behaved so rudely to Nativa was the Viscount Charlesworth ; he was twenty years of age, had a good income, and held a situation in the royal household. This young gentleman was by anticipation a type of the dissipation that gave such fearful notoriety to 'the Mohawks.' Extremely ignorant, and therefore affecting to believe in nothing, he took infinite pains to squander his fortune and injure his health. Insolent, and a jester, not to be unlike his friends, he nevertheless was naturally keen and brave. Brankhouse and the Marquis of Rothesay were gently chiding him, when seeing Morgan approach, they fell silent.

'Gentlemen,' said the Cornishman, with a low bow which all returned hastily, 'I was much engaged when you lately did me the honour to address me, and I do not know which of you promised to await my return.'

'It was I,' answered the viscount, coming forward. 'You find me still dazzled with the flounces of your divinity. A lady who shows such magnificence in her love is a desirable acquaintance.'

These insolent words brought the blood into Morgan's face, but feeling that any exhibition of anger would only expose him to ridicule, he stifled his feelings and replied calmly,—

'I am a stranger in town, and, therefore, must request you to inform me where we can measure swords.'

'Measure swords!' cried the viscount, with irony; 'such an expression could only come from a shepherd swain. Why, I could fancy I heard my great-grandfather talk.'

'Your great-grandfather would no doubt have answered, "On the spot!" but as words, not deeds, seem the fashion now, let us talk as much as you please, the principal point with me is that you shall not escape me.'

'You country gentlemen must have a vile opinion of us town gallants; but pray be assured that we know how to keep our word—except in love; so that when I promised to meet you, you might have counted on me. But really, in regard to a sword,' continued the viscount, turning to his friends, 'look what a fine kitchen spit this gentleman wears. I could never load myself with so much iron.'

'No, my sword would be rather too heavy for your delicate fingers, already tired with the weight of your cane. But really, gentlemen, we are losing time. I am as much dazzled with your wit as you were with the lady's attire, and now as you have had your turn in eloquence, let us turn to measuring blades, as your great grandfather would have said.'

'Directly,' answered Charlesworth coolly enough; 'but allow me to remark that as you seem an amusing fellow, and I should be glad not to lose your acquaintance, I will only prick you slightly, egad!'

'And I, in gratitude for the amusement you have given me, will only run you daintily yet cleanly through the arm.'

'Run me through the arm? capital,' cried Charlesworth, laughing.

'Come, come, viscount, a truce to joking! you have made a pretty good attack, and this gentleman has not behaved amiss. He is country bred; let the joke end here.'

When Morgan, who counted upon his greater address in action making up for his disadvantages in words, saw Brankhouse striving thus to give a peaceful issue to the matter, he gave way to his passion.

'What is your name, sir?' he challenged bluntly. 'Brankhouse? Good. Well, then, by Heaven, if you delay five minutes longer to draw your sword, I proclaim the Viscount Charlesworth as much of a coward as you.

At this insult both Brankhouse and the viscount turned pale, and the latter clapped his hand to his sword.

Brankhouse stopped his hand.

'Dear friend, you forget two very important matters: first, a quarrel in the streets would bring us all into trouble; the second is that we must ask the gentleman his name.'

'Whether he be base-born or not,' answered Charlesworth haughtily, 'I will measure swords with him.'

'You can do as you please,' answered Rothesey, 'only in that case your must excuse my being your second.   All that I can do is to be present at the meeting.'

'My name is Lewis, Knight of Morgan,' replied the Cornishman.

'I only know one Morgan,' said Daunce, 'the knight of that name who was compromised in the state trials of 1675, and has never been heard of since.'

'That was my father,' said Morgan proudly.

On hearing this answer, the other young men bowed, and Rothesey said, 'His was a fine and truly English spirit.   My father was a judge over him.'

'My friend, I am sure, regrets profoundly having treated his son with disrespect.'

'I am sorry,' observed the viscount.

Morgan hardly knew what answer to give, or how to behave, but his antagonist soon relieved his embarrassment by adding, 'Now that my apologies have rendered all explanation useless, and a meeting inevitable, I warn you that I shall do my best to kill you. If you will do me the honour to follow me, in a few minutes we shall be in Birdcage Walk.'

The park was not ill frequented at the moment.

'Do you not fear, gentlemen, that we shall be interrupted?' asked Morgan ; 'there are so many people about.'

'You need not be uneasy,' said Rothesey, 'our precautions are taken.'

Whilst speaking, he knocked at the door of a small lodge surrounded by a garden around which was a thick, quick-set hedge, impenetrable to the most curious eye.

The door opened immediately, and the party entered.

'Tony,' said the marquis to the quiet-looking old man, 'go and prepare a bed and get a doctor.'

Tony was no doubt well used to such orders, for he evinced no surprise, and the gentlemen passed on into the little garden.

A broad walk well rolled and gravelled divided the grounds, and made a convenient place for sword exercise. Morgan hastened to take off his coat, his adversary did the same.

'Sir,' said the viscount, 'I repeat that I fully intend to charge you vigorously and without quarter. You are too much my match for me to spare you.'

'Thanks for your kind intentions,' answered the Cornishman, 'I beg permission to adhere to my resolution.'

'Which was——'

'To perforate your shoulder.'

By tacit agreement Steinkerque and Daunce placed themselves by Morgan, who thanked them with a nod. Rothesey and Brankhouse remained by Charlesworth. Both adversaries immediately drew swords.

'Begin, gentlemen,' cried Rothesey, when the combat commenced.

Morgan, as he said himself, had considerable skill in arms; he possessed also that coolness which, leaving nothing to chance, was able to turn the slightest circumstances to advantage. Still, as he fancied he might in some things be inferior to the young courtier, he prudently kept on the defensive to feel his power. Lord Charlesworth was also a proficient in small sword exercise, but he very soon became aware that he had now met more than his peer.

'In faith, chevalier,' he said, throwing himself back to escape a thrust, 'I own the length of your sword puts me out—it is a perfect lance.'

'You are right,' answered Morgan, who, lowering the point of his sword, asked his second to hand him his, which that young gentleman did at once. 'Kitchen spits are dangerously lengthy!'

The combat began afresh.

It soon became evident to the witnesses that victory would not be on Charlesworth's side. Morgan, cool and collected, still kept on the defensive, however.

'Really,' cried the viscount, 'I don't know what is the matter with me to-day. Will you allow me, chevalier, to take breath?'

'As you please; there is no hurry.'

'Thanks; but please to remark that the truce you grant me is mine by right, which I might have exacted.'

'Oh, my lord,' cried Sir Lewis reproachfully, 'do you think me so completely of your great-grandfather's times as not to understand the language of to-day? The commentaries on politeness with which you favoured me were needless.'

'Well retorted,' replied Charlesworth, wiping his sword on his embroidered handkerchief. 'I don't want to flatter you, but you improve upon acquaintance. When I met you with the lady you seemed to me a relic of the Deluge! Later, when you drew your sword, I took you for a pikeman, but now——'

'Well, what now?' asked the Cornishman, as Charlesworth stopped short.

'Now I am quite rested, let us begin again.'

Morgan still kept on his guard, whilst his adversary, exasperated at the resistance which he met with, made more violent assaults.

The witnesses could no longer understand Sir Lewis's play.

'Stop my vitals!' cried Charlesworth, now really in a rage, 'it seems to me, chevalier, that you are sparing me.'

'Not at all. I only watch for a good opening.'

'Which does not come, it seems——'

'I beg your pardon, I have it now.'

Morgan parried with admirable skill his adversary's thrust,

and launched a decisive response. Charlesworth's sword fell from his hand. But attempting to smile, he said,—

'I don't understand that trick, but it has succeeded, at all events. Your swordsmanship is rather rough, but certainly clever. It was lucky I asked you to relinquish your due; you could have killed me outright.' Here he turned pale, and his supporters rushed forward to catch him; but, pushing them gently aside, he said to his victor,—

'Let us shake hands, sir. And may I ask you why, when you had the opportunity, you did not kill me?'

'Do you really wish for the reason?' said Morgan hesitatingly.

'Certainly.'

'Because I had promised merely to wound you in the shoulder.'

'Oh, chevalier, your candour and delicacy are beyond all bounds! And then not to have even returned my sally about my great-grandfather when I was at your mercy. Well, let us be, if you consent, fast friends in future.'

The viscount, probably feeling that his strength was failing him, now turned to enter the house, saying to his friends,—

'Pray do not let me keep you here. I should be grieved to spoil your evening's amusement. By-the-by, Rothesey, do me the favour to send me a nurse. Little Delia, for instance; she is so excessively stupid, she will talk me to sleep.'

As soon as the wounded man was in bed his friends left him.

'I hope, sir,' said Rothesey to his victor, 'that you will join our party! We are going back to meet some ladies from the French plays in the little theatre in the Haymarket, and we shall finish the evening with a game at hazard.'

Morgan's first thought was to refuse, but his desire was so great to have an insight into the life of the young nobles that his curiosity got the better of his prudence, and he accepted.

Four hours later, having played his part at a magnificent supper enlivened by several theatrical divinities, Morgan's brain was rather confused with wine. He sat down at a card-table.

'What do you stake?' asked Daunce, who held the bank.

He answered at random; but, as often happens with novices, he won.

Ashamed of seeming poor, he staked the whole sum again. He was again and again successful, and some time later found himself possessor of one hundred and twenty pounds.

The ladies from the theatre, who hitherto had paid him little attention, now flocked round him.

By eleven o'clock Morgan had won four hundred pounds; the foreign nymphs were more amiable than ever, one of them even winding a white dimpled arm round his shoulder.

The cards had just been passed to Morgan, whose turn it was

to hold the bank, when a stranger of a rather used-up appearance entered the room.

A cry of pleasure arose from the gambling-table, and the ladies for a moment left the Cornishman to welcome the newcomer, who received graciously, but with a *blasé* air, their blandishments.

'Come and sit by me,' cried Steinkerque, 'it is an age or, at least, two days since I have seen you. It was said you had set off for Amsterdam. But what is the news?'

'Nothing stirring,' answered the stranger. 'Only the Duke of Marland is said to have fallen desperately in love.'

'But who can know the truth better than you?'

'I! what have I to do with such things as love?'

The new-comer glanced carefully round the gambling-table, and proceeded gravely,—

'Who, amongst my friends here, knows the Conde de Monterey, and can give me any information about his lovely daughter, Nativa?'

At this question Morgan's blood ran cold.

The last speaker was the ill-famed Dean of St. Maurice's, once tutor to Lord Wharton, the notorious *roué*.

Morgan could scarcely resist asking an explanation of the dean's words about Nativa ; still he forced himself to silence in hopes that the conversation might afford the explanation he longed for.

'Come, tell us, then, Jannekin,' asked Rothesey. 'Is his grace seriously in love?'

'So it is said,' answered the gay prattler.

'Impossible,' cried in chorus the theatrical dames.

'Why impossible?' asked the cynic. 'I know well enough, dear harpies, that women are all the same, and the most hypocritical are thought the best, and therefore there is no reason for falling in love with one more than another ; and a sensible man ought to despise them equally. That is the fact; but the tamer mind is subject to certain maladies, and some momentary affection, a softening of the brain, for an example, will prevent a sensible man, for the time being, from seeing things as they really are, and he fancies he has found a phœnix in a woman. So my lord may just now be brain-sick. You, Celeste, who jest at my words, I would wager twenty to one, even you have met with the man who believed in your fidelity.'

'I have met with a dozen,' answered Celeste proudly ; 'still it sounds so odd to hear the dear duke is in love.'

'Who is this Nativa,' interrupted Daunce, 'who is such a phœnix?'

'I only saw her for a moment,' answered the dean ; 'she seemed to me so wonderfully beautiful and attractive that I should not wonder if the duke's passion for her lasts a whole fortnight.'

'I long to see this wonder,' cried Brankhouse.

'A little patience, and I'll contrive to have her at the concert next Monday at Kensington Palace.'

'And do you pretend, sir, 'interposed Morgan, with difficulty hiding his emotion, 'that the daughter of the Count of Monterey is likely to love the Duke of Marland?'

'Oh, not at all—I know the contrary. Women never love; they only let themselves be loved,' answered the dean, eyeing Morgan with curiosity.

'Then you imagine that Lady Sandoval will become the duke's prey?' asked Morgan, with flashing eyes.

The dean viewed him attentively, but answered carelessly,—

'How can I tell? If the young lady has a lover already, perhaps she may repulse the duke's addresses, though it is hardly probable.'

'That lady a lover!' cried Morgan in a rage, 'it is a lie.'

'Oh, chevalier!' put in Rothesey, between jest and earnest, 'take care, or you will frighten away the reverend gentleman, and we are very fond of godly society.'

Morgan's violent conduct had startled the gamblers, who had ceased playing. There was a dead silence.

The dean was the first to break it.

'Thanks, marquis,' he said; then turning to the Cornishman, he proceeded: 'You wish us to believe, young man, that you are in favour with the Earl de Monterey's daughter, whom, probably, you do not even know by sight. The plan would be ingenious if not already worn threadbare. Believe me, you are young and good-looking enough to make your way without having recourse to such artifices, which I assure you are quite out of fashion—quite, egad, quite!'

This cunning yet pertinent answer disconcerted Morgan. If he took offence, it would be attributed to disgust at being unmasked, or he must compromise Nativa. On the other hand, to endure such raillery in silence was more than his patience would bear, so he resolved to watch an opportunity of taking his revenge on the wit.

'Come, dean,' cried Rothesey, 'get these ladies to pour you out some wine, and take a hand at our table; play is much better than discussion.'

'You forget that I never drink anything but water, and never touch a card,' answered Jan Stœpel, 'but don't mind me: I came to say two words to Daunce, and then shall go away.'

'What, you roam at midnight?'

'Well, that is not sacrificing too much to Morpheus, when one has to rise at half-past three.'

'The fact is, you are the most extraordinary person I know. You take part in all the revelries, and pursue your serious business just the same. You are the most industrious rake and most rakish man of business in the world.'

'Very likely,' answered the dean, laughing. 'As I have always thought I shall die young, I manage thus to double my time. I am only thirty-nine, and I have lived full sixty years.'

Seeing the gambling about to recommence, and thus losing hope of avenging himself on his insulter, Morgan turned to one of the ladies, and said,—

'Who, madam, is this sarcastic priest?'

'What,' she answered, giving him a tender glance, for this ignorance of Morgan's proved how little the young man knew of life, and gave her hopes of a victim, 'do you not know the Dean of St. Maurice's?' and then, lowering her voice, she whispered a few words.

Morgan turned red, then pale.

'Impossible,' he cried; 'gentlemen like these around us would never admit such a hypocrite into their society!'

'Oh, chevalier, if you only knew gentlemen as well as I do,' replied the dancer, still laughing, 'this intimacy would seem the most natural thing in the world. And then the panderer is a good fellow, and often very useful.'

'Chevalier,' cried Steinkerque, 'we passed you over by mistake; it is your turn now!'

'I regret that, having been a winner, I cannot continue the game,' said Morgan, rising, 'but I must leave.'

'You have quite the right to do so,' said Brankhouse. 'Winners who leave off play nowadays are praised for their prudence, and called men of character.'

'But I pray you to believe that if I leave off playing it is from a very different reason.'

'Oh, an appointment, no doubt, with the beautiful Nativa!' sneered Stœpel; 'you *are* a happy fellow!'

These words rendered the Cornish knight still more indignant.

'Sir,' he answered, looking on him with supreme contempt, 'if you were of my station, or even an honest *man*, my sword should chastise your insolence, but with such as you, you must be aware, shameless as you are, such a thing is impossible. If I refuse to continue the game, it is because I have just learnt what a vile wretch you are, and I should consider myself disgraced by remaining a moment longer in your company.'

This severe speech was followed by a dead silence. The courtiers, feeling that Morgan was right, and though his words were an indirect insult to them, not being at all inclined to take up the cudgels for their guest, found themselves at a loss.

The wretched pimp, with livid cheeks, dilated eyes, and clenched fists, vented his rage at this direct and public insult in a volley of oaths.

'Thou foul-mouthed carter!' he screamed, 'do you think to bully me, you country bumpkin? Dare you give me your address?'

'I repeat,' replied Morgan coldly, 'that between us there can be nothing in common. And if I don't cane you into silence, it is only out of respect to the present company. As for my address, I live—— '

'It is useless to give the dean your address,' interrupted Steinkerque quickly; 'what use would that be to a Churchman?'

'My lord,' exclaimed Stœpel, turning angrily to his country-man.

'Well, fellow, what?' rejoined the Dutchman. 'Don't try and quarrel with me because I want to smoothe over the matter. What do you expect? the chevalier is in the right: you are a worthless cur, and only such reprobates as ourselves could have kept company with you so long.'

'Come, that is good! Steinkerque gone over to the enemy,' said the dean, controlling his features and changing his tone. He pretended to take the courtier's unpleasant frankness as a good joke, and, with a sigh, said, 'Steinkerque, hereafter I shall remember this.'

The wretch spoke truth: twenty years later, when George was in power, Steinkerque suffered exile for this evening's insult. Morgan was going, when the Marquis of Rothesey said to him coldly,—

'Chevalier, as you do not belong to the Court, and we have not the honour to be personally known to you, will you be so good as to take the four hundred odd pounds that belong to you?'

He took the money from his companions and gave it to the Cornishman, who left the odd coins to the lackeys.

'This wrangle has so interrupted our pleasures that it has given me the blues,' observed Steinkerque; 'so good night, my friends.'

'We part friends, eh?' said Stœpel, grinning on the speaker.

'Heaven forbid I should bear malice! Are you not endowed with the blackest heart and the most brilliant wit of any one in England? I am yours ever.'

He and Morgan left together.

'Chevalier,' said the former, 'when one carries four or five hundred in one's purse it is not prudent to go about on foot at midnight. Will you allow me to put you down? Chevalier,' continued he when they were seated in the carriage, 'when I am at standstill about anything, I take the dilemma by the horns, and face the matter at once. Do you know you have pleased me greatly to-day at the duel? and your indignation this evening, though a reproof to my folly, delighted me also. I like to see gentlemen keep their place. We courtiers are much too easy. When there is no question of precedence, and we are not jealous of an equal to whom the king gives the honour of holding his candlestick, we care little about our station. We let the greatest knave into our company. This wretched mocker of the Church, whose gown he wears, is powerful; one is forced to bear with him. Believe me, if you can leave town for a time, it would be well to do so. This man is to be despised, not disdained. He is clever, cunning, and capable of any crime; moreover, violent and cowardly; therefore to be feared. I repeat, try to avoid him.'

'Thanks for your advice,' answered Morgan, touched by his kind interest. 'From what you have seen to-day you may believe me that I feel truly grateful for your kindness.'

'Oh, nonsense about gratitude! will you follow my advice?'

'No, viscount, I cannot do so.'

'I know you are wrong, yet I respect you. But when one has to deal with a viper, it is mere folly to leave one's heel naked; the poison mounts so quickly to the heart. When one cannot crush such a reptile's head, one must keep out of its way. Believe me and beware.'

He was still speaking when the carriage stopped. Morgan and his friend parted, and the former, as he stood on the pavement, heard him once more call to him from the carriage,—

'I say, chevalier, beware of the serpent!'

Allan was awaiting his master's return with the greatest impatience. Since his adventure with Dowlass his natural distrust had greatly increased.

'If even honest folks like me turn to robbing in London,' he said to himself, 'who is to be trusted?'

Morgan's return therefore gave him much satisfaction.

'Have you met with any mischance, master?' he asked; 'have they tried to rob you?'

'On the contrary, Allan; look here!' answered the gentleman, displaying his money to his astonished follower.

'Oh, good luck, master!' cried Allan, 'have you, too, been— ahem!'

'What do you mean?' asked Morgan, as Allan stopped short.

'Oh, this is too much!' murmured the peasant; 'besides, my master would rather blow his brains out than prig a coin.'

Fatigued with the excitement of the day, the knight retired to rest, but could not close his eyes. He had seen Nativa again, and he possessed four hundred pounds. We may safely aver that all that night the thought of Stœpel never troubled his brain.

As for the latter, no sooner had he reached home than he began devising means of revenge, which kept him awake all night, too. On one side, therefore, the attack was planned, on the other no defence was meditated.

CHAPTER XVI.

QUEEN AND FONDLING.

ABOUT eight the next morning Lord Menzil descended from his coach at Kensington Palace. The first person he met was Huysem, the head valet of the king.

'Dirck!' he cried, with a familiarity which not one of the great lords would have used to so important a person, for every one knew how much the king loved and respected his head valet.

The latter bowed low, almost with dread, for the sight of the queen's favourite was always disagreeable to him.

'How are all the family this morning?' continued Menzil, without appearing to notice the man's uneasiness, though he enjoyed it mightily.

'What family do you mean, sir?' asked the latter, pretending not to understand.

'Oh, my godmamma and his Majesty! but the fact is, my good fellow, they keep me so short of money that I can no longer consort with the nobility, and have to make acquaintance with the lower orders; so my manners have degenerated in consequence. I might be mistaken for a Cheapside silversmith!'

'I regret extremely, sir, that I cannot stay a moment longer,' answered Huysem, who had blushed scarlet, 'my duties oblige me at once to attend his Majesty.'

'Which means,' remarked Lusthoos to himself, as the valet hastened away, 'that you are going to warn my patroness of my arrival. But what matters? Thanks to my friend Legaff, I am well provided with the ready, and need not trouble my good adopted mother for two months to come. So, if she denies me, I'll e'en make a pretty hubbub! We shall be the scandal of the day, and I shall be all the fashion again.'

With such grateful feelings Menzil sought the queen's apartments, where, to his surprise, he was admitted at once.

Queen Mary had at this time passed her thirtieth year, but thanks to the severe style of her dress, she looked much younger, for one was induced to think that had she adopted a gayer and more graceful fashion, she would have looked still younger than she did.

She received her always-forgiven favourite in the room where the king usually transacted business with his ministers.

'Madam,' began Menzil, who treated his befriender with all the more respect as his intentions were hostile, 'Huysem fled from me so quickly that I feared I might not have the pleasure of seeing you this morning.'

'Wherefore this reproach, dear child?' said the queen, with much sweetness; 'do I ever refuse to see you? Do you not come almost daily to tell me your mischances at cards, and ask my help? Speak, what do you want to-day? What yesterday's fault have you to confess?'

For a moment the scamp felt tempted, seeing the lady so favourably disposed, to pretend a momentary loss, but fearing the soft tones might be only a blind, he was on his guard, and answered,—

'Dear madam, will you always judge me so severely? What, you overwhelm me with reproaches, when it is you who do me injustice.'

'You have come to ask for some high office, I see,' said the queen, preferring to brave the storm at once to hearing it rumble in the distance.

'No,' said Menzil, 'not at all.'

'Then you want money?'

'Still less,' said the other with an effort.

'Indeed!' remarked Mary, with astonishment; 'I had to sell my stables yesterday.'

'What made your Highness do that?'

'To set an example of devotion, and to aid, as far as my means would allow, the complicated finances and empty coffers of the state.'

'What, the Government is reduced to such extremity,' said Menzil, with an accent of real reproach, 'and you told me nothing about it? There should be sworn confidence between us, methinks. And what sum did your stables bring, pray?'

'Nearly twenty thousand pounds, I believe. Enough for the hospital for poor friendless women which I contemplated.'

'Well, that is a pretty sum; it would have made me happy for life.'

'Fie! that sum would only have lasted you two months.'

'Possible! still, every day during that time you might have had the pleasure of thinking that your dear godchild was happy.'

On her side the queen was almost frightened at her caller's unusual amiability, and longed to know the object of his visit. She said at last, 'I know you too well to ascribe this visit to dis-interested affection. What is it you want?'

‘Well, my dear queen, to be frank with you, a great friend of mine—indeed, my best and only friend—wishes to have a private audience with his Majesty the king. This friend has rendered me the greatest service, and I must insist on your kind offices to facilitate his wishes.’

‘What is his name?’

‘Baron Legaff,—a—a Hungarian noble—irreproachable—”

‘What does he want? what is his position?’

‘Two very short questions, but difficult to answer. Who is he? The devil, for aught I know! What does he want? I don’t know. What is his position? That of a Bentinck, who sows his gold by handfuls.’

‘And are you not ashamed, Menzil,’ cried the queen, reddening with anger, ‘to ask me to obtain a private audience of the king for such a man?’

‘Oh, to speak frankly, the best man with me is the richest and the most generous. And who is our king?—not a Stuart or Bourbon? But I have a far more cogent reason for making this request which concerns us both.’

‘Well, name it,’ said the lady resignedly.

‘My good Mary,’ continued Menzil gravely, ‘the parsimony that the king in his Hollandish prudence has shown towards me has embittered my life and reduced me to such a state of poverty that I was ready to do anything for gold.’

‘You frighten me; what have you done?’

‘Conspired against the crown—that’s all! call me a Jacobite, if you will! The Pretender thought I might be useful to him, and for his interests he did what my liege lord ought to have done for his own dignity; he enabled me to pay my debts. You see before you a partisan of the Stuarts. Now, godmamma, my downfall must affect your peace and standing. This Legaff holds a proof of what you would call my treason and I my revenge. If to-morrow the king refuses a private audience to this man, the king will be warned that his wife’s favourite has conspired against him; you will know whether the royal vengeance will stop at you.’

‘Oh,’ cried the queen, in tears, ‘how wretched you make me! I wish I were dead!’

‘Dead,’ cried her tormentor with a sneer, ‘do you expect some higher crown in heaven than that you wear?’

‘I will do as you wish. Bring this Baron Legaff here at three to-morrow, and he shall have the audience.’

She rose to leave.

‘One word more, dear madam. Whatever gratitude I owe to the baron for his generosity, it would not be quite pleasant to have Damocles’s sword always over my head. May I hope that you will get me to-morrow, if possible, a blank warrant of arrest.

signed and sealed, for service of the state. I dare say I can fill
it up, and I defy him to mate me with a *habeas corpus.*'

'You are acting madly,' Menzil, 'this is not Holland!'

'But there are many dykes here in which to drown your
man.'

'You shall have the paper.'

CHAPTER XVII.

KING AND CORSAIR.

WILLIAM THE THIRD was walking slowly up and down his
room dictating a letter to Queen Mary, who was writing at a
table covered with papers. Though her hearing was excellent,
and the king spoke very clearly, yet she several times repeated
the phrases, slightly altered, in an interrogative tone. After a
moment's consideration he usually accepted the alteration.

King William was at this time in his last stage of consump-
tion ; his careworn brow and hollow cheeks made him look still
older, but his eye retained all the brilliancy and ardour of his
martial youth. What especially marked the royal person was
the gloomy dignity of his deportment.

At a pause in his dictation his royal amanuensis remarked,—

'Your Majesty remembers doubtless that the Conde de
Monterey is promised an audience to-day ? The earl has been
an hour in waiting.'

'Right, Mary ; Huysem has the order to bring him here.
My position in regard to Spain will not allow me to receive
Montcrey as his high rank and qualifications demand, but I will
explain this to him ; he is a man of high ability who might be of
great use to England.'

'In order to render the interview less formal and diplomatic,
sire, I invited him to bring his fair daughter with him ; she is
the godchild of the unfortunate Queen Maria Souza.'

'You did well, Mary ; I have heard Wharton speak
enthusiastically of the young lady. I shall be pleased to see
her.'

A quarter of an hour later the Earl of Monterey and his
daughter were introduced.

'Count de Monterey,' said the king, 'I am happy to receive you in a friendly manner.'

The Spanish noble bowed low, and in a grave, almost solemn
tone, replied,—

'Sire, contrary to custom, and in spite of the wars ever
current between our two nations, I have the honour to be

accredited secretly from my master, Charles the Second of Spain, to your Majesty.'

William concealed his surprise, and answered,—

'My well-beloved brother of Spain could not have made a choice more agreeable to me. Only, a secret ambassador, sir count, is so contrary to all Court etiquette that I cannot at once consent to receive one. At present I can only consider you as a gentleman sent on some important private mission from his very Catholic Majesty. Do you agree to this?'

'Yes, sire.'

'Then, count, speak as you list.'

'Sire, my master, the King of Spain, entreats your Majesty, notwithstanding old feuds of Holland and England, to unite your marine forces with his to exterminate the pirates infesting the Antilles. This is no question of policy, but one of justice and humanity, which my master has much at heart.'

'Count de Monterey,' answered William, 'on the contrary, I consider this question entirely one of policy. In the first place, the French buccaneers of the Antilles only act in accordance with the commissions granted them by King Louis; the Dutch and English cruise unwarranted, but spare their countrymen. Moreover, since my brother of Spain attaches such importance to their devastations, it is a proof that the efforts of these ocean vagrants are not to be disdained.'

'Sire,' said the count, 'will your Majesty permit me to lay before you the most powerful consideration which has induced my master to send me here?'

The king nodded, and Monterey continued,—

'This consideration, sire, is the most sacred in the world; the buccaneers of the Antilles commit every day the most fearful horrors. The buccaneers not only pillage and desecrate our churches, but they persecute the clergy.'

'I regret the sacrilege, my lord, but that is no cry in Protestant England. Is there not in one of our temples—perhaps within hearing—a bell taken from Cadiz Cathedral by Drake or Raleigh? Well, believe me, there never was a king, from Rufus to Charles the Second, who would dare to offer to restore that trophy to the fane! No, base not your plea on the rudeness of the sea-rovers to holy men—put before us the tables of the losses to commerce! That will touch our pocket; and then we shall see.'

Nativa and the queen had entered into conversation. King William, not being prepared to debate so important a question, advanced towards Nativa, and addressed a few graceful compliments to her; then turning to the count, again said,—

'I hope soon to have the pleasure of seeing you, when we will discuss these matters more at length. I beg you not to be surprised at the manner in which you have been received. Ignorant that you were a *chargé d'affaires* from my brother of Spain, I wished to receive you with the esteem you deserve.'

As soon as Monterey and Nativa had retired, the king, with unwonted animation, observed,—

'What is your opinion, Mary, of all this? Don't you think that this crusade against the buccaneers which Charles proposes to me so secretly is a very important matter?'

'I am entirely of your opinion, sire, there.'

'To chase the freebooters from the Indian Seas in the present state of my navy would be an absurdity. By forcing Spain to keep a large fleet to defend her colonies, the buccaneers do us a great service.'

'I have some one to present to you before you cease business, William.'

'Whom, Mary?'

'I cannot tell you.'

'Well, if it is to be a surprise, let the person come in.'

Five minutes later Legaff entered the chamber, and having bowed low, stood there, calm and unmoved.

William had the soldierly habit of looking earnestly at any one presented to him for the first time ; if the person flinched beneath his gaze, he contemned him.

Whether Legaff did or did not know of this peculiarity, he bore the king's scrutiny easily.

'What do you desire, sir?' asked the monarch.

'Sire,' answered Legaff, 'I desire to open up to your Majesty such horizons of glory that your eagle glance will not be able to take in the splendours ! I wish to be the Fernando Cortez of your reign, and leave my name united to the age which posterity will call yours.'

This mixture of boldness and adulation was a real surprise to the king, who turned an inquiring look on the queen, who, in agonies at what might come next, only smiled in return.

'And who are you, sir?' continued the king, examining Legaff with much curiosity.

'Sire, I call myself here Baron Legaff. The name by which I am better known on the open seas, and I may say respected and feared, is that of Morgan the Second.'

The queen turned pale, and William, giving way to his wonder, cried,—

'Morgan ! that is the name of a noted buccaneer, who died some years ago.'

Legaff smiled, and answered,—

'Morgan resembles, if you will allow me the simile, those kings of France who never die. The king is dead ! Long live the king !—Sir Henry Morgan is dead ! Morgan for ever !'

At this extraordinary answer William turned again to his queen, but she was so frightened at introducing such a person that she turned away abashed.

'Please to explain, sir,' said the sovereign.

'Sire,' answered Legaff, 'your Majesty is no doubt so entirely absorbed in important affairs that perhaps you have never found time to inquire who these buccaneers of the Spanish Indies are, who extend the power, venerate the name, and, without any hope of recompense or ambition, add to the glory of maritime England. These buccaneers are not isolated pirates, as is generally thought, whose only profession is to pillage Spanish vessels. No! The buccaneers have formed among themselves a secret and powerful association, whose chief is an absolute despot, and takes the name of Morgan, from the illustrious founder of the league! I am that present admiral!'

William looked with increasing curiosity on a man at once so bold and so tranquil, the type of those famous freebooters of whom such wonders were related. Come of the watery kingdom Holland, he sympathized with those who dared the ocean.

'Master Morgan,' he answered slowly, 'you are mistaken in thinking that I am ignorant of the great deeds of the buccaneers ; are there not Dutchmen among them ? And as chance has brought you before me, I shall question you concerning several acts brought against you, and for which, if true, I shall demand signal justice.'

'Sire,' cried Legaff, boldly interrupting the king, 'people like us, who bravely and loyally serve their commander, are incapable of wanton outrages. We are sea soldiers, and we ourselves punish the faithless and the ruffianly.'

This audacity pleased the king, and seeing his grim smile, Mary began to lay aside her fears.

'Are you noble by birth ?'

'Yes, sire, I am. I belong to that antique Saxon squirehood who, shunning the Norman and Tudor Court, has always stood up for the privileges of its order, and oft for its serfs.'

'The privileges of rebels, which has cost much blood on the scaffold.'

'Your Majesty must permit me to think otherwise : in my eyes these rebels were victims and martyrs. If we had won we should have changed the succession to the original strain from Harold.'

Astonished at the buccaneer's audacity, William did not answer. He was the head of his line, and had his Pretender opposed to him.

'Since you are of gentle blood, I cannot let you enjoy the advantage of concealing your birth. As a gentleman, you have no right to appear before me under assumed names.'

'Sire,' answered Legaff, 'to give up my name would be to endanger my life. If you require it of me, I will obey *you*, but reflect : clemency is the divine right of kings, and it would ill accord with your greatness to provide for the executioner.'

'You are, then, an outlaw ?'

Yes, sire, doubly an outlaw.'

The queen again turned pale, and fumed against her godson.

'For what crime were you condemned ?' asked the king,— 'for murder or for sacrilege ?'

'For disputing the royal authority, and upholding old privileges of the nobility and the rights of the people.'

'The crime of rebellion ?'

'So my judges decided.'

'Sir,' after a moment's thought, said the king, 'I am willing, out of respect and affection for my wife, not to insist on your name. But as you say clemency is the divine right of kings, it is possible, that if you appeal to my clemency, confess and repent of your crimes, I may be induced to pardon you.'

'Pardon !' cried Legaff, in a thrilling tone. 'My faults were against your predecessor—the vain trifler you have displaced ! Pardon ! I entreat your Majesty not to grieve—I dare not say outrage—me so far. I pardoned like a criminal, by either him I offended, or you his successor ! No, sire, do me not so much wrong ; let me retain the memory of my injury ! It is my strength, my inspiration. Do not dispel the dream that has supported me through twenty years of exile, that of a noble revenge on royalty.'

'What is your meaning, sir ?'

'Accused wrongfully of having failed in duty to the throne, when I only defended the privileges of the nobility and the people's rights, I wish to prove by glorious deeds redounding to England's credit that I have never ceased to be a faithful subject.'

William, with that tact in judging men for which he was noted, perceived and appreciated the nature of the buccaneer ; therefore he said graciously,—

'In consideration of the respect and devotion you express for us, we are willing that you should retain your mask. What is your request ?'

'Permission, sire, to devote myself to your service, together with the immense resources which are at my command.'

'Explain yourself more clearly.'

Concisely, and with manly earnestness, Legaff unfolded a plan for the conquest of the Spanish West Indies. Stimulated by the presence of the king, and anxious to gain his point, the energy and dauntlessness of his soul breathed forth in his words.

The king and the queen exchanged glances of wonder and admiration.

When he ceased speaking, William III. said,—

'Sir, I have listened to your projects with all the attention that earnestness, your good faith, and the greatness of the enterprise deserve. I shall consider carefully the plan that you have submitted to me, and also beg you to give me a private memorial on the subject. Have you anything more to say to me?'

'I have an unpleasant subject to speak of which, did I not know that I was addressing the greatest king in the world, I dared not touch upon. However distant, sire, we buccaneers may be from our native land, believe me, on the other side of the globe, we glory in England's successes and bewail her disasters. Your Majesty must pardon my boldness, as it is inspired by love of my country. I thought it only a duty at this juncture of financial distress to offer my aid, and I came.'

'To offer me your assistance, doubtless,' said William, ironically, but his lip relaxing at the idea of money.

'Even so, sire,' answered Legaff quietly. 'Your Majesty is too great not to have unbounded confidence in the protection of Heaven. Lately the United Kingdom has endured signal reverses; why cannot you believe that I, a humble instrument in the hands of Providence, may be sent to help you in your need?'

These words, pronounced with fervent conviction, made a visible impression on the king, who answered,—

'I own, sir, that your words astonish and delight me. Explain yourself without fear; how do you propose to succour the exchequer, to replenish which we pay the bankers so dearly?'

'First by entreating your Majesty to accept this half-million,' said the captain, taking a sealed packet from under his cloak and presenting it to the king. 'This sum, employed in a manner that I would point out, might be twice doubled in five months.'

'In what way?' asked the king.

'Sire,' answered Legaff, 'my plan would be to take the powerful and flourishing town of Carthagena.' He then entered into details which appeared so plausible that ere Legaff had ceased speaking, William was convinced of the practicability of so vast and bold a project.

'My only objection to this enterprise,' said the king, 'is the complaints which I mentioned to you before of the want of morality of your men. Who can assure me that in the sack of Carthagena the most fearful outrages may not take place, as happened when your predecessor Morgan overcame it?'

'I, sire,' answered Legaff proudly,—'I can prove to you that many of the tales against Sir Henry were only a contrivance of Spain to deprive us of the great advantages England might have derived from the support of the buccaneers. With thousands at one's disposal it is easy to learn everything. Should your Majesty still retain any doubts of my loyalty and good faith, and wish to know the hidden ambassador in the Jacobite interests, I can name him to you.'

'Take care, sir, not to jeopardise the good opinion I have of you.'

'I can make my words good, sire.'

'Then, who is this secret ambassador of St. Germain's ?'

'Señor Sandoval, Conde de Monterey.'

This answer struck the king with superstitious terror.

Morgan knew things that William was ignorant of, spoke with boldness of mighty projects worthy of a powerful monarch's consideration, and notwithstanding his outward respect, treated on an equality with the King of England himself.

'Master Legaff,' said the latter, 'take these bills. A British sovereign cannot accept money from a subject. You can arrange about the loan of it with our Chancellor of the Exchequer. One last word : should I, as is not unlikely, decide upon the Carthagena expedition, what terms do you demand for this monetary advance of yours ?'

'Three things, your Majesty : first, that my officers should hold the same rank as those in the royal navy. That whoever your Majesty may choose to command the expedition, he must, in one circumstance, that may not arise, obey me. I agree to give no order to the admiral that shall not be approved by the king or by Captain Bloxam. And lastly, that my freebooters may have one-third of the spoils.'

'Sir,' said the king, 'I authorize you to go and explain matters with Barstairs.

Legaff bowed low and retired, grave in demeanour, yet joyful at heart.

As he crossed the court to his carriage whom should he meet but Sir Lewis Morgan.

'You here, young gentleman,' exclaimed Matthewson, with a frank, pleasant air ; 'we seem destined to meet.'

'This meeting is the more agreeable to me,' answered Morgan, 'as it gives me the opportunity of paying what I owe you. Be so good as to let me know what loss you sustained by the stupidity of your groom. I am well provided, and shall have pleasure in indemnifying you.'

'You, sir ; I was right in saying that fortune would come to you. I am delighted at your success. You remember how poor you were a few months ago, and now——'

'Never mind what I was, Master Matthewson,' answered the Cornishman, blushing, 'I only want to pay my debt.'

'As hot as ever,' cried Matthewson, with a hearty laugh. Come, young gentleman,' he continued, taking his hand in both of his, 'I know there is a great distance in rank between us, but that does not prevent my loving you as if you were my son. Shall we be friends? I know my manners are not polished, but my heart is true as the star.'

Already respecting him highly for his intrepidity in rescuing Nativa, Morgan was too lonely in the world not to accept willingly this offer of friendship.

'If nothing detains you at Court,' said the latter, 'perhaps you will return with me to town. My carriage is waiting.'

'Carriage!' echoed Morgan, surprised; 'I perceive you are splendidly dressed for a horsedealer! You look as if you had been to see the king.'

'Yes, I have just had an hour's private audience of his Majesty,' answered Matthewson, as they entered his carriage.

CHAPTER XVIII.

THE REVELATION.

LEGAFF took his companion's hand, and said gravely, 'Although we have met so rarely, I have seen enough of you to appreciate your high honour, probity, and courage. These qualities render you a gentleman in the true sense of the word; but to make of you a man one thing is wanting, which neither birth nor instinct can give—that is, experience. When your bleeding heart will have thrown aside its dearest illusions like weeds on the roadside, and your mind feels neither anger nor pain at treason or perfidy, and you have learnt to see in the bewitching smile of woman interest or ambition—cupidity lurking behind it, you will then be able to value such a man as myself. Know me no longer as the horsedealer who practised on your inexperience, but as Baron Legaff.'

'And if, Baron Legaff,' answered Morgan, with wounded pride, 'under your assumed character you received any insult from me, I am ready, in spite of newly-sworn friendship, to give you satisfaction.'

'Take care, dear Lewis,' answered the buccaneer, with melancholy tenderness, 'how you taunt a man who could retaliate. Between you and me strife is impossible. Towards you I must be gentle, though Heaven knows'—a sinister fire glowed in his dark eyes—'that tenderness is no part of my character. Only fools tempt my anger. My hand is swift as thought, irresistible as fate.'

'Your feelings towards me, baron, will only make me more careful not to offend you. But will you kindly explain the cause of the interest you take in me?'

‘My dear Lewis, you are the only being I love in the world ; the only tie that binds me to mankind. One word will explain the tenderness I feel for you. I was the disciple, then the intimate friend, aye, the brother in arms of Sir Henry Morgan, your uncle ; and your father was not unknown to me.’

‘You have known my father !’ cried Morgan eagerly. ‘Oh, pray speak ; may I hope to see him again ?’

‘He died assassinated in these my arms,’ said Legaff, with deep feeling ; ‘his last words were, “ I leave my dear son Lewis to your care ; be his father ! ” ’

A pause ensued. Taking the weather-beaten hand of Legaff in his, Sir Lewis put it to his lips. Then giving vent to his emotion, he threw himself into the buccaneer’s arms.

‘Oh, sir,’ said the young man, ‘you weep too.’

‘Aye,’ answered Legaff—over whose sun-burnt cheeks tears were fast falling, which he attempted not to hide—‘your father, my brave Lewis, was a noble fellow, and he loved me as I shall never be loved again. In Sir Henry’s affection was something paternal, as he was older than I ; but your father and I were brothers.’

‘I will do my best to replace him,’ said Sir Lewis.

‘Yes, you are brave, Lewis, and will be grateful for my devotion ; and willingly would I sacrifice my life for you, but never can you be to me what your father was. And what cuts me to heart is, that during the fifteen years since your father’s death never has my hand been able to reach his murderer. Your father is still unavenged. Now do you understand why I need you ?’

‘Yes,’ cried Morgan, ‘and I swear that wherever I may be I will abandon love, fortune, everything when I can help you to avenge my sire.’

‘I take you at your word, young man,’ said Legaff solemnly.

A long silence followed, and it was only as the carriage crossed the bridge over Tyburn brook that Legaff said,—

‘My dear Lewis, without being indiscreet, may I ask you what brought you to Kensington to-day ?’

‘I went to watch a young lady pass whom I love deeply,’ answered Morgan, blushing, yet still pleased to have met some one with whom he could speak of his love.

‘Nativa de Sandoval, do you mean ?’

‘The same,’ answered the Cornishman, with wonderment ; ‘but allow me to ask how you could guess her name ?’

‘I cannot satisfy your curiosity ; I know all that is going on ; I ask questions, but I never answer any. Still, if the news interests you, I can tell you that I have known Nativa some two years.’

‘Two years !’

‘Yes, about that time. She is very pretty and loving. The first time I heard of her was when she had fallen deeply in love with a buccaneer on Tortoise Island. A pretty fellow enough, as brave as he was handsome : the young lady showed taste.'

'I know the story,' answered Morgan, turning pale, 'Nativa told me.'

'Oh, then, the young lady has keener wit than I gave her credit for. And did she also tell you, my dear sir, that the remembrance of this man was still so dear to her that only six months ago she wrote to offer him her hand ?'

'A vile calumny !' cried Morgan.

'Well, that is a gratuitous insult !' said Legaff, laughing, 'but who could expect reason from a lover ? After all, Nativa having been so frank with you, and never having mentioned this letter, perhaps it never existed.

'I repeat, baron, it is an infamous scandal.'

'In faith, I should incline to your opinion if one thing did not stagger me. I have seen the letter in the hands of the man to whom it was addressed. But, who knows, it might be only a forgery of his ? Still, if you would trust to my experience you would break with Nativa. There is something in the young lady's expression which does not suit her age, and gives me a bad opinion of her. Well, I see by your looks that you are obstinate on this point ; so let us drop the subject.'

'But tell me,' said Morgan, 'how it happens that if my father has been dead fifteen years you never acquainted me with the news before ?

'My dear Lewis, when my poor partner* died, you were only a child. What lasting impression could the news have made on your mind ? No, I preferred waiting until, arrived at manhood, you could share my thoughts of vengeance. Perhaps you consider it unkind of me to have left you so long in obscurity, almost in poverty. In this also I had my end in view. I feared that riches and luxury might make you effeminate and unfit you for taking and carrying out a noble resolution.

'I was satisfied that you should be only kept out of want, and it was by my orders that Compton paid you your modest allowance. Let not your pride suffer at being so far under obligation to me. One hour's boldness, if you will follow my advice, will repay far more than you owe me. One thing more I have to beg you in the name of your father, never ask me any questions ; I am so used to act alone that any intervention would only do harm.'

'Still I must entreat you, baron, to tell me by what means you hope to find out my father's murderer.'

'I know him already, Lewis.'

'And he still lives !' cried the knight bitterly ; 'you have not loved my father really.'

'If this murderer still lives it is because his punishment

* The buccaneers paired off with life-sworn *companions* or partners.

would not have equalled his crime.   It is not his death only that
I want ; death is nothing.   I must *avenge* your father !   But
now I repeat, you must ask me no more questions.   In everything
else dispose of me ; I have credit, money, audacity, all at your
service !   Do you desire anything?'

'Nothing, thank you.'

'What ! not to be invited to the concert next Monday at the
palace ?   Come, my dear boy, you do not treat me with frankness.   Well then, adieu, till Monday,' said Legaff, embracing our
hero as the carriage stopped at the White Horse.   'Be ready, I will
call for you at nine ; that is agreed?'

'Yes, on Monday,' answered Morgan, blushing.

CHAPTER XIX.

ANOTHER EVENING OUT.

OUR hero had received a note from Nativa, telling him of her
visit with her father to Kensington, and on this would depend
the fulfilment or present abandoment of the plan she had spoken
of to the Englishman.

Three days later—that is, on the following Monday—Morgan
rose at four, was quite dressed by six, after having taken infinitely
more pains than usual with his appearance, and was already impatient for Legaff's arrival.

Allan eyed his master's preparations with surprise and also
with sorrow.   Since his marvellous adventures Allan had become very thoughtful.   His conscience accused him of his conduct to the clothier ; he felt he was not blameless.

'Master,' he observed sheepishly, and with an effort, 'for
several days I have wanted to tell you something and I dare not.'

'You are wrong, my good fellow,' answered Morgan ; 'in whom
can you place your confidence if not in me ?'

'But what I want to tell you, sir, sticks in my throat ; I fear
to make you uncomfortable.'

'Speak up, man, don't fear.'

'Well, sir,' faltered Allan looking down, 'since you have become so rich you might have returned my twenty crowns that
I lent you.'

'You are right,' said Morgan, slightly embarrassed.

'Pray don't be angry, sir,' eagerly said Allan ; 'I assure you
that if I had not wanted to repay the money I would not have
spoken of it for—a whole week.'

At this moment Legaff entered the room.   The buccaneer wore
a plain but rich dress, every button of his coat was a diamond,
and a splendid row of pearls ornamented his sword handle

'I knew I should find you ready,' he said, embracing his *protégé,* 'yet it is scarcely eight.'

'Shall we go at once?' asked Morgan.

Legaff took the speaker's arm and was leaving the room when Allan rushed after them, crying out,—

'But, master, my twenty crowns.'

'You can take them out of my box; here is the key,' said his master. 'Don't be long away from the inn, and when you go out be careful to double-lock the door.'

'And above all, friend,' remarked Legaff, laughing, ' don't bring your sweetheart here.'

At this frivolous command Allan's eyes glistened with anger, and looking indignantly at the buccaneer, he rejoined,—

'That is not likely, sir. But is it indeed you, friend Matthewson, rigged out so fine? What pretty glass buttons you wear! I dare say, too, they cost a pretty penny. Horsedealing must be a paying trade here. But every one makes a fortune except myself.'

'Come, baron,' cried Morgan impatiently, and the two departed, leaving Allan in bewilderment.

'Well, one must be strong-headed not to lose one's senses in this city. Now there is master, at one time so plain in his dress and so proud, now, forsooth, he titivates himself out like a tragedy queen, and makes a friend of 'a horse-coper. And it seems, too, that Matthewson has become a baron. Where will it all end? I wonder what the folk at Penmark would say if I told them such tales!'

Allan took out the twenty crowns, and having carefully locked the box and room, wended his way to Dowlass's shop.

'What shall I say to him?' he argued with himself, 'for I see now it was a theft on my part. Still, could I let my master break his heart? But what if Dowlass should be angry and have me taken up? Bah! I have my staff, and can defend myself. But it will be best to explain the matter quietly to him.'

With this doughty resolution, Allan entered, where his arrival caused such consternation to his victim that the draper sat with his mouth and eyes wide open, without saying a word. Allan felt sure that as soon as the man recovered his speech he would call for help, so with a desperate effort he approached the counter, threw the money upon it, calling out, 'Here are the twenty crowns I owe you!' and ran off at full speed.

'Whew!' he cried, when he stopped to take breath, 'any one would think I was bewitched! Every time I go into the street I have to run like a hunted stag. Never mind, though: I am heartily glad that is done. I dare say I might have explained myself clearer to Dowlass, but what matters a few words more or less?'

When Sir Lewis Morgan arrived at Kensington Palace, the first carriage that passed them was one containing the Earl of Monterey and his daughter, and by her side the infamous Dean of St. Maurice's. The young noble could not repress a cry of rage at the sight. That vile wretch had then so far succeeded in his detestable scheme as to. have insinuated himself into the acquaintance of Nativa's father, and, thanks to his perfidy, now occupied a seat which Morgan would have paid for by any sacrifices and dangers.

'My dear Lewis,' said Legaff, 'don't ruffle yourself! You will throw your attire awry, and remember that women care more for an elegant costume than a tender heart! A crumpled feather, an ill-chosen sword-knot, and a rumpled ribbon are unpardonable crimes in their eyes. And I do not want you to cut a sorry figure before little Nativa. Break her heart, if you please, but respect your ruffles! Women don't mind being hurt, but they despise negligently-apparelled men.'

'But, baron, do you understand how that ignoble hypocrite can have become intimate with the Conde de Monterey?'

'Perfectly! that man knows his business. Come, courage, lad; what, are you going to strike your flag to Spanish colours? I won't let you show yourself ridiculous before the Creole!'

'Ah, dear friend, if you knew how much I love her!'

'Oh, I know all that, well enough!' answered Legaff, smiling.

Although he assumed a gay indifference, a closer observer than Morgan might have perceived that his sunburnt cheek was pale, and his lips quivered with emotion.

Two hours later Legaff and his *protégé* were walking arm-in-arm in the palace park. The gardens were filled with nobles and gentlemen of all classes when they entered. About two the king came forth, coughing hollowly.

He gave his arm to the queen; on his left was the Duke of Portland and Lord Godolphin, and the Keeper of the Seals followed. Morgan, with mournful curiosity, saw the king pass who had signed the death-warrant of his father, and thus obliged him to fly from England. In other respects, the young man felt neither surprise, admiration, or embarrassment. The king was exactly the asthmatic anatomy that he expected.

'Dear chevalier, I am delighted to see you,' exclaimed a courtier magnificently dressed.

'Lord Rothesey!' exclaimed the Cornishman.

'The same, but I little expected to meet you here! you have not, it seems, followed my advice.'

'What advice?'

'To beware of the reptile! the dean is here.'

'Oh, is he?' said Morgan between his teeth; 'where, if you please?'

'I just passed him in company of one of the most charming creatures I have ever seen.'

'Lucky being!' said Morgan, 'I really think, if I saw him, I could ask his pardon.'

'You had better keep out of his way; but if you stay here, what you propose in joke would not be unwise in earnest. You see, chevalier, I am an older courtier than you. It is my notion that you wish to see him to punish him; and, frankly, if you won't fly, I think it is your best course. They say vipers don't bite lions! be a lion then, for I warrant you Jannekin is a most venomous viper.'

'Still, my dear fellow,' said Morgan with impatience, 'you have not yet told me where I shall find this scoundrel.'

'Come with me and I will show you; only, when I have put you in the way you must permit me to retire. If I am mixed up in the matter I shall get in Wharton's black books, and that would be troublesome. Your arm, and we will walk towards the enemy.'

'I will leave you for the present; you will find me by-and-by at the twin oaks,' said Legaff, who had listened to the young men's conversation without comment.

Rothesey soon stopped, and hiding behind a tree said, 'Do you see that man with his back towards us?' pointing to a person a hundred feet in advance; 'that is the dean. I wish you success.'

As he was returning, a youngish man of elegant figure and most prepossessing appearance stopped him, crying, 'Odslife! is that you, marquis? I have no time to stop and talk, for Jannekin is waiting for me in company with such a divinity.'

'I wish you success, my lord,' said the other coldly, but with deference. 'In truth,' he muttered to himself as he went on, 'that poor Cornishman makes me unhappy. A noble heart like his knows how to love; and who doubts,' he added with a sigh, 'whether true love does not yield the happiness that I have never felt?'

When Morgan approached the place where Nativa and the dean stood, he felt that not to play an absurdly jealous part before Nativa he must moderate his anger and calm his feelings. He therefore walked slowly forward, assuming as indifferent an air as he could.

Scarcely had he made this resolve when he saw the Churchman approach Nativa and whisper in her ear.

Forgetting his resolution, he rushed forward with the impetuosity of a tiger. Probably his face reflected the rage and grief that gnawed his heart, for Nativa uttered an exclamation of affright, and the dean's face turned deadly pale.

'Lady, do you know to whom you are talking ?' cried Morgan, pointing to the jackal with unfeigned contempt.

'Yes, with the reverend Dean of St. Maurice's, for whom my father has great esteem,' answered Nativa ; 'and, regarding your manner of questioning me, allow me to observe, Sir Lewis Morgan——'

'It little matters—forms and ceremonies, when your honour is concerned !' retorted Morgan violently.

'My honour, chevalier——'

'Yes, Nativa, I repeat, your honour ! You do not know that one word exchanged with so vile a man is dishonour to any modest woman.'

'Chevalier,' cried Nativa proudly, 'do you intend to insult a gentleman of the Church and a lady of rank ?'

'I wish to save you.'

'Master Orlando !' sneered Jannekin, 'I will not deny that had I not the highest trust in this lady's honour your violent conduct would lead me to suppose——'

'Silence, sir !' cried the knight with such energy that, in spite of his rage, the dean was forced to be hushed.

Morgan turned to Nativa, and went on :

'I intreat your pardon beforehand for what I am going to say, for rather would I shed my blood than sully your ears—so great is the respect I bear you—with such words, but my duty must be done.'

'If these extravagancies are your only means of proving your respect, I decline to listen to one word you have to say.'

But Sir Lewis seized her arm to detain her, and said with the energy of conviction :

'Nativa, you shall hear me ! Hate me for my violence if you will, but I will hazard everything to save your fair fame. That trembling dog is not what is called a man of gallantry. Were he so, there would be little danger for *you*. But he is a panderer, who provides his master's depraved appetite for money. There is not a woman of ill-fame unacquainted with him ; there is not an honest mother who would not screen her daughter from his sight ! My heart bleeds to tell you of such vileness, but my duty urges me on : believe me, it would be better for a lady to proclaim in the court that she has a favoured lover than to be seen talking with that man. In the first case, love might be her excuse ; in the second, she would be considered a courtesan. Stand back, wretch !'

'Well, young spark,' said the dean, pretending to turn this off with a laugh, 'if your manners are not in good taste, at all events they are energetic.'

'Nativa,' cried Morgan, 'I entreat you leave us ! My indignation gets beyond my control, and I could never forgive myself if I chastised such a hound in your presence.'

'You have observed then,' said Jannekin, 'that men of my profession do not carry swords?'

'What! use my sword on you?' cried Morgan, with ineffable contempt. 'You too well know for what gentlemen carry canes!'

'In good faith, dean, you are not in luck,' cried the young gentleman who had met Rothesey. 'This is the second rebuff you have had in three days. All the canes in London seem at war with you. I arrive in time.'

'Very true, my lord, I was near being carried off by a west country tornado.'

'If you deign to accept my arm,' observed the new-comer to Nativa, with a graceful, but rather familiar bow, 'I will lead you away from this scene of carnage.' Then turning to Morgan, he added, 'As to you, sirrah, be off!'

'Sir,' cried the latter, turning pale, 'your dress is that of a gentleman, your behaviour that of a bully! Pray, as which am I to treat you?'

'As Thomas Lord Wharton,' answered the other.

'Sir,' answered Morgan, 'by dismasking a villain I have not invited such an insult from a man of rank.'

The other shrugged his shoulders and again offered Nativa his arm, but she drew back.

'My lord,' cried the chevalier, 'you have insulted me unjustly, and you force me to remind you that I also am a gentleman.'

'What do you mean, sir?' cried the courtier angrily. 'Do you want to fight me?'

'And why not?' answered Morgan, with provoking firmness.

'You must be very daring, or very ignorant, to dream of such a thing.'

'Then make me the reparation I demand.'

'Oh, this is going a little too far! I don't know what should prevent my caning such insolence.'

'By heavens, then, you shall fight now!' cried Morgan in a fury. 'I am afraid I remember you now; and your name is often coupled with this, your trainer—and I am forced to see all the truth in the old saw: "Like master, like man!" Lord Wharton, since it comes to caning or fencing, shall I beat you before your jackal or after him?'

Wharton was an 'universal rogue,' and even could defend his profligate acts with steel; he drew his sword to the joy of the Cornishman, who had already unsheathed his, and there, in the royal precincts, their weapons clashed.

Jannekin wished to part the combatants, but before he could do so a man rushed forward between them, and seizing Morgan's sword, cried out 'Stop!' This was no other than Baron Legaff.

'Away, sir!' cried Wharton, in a white fume,

'I am sorry I cannot obey you,' answered Legaff firmly; 'I cannot allow a crime to be committed.

'A crime!' echoed Lord Wharton.

'Ay, my lord, a crime! You know what your life has been off the stage of politics—I follow you not there. But in an age when the highest in camp and church, the pseudo-friends of the king, are pensioners of his dethroned rival, you are conspicuous for your fidelity! Mothers may curse you, injured husbands seek your life, but the men of your party, through years upon years, have trusted you with much that is dearer than life. Such a politician is rare! and you have but to live to redeem your past career! an aged profligate is an anomaly. I believe better of you, and you must not fall in a private quarrel! Live for England, Lord Wharton! Lewis, put up your sword.'

The courtier smiled with some perplexity, and studied the interposer with the eye of one who could weigh and measure men. Then he observed drily,—

'This offence to etiquette shall pass. The rule does not affect madmen!'

CHAPTER XX.

THE DOUBLE ARREST.

OF all the courtiers whom curiosity, ambition, duty or pleasure had brought to the concert Sir Lewis Morgan was by far the happiest. He loved Nativa with all the fervour of an earnest, simple nature, and she had now united herself to him by an avowal which to him seemed an indissoluble bond sacred as an oath.

He held Nativa on his arm in the sweet intoxication of first knowing himself loved : his heart expanded in bliss ; he told her his past sufferings, his future prospects, and ever and anon reverted with fresh delight to his delicious present, the lovely Spanish girl answering with gentle words and still more bewitching glances.

When her cavalier had conducted her to her father, he was beside himself with joy. One thought alone absorbed him entirely—the knowledge that he was loved. The world for him at this moment contained only Nativa.

Legaff, who had watched at a distance his interview with Nativa, was the first to draw him out of his ecstacy.

'My dear Lewis,' he said, as soon as he had parted from the young lady, 'I hope you do not now repent coming. How delighted you look! If your constancy only equals your fervour, your love will go with you to the grave!'

'Say to heaven, dear Legaff,' answered Morgan.

'Oh, your love is to be eternal, is it? Well, happily, at your age, eternal love never lasts more than three months. That is pretty well!'

'Oh, baron, how can you speak so?'

'Oh, I speak from experience. I never was in love longer than a fortnight ; so you see it is pure complacency on my part to allow you three months. Now let us speak reasonably, if it is possible. What are your projects?'

'Projects, baron ? Why, I have none. I love Nativa, and am beloved in return : a blissful future is before me.'

'My dear Lewis, folks who neglect the present to build on the future never do well. If Nativa loves you, she will not refuse to fly with you. If she is only tampering with your affections, throw her off with disdain.'

These words, said in the genial way that Legaff could assume so well, struck Morgan with pain.

'Baron,' answered he gravely, 'your friendship to my father makes you sacred in my eyes, and I would wish to love and obey you. But my love for Nativa is holy. Be generous, and forbear to jest.'

'Well, dear Lewis, I agree never to mention this subject again, as it distresses you, if you will allow me, once for all, to give my opinion upon it.'

'On that condition I will listen.'

'My dear boy,' continued the buccaneer affectionately, 'I cannot without deep sorrow see you pursue so dangerous a path. If a young fellow at the beginning of life meets with a woman, she plays with his affections, and all his after-life is darkened and embittered. Well, on my soul and conscience, I believe Nativa does not love you. Oh, you may smile incredulously. My experience is less blind than your love. Nativa, I vow, is very captivating. Nowhere could you meet with more sovereign beauty, more perfect grace, more enchanting smiles. I am neither a fool nor blind, Lewis ; I can read her well. In spite of all these perfections, which I frankly allow her to possess in so high a degree, this Creole has a cruel heart, a force of will to overcome all obstacles, and extraordinary perseverance in carrying out her plans. Believe me, boy, if you give yourself up to be her willing slave, she will use you as an instrument in her hands, as a lever to remove obstacles in her path, or as a dagger with which to free herself from an enemy. But she will never love you, Lewis.'

'I will keep my word, and listen to you,' was Morgan's only answer.

'A woman, believe me, Lewis, never loves a man who is her dupe ; she feels too much his superior, and despises him. If you cannot shake off her influence and the passion that now absorbs you, I foresee dreadful consequences. Perhaps, Lewis, I ought not thus to speak to you ; but what I never experienced for myself I feel for you : I dread what may happen to you. Lewis, in your father's name, the only being whom I ever truly loved, I conjure you to renounce this Spanish girl ! Between you there is an insurmountable obstacle which separates you for ever. Pride sparkles in your eyes ; you trust in your youth and bravery ! Alas, Lewis, it is not the want of fortune that places an abyss between you, for if a million sterling could make you happy, you should have it ; but no———.

'Come, Lewis,' continued the so-called baron, after a pause, 'perhaps I did wrong to speak in your father's name ; yet for his sake let me conjure you.'

'Baron Legaff,' answered the young knight coldly, 'you cannot doubt the reverence I feel for my father. In his name I put up my sword. Do not abuse so sacred a remembrance. My father, were he alive, would approve my sentiments and bless my choice.'

'Your father bless this choice ? Oh, unhappy boy, if you knew all,' cried Legaff, in a voice of thunder, little minding who might hear him.

But after a short time he recovered his composure, and added,—

'Well, it is no use combatting destiny ; what is written must come to pass ; and who knows whether this love that I dread so much may not aid my plans, and work out the designs of Heaven ? Its ways are inscrutable, and crime sooner or later is punished.'

At a few paces behind Legaff and Morgan were two men who appeared to follow them ; they were Lord Menzil and the Rev. Mr. Jannekin. They had met half an hour before, and had been conversing ever since.

'That young springald, my lord, is an unchained tiger ; dangerous to leave at large,' said the dean. 'He was nearly devouring me awhile since.'

'What nonsense are you talking, man ?'

'A positive fact, and when Lord Wharton interfered he drew his sword and wanted to fight him.'

'In the palace grounds, swords bared ? And they were not arrested on the spot ?'

'Oh, my lord is so good-natured ! Besides, the audacity and ferocity of the tiger had a charm for him ; you know he likes anything that borders on the wonderful, being so palled with common-places.'

'But you are not your lord.'

'No,' answered the dean, with a sinister smile, ' I am another guess sort of man.'

'And therefore mean mischief. What do you propose to do ?'

'Have the young swaggerer arrested.'

But a gentleman cannot be arrested offhandedly, sir.'

'Why not, pray, when I have a blank warrant that will do for him in my pocket.'

'How long have you had it ?'

'Since yesterday.   The tiger offended me two days ago ; but what is your lordship laughing at ?'

'Oh, this is too good ! ' laughed Lord Menzil.

Jannekin looked uneasy, and already regretted his confidence.

'Are you interested in the young fellow, then ?'

'I?   No, indeed, I don't know him from Adam ; but what tickled my fancy was that while you were after the young man I was after the old one.   I also have a warrant in my pocket !'

'Oh, that is delightful ! we shall bag our game together.'

'With pleasure, dean ; and as your detestable reputation makes you no favourite with the king, I shall have the satisfaction of making him angry by walking with you.'

'Ah,' cried Jannekin, pretending not to have heard the last words, ' our game is nearly hunted down ; once beyond the gates we can have them arrested, there are plenty of Bow Street officers about.   Let us hasten on.'

In fear of losing their prey, the two accomplices were now almost on Legaff's and Morgan's heels, when they saw Mr. Secretary Barstairs address Legaff in a friendly manner, and draw him into conversation.

'Oh, the deuce ! ' exclaimed the dean, 'it seems your man with the diamond buttons is in favour at Court.   See how animated and agreeable Barstairs is with him !   I never saw the bear in office so amiable.   I don't understand how you can have got your blank warrant.'

'One thing is evident,' answered the other, ' it is lucky that I have the letter safe in my pocket, or there would be little chance of my getting one now.   That man, dean, is Satan himself, and I almost regret the useless warring with the devil.   I should not wonder if he hears every word we say.   Come, dean, I think we had better tear up our papers.   My Lucifer, if you have his imp arrested, will soon get him out again.'

Jannekin reflected a few moments ere he said,—

'My lord, is it of much moment to you that your man should disappear ?'

'If it were not so, do you think I should have troubled ?'

'Well, if you will help me, I promise that you shall never hear of him again.'

'I know that your reverence is ingenious in resources.   What must I do ?'

'Only find me a retired non-commissioned officer ; some shameless beggar and great gambler, almost dinnerless ; but one who has not had too many conflicts with the police.'

‘Nothing easier, dean ; you have drawn the portrait of half of my clients.   Only, instead of a non-commissioned officer, I will give you a captain.’

‘All the better.’

‘And you can assure me that my friend with the diamond buttons shall not come out of prison.   Think for a moment how angry he will be.’

‘My prophecies are usually correct,’ answered the dean, with a malignant look, ‘and they tell me now that we look for the last time on your enemy and mine.   Only, as it is possible that Barstairs may wish to see your Satan to-morrow to finish accounts with him, we will only have him and his companion arrested the day after.   I will give orders that they are well watched, so that no lawyers see them.   And my lord will find me to-day the captain he spoke of, and send him to me to-night ?   I kiss your lordship’s hand !’

The Dean of St Maurice’s was right in putting off Legaff’s arrest, for the last words the secretary said to him, were, ‘Well, baron, it is agreed then that you shall come to me at seven in the morning, without fail ?’

Deep as Morgan was in his love-dreams, he could not help observing the extraordinary impression that the naval official’s conversation with the buccaneer had on the courtiers around them.

‘Who is that excessively ugly man whom every one treats with such respect, and with whom you have been talking ?’

‘Barstairs—at the head of the Navy Commissioners.’

‘What, talking to you so familiarly !’

‘Why not ?   His superior, Lord Russell, is a sailor—so am I, and he would have treated me as a mate.   Barstairs needs me, I could do perfectly well without him ; so you see the con-descension is on my side.’

‘But, baron, what an enigma you are !   When I think of you as the horsedealer Matthewson in my poor place at Pen-mark, you seem enveloped in mystery.’

‘Well, my dear boy, I have confidence in you ; but a secret known to three persons is soon made public.   However, you shall know all soon.’

‘Then some one else knows your secret ?’

‘Yes, Compton, the banker, who owes his fortune to me.   I can count on his fidelity.’

The remainder of the day passed very pleasantly to both ; not that they took much interest in the concert, but they carried in their own hearts the source of their happiness.   Morgan was thinking of Nativa’s soft confession, Legaff of his victory over the Red Tape ; for the secretary had promised the next morning to give him the commission for Bloxam.   Dazzled with the loan

which Legaff offered, William, who loved money, had agreed to
the attack on Carthagena, though there was no war proclaimed
against Spain. The next morning the buccaneer left the minister's presence with his three demands satisfied.

As soon as Morgan the Second had his treaty given him,
he sent a copy of it by special messenger to Compton.

' Well, baron,' asked Morgan, who had scarcely risen when
Legaff returned from his interview, ' what success have you
had with the Government to-day ?'

' I obtained what I wanted ; but I am not satisfied.'

' Wherefore ?'

' Because the victory was too easy. But what do you say ?'

As Nativa remained with the Court, they stayed for another
day at Kensington.

During the time Legaff showed himself to Morgan under
another point of view—that is, in his great skill and knowledge
in nautical affairs. He questioned the young man about his
voyages to Ireland, and seemed pleased with Morgan's predilec-
tion for a seafaring life, common enough in Cornwall.

' My dear Lewis,' he said, ' on board of a cruiser you will
the most readily find the fame and fortune that you dream of.
Do your best then to become acquainted with maritime matters.
I hope soon to see you fit to command a vessel, and I shall put
you to the proof before long.'

In vain Morgan questioned his friend on his past life and
his future prospects. Legaff was as silent as the grave.

On the following day the friends returned together to town.

' Will you let me go to your room, Lewis ?' said Legaff ; ' I
want to write a letter.'

On reaching his humble quarters, the knight knocked repeatedly without gaining admittance.

At last he heard the click of a firearm, and Allan's voice cried
out,—

' Who is there ? what do you want ?'

' It is I, Allan ; open the door,' cried his master.

A key was twice turned in the lock, and the door opened
cautiously.

' Oh, master, is it indeed you ?' said Allan ; ' I was afraid some
one had imitated your voice ; these cockneys are so deceitful.'

He then retired behind the door and put down a musket with
which he had armed himself.

' Egad,' exclaimed Legaff. ' this fellow is worth his weight in
gold.'

' What is the matter, Allan ?' asked his master; ' you look quite
pale and upset.'

' I am hungry,' replied the man laconically.

' Hungry ?'

‘Likely enough, when I have tasted no food for two days.’

‘Not eaten for two days? have you been ill?’

‘Had I any money to buy food with?’

‘What the deuce do you mean when I gave you the key of my box?’

‘And did you tell me to take out any money except the twenty crowns.　Ah, if you had only returned the five crowns I lent you!’

‘Poor fool,’ sighed Morgan, ‘your honesty shall be rewarded; here are thirty crowns instead of the five you lent me.’

‘Stop, master, stop,’ cried Allan, locking the door.　‘No one must know you have money here.’

As he spoke a sharp altercation was heard on the staircase, followed by a loud knocking at the door.

‘Open, in the king’s name,’ was the cry there without.

Legaff and Morgan looked at each other; one thought of Menzil, the other of the Dean of St. Maurice’s.

‘Chevalier,’ said Legaff, without showing the least emotion, ‘desire Allan to hide himself behind your bed, and remain as motionless as if he were dead.’

‘You hear, Allan? make haste,’ said the Cornishman.

Allan hastened to do as he was bid.

More violent knocking followed, which seemed as if it would beat in the door.

The buccaneer opened it.

‘Welcome,’ he said, ‘if you come in the king’s name; what are the royal commands?’

‘That you should deliver up your sword and follow me,’ said the officer who appeared.

‘At least you must show me the order on which you act,’ replied Legaff coolly, ‘or else I shall be under the necessity of blowing out your brains unless the watch seize you between-whiles.’

The officer, without noticing this threat, presented two orders, one for the arrest of Legaff, the other for Morgan’s.

‘Your papers are quite correct, sir,’ said the buccaneer; ‘here is my sword, a Court weapon, that I bought the day before yesterday.　Had it been the one I have so often drawn, I should have broken it rather than given it up.　Here also are a pair of pistols, and now will you allow me to take a few clothes?’

‘As you like, sir,’ answered the officer, ‘I have no instructions to interfere,’ and Legaff and Morgan passed into the bedroom. The officer followed them. ‘You need be under no alarm, sir,’ he said to the latter; ‘this room, as you see, has no other door, and only one barred window looking on to the yard where I see your men are stationed.’

The buccaneer turned to Morgan, and said in Cornish,—

'You and Allan pay particular attention to what I say.'

Legaff began looking over some clothes ; then, turning to the officer, he said :—

'Sir, your appearance denotes you a gentleman ; and between gentlemen some courtesy may be expected. Will it infringe on your duty if I request you to inform me what your instructions are in regard to this gentleman and myself?'

'Not to let you hold communication with any one by writing or word of mouth, and to conduct you at once to your destination.'

'I am happy we shall have the favour of your company so far ; but will you allow me one more question?'

'I am at your orders,' said the officer, delighted with the courteous politeness of his prisoner, who had been represented to him as a violent and dangerous character.

'You were desired to take my sword, but that need not include the row of pearls round the handle ; allow me to offer them to you in gratitude for your civility.'

'Sir,' answered the officer, 'these pearls appear to me of great value.'

'Why,' said Legaff, 'for a scurvy fellow who wanted to sell them they might be worth some eight hundred pounds. But to you, sir, they will be only a trifling keepsake for your courtesy. You won't affront me so much as to refuse them. Have we not made mutual concessions? I gave up my pistols, which you did not ask.'

The officer whom Jannekin had chosen was a resolute fellow, but possessed of little delicacy. His instructions said nothing about accepting or refusing a present, and eight hundred pounds sounded pleasantly to his ears.

'I think,' continued Legaff, 'that your instructions do not forbid you to inform the chevalier and me where we go.'

'But, baron,' objected the officer.

'Since it is agreed,' interrupted Legaff, 'that neither my friend nor I am to hold any communication with any one, and as we are willing to respect this order, surely you cannot object to satisfy us on this insignificant point.'

'That is only just,' said the officer, who was frightened lest his refusal might exasperate the baron and compromise his right to the pearls. 'Well, baron, I am ordered to conduct you to Dover Castle.'

'A thousand thanks! Now that we know where we are going we can arrange our toilet in consequence. You are aware that it makes a great difference if we are to be carried north or south.'

Legaff, then turning to Morgan, continued in the Cornish tongue,—

Allan, listen with all your ears, and don't lose a word of what I tell you! On you depends your master's safety. As soon as we are gone, take all the money in your master's box, dress yourself like a gentleman, and paying double for speed travel post night and day to Bristol. At Bristol ask for Mr. Compton, ship merchant, and tell him what has happened to Baron Legaff; and now, chevalier, tell your servant to obey me.'

Legaff, while speaking, had been examining and selecting different articles, Morgan imitating his example.

'Allan, by your attachment to me, obey implicitly these orders; don't stint the money! the more you spend the better I shall be pleased. Leave town to-night! farewell!'

Legaff and Morgan then declared themselves ready.

A close carriage awaited them in the yard; all three entered it, and it set off at a rapid pace, followed by a dozen mounted guardsmen, leaving the whole inn in a great state of consternation over the arrest of 'Jacobite emissaries who had come to fire St. Paul's, and blow up the palace, no less.'

No sooner had they left than Allan came out of his hiding-place.

The poor fellow, with tears in his eyes, took all the money out of the coffer; but, grieved as he was, a smile passed his lips as he counted out the thirty crowns his master had given him.

The evening before Legaff and Morgan were arrested 'Captain Chafferex' was sent by post to relieve the governor of Dover Castle for a fortnight. The captain has been known to us under the title of Viscount Charmarand. Of such rascalhood were composed the myrmidons of Lord Wharton, and his familiar, the dean.

CHAPTER XXI.

THE TRAP.

THE second day, at nightfall, Legaff and his companion reached Dover Castle.

No incident had occurred. Legaff showed the utmost politeness and amiability to the officer. Morgan, engrossed with his love, scarcely spoke a word. As for appeal to the civil authorities, not a whisper.

'Really, baron,' said the officer on taking leave, 'I cannot recover from my amazement and delight; you were represented to me as a desperado, and yet I have found you to be most agreeable and affable. Believe me, I shall always retain a pleasant remembrance of our journey, and shall be most pleased to hear of your deliverance.'

'When one has enemies of course one is calumniated. But, really, I don't know a greater lover of peace than myself. Anything for a quiet life, is my motto. The governor won't have much trouble with me.'

'Be satisfied, my dear baron, that I shall not fail to acquaint him with the excellent opinion I have formed of you. As for your companion, there is something in his eyes murderous enough—pardon me.'

'Oh, my friend, you are wrong for once! my mate, Sir Lewis, is in love. Therefore you can understand that a young gentleman about to marry the lady of his affections cannot be very gay when carried off from her arms. Of course he fancies himself supplanted by rivals.'

'Which sometimes happens, baron,' chuckled the officer.

'Always, my friend; a little hunchback on the spot would be better to any woman than an Adonis in gaol. All women are alike in that.'

'Poor chevalier!' said the officer; 'considering he is so unhappy, and likely to lose his lady love's heart, I will make a favourable report of him, too, to the governor.'

'Thanks, comrade,' answered Legaff, squeezing the officer's hand. 'Sir Lewis is worthy all your kindness; he is really a fine fellow, and merits better than to be superseded by a hunchback.'

A few minutes later Legaff and Morgan were conducted into a large room tolerably furnished for a prison.

'Well, chevalier,' said Legaff, 'what do you think of our home?'

'I was thinking,' said Morgan, 'that as we only mounted thirty-four steps to reach it, that yonder barred window cannot be more than twenty feet from the ground.'

'Well done, Lewis!' cried Legaff, 'your answer shows as much shrewdness as hope. Only, you are wrong in one step; there are thirty-five, not thirty-four.'

'What, you counted also?'

'Eh, boy! would not an eagle confined in a cage seek to mount again in the free blue?'

'Well,' cried Morgan, catching his enthusiasm, 'I will aid you with all my might. May we soon be free!'

A gaoler soon made his appearance with several dishes carefully covered with napkins, and followed by another carrying choice wines.

'Gentlemen,' said the principal gaoler, 'if your dinner to-day does not please you, pray inform me. I have the new deputy governor's orders to treat you with every consideration.'

When the friends were again alone, Legaff observed,—

'Lewis, we must be on our guard against the new deputy's

politeness. If I am not mistaken, there lurks treachery beneath. New brooms sweep clean, and they shall not make a clean sweep of us so easily.'

A whole week passed and no change occurred in the position of the prisoners. During this age, for too slowly drag on the hours of captivity, Legaff's cheerfulness never forsook him, while Morgan, tortured by jealousy and burning with impatience, rose every morning full of a fresh plan for escape, which he had concocted during the night.

Legaff listened patiently to his schemes, and only said as soon as he had heard each new plan,—

'My lad, this idea is no better than yesterday's.'

One day the gaoler, having sent away his subordinates, observed to Legaff,—

'My lord, I hear that you are very rich, and extremely generous. If I could count on your discretion, I could give you a great pleasure.'

'What pleasure, friend?'

'I could give you a note that I received for you—from your mistress, perhaps.'

'Oh, you have received a note from her for me?' said Legaff carelessly; 'then you had better take it at once to the deputy. It may give you a lift.'

'Indeed,' answered the gaoler, 'I never expected such an answer from you; but it is a good notion. I'll take it to the governor.'

'Go, friend, and good luck to you.'

The gaoler, evidently annoyed, moved towards the door, but a sudden thought struck him, and he turned and said,—

'I cannot take it to the captain, for he will ask me why I kept the note so long, and I shall, perhaps, lose my place.'

'Oh, then you have had the note some time?'

'Only since yesterday.'

'And you delayed so long doing your duty, sirrah?'

'Well, my lord, I counted, I vow, on your generosity.'

'Then it was your good opinion of me that prevented your showing your zeal in the service. In that case you deserve some reward; here are ten pistoles for you.'

'And here, baron, is the note. Only I beg that when you have read it, you will tear it to pieces, or better still, burn it.'

'Unless, friend, I don't care to read the note at all. Take it unread, and burn it yourself.'

'Then I shall have to give back your ten pistoles?'

'Well, if you make it a matter of conscience, I will open the note.'

The buccaneer tore it open, smiled contemptuously, and tore it into atoms.

'The note does not seem to please you much, sir ? '

' My light-o'-love, who takes the trouble, too, to write in cypher, tells me that she loves me still, and wants more money, of course. Really such mystery is absurd about such a matter-o'-course. The next time, turnkey, that you are asked to take charge of such a letter for me, I hope you will decline doing so. What do I care about such stuff in my situation ?'

'Lewis,' cried Legaff, as soon as the man had retired, and he had heard several doors locked behind him, ' Allan is a first-rate fellow : he has warned Compton. A vessel is on the look-out for us. To work ! in a fortnight's time we must be free, or dead.'

Morgan gave a cry of joy, and exclaimed,—

'Ah, now I understand your calmness ! you were expecting?'

'Yes, dear Lewis ; and though each hour spent here seems to grow into my heart, I put a calm face on it, not to increase your sufferings. Now that we have news from outside, and a secure refuge in case of the worst, I will join heart and hand in your hopes and plans.'

' But why, dear Legaff, did you show such indifference about this said note ?'

' Because I doubt this turnkey ! The fellow treats us with obsequious courtesy that I know is not in his nature, and he never dares look us honestly in the face. He evidently had some reason for wishing me to read the note, but what his motive is I have yet to learn.'

' A very simple one, perhaps,' answered Morgan,—' that of gaining money.'

' I think not. Ten pistoles is a small sum to risk his berth for. There is some mystery here which I cannot penetrate. I will try again the next time I see him, and you take care to watch him too.'

The captives then proceeded to a minute examination of their prison. It offered little to their inspection : four stone walls and a narrow window, guarded by stout iron bars, raised nineteen feet above the floor. At this moment, though at an unusual hour, the gaoler appeared.

'My lord,' he said to the elder, ' people fancy that gaolers have no hearts, but I could not rest till I told you what comfort your ten pistoles have been to my sick wife. She sends you her best thanks, and——'

' Your wife rates a small present too highly !'

'Ten pistoles is a very large sum to us, sir, with four children to feed.'

' Why did you not tell me of your poverty ? I would have helped you.'

'Oh, baron, poor as I am I have some pride. If the king

lets me starve in his service, so much the worse for him. I should not mind betraying him, though I could not receive charity?'

'The deuce, friend! what you tell me is rather serious.'

'I only say what I think, sir,' answered the man, embarrassed.

'Chevalier, this looks rather like an offer of freedom.'

'Well, sir, that is what I do mean,' answered the gaoler earnestly. 'Hunger brings wolves out of the woods, and makes an honest man deaf to his duty. And frankly, sir, I should like to prove my gratitude to you.'

Morgan's heart beat violently, and he was about to speak, when Legaff forestalled him by saying to the speaker,—

'We thank you, friend, for your kind intentions, but I frankly own that I am much less rich than is supposed, and that I should not be able to pay the sum you expect.'

'But I never fixed any sum, my lord.'

'That is true; but as our escape will make you lose your place, it is natural that you should need ample recompense; therefore, as I am not rich enough to indemnify you, I must refuse your offer.'

'Good gracious, sir,' answered the gaoler, in a vexed tone, 'there is no certainty that your escape will cost me my place. Prisoners escape every day. Now, what could you give?'

'I am ashamed to say, friend, that I could not dispose·of more than fifty pounds, and that at some sacrifice.'

'Fifty pounds is a goodly sum,' remarked the turnkey delightedly.

'Do you think so? Then you consent for fifty pounds to aid our escape?'

'My lord, I don't get more from the king in four years! Aye, I accept your terms! I thought we should understand each other at last, so I brought a file with me. You can set to work without delay.'

The baron examined the edge, and found it well-tempered.

'Now I will leave your lordship, for fear my absence should be remarked,' said the traitor. 'We can talk more to-morrow and make arrangements. At nightfall begin to file the bars, but work as silently as you can, for a sentinel keeps guard beneath your window.'

'What do you think of all this, Lewis?' asked Legaff, as soon as they were alone.

'I think as you do, sir; the gaoler is evidently tampering with us.'

'What had we better do?'

Cut the bars of our cage. We shall, at all events, get a little more light and air. Our time will not be lost.'

Morgan moved the table against the wall, mounted on it, and saying, 'Now, baron, you begin,' offered his back.

Legaff was up in a moment; his strength and agility were immense.

The next morning when the gaoler brought breakfast two iron bars were sawed through, so that a quarter of an hour's work would get them out. The sentinel had heard no sound, as he had not interfered.

'My good friend,' said the baron, 'you are such a faithful fellow, and so kind-hearted, that I don't like deceiving you. Yesterday, excited by hopes of gaining my liberty, I gave you a false account of my finances. My friend and I by clubbing our moneys together cannot make up more than twenty pounds.'

'Only twenty pounds!' said the gaoler.

'Therefore you perceive we must renounce our intention, rather than get you into trouble.'

'Oh, not so, gentlemen,' answered the man hastily. 'Your generosity moves me to tears; but I will not prove myself less generous than you. After all, twenty pounds will be a large sum to me.'

'Then you still consent to aid our escape, and for a score caroluses?'

'Here is my answer, sir,' said the gaoler, drawing a rope-ladder from his pocket.

'How lucky!' cried Legaff; 'what a fine thin, yet strong cord!'

'This ladder would bear ten men,' said the gaoler. 'No danger of its breaking; and it is three or four feet longer than the turret from the window to the ground. Did you work a little last night?'

'We sawed furiously at our bars last night,' answered Legaff, 'but as they are very thick, and we were afraid of exciting the attention of the sentinel, we have not finished. Perhaps we may do so to-night.'

'Courage, gentlemen! I must leave to avoid suspicion.'

'Well, Lewis,' said Legaff, 'this is an accommodating turnkey, who seems more anxious than ourselves for us to be free.'

'It is certainly very odd, baron; the man evidently plays a part.'

'And is laying a snare for us.'

'Why a snare?'

'That is what we must learn. We shall have to wait.'

'But, baron,' proceeded Morgan, 'one thing astonishes me greatly. Why has not Compton, instead of wasting time in equipping a vessel, applied at once to the king or authorities to set you at liberty? On such good terms as you are with powerful ministers, this proceeding would have soon opened for you the prison doors.'

'Compton has too much experience of men not to know that the great are almost always ungrateful. How am I sure that Barstairs himself is not the cause of my arrest? or even higher powers? The Dutchman himself is under obligation to me, and may think this a convenient way of paying off the debt. No, believe me, Lewis, we must trust to ourselves to effect our escape, since I have not chosen to make a case for the courts of justice.'

The next day the gaoler came earlier than usual.

'I was uneasy,' he said. 'Did the sentinel hear nothing? Have you sawn through the bars?'

'Yes, friend, the bars are sawn through.'

'When, then, shall you make the venture? this evening?'

'Never,' answered Legaff, quietly; 'this gentleman and I, having full confidence in the king's justice, have renounced all intention of escaping.'

'Impossible!' groaned the gaoler, in vexation which he could not hide. 'You well know, gentlemen, that a man may be kept years in prison in spite of his innocence. Don't talk to me of the king's justice! I am sure that cannot be your motive.'

'Well, friend, I will own another idea struck me.'

'Ah, you see I guessed right; and what idea, may I inquire?'

'One of your own suggestion. You recommended us twice to work as quietly as possible, not to alarm the sentry under the window. Now, this deters us, for sweet as is liberty, it may be too dearly bought by a bullet in the head; so my friend and I have decided, as long as the sentinel remains there, to forego our chance of escape.'

'If that is your only drawback, gentlemen, you may make yourselves easy on that score. I am too honest to expose you to such a danger. I will manage the day you fly to decoy the sentinel away.'

'That is well said, my good fellow; but as your new governor might insist on the sentinels remaining, and as prudence is the mother of security, if you could procure us two brace of pistols, gunpowder, and two daggers, we should not hesitate to try our fate.'

'I can steal them for you out of the armoury,' answered the gaoler, after a moment's thought, 'and will set about it at once.'

'Indeed,' observed Legaff, 'was there ever a gaoler so anxious to get rid of his lodgers? What zeal he shows! Certainly not one, but two traps must be laid for us. But what matters it? Once armed we can fight our way, can't we, Lewis?'

'We will do our best,' answered the young man.

Scarcely had the chevalier uttered these words than the gaoler came back.

'Here are your arms, gentlemen: two pairs of pistols, two daggers, the powder—all you asked me for. For to-morrow, eh?;

'For to-morrow,' answered Legaff joyfully.

As soon as the turnkey quitted them, Legaff and Morgan seized the weapons and examined them with care.

'Now let us review our resources ; the pistols are in first-rate order, and this dagger has a splendid edge.   We'll try its temper.'

Placing a crown piece on the table, Legaff cleft it in half in a moment.

'Truly our custodian is the most generous fellow living; for twenty pounds he gave us arms that are worth, at the lowest, fifty.   Oh, I forgot the powder !   That is as good as the rest. Well, dear Lewis, shall we do battle to-morrow ?   The bout will be rather rough, but I have passed through worse dangers, and I still live.'

' Now, do you see what trap was laid for us ?' asked Morgan.

'Oh, yes, clearly.   A king has nothing to do with such villainy.   That rascal, your dean, and my knave, Menzil, are at the bottom of it all.   They are afraid that William may learn of my captivity.   As to the trap laid for us, it is probably only an officer and a dozen sleepy soldiers that we shall have to frighten. Five minutes will finish them off.   Armed to the teeth as we shall be, we need not fear a troop of such fellows.'

CHAPTER XXII.

THE ESCAPE.

At six o'clock Legaff and Morgan sat over their dinner.   The weather had turned cloudy.

'Then, dear Lewis,' said the former at midnight, ' it is agreed we try to escape ?'

'Yes, all is ready ; the gaoler has brought us a good plan of the route, and the bars are removed.'

'My dear boy,' responded the mariner gravely, 'though I feel almost the conviction that we shall succeed, and I have full faith in my lucky star, yet should anything happen to me, and you have the good fortune to escape alone, it is right that you should know the name of the man who will leave you heir to his immense fortune.   Lewis, I am your father's brother, Randolph Morgan.   Sir Henry was thy father.'

'You my uncle, whom I thought dead long ago ?' cried Morgan, much moved.

'The same, my boy, and I love you dearly.   You are very much like your father, Lewis, and I loved him well.'

Tears fell from the buccaneer's eyes, but ashamed of this weakness, he dashed them off with his hand, and steadied his voice as he proceeded,—

'Now, Lewis, sit down by me and listen to what I say. You must keep my name a profound secret. To the world, to yourself even, I must be only Morgan's heir and successor, by his authority, not by my name and birthright.'

'Oh, uncle,' cried Morgan, with tears, 'why did you let me remain ignorant until now that I had any one to love me?'

'It was necessary, Lewis. A man becomes strong only from self-reliance. A nature like yours could rise above circumstances. I felt this. To be your father's avenger you needed a stout heart and a strong hand. Had I found you unworthy of this trust I would never have made myself known to you. I would have heaped wealth upon you, but my hand would never have pressed yours.'

'And my father died in your arms, uncle?'

'Yes, Lewis, your father died, murdered by a villain. Now listen to me. In 1675, when much blood was shed in the West, your father was so much compromised that he could expect no pardon. Nevertheless, it was only by earnest persuasion that I induced him to fly for his life. A vessel was leaving for the colonies; we took the passage on board. We were already close to the Antilles when a Spanish frigate took us prisoners. Your father and I were carried on to Cuba and sold as slaves.'

'Poor father,' sighed Sir Lewis.

'Then began for us a most wretched existence; however, the overseer, seeing something in our looks which told him we would not brook insults, spared us the outrages he heaped on the rest.

'We had groaned above a year in this bondage till your father and I resolved to escape, and had all but succeeded when a fearful event took place.

'The wife of our master, a woman as beautiful as she was infamous, had as a lover one of her husband's secretaries. Surprised one night in a secret interview, she contrived her lover's escape, and succeeded in laying the blame on your father. Our master, as proud as he was pitiless, knew well enough that his wife lied, but he affected to believe her, because it allowed him to save her honour.

'Your father was instantly made prisoner, and dragged before his master. In vain he tried to defend himself; he explained his conduct, and proved his innocence; but his master refused to listen. Then I threw myself at the proud Spaniard's feet— think of that, Lewis!—I entreated, I conjured, all in vain. His wife's honour could only be saved by throwing the guilt on some one. The noble Spaniard did not hesitate to sacrifice an innocent man to his pride. Your father was condemned to be flogged to death.'

'My father? oh, it is impossible!' groaned the young man.

'And the sentence was executed,' added Morgan, with fearful calmness.

'Oh, uncle, the assassin's name ? his name, I conjure you ! Now I know that I shall escape ! nothing shall keep me here. I will avenge my father. But the name, uncle, tell me that !'

'Lewis,' answered Randolph Morgan firmly, 'it is not yet time to tell you that ; before we leave here I will give you a letter, which, if I die, you may open ; if not, you must return it to me unopened.'

The evening passed rapidly ; the young man asked many questions about his father and his famous relation, which his uncle answered readily.

As the clock struck twelve, old Morgan said,—

'Now ! stand ready !'

The buccaneer placed two chairs, one upon the top of the other, upon the table, then, mounting with the rope ladder, fastened it securely to the window bars.

'Now, Lewis, I will pass first.'

'No, no, uncle ! if a trap be laid for us, let me be the first victim ! You are powerful, I am nothing ! My father's vengeance will be safer in your hands than mine.'

'Lewis,' answered the adventurer, 'once for all, you are the only one in the world that I love still ! If you resist me I shall think you without pity. You must take your friend with all his faults. Forgive my roughness, but the habit of command is become a second nature ; everything must give way to my will. Come, Lewis,' continued the freebooter gently, 'between you and me insult is impossible, and self-love should not exist. Let me pass, I say ; if I die you can avenge me.'

Legaff felt that the pistols fastened in his belt were safe, wrung his nephew's hand, and putting the dagger in his mouth, seized the cord with both hands, and flung himself out of the window. Morgan hastened after him.

At the same moment a loud clap of thunder reverberated through the old castle.

Although the gaoler had assured them with a solemn oath that the sentinel had been removed, old Morgan waited for a moment on the ladder to take his dagger in his hand before jumping on the ground. The weapon eluded his grasp and fell. Fancying that the noise would rouse the sentinel, he still kept on the ladder, Sir Lewis close behind.

When the buccaneer reached the lower end of the ladder there was no ground beneath his feet.

'Treachery !' muttered he.

At the moment a horrid thought struck him ; he took a heavy purse from his pocket and let it fall ; a quarter of a minute elapsed before he heard it clink against a sea-beaten rock.

‘Lewis!’ he cried, ‘take care, we are hanging over the cliffs.’

Morgan, though brave, when he heard these fearful words shuddered involuntarily.

‘Come, boy, cheer up,’ cried Randolph, ‘and climb up again.’

‘Oh, I cannot! I cannot!’ murmured the youth.

‘What, afraid?’

‘Yes, uncle! I am afraid! don’t despise me—my heart is calm, I could face death, but I cannot mount.’

‘Hold hard, my child, hold hard! here I am,’ cried the buccaneer, eagerly mounting the ladder where Lewis was dangling. ‘Now pass your arms round my neck.’

‘No, uncle, you shall not endanger your life for me; try to get back to the cell; make haste, my strength fails me.’

‘Heavens! what loss of time! quick, your arms round my neck, I say, and fear nothing; why, this is child’s play for me.’

‘No, no; you must live to revenge my father! Tell Nativa my last thought was hers.’

‘Curses on your generosity! you don’t think I would leave you, Lewis; every moment makes me less able to help you; run your arms round my neck, I repeat.’

A fearful pause followed; the ladder swung backwards and forwards with the wind and the weight of the two men suspended over a precipice.

‘Uncle Randolph,’ cried young Morgan, the hard breathing of both sounding like the death rattle, ‘I am myself again. Now the fit has passed I can climb back easily.’

He mounted the five or six rattlins that brought him back to the window.

‘There; now give me your hand,’ said Randolph coolly, ‘otherwise I shall fall myself.’

Morgan clutched the bars tightly with his left hand, and stretched out his right to his uncle. A minute later and they were both safely within the cell again.

‘Well, what do you think, boy, of our little escapade? Not badly contrived, anyhow. Why the deuce did I never suspect that? My head so ran on ambuscades, that my conjectures were at fault. Oh, you rascally gaoler. There is a noise of approaching footsteps.’

Morgan instantly seized one of the bars, and calling out, ‘On your guard, Lewis!’ placed himself before the door.

A key grated in the lock, and the gaoler, carrying a dark lantern, half opened the door.

‘No one here, sir; the trick has succeeded,’ cried the wretch joyfully; ‘you can come in, governor!’

Scarcely had he said these words when a blow from the crow-bar clove his skull, and he fell heavily to the ground.

At the same moment the deputy-governor entered. The

buccaneer, seizing the lantern, placed himself between the new comer and the door, while Sir Lewis, catching the wretched instrument of their enemies, cried out in amazement: 'Charmarand! you here! you the governor? However, no movements. Not a word or you are a dead man.'

This threat was unnecessary, as so completely was the man stupefied with fright, that he could not have uttered a word.

'Mercy,' he moaned at length, falling on his knees.

'And to think that such a vile wretch had nearly triumphed over two men like us,' said Morgan.

'Scoundrel,' continued he, 'your warder probably told you we were prompt enough. You cannot complain of our severity.'

'Mercy, mercy,' gasped the captive.

'Really, you don't do credit to our generosity. Life for life. He took out a pistol and pointed it at his head.

'Mercy, mercy,' was all the trickster could say.

'Your cowardice makes me blush,' returned Randolph. 'Shall we spare this man?'

'I know him of old; he has already robbed me. But still let him loose if he repents and helps us.'

'I will be your slave,' chattered the once-called viscount.

'You will lead us out of prison?'

'Instantly! I swear it.'

'Well, then, let us be off,' said the buccaneer coolly.

Charmarand gave a sigh of relief.

'Now, hark ye, dog! I will take you by the arm, and at the first sign of treachery I blow your brains out. I don't think you will escape me now.'

The governor *pro tem.*, escorted by the two fugitives, conducted them through a number of rooms and courts. Each time they met a sentinel Sir Lewis pressed his dagger to his throat, and Morgan brought his pistol forward.

'Friend governor,' said the captain, when they had reached the shore, 'will you kindly inform me who invented this clever trap to which we had both so nearly fallen victims?'

'Jannekin, the Dean of St. Maurice's,' answered the myrmidon. 'It takes a churchman for such tricks, not we men of the sword!'

'And what was to have been your reward had it succeeded?'

'I should have perhaps been confirmed here as lieutenant governor. That is all.'

'Have you the conventional wife and children in want?'

'No; Mistress Baggot is not my wife. I have only gambling debts, which are always crying out: "Pay me! pay me!"'

'Then it was only to fulfil your duty that you plotted against us?'

'Yes, my lord, only that!'

'In that case you are not so much to blame! You may lie there till dawn!'

At these words Morgan bound and gagged the miscreant, and left him on the sands.

'That rascal is safe for an hour, at least; if he even gnaws his mouth free,' he said quietly, 'we shall have time to get off.'

'Provided we are not watched; for I have seen a human figure gliding over the beach. Lo, there it is!'

By the glare of the lightning the elder man saw a form trying to hide behind a rock.

'Ahoy, friend!' he challenged, rushing forward.

Two minutes later Morgan clasped the hands of his faithful servant Allan, for the prowler under the castle cliffs was he.

'How is it, Allan, that we find you here?' asked the knight.

'Oh, I have been watching for you ever so long,' answered he. 'Mr. Compton told me that you would try to escape, and since then I have spent every night on the shore. Oh, gracious! how happy I am! as happy as if I had a whole sack of crowns. I can't contain myself for joy; and, master, I only spent fifty pounds. But come, the boat is waiting.'

On their way to the boat Sir Lewis, with some hesitation, for the buccaneer walked by his side, asked Allan if he had heard anything of Nativa.

'Oh, yes, the young lady at Penmark? Yes, I have heard about her; she came to see you.'

'Lady Monterey come to see me? Impossible!' cried Morgan in delight.

'Oh, it is true, master, and she gave me a bit of a paper for you.'

Two hours later the fugitives were on board the vessel which Compton sent, and which was lying in the offing.

Morgan's first care was to read Nativa's letter.

The charming Spaniard told him that her father had failed in his mission, and therefore they were about to embark for Spain, and thence proceed to Saint Domingo. What was Morgan's transport when he heard from his friend that their vessel was bound to the same island!

CHAPTER XXIII.

THE NEW LIFE COMMENCES.

ON the 20th of April, 1696, a beautiful ship of 500 tons lay in the straits of Tortoise Island, lately arrived from England; on board were the Morgans and Allan.

It was eventide, and the horizon was illuminated with one of those magnificent sunsets seen only in the tropics, and which pen or brush must ever fail to paint.

'Well, dear Lewis,' said Randolph Morgan, as the two stood on deck inhaling the refreshing breeze, 'what do you think of your new country, its luxurious vegetation, its dark forests, its golden and ruby sky?'

'No words can express my admiration. Before this sublimity of nature the tongue of man is dumb, but his heart sings a hymn of praise to the Creator. Oh, this is the land of my dreams!'

'So, uncle,' continued the youth, his eyes still lingering on the splendid prospect, 'this is the Tortoise Island, so famous for the daring exploits of the buccaneers?'

'Yes,' answered Morgan, 'this little rocky island, not more than forty miles in circumference, has made Charles the Second's crown tremble, and has long been a dark blot on the sun of Spain. The wretched huts along its shores have contained more gold than Louis has ever seen in the Escurial.'

'But if this little island is so formidable to Spain, how is it that she has not conquered it?'

'She has tried, and several times has succeeded in doing so, but we have been conquerors at last. Not a spot of land here but has been watered by human blood. Spain has not yet recovered the defeat she suffered from Captain Lewis the Scot, and now a whole armada could hardly take from us a spot so bravely defended and so dearly bought.'

A boat from St. Domingo came alongside, and five men mounted on board; they were dressed in loose dark cotton shirts, leather leggings, and sombreros. They all bore in their girdles three or four long knives, a bayonet and powder-flask, and had in their hands long rifles. Their arms were evidently of first-rate workmanship, and the men altogether presented a picturesque but savage appearance. They welcomed Morgan in the most hearty manner, who seemed equally rejoiced to see them.

'Well, my lads,' cried the latter, 'what cheer with you? Do the Spanish galliards still vex our mates? Have you had good success in fishing and hunting?'

'If the hidalgoes attack us while you are here, Morgan, it's not likely they will leave us alone when you are away,' answered one of the new-comers. 'The rascal dogs destroy our game, so that soon there will not be a wild boar left, and we shall have to join your freebooters to save ourselves from starving.'

'And your best plan, too, friend. Why, in an hour on board our ships you would gain more than in a month with your rifle and nets.'

'True, captain; yet our wild, free life has a charm which no riches can purchase. And then, after a long, dangerous cruise or chase, to see the smoke curling up from my small cot and know that those I love are watching for my return. Oh, I would not exchange this delight for all your wealth.'

'And who,' asked the Cornish knight, after the men had left, 'were your strange visitors?'

'Men of education and station, aweary of tyranny and priest-craft, who have emigrated here. At St. Domingo you will see men belonging to the highest families in Europe in rags, and others of the lowest class rolling in riches. Here, the only distinction springs from courage and success.'

'Then the hardest blows gain the most money?' inquired Allan, modestly putting in his word.

'Yes, my good fellow, that is the rule,' answered the rover.

'Odzookers!' exclaimed the rustic. 'How I long to have at those vile Spaniards who roast the poor Indians as if they were chestnuts.'

When the vessel cast anchor in Tortoise Bay and the Morgans went on shore, the elder was received with the most joyful enthusiasm, a proof of his great popularity among them. For these freebooters are too well used to pass their life in daring adventure to waste much excitement over common events.

At a little distance from the fort was a beautiful habitation belonging to the admiral. Thither he conducted his nephew, after he had dismissed his numerous friends and followers.

He led Sir Lewis into a chamber filled with the most costly works of art, and opening into a delicious garden.

'Lewis,' said he, pointing to a luxuriant lounge, 'sit down there, take a pipe, and listen to me. I have something important to tell you. But first you must promise me secrecy. My duty and my position demand it.'

'Then, uncle, I swear it.'

'Already, my dear boy, you know the power we buccaneers possess in these seas, but you have yet to learn how few we are in number. Yes, these men who set the power of Spain at defiance, and to-morrow could free themselves from the control of the rest of Europe, are only a hundred and fifty in number. Our union is our strength. By means of our league the Brothers of the Coast acquire immense riches, and a power all the greater that it does not interfere with the personal independence of each member. I am the absolute and sovereign head of these hundred and fifty members. When the disasters of war cut down one or many of our people, we choose among our allies in whom we have the greatest confidence, men to succeed them. But before any one is admitted among us, he must pass through a novitiate of three years. For not only do we require him to possess great physical courage, but we exact a strength of mind and force of character almost superhuman.

'While artfully exciting his passions, we sow his path with
snares. If he yield to the temptation, and neglects for a moment
the commands of his master, we discard him for ever and without pity.'

'And you do not fear, Morgan, the indiscretion of a man
once admitted to your secrets ?'

'The dead tell no tales, Lewis ; the grave is dumb.'

'What !' cried Sir Lewis, with horror, 'do you kill off-hand ?
do you become murderers ?'

'Child,' answered the buccaneer slowly, 'wait till you know
the life before you condemn. Your blood is still too hot, and
your hair too dark, to judge and condemn men who, like you,
have been young and generous. Experience is often a severe
counsellor, but always infallible. You forget, also, in what sort
of world we live. Outlawed by the rest of creation, we must
protect ourselves by means that society reproves.

'Our strength lies in our strength, not in our morality. But
that is not now the question. Among the advantages which as
chief I possess, is that of the right of admitting to our ranks,
without apprenticeship, any one whom in my soul and conscience
I consider worthy of the honour !

'Will you become one of our band ? To-morrow you will
be made acquainted with all our resources, our plans and projects,
and admitted to our mysteries. Only, Lewis, listen to what I
say : if you accept the immense favour I offer you, I require and
exact from you absolute obedience. My will must be law, and
break down all obstacles. You must become my property. If
an hour hence I said to you, 'Lewis, you must give up your
love,' would even heart-strings snap in the effort, it must be done
I speak frankly, for I love you too well to attempt to deceive
you. Reflect before you answer and decide. My offer, once
accepted or declined, is final.'

'I thank you sincerely, uncle, for the confidence you place in
me,' answered the chevalier gravely, ' but I need no consideration. My choice is made, and is irrevocable. The most sacred
feeling that exists in the human mind is the love of liberty. I
refuse your offer, though it leads me in the steps of my famous
forefather. And now, listen to me. I will speak as plainly as
you did. I believe in your friendship, and return it, but I will
not hide from you that on some points your character repulses
me. Brother of my father, you change your name, and oblige
me to call you captain. I have obeyed you, but from this
moment you cease to be my uncle, and henceforth I see in you
only my father's dearest companion, and my surest friend. To-
day I only desire one thing ; to carve out my own prospects
while retaining my independence. Your advice 1 shall always
receive with gratitude, but I refuse your support. The day that

you shall say to me, " Lewis, there stands your father's murderer! you must revenge him," I will implicitly obey your orders. Except in this way, I desire to remain entirely free.'

The frank, bold language, instead of offending his uncle, seemed to give him satisfaction.

'Good blood never lies!' he said kindly; 'I could fancy, my dear Lewis, that I heard my poor brother speak, for he liked not Sir Henry's reputation! Well, let 'it be as you say: perhaps you are right in refusing my help. Fortune to a noble heart is only valuable when it is toiled for or won. Your father only left you his name and honour—be the son of thy works!'

The next evening the two went again on board the vessel that had brought them from England, and sailed for Seogane, the most important town in the colony; there the governor lived.

'My dear Lewis,' said the buccaneer, passing his arm through his nephew's, 'before we part, and you follow your own course, I wish to give you some idea of the new life that opens before you. Since it is decided that you do not cast your lot with us, you must at least understand the freebooters among whom you dwell. You will soon have a high sense of their independence. Out of the service, each does as he likes without troubling himself about neighbours.

'They keep up the same sort of freedom on board ship as on expeditions. Each one pleases himself without thinking of his comrades. If a freebooter likes to sing while his companion sleeps, the sleeper has no right to complain. All annoyances that serve to exercise patience and fortitude, and accustom them to privations, must be borne without a murmur. This resignation is an essential part of their discipline.

'Freebooters are bound by unshaken faith and honour to each other. If one, which is rarely the case, in the slightest degree cheats his neighbour, he is most severely punished. He loses his name and rank as a freebooter, as also his property, and is marooned; that is, left without clothes or food on a desert island. To prevent all jealousy and cause of quarrel, no woman is allowed on board any vessel. The infraction of this rule is punished with the same severity as abandoning a post :—Death for both.

'The chief in command has no power to show mercy. The best sailor on board, if guilty, suffers death like a lubber.

'To avoid quarrels on board ship, the dispute is always put off till they land ; then duels often take place, and generally one falls.

'Each buccaneer is obliged to keep his arms in the most perfect condition, and in this they emulate each other.

'Fire and light are put out on board all vessels at eight

o'clock, and no more liquor is allowed to be drunk. It is also forbidden to play at cards, or games of chance.

'When a freebooter possesses a vessel, and undertakes any expedition, the men who serve under him are forced to obey him, or be deprived of their share of booty. A certain sum is first put aside out of the prizes for the person who advanced money for the expedition; and his profits are enormous. Besides lesser sums for the surgeon and chief carpenter on board.

'The daring and audacity of the buccaneers your own experience can alone acquaint you with. Many Spaniards think them demons, and invulnerable, and this belief contributes not a little to our success. In Sir Henry's day, we have held a gap, sixty of us against thousands of the Castilians, and hardly required a patch of plaster or a plug of tow for our wounds.'

CHAPTER XXIV.

THE FREEBOOTERS AT HOME.

On his arrival at Seogane, Morgan was astonished at the style, luxury, and wealth which it contained. On all sides rose beautiful mansions, and splendid shops filled with the most costly wares; young men dressed in exquisite taste lounged about, or rode magnificent horses, while lovely creoles, covered with lace and jewels, were carried in rich palanquins. Everywhere abundance, and all the refinements of advanced civilization.

'What a contrast is this to Tortoise Island!' said he to his Nestor.

'The difference is easily explained,' answered the seaman. 'At Seogane is dissipated what has been gained on Tortoise Island. This town is a place of rendezvous and amusement for buccaneers, and besides, carries on a considerable trade with Europe. But here we are at the governor's house; wait for me five minutes.'

As soon as Captain Morgan left him, Lewis's attention was attracted by the sound of music approaching, and immediately the creole ladies came to the windows, and the negroes in the street began to dance, joyfully clapping their hands.

'Would you be so good as to tell me the meaning of this excitement?' he asked of a young man passing by.

'Oh, it is Handsome Lawrence, who landed last night, and is taking a turn round the town to-day.'

'But who is Lawrence, if you please?'

'Why, where can you have dropped from, not to have heard of Lawrence?'

'I came from England.'

'Is not Handsome Lawrence known in London ?'

'Not to my knowledge.'

'It is really incredible !' answered the stranger ; 'I have never quitted St. Domingo, but I should have thought that Lawrence was known everywhere.'

'My goodness !' cried Allan, who followed his master, 'the musicians are coming our way. What a pity, instead of scraping fiddles they don't play the Welsh harp ! How I could have danced !'

Morgan now saw a young man, tall, very handsome, and superbly dressed, walking along escorted by the band, and sheltered from the sun by a canopy of rich silk embroidered with gold, carried by four negroes gorgeously appareled. The crowd respectfully made way as he passed.

'Be off ! you don't leave me air to breathe,' said the man under the daïs to a party of negroes who, with eyes and mouths open, were staring at him with unbounded admiration. 'Here, fellows, here is something for rum,' he continued, throwing them a handful of thick gold coins.

'Long life to the handsome gentleman !' cried the negroes in chorus. At the same instant a window opened, and a nosegay of lovely flowers was thrown at the feet of the hero.

'These flowers are bright, but have no perfume,' he said, pushing them away with his foot ; 'still, good intentions deserve their reward.'

This singular personage took a string of emeralds from his neck, and threw them up into the balcony.

The blind was instantly closed, and a loud sob was heard.

'It seems,' said Lawrence, raising his voice in contempt, that diamonds would have been more acceptable. Madame ought to have been clearer. I don't understand the language of flowers.'

The crowd laughed, and the hero of the self-bought triumph continued his progress.

As one side of the street was very sunny, the whole party crossed ; and Morgan, to make way for them, stood up close to Government House.

'Hoy, there, rogue, do you know who I am,' cried Lawrence, 'that you take the right side when I pass ?'

'Did you speak to me ?' asked the Cornishman bluntly.

'Of course ! no words about it, if you please ! I kick rogues out of my way.'

Patience was not one of the west countryman's virtues, but the impertinence of 'Handsome Larry' seemed so gratuitous that the youth only stared in amazement.

'Well, mate, have you come to your senses yet, or am I to throw you to the other side of the road to clear your wits and my path ?'

'Sir,' cried Morgan, putting his hand to his sword, 'I know nothing of the customs of this place, but you have insulted me grossly; so draw, and defend yourself.'

'What, fight with you, so hot as it is? No, indeed; far too much trouble. Draw back, or I'll shoot you down!'

'Wretch!' cried Morgan,'in a rage, advancing towards the other. Lawrence glared at him with the ferocity of a tiger, and drawing a pistol from his belt, took aim.

Morgan felt he was powerless, so he folded his arms, and looking his adversary full in the face, cried:

'Cowardly murderer, my curse on you; but if you miss me, I shall cleave you in twain!'

Scarcely were the words uttered, than by a violent blow Lawrence was stretched on the ground.

'You thought you could shoot my master, though he had his faithful Allan behind him, did you?' cried the servant. 'I'll teach you better manners.'

'Stop, Allan,' cried Morgan, 'he is stunned! He cannot defend himself.'

'And could you have parried his bullet with your sword, master? He is a coward, and deserves no pity. A few thumps will do him no harm.'

'Is it because you have saved my life, you refuse to obey me, Allan?"

'Oh, master, don't talk so cruelly,' cried Allan, blushing; 'I so long to pummel him a little, but I won't if you say not.'

The bystanders, seeing Allan lower his cudgel, were about to lift up Lawrence, when a young girl rushed from the house whence the nosegay had been thrown, threw herself on the ground by his side, raised his head, and strove to staunch the blood with her scarf.

'Pray be not uneasy,' said Morgan, with respect, 'he was only stunned; see, he recovers his senses.'

The wounded man opened his eyes, and fixing them on Morgan, said:

'To knock a man down like an ox is the deed of a dastard! You shall answer for this.'

'Sir,' responded Sir Lewis, 'to fire on a man who has only a sword to defend himself with is the extreme of cowardice, and this I will maintain at the point of the sword. Only, as you are hardly capable of holding yours now, we will put off our meeting till to-morrow.'

'Lawrence, I entreat you, do not meet him,' cried the young girl, in tears.

'Silence, Marienne,' answered Lawrence roughly. 'Instead of interfering with what does not concern you, you had better stay at home. A girl ought to have more self-respect than to parade herself in public. I am neither your husband, your father, nor your lover.'

'Oh, this is cruel!' moaned the girl, covering her face with her hands.

'As for you, sir,' continued Lawrence, 'if I let you go now, who will answer for my finding you to-morrow?'

'I!' rejoined the sonorous voice of Randolph Morgan, who, leaning against the door of Government House for the last few moments, had watched the scene in silence.

The voice of the celebrated buccaneer made Lawrence start.

'Do you know this man, and answer for his appearing?'

'I know him to be fully capable of chastising your insolence, and I answer for him as for myself. I would give ten years of my life, Lawrence, to take his place, and pit my strength against yours, you French coxcomb!'

'Very likely,' replied Lawrence coldly, 'our association unluckily forbids that; but who knows if a time may not come?'

'No more of this!' cried the captain. 'Name the day, the hour, and the place.'

'The day after to-morrow, six in the morning, at the foot of Mount Pithon, at the entrance of the wood.'

'It is well; he shall be there. Heal your cracked pate, man! and beware: you may now receive due punishment of all your crimes!'

'I know,' answered Lawrence, 'that my death would please you, but I fear your charitable wish may not be granted. I have fought thirty duels or so, and each time *killed my man!*'

Lawrence was departing, when he turned, and added:

By the bye, who gave me that cowardly backhander on the head?'

'I,' said Allan; 'I struck hard, I dare say, but you should not have tried to murder my master.'

'You prevented my committing a dastardly act, for which I thank you, and here is your reward!' He threw towards Allan a purse of gold.

'My brave Lewis,' said old Morgan, as he drew his nephew out of the crowd that had now anxiously collected round them, 'you have a sad matter on your hands. I would rather have given my whole fortune than you and Lawrence had met.'

'You are wrong, sir, to care so much about the matter. I feel sure I shall conquer; but who is this handsome swaggerer?'

'Handsome Larry, as he is called, after myself enjoys the highest repute among the freebooters. His boldness, strength, and knowledge are extraordinary. Nature has endowed him with her choicest gifts, but they are perverted by boundless pride and implacable cruelty. For some time I have suspected that Lawrence covets my authority, and tries by underhand means to sap it. But he had better beware. I own he is extremely popular, especially among his countrymen. His munificence is unbounded, and his purse is open to all the luckless. A strange fellow! Sometimes I think there must be some good in him. Some great grief must weigh over his past life, for he treats·women with the greatest contempt, and yet they all fall in love with him. That girl who rushed out to help him belongs to one of the richest and most important families on the island, and still you saw how he treated her. Lawrence is a mystery, even to me.'

'His name at least does not denote any high birth.'

'You are mistaken, my dear Lewis. In all St. Domingo there is not one freebooter, except De Grammont, who goes by his own name. Yet among us is some of the best blood of France and England.'

The next morning the uncle and nephew set out for Mount Pithon, as the former wanted to examine the duelling grou. l. Allan followed, very sad and anxious ; with Lawrence's present he had bought a buccaneer rifle, some powder, and shot.

CHAPTER XXV.

WILDFLOWER.

ALTHOUGH the gentlemen were mounted on thoroughbred horses, yet they were nearly three hours going the short distance of six miles. Attracted by the wondrous beauties of the tropical landscape, the younger man stopped continually to admire. His ardent imagination dwelt with ecstasy on the supreme happiness of living in these delicious solitudes with one loved being far away from the cruel passions of men. The form of Nativa naturally arose to his memory, and he felt sad.

'My dear Lewis,' said his uncle, 'I could tell you something that would make your anger against Lawrence still more implacable. You have full faith in my honour, have you not?'

'As perfect as in my father's, if he were alive,' answered Morgan.

'You still love Nativa?'

'More than ever.'

'Then Lawrence has done you a still greater injury than the insult he offered you, in the contemptuous and shameful manner he speaks of that young lady. In this meeting, you will avenge her honour as well as your own.'

'Then he shall die, though my own life be forfeited.'

Before reaching Mount Pithon, our travellers passed through

Roger's Wood. Entirely planted with wild orange trees, and carpeted with the softest verdure, interspersed with brilliant cactus flowers, this wood was the most enchanting solitude in the world. From the bright green and white flowered canopy overhead hung festoons of elegant parasites, among which fluttered birds of the most brilliant plumage and vivid colours.

'My dear son,' said the pirate admiral, 'we are now close to the dwelling of a buccaneer who will be delighted to have us for his guests ; here we will leave our horses, as the road further on is too steep and rough for them, and proceed to the place on foot.'

The buccaneer's cabin struck Sir Lewis with admiration. Partly overshadowed by thick woods, it had in front a well-arranged garden, radiant with the brightest flowers.

'What sort of person is the owner of this lovely place ?' asked Morgan.

'One of our countrymen who calls himself Greybeard ; he is a queer fellow, as you will soon perceive, and for the last thirty years has lived here secluded from the world. But he has an excellent temper, and he and I are great friends. He is considered one of the best marksmen among us, and will be able to give you very useful hints about your meeting to-morrow.'

'But are we not to fight with swords ?'

'No, my boy ; here duels are settled with both weapons. Do you know how to use a rifle ?'

'I was thought a good marksman in Cornwall.'

'All the better ; but here are Greybeard's servants.'

About a dozen hunting dogs bounded towards them.

'Ho, ho, boys ! down ! down !' cried old Morgan ; 'we are old friends, but it is long since we have met.'

As if the animals had understood his words, they fawned upon the speaker.

'Good dogs ! see how they remember me,' said the buccaneer to his nephew. 'How few of my friends, after so long an absence, would have received me so well. But here is Greybeard !'

The buccaneer who came towards them was about fifty years of age, of small and insignificant figure ; he wore the usual dress of his profession, only much neater and cleaner.

After the first salutations, the captain pointed to Sir Lewis, and said :

'Here is a young man who wishes to make your acquaintance, and desires your advice. He is going to fight a duel to-morrow with Lawrence.'

'Then he will certainly be killed,' said Greybeard, as coolly as if he were speaking of the most trivial matter. 'But, never mind, he is welcome to my services. But you must need refreshment ; you will find a bottle or so of rare old rum in the house.'

The interior of the dwelling was beautifully neat and clean.

Greybeard opened an old cellarette, and took out several bottles.

'Rum is well enough,' said Allan, as he helped to place them on the table, 'but what a fine thing is English beer !'

A minute later their host placed before Allan a jug of that liquor.

'I like that fellow,' said Greybeard to the rover ; 'I wish you would leave him with me !'

'Allan is my nephew's servant, not mine ; and I don't suppose they are willing to part.'

'I would give you a black man, two of my best dogs, and a barrel of pork or rum in exchange,' said Greybeard to Morgan, who was much surprised at so strange a proposal.

'Allan will only leave me at his own wish,' was his answer.

'Well, then, if I can't trade for you as a servant, you must be my friend, Allan.' Greybeard took his rifle, and followed by his dogs, accompanied Morgan and his nephew to Mount Pithon.

Under Greybeard's instruction, Sir Lewis passed several hours in practising with the rifle, unlike those of any European country. At length his tutor pronounced, with an animation that he showed on no other subject but that of arms, that he thought it was just possible that he might hit Lawrence.

The party then returned to the cabin, where an abundant dinner awaited them. They were about to do justice to it when a soft west-country ballad sounded from the neighbouring thicket.

The sweet melody so far from home brought tears into Morgan's eyes, and Allan was not less moved.

Even old Greybeard smiled when he heard it, and said :

'Why, there is Jennie come back again.'

In a few moments a girl sprang forward and kissed Greybeard. She was scarcely seventeen, of slight, agile form, and her complexion, lightly kissed by the sun, glowed with health and exercise, setting off to the best advantage her glossy brown hair, slightly tinged with gold. Her large black eyes beamed with feeling and intelligence, and her whole appearance was that of a beautiful Hebe or graceful Diana.

'Good evening, father,' cried the girl in clear, joyful tones ; 'you did not think to see me home so soon ?'

'No, pretty one ; but why is Leathercap not with you ?'

'He found the trail of a boar, and won't be here yet for an hour.'

The girl threw down her hat, and running to old Morgan, said :

'I am so glad that you are come back! Do you know, Leathercap and I met to-day a party of fifty Spanish lancers! And tell me, captain,' she continued, after a moment's pause, 'who is that young man by your side? I like his face very much; he looks kind. Is he come to fight against the Spaniards? And that other man,' pointing to Allan, who coloured up to the eyes, 'good gracious! how ugly he is!'

'These new-comers,' answered the rover, smiling, 'are Cornish, like your father and mother. They both deserve your liking them, for they are honest and brave. The one who pleases you most is my nephew.'

'Since you are good and handsome,' said the girl, sitting down by Morgan, 'we will be friends, if you like.'

'It is a great honour to me, fair mistress,' stammered Morgan, astonished and confused.

'Why do you call me mistress—won't you be friends with me?'

'Lewis,' interrupted old Morgan, laughing, 'you don't know Wildflower. She is so unused to the forms of society, and is so completely the child of nature, that she says exactly what she thinks. You must not be too vain of her preference, for she sees in you a companion; nothing else. Wildflower is a great favourite with all our people, and is treated by them with the greatest respect, so that in the midst of our corrupt society she lives as pure and innocent as an angel.'

'Captain,' remarked Jennie, 'I don't like the way you put things, so I shall talk to your nephew. Your uncle says that you are good, and you must be brave too. Was your last cruise against the Spanish dogs successful?'

'I have never been in battle at all,' answered Morgan.

'Oh, then, in your first voyage I will go with you.'

'I thought, Jennie, that women were not allowed on board?'

'That is true, but with me it is different; I am a buccaneer. How astonished you look! Do you think it is false? You cannot be my friend if you doubt me.'

'Jennie is right,' explained old Morgan, 'the only exception to the rule is made in her favour; indeed, we buccaneers are so superstitious, that we think that Jennie's presence brings us success, and part of the booty is always put aside for her.'

'Oh, yes, I bring success,' added Wildflower, 'because I always take care of the wounded of either party.'

'Oh, young lady,' cried Allan, gallantly, 'I am delighted to hear that; and ugly as I am, if ever you want a fellow who can hit hard, I and my club are at your service.'

'Are you attached to your master?'

'If a man asked me that, he should taste my club.'

'Then I like you! and now I look at you again, you don't seem so very ugly.'

In a short time Leathercap, as he was called, entered the chamber. He was an immensely tall, stout fellow of about thirty, with a bullet head and unmeaning face ; he showed a snowy row of teeth as he entered, which was his way of smiling, but on seeing Sir Lewis he put on a sulky look.

'Who is that young spark ? ' he asked Greybeard.

'He is Sir Lewis Morgan,' answered Jennie ; 'we are already good friends.'

'Then he had better keep out of my way, if he does not want a bullet through his head.'

At this undeserved attack Morgan rose angrily, but Jennie throwing herself between them, said :

'Leathercap is rough, but he is not wicked. I insist, sir, that you ask Lewis's pardon.'

'I?' cried the hunter, with the growl of a bear.

'Yes, and straightway.'

Leathercap made no answer, but shouldered his rifle.

'If you don't do so, I will not speak to you for a fortnight,' threatened Wildflower, stamping her pretty foot, 'and you know I keep my word.'

The giant looked angry, but said, in a voice of thunder :

'Forgive me.'

'I cannot forgive you, as you have not offended me,' said Morgan, offering his hand.

'Wildflower wishes you to forgive me.'

'Well, then, I forgive you.'

'You see Leathercap is very gentle,' remarked Jennie, 'Folk say he is in love with me, but I think him uglier than your servant, but that does not signify, for he is brave and good.'

'Thanks, Jennie,' said Leathercap joyfully.

'My dear Lewis,' said Captain Morgan, 'as your duel with Lawrence is to take place at six, and we shall have to leave at daybreak, we had better rest now.'

'Going to fight Lawrence ! ' cried Jennie, turning pale. 'Oh no, he will kill you! you must not meet him! Sir Lewis,' she added, a few moments later, with tears in her eyes, ' you must not mind what I say. Your honour requires that you should fight. Fight, then, you will, alas !'

CHAPTER XXVI.

SAVED FROM THE SPANIARDS.

NOTHING is so poetical and enchanting as sunrise in the American forests. As the sun's first beams kiss the horizon, the twittering of hundreds of birds, the buzzing of thousands of insects, the rustling of reptiles and the larger animals break the solemn stillness of night, and make a harmonious concert, nature's first hymn of thanksgiving for life and light.

The immense fan-shaped leaves, glistening with myriads of dewdrops, form a canopy of jewels that exceeds in splendour even the dream of the Diamond Valley of the Orient.

Such were the sounds, such the sights, that greeted Sir Lewis on the morning after his arrival at the cabin. Having risen at four, he waited in calm pensiveness his uncle's waking. He thought of his life, so quiet and peaceful until the last few months; of the stirring events since, in which he had been little more than a passive instrument in another's hands; of his love for Nativa. Soon a gentle knock at the door roused him, and Jennie entered with a basket of fruit and flowers in her hand. 'Lewis,' she said, 'I could not sleep all night for thinking of you and of your duel with Lawrence; and did that keep you awake too? Do you fear Lawrence, or have you good hopes of being successful?'

'Yes, Jennie,' answered Morgan, 'I also was wakeful, and thought of you as of a beloved sister. The interest you so kindly express for me softens and rejoices my heart. It is so sweet to have a friend that I gave myself up to the pleasure without considering that the friendship you so frankly offer me is too sudden perhaps to last.'

'Lewis,' went on the girl, 'do you know that though we met yesterday for the first time, it seems as if we had known each other for years, as if we had grown up together; and only that you will laugh at me——'

'I promise not, sister. Come, tell me.'

'Then, is it not strange that when I first heard your voice yesterday it seemed quite familiar to me? I am sure I have heard it in my dreams. And that made me ask you at once to be my friend.'

Captain Morgan interrupted the conversation, bidding his nephew get ready.

'My friend,' cried Jennie, trembling and in tears, 'I fear I am not strong enough to go with you.'

'You come with me, Jennie?'

'Do you think I can wait here to learn your victory or your death? Oh no, I must go; but you will conquer! Oh, I could never be happy again if you were to die. Lewis, you will conquer. Lawrence, so rough with others, is gentle with me, pretends he loves me; but I will beseech him——'

'My dear child,' cried Morgan, gently interrupting her, 'you must remain here. All your efforts to interfere would be worse than useless. In England, Jennie, women never mix themselves in affairs of honour; they weep over those who die, but they despise cowards. Jennie, I will not be despised.'

'Yes, Lewis, you are right,' sobbed the poor girl; 'I will remain here.'

'Come, Lewis,' cried his uncle, 'Greybeard is waiting.'

The three men were already on the threshold when a negro approached.

'Cap'en,' he said, 'hyah am a package dat Mass' Lawrence send yer.'

Negroes, less accustomed than they have become since to the usages of civilized life, imagined that a slip of paper or letter could not be of the slightest consequence, therefore persons were in the habit of placing a letter between two heavy stones, and the negro, convinced of the importance of what he carried by its weight, delivered it faithfully.

Lawrence had enclosed his note to the admiral, not between two stones, but between two ingots of silver. Its contents ran as follows:

'Captain, the blow that I received yesterday prevents my setting out; but to-morrow, without fail, I will be at Mount Pithon. Beg Wildflower's acceptance of the silver bricks.'

Morgan read this letter aloud, and Jennie gave a cry of delight and said to Sir Lewis:

'My friend, this delay is of good omen for you; for never has Lawrence been inexact to a duel. But I will not accept his bars; I hate the sight of them.'

This delay was not agreeable to Morgan; though he was brave, one day's longer suspense was painful to him.

'Lewis,' said Jennie, 'shall we spend the day together in the woods?'

The youth was delighted with the idea of a long ramble in the virgin forest with so charming a companion; it offered besides a pleasant distraction to sad thoughts; still he hesitated.

'I am afraid, Wildflower,' he returned, 'that your father would not approve of your proposal.'

'Not approve—why should he not?'

'Because it is not what we call " the thing."'

'What can you mean?'

'Only that your father knows so little of me, he might not have enough confidence in me to trust you to me.'

'I don't understand a word,' answered Jennie, pouting. 'Why should my father be afraid? The nephew of Morgan the Second would defend, not injure, a buccaneer's child! Come, take a rifle and follow me.'

Seeing that Morgan still hesitated, Jennie ran after her father and said: 'Father, lend Lewis your rifle; he is going shooting with me.'

'What, are you going alone?' asked the wild hunter.

'Certainly, father; don't I know the paths through the forests as well as you?'

'So you may, child ; but as our guest is not used to Spanish ambushes, I advise you to take Leathercap with you.'

'Oh, Leathercap would spoil our pleasure ; he is jealous of all those I like.'

'Oh, if he is in the way, that is another thing ; but what makes him jealous ?'

'Oh, because he says he is in love with me,' answered Jennie, with a ringing laugh.

'Well,' said her father, 'if my companero is in the way, you had better take the dogs with you, my girl.'

Before they set out, Jennie took young Morgan into the house, and placed before him a piece of wild boar baked after the fashion of the buccaneer, bread, and fruit.

After breakfast they set off. During the first ten minutes Wildflower kept silence. Then, turning to her cavalier, she said :

'If you were not going to fight a duel to-morrow this would be the happiest day of my life.'

'What makes you happy, sister ?' asked her companion.

'Because you are with me,' she answered with a smile.

This speech troubled Morgan, and it was only after a while he remarked :

'Jennie, have you been long here ? Have you ever lived in towns ?'

'Never, Caballero Luis, except for a few months at Pontpier and Seogane. I can't bear towns ; I can't breathe there, and the flowers have no scent. I am only happy in the woods. I was born here, and here I hope to die.'

'You have never known your mother Jennie ?'

'Never ; I was too young when she died to remember her.'

'And have you been happy on land and sea ?'

'Yes, for I brought good fortune to the shipmen.'

'That was not exactly what I meant. Did you like the sea ? And,' added the young man with some hesitation, 'did you like your companions there ?'

'Oh, I liked the buccaneers well enough ; they treated me as if I was their daughter ; only the last time——'

'Go on, Jennie.'

'Some of them frightened me.'

'Frightened you ?—how ?'

'When they had drunk too much. I will never go to sea again except to bear you company, Lewis. But what voice is that ? Listen. Yes, there is certainly some one near us ; yet the dogs are quiet.'

Wildflower stopped and looked eagerly through the brush-wood, then stamped angrily and attempted to frown.

'It is that plague Leathercap. Wait for me, I will be back directly.'

So saying, Jennie disappeared in the *chapparal.*

'Did I not tell you not to come? Why did you follow us? If you don't answer me, I shall be angry.'

'I followed you,' answered the giant gruffly, 'because I am jealous.'

'And what makes you jealous?'

'Because you take the stranger for a lover.'

'Certainly he loves me, and so do you too. Will you let me be?'

'I your lover indeed!' said Leathercap with wonderment, showing what a different interpretation he put on the words.

'Really, you are quite absurd,' said Jennie. 'Are we not lovers and friends? We shoot together, and I am always happy to see you; so what can you want more?'

'You are very kind sometimes, Wildflower, it is true,' answered the strapping fellow; 'but if Sir Lewis escapes Lawrence, let him beware, that's all.'

'If you do him the least harm I will never forgive you as long as I live. I shall hate you.'

'Then I shall kill you, Jennie,' answered Leathercap curtly.

'You silly fellow!' said the girl scornfully; 'why, what could you do without me?'

'That's true,' sighed the colossus, 'I could never live away from you.'

'Then be good and do as I bid you. Sir Lewis, I bring Leathercap here to tell you that he wishes to be friends with you. Come, say so, sir.'

The giant hesitated; but seeing Jennie get angry, he came forward and said in a rough voice, 'Caballero, I wish to be friends with you.'

'Very well, Leathercap, let us shake hands on it. Now do we not depart?'

The hours that followed were delicious to Morgan. Jennie led him to the most lovely solitudes, and in her gentle society he felt a calm contentment which he had never experienced with Nativa.

About midday the great heat warned them to rest themselves. Jennie seated herself on the root of an old tree, and leaning back against its trunk was soon asleep; the dogs lay round her. For some moments Morgan watched her; never, except Nativa, had he seen any one so beautiful; but while Nativa's beauty dazzled the sight, Jennie's captivated the heart. Morgan sat down, but he could not sleep; he rested his head in his hands and mused. The strong perfumes of the flowers gave him a strange feeling of intoxication. Suddenly a great noise roused them both.

'What uproar is that, Jennie?'

'The Spaniards, who no doubt have met with some unlucky buccaneer ; come, let us fly to help him !'

'If I were alone, Jennie,' answered the Englishman, 'I would not hesitate a moment, but I fear for you.'

'Oh, never mind me ; it would be dastardly to let the Spaniards murder one of us, and not try to help him ! Come !'

Pale, but with gleaming eyes, Jennie called the dogs and rushed forward in the direction whence the cries proceeded.

Scarcely had they gone a hundred yards before they heard a shot.

'Courage !' cried Jennie, with all her strength. 'Help is near.'

A company of Spanish lancers surrounded a buccaneer, who was armed only with a pistol, and stood in the midst of them calm and collected, his head high, and a proud sneer on his lips.

'Heavens !' cried Jennie, 'it is Handsome Larry ; the Spaniards will kill him, Lewis ; in five minutes your enemy will be no more.'

'Jennie,' cried Morgan, 'if I risk not my own life to save his, I shall be dishonoured. If I fall, farewell, child !'

The youth levelled his rifle, took aim, and fired—a Spaniard fell dead. He then rushed forward towards the enemy, already in disorder at the surprise.

Morgan saw Lawrence's plan of defence : he had emptied all his powder in his hat as well as his bullets, and stood ready at the advance of the Spaniards to set light to this new description of mine, which, though certain death to him, must involve that of many of his foes.

As soon as they perceived the new-comer, several rushed forward, lances in hand. The moment was critical ; if he waited to reload, he felt that he was lost.

The lances were almost upon his breast, when a shot from the wood brought one of the foes to the ground, and Morgan recovering hope, cried with all his might :

'Hither, friends, this way, or the villains will escape.'

A dozen furious dogs now rushed from the brushwood, and the Spaniards, fearing to fall into an ambuscade of buccaneers, rode off.

'Thanks, a thousand thanks, my kind Jennie,' cried Morgan warmly ; 'I owe my life to you, you saved me from a dreadful death.'

Lawrence stood unmoved, and quietly poured his powder and shot back into his flask and pouch. Then turning to Morgan he began :

'Thanks, friend ; if ever Lawrence can serve you'—then recognising the man with whom he was to fight the next day, he said curtly, 'You are unlucky. What the deuce made you come to my help ? The Spaniards would have saved you all trouble

to-morrow. What extraordinary want of sense on your part!
But perhaps you did not know whom you were helping?'

The knight was silent, not wishing to entangle his adversary.
At that moment Jennie appeared. Lawrence smiled on her.

'Dear Lewis!' cried the girl, 'how glad I am you are safe!'

'And have you not one word for me, pretty one?'

'You know I don't like you,' was her frank answer.

'You are wrong, child, for I like you very much.'

'Oh, but you are so cruel; everyone is afraid of you. And
if Sir Lewis had done as I bid him, you would have been killed
by the Spaniards.'

'What! did the caballero know who I was?'

'Certainly! Now was he not wrong to save your life?

Lawrence was silent a moment; then turning to his preserver
he observed:

'Your conduct has been admirable, and I honour you for it.
Still, I hope you will not make it an excuse for not meeting me
to-morrow?'

'You need feel no alarm on that score,' answered Morgan;
'in putting off the meeting until to-morrow you have shown less
eagerness in the matter than myself.'

'Señor,' answered Lawrence politely, 'I was really too much
shaken yesterday to set out. As soon as I was able I mounted
my horse. If you are impatient, we can settle matters *here.*
Only I think we should spare Wildflower such a scene, besides
depriving her of an escort home, for probably the Spaniards still
lurk in the neighbourhood.'

'Your excuses are accepted,' answered the Englishman.

'Then shall we converse like men,' asked the other, 'without
thinking of to-morrow?'

'Willingly; any allusion to it before a lady seems improper.
Let us change the subject. Pray tell us how you were able to
keep so many at bay; and how was it the Spaniards did not
riddle you with balls before they closed in?'

'The lancers never carry firearms; they fancy the Brothers
of the Sea are bullet-proof! Ha, ha!'

During this conversation Jennie looked at Lawrence with
astonishment.

'Lawrence,' she said at length, 'you quite surprise me. Never
have I seen you so agreeable. You are generally most rude and
uncivil!'

'My pretty Wildflower,' answered the handsome freebooter,
'such an observation from you I do not deserve, for never have
I said a word to vex you.'

'Perhaps not to me, but to others.'

'If I have behaved well to you, Jennie, it is because you are
the only one of your sex whom I can respect. When I was

young I loved everyone, but experience has taught me a cruel lesson. I have learnt to consider men as monsters of selfishness and ingratitude.   If I talk differently with Señor Lewis, it is because he seems to me less bad than his fellows.   Do you understand ?'

'Yes, I know that Lewis deserves everyone's love,' said Jennie enthusiastically.   'And now, Lawrence, I don't dislike you quite so much.'

'What, have you disliked me ?' cried Lawrence sadly.

'I should think I had !' answered the girl.

Handsome Lawrence treated her with the most refined delicacy, and Morgan with the easy politeness of good society. It was nearly dark when they reached the cabin.

Greybeard seemed to think little of the danger his daughter had incurred, and showed no surprise at Lawrence's arrival ; but h's face reflected a strange anxiety when the buccaneer remarked :

'Yesterday, I had news from England.'

'Indeed !' cried the other, 'what about my lawsuit ?'

'Not finished yet, of course.   Here is a letter from your lawyer, who wants more money to carry it on with, equally of course.'

'As much as he wants,' said Greybeard ; 'if I have not enough I had rather pillage a town than the suit should be lost for want of money.'

The word 'lawsuit' sounded so odd in the mouth of a pirate, far away from civilization, that at the first opportunity Sir Lewis asked his uncle about it, who answered :

'The human heart is truly unfathomable.   This fellow, so indifferent to everything, who leaves his daughter in such perfect ignorance ; this man, who would not go out of his way to secure a fortune, would risk his life to gain a lawsuit, which has been going on for nearly thirty years.   And about what, do you think ? Whether he is really descended from the Duke of Buckingham, and has a right to bear the arms of their head, attainted under Henry VIII.'

Morgan was pleased to think that Jennie was of good family, though he hardly knew why.

The next morning, both adversaries, accompanied by the buccaneer chief and Greybeard, took their way to Mount Pithon.

———

CHAPTER XXVII.

THE DUEL COMES TO AN UNEXPECTED END.

DUELS in St. Domingo were at this time very frequent.   Those among the buccaneers came off without witnesses.   The adversaries were obliged to tell their comrades the day and place of meeting ; they then went out alone, and fought as they liked, at a long or short distance.   When one fell, which was the case nine times out of ten, a surgeon was sent by the buccaneers to examine the deceased, and if he found the ball had entered from the back or side, the shot was, according to the expression in use, 'imputed to malice'; then the victor was tied to a tree and his neck broken. Several buccaneers having been thus condemned and executed, the first governors ordered that no duel should take place without witnesses, but their successors generally remained passive, and let the duellists make their own arrangements.

When they reached the spot, Sir Lewis Morgan, with his usual gallantry, said:

'Sir, as you are more used to these affairs than I am, will you settle how we are to fight?'

'Sir Lewis,' answered Lawrence, as cool and indifferent now as in the ordinary occurrences of life, 'although we here stand to take each other's life, and I feel almost certain that it will be my fate to take yours, yet I cannot even at this moment repress the esteem I feel for your gallant conduct. You are the only really honourable man I have met these ten years.'

'Lawrence,' answered the Cornishman, 'yesterday I longed to ask you a question, but our mutual resolution not to speak of the subject prevented me. Will you listen to it now?'

'Certainly,' answered the other. 'A quarter of an hour more or less, when one of us stands on the brink of eternity, is of little consequence. But allow me to tell you, that should you be the conqueror, the thought of my death need cause you no compunction. You will have rid the world of one who has done far more harm than good in it, and is, moreover, tired of life. But what is your question?'

'Do you know Nativa?' asked Sir Lewis, with hesitation.

'You mean El Conde de Monterey's daughter?—yes, what then?'

'What then!' cried Morgan angrily, 'you have dared to vilify that lady, sir, and I love her.'

'My dear sir,' rejoined Lawrence, half in joke, half in earnest, 'I am glad you think you have some complaint against me. Still, were you the accepted lover of the young lady, my conduct towards her need not make you jealous, and I believe, moreover, that she will be grateful to you for killing me. Is there anything further that you wish to know?'

'Nothing; I await your decision.'

'Then let chance decide who is to fire first. The distance shall be fifty paces; but if the first shot misses, the one who fires second may come as close to his adversary as he chooses. In other respects, we will keep to the buccaneer conditions. By the bye, I must tell you, that if your piece flashes in the pan it counts as a shot, so that if you have any doubt about the loading of your piece, you had better look to it.'

'I answer for the loading,' said old Morgan, attending to his nephew's gun.

Lawrence counted fifty paces, and marked each extremity with a pistol on the ground.

'This quadruple piece shall decide which of us fires first.' He threw it in the air.

'Cross!' cried Morgan, who knew how Spanish money was marked.

Fortune was against him. 'It is for you to fire first,' he said quietly, and stood leaning on his gun, very pale, but eyeing his adversary with a proud, unflinching gaze. Life was very sweet to him, but he thought only of his separation from Nativa.

As for Captain Morgan, though stern and motionless as a statue, it was easy to see from his contracted brows, and the fierce fire in his eyes, what a storm of feelings was raging in his breast.

Greybeard looked on with the utmost indifference; all the interest to him lay in whether the shooting would be good.

When Lawrence reached his place he took aim without pity or anger, as if he aimed at a bull's-eye.

After a few seconds a sharp crack was heard, and a little smoke rose. Lawrence's rifle had missed fire.

'Señor,' he said, with a surprised but mocking air, 'you must be born under a lucky star! How very ridiculous I must appear after my boast a little while since. But this is the first time my hand has ever missed. I took aim at your forehead. Well, it is your turn to fire now.'

'Lewis!' cried old Morgan, coming close, 'think of Nativa! Be pitiless.'

The knight so little expected such a miracle, that at first he felt neither joy nor wonder; but Nativa's name acted as a spur. Almost unconsciously, he advanced towards his adversary, who stood motionless, with a smile upon his lips. But a soft voice suddenly sang out from the woods:

'Lewis, would you kill Lawrence, defenceless?'

Morgan started, and seemed to awake from a dream.

'I was a brute! Thanks, dear Jennie, you have saved me from committing a great crime.' He fired in the air.

'By all that is holy!' shouted Lawrence, with a sudden burst of anger, 'I won't accept my life as your gift! Load again and fire, or by all the furies of hell, I will blow my brains out.'

'Lawrence,' cried Lewis, 'our meeting was caused by my calling you a coward and a murderer. I retract my words, and here, in the presence of the admiral and Greybeard, I crave your pardon. What can you ask for more?'

At these words, spoken very gravely, Lawrence threw away his pistol and caught the speaker by the hand.

'Companero,' he cried, 'to you I owe the first good feeling I have experienced for the last ten years. I own there may be some few men worthy of being loved. I have always until now refused to have a partner, but will you be my mate?'

With the instinct of a pure, upright nature Morgan saw at once that Lawrence was sincere, yet this seemed so solemn an engagement to take that he hesitated.

'Lewis,' said his uncle, 'it is no reason because Lawrence and I don't hit it off that I should not do justice to his great qualities. Proud, passionate, revengeful as I know him to be, he is most honourable, and generous even to a fault; and if you accept his brotherhood, you need fear nothing from his faults, but may gain much from his skill, his valour, and experience.'

'Lawrence,' said the knight, 'although it is my ardent wish to carve out a career for myself, believe me it is not the belief that you could aid me much in doing so which induces me at this moment to accept your offer—it is because I feel drawn towards you because you have suffered much and still suffer. Here is my hand again and for ever.'

'Thanks, brother,' answered the handsome fellow, shaking the hand warmly; 'now there can never be between us quarrel, jealousy, or strife. Our past life only is our own, our future belongs to each other. But I beg as a favour that you will not question me on the past, and I will only add, as, coming so lately from Europe, old world notions probably still cling to you, that my birth is as noble as your own, however high that may be.'

They were all about to return to the cabin when they saw Allan come out of the wood, who looked delighted, and carried his gun in his hand.

'Whence do you come, Allan?' asked his master.

'From the brushwood yonder,' answered the man.

'And what made you hide yourself there?'

This question greatly embarrassed Allan, who coloured up to the eyes.

'Come, lad, I want an answer.'

'So much the worse,' answered Allan, 'for it will make you angry. But, if you must know, I went there to bring down Master Lawrence if he had hurt you.'

'Mate,' said Lawrence, 'your servant's answer proves to me how worthy you are of being loved. Here, friend,' turning to Allan, 'here is something as a reward for your affection to your master.'

'Oh, this is too good a fortune,' cried the servant, seizing eagerly the gold pieces the freebooter tossed towards him, 'what would you not have given me if I had killed you?—a treasure perhaps.'

'Mate,' observed Lawrence to Morgan, as they walked back

side by side, ' you will hear strange tales of me, but you must not believe more than half, though that is bad enough. I need noise and excitement to distract me and make me forget. In hazardous expeditions, in the strife of war, I am in my element: without these I should have long since committed suicide. Except yourself, there is but one person in the whole island whose presence is endurable to me, that is Wildflower. There is a purity and innocence in that girl that has a great charm for me.'

On reaching the log hut they found breakfast waiting for them. After that meal Lawrence asked Greybeard to lend him a horse, and he went off at once for Seogane.

'Mate,' he said, on taking leave of Sir Lewis, 'I have only twenty thousand crowns left from my last voyage, so I shall soon put to sea again ; I will let you know when I am going. In the meantime I would say, though I fear you will refuse, that if you need money, it will be doing me a pleasure if you dip into my bag. May we meet soon again.'

' Sir Lewis,' said Jennie, ' shall we go out and shoot in the woods ; and may Leathercap come with us ?'

Morgan did not look too well pleased with this arrangement; and Jennie perceiving it, went on to say :

' Oh, I had rather go with you alone, we understand each other so well, but we must be just ; without Leathercap I should be the most unhappy creature in the world.'

' What can you mean, Wildflower ? I don't understand,' said Morgan.

' It was Leathercap who saved your life, for, taking advantage of a moment when Lawrence was talking to me, he shook out the priming in his gun. It was not an accident that saved you ! That is the reason I begged you not to fire at Lawrence. You had been in no danger, and I could not leave you to commit a murder.'

This confession of artifice made Morgan's face flame with shame and vexation.

' Jennie,' said he, ' how could you do so ? to what dishonour you exposed me !'

At the severe tone, the savage girl hung her head, and silent tears coursed each other down her pale cheeks.

' Dear Jennie,' said Sir Lewis, much moved at her grief, ' pardon me a moment's anger.'

' Perhaps I was wrong to do what I did, but I would do the same thing again. How could I bear to see you killed ?' said Wildflower eagerly ; then in a sweetly entreating tone added she, the tears still glistening in her eyes, 'Sir Lewis, when you are vexed with me, I beg you not to scold me ; that tone makes me so unhappy. If you knew how I love you, you would be sorry you hurt me."

' I am very sorry, Jennie,' said the Cornish gentleman, much moved.

CHAPTER XXVIII.

A DAREDEVIL PROJECT.

DURING a month that he continued Greybeard's guest, our Englishman had not once heard from his comrade Handsome Lawrence.

Full of enthusiasm, the chevalier at first counted the days with feverish anxiety, which gradually calmed down, until at last he thought of going to sea almost with regret.

Wildflower had much to do with this change. He had remained so isolated hitherto in his solitary life that he could not be insensible to the charm of the tender intimacy which had sprung up between him and Jennie. Every day he beheld some new attraction in her lovely and loving nature which strengthened his affection for her.

Jennie had been so entirely neglected by her father as to have grown up in the most complete ignorance. Morgan ardently set himself to instruct her.

At first the girl showed great repugnance to learning.

'What do I care, Sir Lewis,' she said to her professor, 'for what is contained in books? Life is so simple. To trust in Heaven, to love good and avoid evil. What is there in your books as beautiful as these forests? Come, let us leave this tiresome reading. The weather is delicious, the birds are singing joyfully. Take your gun and come away.'

'Jennie,' said her tutor, 'would you not be glad when I was away to be able to write to me, and to make out my letters?'

'Oh, Señor Luis, I never thought of that! You are right! Why did you not tell me that sooner? I should have learnt so quickly!'

From that time Wildflower set assiduously to work, and in a fortnight could read tolerably well.

One evening, on their return from a ramble, they found a stranger at table, who brought a letter from Lawrence.

'Mate,' wrote he, 'thanks to my evil genius, which made me win, I have taken longer than I expected to get rid of my crowns. But yesterday the dice robbed me of my last diamond and my last doubloons. Come directly, for I am in the vein to fight, and shall sail against the Spaniards at once. I shall expect you to-morrow.'

The contents of this letter chagrined Morgan not a little, and poor Jennie turned pale and almost fainted.

'Sir Lewis,' she cried, 'why should you go? You do not care for riches. You are not like other men : you don't care for gambling, nor luxury, nor costly wines. Have you not here splendid forests, lovely flowers, a rifle that can kill a buffalo at two hundred paces, and a sister who loves you? And besides, have you not elbow room and freedom? Why coop yourself up in a ship and run immense risks to gain wealth which you do not need? Oh, stay with me, I will never vex you; I will do all you wish, and obey you in everything. Oh, I shall be so wretched if you leave me!'

Morgan, really moved, knew not what to answer, when Greybeard interposed.

'My child, don't make yourself so unhappy. Though you are fond of Sir Lewis now, you will soon meet with some one else you will like just as well. Still, if Morgan's nephew likes to remain, he is quite welcome to do so. Let everyone do as he likes, it is all the same to me.'

Her father's words made a strange impression on Jennie, who looked confused and remained silent.

The next morning at daybreak the young gentleman and Allan set out. Wildflower accompanied them through the forest. She was silent and pensive. As for our hero, he tried in vain to persuade himself that he parted with her without a pang. He felt for this untaught child of nature a deep fraternal affection.

'Sir Lewis,' said she, 'if you are killed I could never be happy again, so if you really love me, be not rash; remember you have both of us to save.'

Jennie held out her hand, and with a tender smile left him.

Morgan, almost vexed at her calmness, watched her retreating figure until it was lost among the trees, but Jennie did not once turn to look at him.

Four days later the knight accompanied Lawrence and his servant to Tortoise Island, where the former was to man his vessel.

The following day, as Lawrence was walking along the coast, a sailor said, 'Sir, I am entrusted with a secret and important commission to you; will you tell me where I can meet you alone?'

'Come on the shore, where we shall not be interrupted,' answered Lawrence. 'Now who are you, and what do you want?'

'Captain,' said the sailor, 'I have risked my life many times to get to you; promise that you will not betray me.'

'When was Lawrence ever taken for a traitor?' cried the freebooter angrily. 'I don't know what should keep me from knocking you down, knave!'

'Oh, captain, I entreat your pardon if I said anything to offend you, but I am a poor devil whom you will despise so much when I tell you who I am that I tried to make conditions.'

'Well, as you did not intend any insult, speak out. I promise not to betray you.'

'Captain, I am Lightfoot,' faltered the sailor.

'Oh, the traitor who went over to the Spaniards, and upon whose head a price was put? What do you want with me?'

'Sir, I was sent from Grenada to bring you a letter and take back your answer.'

'A Spanish letter for a corsair?'

'Don't be angry, captain, it's from a lady.'

Lawrence smiled. 'Oh, if it is from a lady, that may alter matters; and pray how much did the lady give you, to bribe you thus to risk your life?'

'Oh, a sum that only a king or a Captain Lawrence could have given.'

'Come,' said Lawrence with a sneer, 'another fool, I suppose, fancies herself in love with the rover.'

He broke open the letter, and, having read it, tore it into pieces and threw to the winds.

'Well, captain inquired the seaman, 'is there no answer?'

'You may tell the lady who sent you that Captain Lawrence forgets the names of his flames, and that the signature to the end of the letter awoke no remembrance. Now, Lightfoot, you will leave instantly. I promised not to betray you, but I did not promise not to blow your brains out if you stay to spy out our movements. You have not an hour to live.'

'Captain, I swear by all that is sacred that my mission this time has nothing to do with politics—but——'

'But what? bear you another letter? That would be charming; don't lie, come, tell me the truth. Ob, this is droll,' proceeded Lawrence, laughing; 'and for whom is the other letter?'

'Well, captain, I don't know—I——'

'Take care, rogue, I am not accustomed to order or question twice. Let us see the missive.'

The spy knew the speaker well enough to be sure that in obedience lay his only safety, so he gave him the letter.

'Is it possible? To the Caballero Luis Morgan! Oh, then, my disdain has borne fruits! Piqued at my conduct, you forget yourself and your duties! I ought to be proud of my work! Poor young fellow,' he continued musingly, 'with his loyalty and his love, how can he resist Nativa's dangerous seductions? I think I see him already broken-hearted, blaspheming, hating men, breathing vengeance, such as I was myself ten years ago. Perhaps it would be better to destroy the letter, but Nativa would soon find other means to enthral her victim. What a bold, daring spirit she has! Sometimes I.fancy I may have been mistaken in her, and ask myself whether I have not found that devoted love that I dreamt of in my youth. But I must be mad to dream of such absurdities. Is there in the world one woman capable of real, deep, true feeling? A thousand times, no!

Women have a lively imagination, a little sensibility, but no heart. I suppose she took me for a hero out of one of her romances; that is the only explanation of her conduct.'

'How do you intend to get away?' Lawrence asked the spy.

'Easily enough, captain; I have a boat hidden under the rocks, and a Spanish vessel is waiting for me in the offing.'

'Well, I shall go with you and see you off. As for the second letter, I promise to deliver it safely.'

'But, captain, I was to take the gentleman back with me.'

'The plague!' cried Lawrence; adding with a sneer, 'Nativa does nothing by halves. Well, Lightfoot, you will tell the lady that you delivered the letter safely, that the gentleman seemed delighted, and was about to embark with you, when you were recognised and obliged to fly.'

'I will obey you, captain.'

'Now a last word, Lightfoot. If you don't carry out my instructions to the letter—and I am sure sooner or later to know the facts—I will find you out even if I have to seek you in the very heart of Spain, and, by my honour, you shall die by slow tortures.'

An hour later, having seen the spy embark, the captain returned to the inn where Morgan waited.

'Mate,' he said, 'here's a letter for you.'

'A letter for me!' cried the Englishman with emotion, for he thought Wildflower might have sent it.

Scarcely had he run his eyes over the page than he turned red and then pale.

'Oh, mate,' he cried joyfully, 'if you knew how happy I am!'

'So much the better,' said Lawrence quietly; 'happiness is so rare.'

Twenty times Morgan was on the point of confiding his love secret to Lawrence, but delicacy towards Nativa prevented him.

'Mate,' said Lawrence, when night came, 'will you go with me to the "Weighed Anchor"? I must complete our crew.'

'Friend,' answered the other, with hesitation, 'I have something unpleasant to tell you. I cannot embark with you.'

'You are mad, or you are joking.'

'No, Lawrence, I am serious. I know that you have a right to be angry and reproach me. I am wrong. But there are solemn hours in life when the happiness or unhappiness of a whole existence is decided. Such an hour has just struck for me. I no longer belong to myself.'

'Well,' answered his friend, with a shade of pity, 'I understand: a love affair—some fancy.'

'Speaking so, mate,' observed the knight, 'is profanation.'

'Oh, of course! Is not the queen of our hearts for the time the most perfect creature in the world? Don't we fancy we alone have the gift of finding out all her perfections, her superhuman virtue, her enchanting grace, her changeless faith! Really, Sir Lewis, I fancied you stronger nerved than this! Why, because you have met with one of those fallen creatures which the Crown so kindly sends us out to help people our solitudes, you will lose such a capital chance of making a fortune, and be faithless to your word!'

'Oh, Lawrence, how much you are mistaken! The one I love is the most divine creature the sun ever shone upon.'

'Oh, yes; one of the perfections I spoke of. We all think we have found her.'

'The one I love is not in St. Domingo.'

'A young lady you were engaged to, perhaps, in England, and who has doubtless already found consolation in another lover. Well, mate, I cannot see why that should prevent your embarking with me, and make you break your word.'

'Listen, Lawrence. Will you promise me secrecy?'

'Between brothers that is always understood.'

'The lady I love with all my soul is Spanish.'

'It shows your good taste: Spanish girls are charming. And in what part of the world does the señorita of your soul live?'

'At Grenada, mate.'

'The deuce! Do you know that Grenada is one of the best fortified towns in the New World; and if you attempted to go there and were discovered—which would be sure to happen, for you don't speak a word of Spanish—you would be hung up in the market-place.'

'Oh, Lawrence, could such considerations stop a brave man like you?'

'Oh, that is another thing, for I possess advantages that you do not. Where you would be ignominiously hung, I should come out with flying colours. But to the point. You don't wish to embark, and you want to go to Grenada.'

'Yes, Lawrence.'

'Well, how do you think of proceeding? It would be quite useless to try and get a vessel at St. Domingo: our laws forbid it. Your best way is to leave the island with me, and trust to chance to favour your wishes.'

'My love is so great that I fear no obstacles.'

'Well, then, do you decide to embark with me?'

'Yes, Lawrence, I am ready.'

'Good! Time presses; let us hasten away.'

The public-house called the 'Weighed Anchor' was a wooden hut containing only one large room, which might hold more than two hundred people.

Lawrence's arrival caused some sensation, for his luxurious and aristocratic habits made him a rare visitor there. His appearance was always the forerunner of some fresh expedition. He was accepted by the freebooters as a man above them, and they tolerated an arrogance in him which they would have borne from no one else.

Lawrence's bravery was so uncommon, his success beyond all probability, and he showed such extraordinary generosity and munificence that the freebooters felt an almost superstitious respect for him. One captain alone, Van Horn, before whom everyone trembled, had dared to blame his conduct, and the next day he was killed in a duel by Lawrence.

Hardly had the handsome pirate passed the threshold, than ne was surrounded by a crowd anxious to see him near.

'Back, lads!' he said; 'a little less noise, I beg. I have something to say.'

There was at once profound silence, and the chief began :

'Brothers of the Coast! I come to free those who had engaged to join my next expedition. What, complaints and regrets? Listen to me without interrupting me. My friends, I want to take a little pleasure ; therefore my expedition will not be what it ought. You know I never deceive any one ; I make this declaration that those who desire to follow me may know what risks they run.'

When Lawrence said he wanted to amuse himself, it meant that he was bent on one of those extraordinary strokes of audacity and temerity which he alone attempted. The most intrepid vied who should follow him ; he had only the difficulty of choosing volunteers.

'My lads,' he continued, 'I have two words to add : let those who think of going with me now, make up their minds to something very tough. Above all, let them not forget that I never answer questions, and hate curiosity and chatterers. Come, who will follow me ?'

A hundred and fifty voices answered, 'I, sir ! I !'

'Mate,' Lawrence whispered to Morgan, 'on further consideration, I think you will also decide on accompanying. Keep it dark. My next expedition is to take Grenada by storm.'

'Lawrence,' cried the Englishman, with an indescribable expression of gratitude, ' I accept your generous help ! By my forefather's honoured memory I swear from this day forward to be your devoted friend.'

'Pooh ! what need is there for gratitude?' answered Lawrence, laughing. 'Don't think it is to help your love affairs. I am going to take Grenada to amuse myself.'

In a quarter of an hour later Lawrence had closed the list of those who voluntarily enrolled themselves in this service ; he had chosen ninety out of those that had offered, the cream of the corsairs.

CHAPTER XXIX.

THE UNSOUGHT PASSENGER.

AN hour after, Lawrence went on board a long boat with twenty sweeps, and having consulted the state of the wind, and given orders, he commanded them to put to sea, and the long, rakish clipper shot over the tops of the waves like an arrow. Lawrence, seated at the stern, steered the vessel. He looked thoughtful.

'So the señorita wishes to see me again? Her wishes shall be granted if only I can manage to overtake Lightfoot. That is of the highest importance, as no one could better give me the information I need. Strike out boldly with your oars, friends; fifty piasters to the first who sees the vessel we hunt!'

Lawrence, whose sagacity equalled his skill in navigation, had calculated both the start of the spy, and also what direction he had probably taken.

"The Spanish cutter which waited for him could not dare to approach nearer than eighteen miles, and as the spy is alone, and wind and tide are against him, he cannot escape me."

For two hours Lawrence continued silently absorbed in conning the horizon. It was a magnificent night, and a bright moon helped his search.

At length the buccaneer cried out joyfully:

'Ho, my lads! are you asleep or indifferent about the fifty dollars, that you have not yet sighted the vessel that lies to port? Her sails stand out clear against the blue sky; see!'

Lawrence was noted for his strong sight. The rest could scarcely discern the vessel. The Spanish cutter carried only five men, and made no resistance to the freebooters boarding her. The first person that Lawrence perceived when he jumped on board was Lightfoot.

The wretched man, as pale as death, trembled in every limb.

'Come with us without a word," said Lawrence to him; 'if you serve me faithfully, no harm shall befall you; if you attempt to deceive me I will torture you to death!'

Lightfoot followed without a word. When he had placed him beside him in the boat, Lawrence said, 'You have been away so long, there is no fear of your being recognised by your old comrades. I shall call you Little John, and represent you as a deserter from a man-of-war. Try not to commit any act of imprudence.'

The first rays of the sun gilded the horizon when the long pirogue reached land. Lawrence dismissed his rovers, only saying, 'My friends, it is all right. We sail to-night, assured of success to our expedition.'

The freebooters, who generally expected a full explanation from their chiefs, were satisfied with these words.

When he got to the house which he inhabited alone, Lawrence said to Lightfoot, 'Now that we have time, tell me exactly what instructions you received from the lady about those letters. I cannot understand how, after the letter that she wrote to me, she could have desired you to bring away with you Señor Luis de Morgan. You must have lied.'

'No, indeed, Señor Capitano! I followed my instructions to the letter. The señorita told me expressly to see you first; and it was only in case you received her letter with disdain that I was to deliver the other to Señor de Morgan. I have faithfully executed her orders.'

'Egad!' muttered Lawrence, 'I can guess all now. My disdain has forced the Spanish girl to extremities: she seeks an avenger. Strange that she should have fixed upon my own mate; but I rely on Morgan's honour. What fun it will be to prove to him Nativa's treachery! This interview will be most interesting. Well, anything for distraction. I strive against past griefs, and steel my heart to every kind feeling and generous thought, and try to persuade myself that I despise mankind; still I suffer. When I awake from the excitement of debauchery or war, I cannot stifle regret for the life I lead. I sometimes ask myself whether rest would not be preferable to this stirring, adventurous life ; and to think that I, whose ambition is so vast as to eclipse that of other men, that I, born on the steps of a throne, cannot overcome a feeling of love for Wildflower, that simple child whose heart the first fool may gain and not know the treasure he possesses!'

Rousing himself from these thoughts, he inquired of the spy:
' How long have you been in Grenada?'
' Three years.'
' Then you know it perfectly?'
' Rather.'
' How many inhabitants are there ?'
' Twelve thousand, captain—there or thereabouts.'
' And the garrison ?'
' Six hundred regular troops and some native soldiers.'
Lawrence looked fixedly on the spy, and said, throwing himself dressed on a bed :
' I forbid you, and your safety requires, that you should not leave this room or show yourself to anyone. If, during my sleep, you have a fancy to shoot me, my pistols are lying on the table'
A few minutes afterwards Lawrence was fast asleep.
When a band of adventurers had determined on any enterprise, the person who supplied the vessel had a right to his share of all prizes, which was fixed beforehand, besides which the

captured guns were his by right. A society of speculators, mostly Jews, was formed on Tortoise Island to cull a profit out of the daring exploits of the rovers.

Lawrence's reputation stood so high in the formidable band of which Morgan was chief, that the Jews were very obsequious to him and let him have their best vessels.

Four days after Lawrence had announced his intentions at the log-house, a frigate, with sixteen guns on board, was ready for him in the offing.

The morning that Lawrence embarked a large crowd followed him to the jetty. Just as he and Morgan were jumping into the boat a murmur arose.

How fortunate Handsome Larry is! He will be sure to succeed now! Here is Wildflower come to embark with him! What good luck!'

'You here, Jennie!' exclaimed Morgan, with as much emotion as wonder.

'What!' rejoined the girl with tender reproach. 'Did you not expect me? Should I have left you so gaily if I had not hoped to see you again soon? You do not love me, then.'

'Yes, Wildflower, I love you as tenderly as a sister, and that is the reason I am grieved that you should share our dangers.'

'Come, let us go on board!' cried the imperious Lawrence.

Jennie leaped lightly into the boat. Morgan followed.

'Is this apparition in answer to my wishes?' wondered Lawrence; 'or is it a new grief that Heaven has in store for me? What matters? Nativa, Morgan and Wildflower together! Something amusing must come of it, happen what may.'

CHAPTER XXX.

THE GUILELESS MAIDEN.

A WEEK had passed since the expedition had left Tortoise Island. The time had passed most rapidly to Morgan. Every day, every hour, made him more attached to Jennie, for he perpetually discovered something new in her to love or admire.

One great advantage he gained by being mate to Lawrence, that he could live apart from the other buccaneers. Generally all lived together, and no distinction was made, except obedience, and a larger share of booty, between the lowest sailor and the captain. But the proud and despotic Lawrence had never chosen to give in to this custom. He insisted upon being treated as a master, and his discipline was as severe as that on board the king's ships. Magnificently installed in the poop cabin, he admitted no one to his table but Morgan and Jennie.

Since they had been at sea, two Spanish vessels hove in sight, but each time Lawrence commanded keeping on their course and not giving chase. This indifference for booty almost within their grasp did not displease the freebooters, as it proved that their commander aimed at something very important.

One evening the chief, his mate, and Wildflower sat on the quarter-deck, apparently watching the brilliant sunset, but not one heeded the splendid spectacle; they were too busy with their own thoughts. On Lawrence's face there was an expression of soft melancholy, very unusual to him.

'Friend,' he said to Morgan, 'the elements themselves conspire to favour your love. Never, since I have known these seas, has there been such a continuance of fair winds. In ten days more, if all goes well, you will be with your lady love.'

Although Lawrence's words ought to have pleased him, Morgan felt uneasy, while Jennie turned pale and put her hand to her heart.

'What do you say, Lawrence?' then stopping suddenly she smiled and added, 'Oh, it is only to frighten me that you speak thus.'

'Frighten you, Jennie,' said the corsair sadly, 'how can the love of the English knight affect you? If you are his friend, you should rejoice at his happiness.'

'What, is it, then, true, that you love some one?' cried Jennie, sobbing; 'I thought you so good, so noble! oh, it is impossible.' Overcome by her emotion, Wildflower cried: 'I don't know what is the matter with me, I am suffocating! Have I been dreaming?'

Little as he knew of love, Lewis could not but guess the cause of Jennie's emotion, which made his own heart beat violently. Embarrassed, and not knowing what to answer, Morgan wished to change the conversation. Wildflower's eagerness did not give him time.

'Oh, I remember now,' she said, 'Lawrence told us that, if fair weather lasted, you would soon see your beloved. You have then another friend besides me? Is she pretty?—is she young? why did you never tell me about her?'

'I did not think,' the Englishman answered with embarrassment, 'that you could be interested about a lady you had never seen.'

'What does it matter, Sir Lewis, if she loves you? I must be interested in her, I wish to try and please her. Is she kind?'

'As kind as you are, sister.'

'How strange it is! My first thought was that she was wicked; that I should hate her. I cannot think what is the matter with me to-day; I feel quite dizzy, I tremble so much.'

'Wildflower,' said Lawrence, gently taking her hand, 'courage; you will feel better to-morrow. You had better go to your cabin and try to rest.'

'Thanks, Lawrence, for your kindness. You are very good, and I like you much better than I used.'

At these words Lawrence smiled, and Morgan thought he saw a gleam of joy pass over his face.

When Jennie had left them, Lawrence after a long silence said gravely :—

'Mate, I wish to come to an explanation with you. I entreated you never to revert to my past life, and you have with great delicacy refrained from doing so. I now briefly tell you that my earnest, impassioned youth was blasted by one of those storms of feeling that morally wreck a man. Too proud to bend my head to the tempest, too impatient to wait for the soothing influence of time, and hopeless of all consolation, I rushed into adventures that were not destined for me, and I have pursued excitement as an opiate to drown all feeling. Heartily despising the whole human race, and believing I had wrongs to avenge, I resolved to make all yield to my will or even caprice. Gold or blood never stopped me in my career, I have been pitiless. Now, whether it be remorse or fatigue, I long to change my life; to begin a better, a nobler existence. A spirit of love, of hope beams upon me, and its wings flutter softly over me. I dare say you are astonished at words so contrary to all you know of me; I wonder at myself, and could fancy I was in a dream. The sweet spirit that wrought this change in me was Wildflower. Thanks to my audacity, prodigality, and reputed insensibility, I have never yet met with a woman who disdained my advances, but so incredulous am I of their fidelity that I have never loved. Well, mate, I have now met with one whom I could love—Wildflower. I have faith in her.'

'Perhaps you are right,' answered Morgan dryly, 'but what have I to do with that?'

'Your ill-humour, Lewis, proves the contrary; it is something to you. To me it is plain that Jennie prefers you, but with time and perseverance, now that she knows your love for Nativa, I believe that I shall be able to replace you in her affection. You see I speak frankly. I desire your esteem; I don't wish that later you should be able to accuse me of abusing your friendship; therefore, from this time forth, I warn you I shall use every effort to win her.'

During the remainder of the voyage, Wildflower remained sad and thoughtful; she passed the greater part of the time in her cabin, and avoided Morgan, turning pale at his sight.

At first annoyed, then grieved, that she should show such coldness towards him, he determined to seek an explanation.

On the seventeenth day the adventurers reached the mouth of the Nicaragua river, where at Lawrence's command they anchored. Towards evening he assembled the crew on the quarter-deck and addressed them thus :—

'My friends, the time has come when I ought to tell you of my project. If its greatness astonishes you, don't forget that I warned you that you were engaging in something more than ordinary. The Spanish seaports, continually threatened by our attacks, have formidable means of defence, and to attack them with success requires larger forces than in the days of old. Our enemies' merchantmen are so frightened at us that they will not leave port unless convoyed by a fleet of men-of-war. Never has it been so difficult for buccaneers to gain their livelihood. Well, friends, I wish by one stroke to make up for lost time. I wish in one day to make you amends for a year's toil, in one hour make you all rich !'

At these words, in a burst of enthusiasm that seemed electric, the crew cried out, 'Long live Lawrence ! Long live our noble captain !'

'Friends,' continued the buccaneer in a thrilling voice, 'my intention is to take possession of the town of Grenada.'

Though the moment for stating his project was admirably timed, yet so little did Lawrence's companions guess his idea that a dead silence followed their noisy applause.

'Friends,' proceeded their chief, 'your valour even exceeds my expectations. I thought that not yet acquainted with the precautions which render our success undoubted, its temerity might excite murmurs among you. By your resolute demeanours, I find I have misjudged you. Friends, five days hence you will be bending under the weight of plunder, the deck of our frigate will be covered with gold. We shall then set sail for Jamaica, the land of good liquor and pretty girls. Our entry will be a triumph, our abode there enjoyment without end. Long live the freebooters of St. Domingo !'

The confidence shown by their chief, the seducing picture of the pleasures in store for them, the thought of the riches they would acquire, all conspired to drown the apprehensions of the crew, and rekindle their enthusiasm. Ardour and impatience reigned on board the corsair.

The next morning they entered the river, and the difficulty now was to ascend it without being discovered.

Lightfoot, who knew the locality well, acted as pilot. The bold chief, as prudent as he was daring, had the frigate disguised as a merchantman. The guns were hauled in and the ports closed, while a Spanish flag floated perfidiously from the mast A few top-men were alone visible in the rigging. At midday they reached their destination.

Lawrence caused the vessel to be hidden among the large trees that bordered the river ; vegetation at this part was so luxuriant there was little fear of her being discovered.

The expedition was to set out at ten at night, so as to reach the town about midnight, when the inhabitants were plunged in their first sleep.

Several times during that day Jennie seemed to wish to approach Morgan, but it was only near sunset that she took courage and called the young gentleman to sit beside her.

The eagerness with which he obeyed, and the colour that mounted in his face, showed that this request both troubled and pleased him.

' What do you wish, sister ?' he asked.

' It is strange,' said the girl musing, 'how your voice troubles me, yet I should like to hear it always.'   She stopped a moment, then looking at Morgan with eyes filling with tears, she went on —' Sir Lewis, though we always beat the Spaniards, yet they are brave people and fight well.   Who knows whether you may not be killed at the assault to-night ?'

' I would it may be so, Jennie,' murmured he sadly.

' What are you saying ?' she cried, seizing the young man's hand ; ' it might bring you misfortune. Why should you hope to die ? You are young, handsome, good ; no one can know you without envying you.   Your life must be happy.'

' No one can know me without envying me ?' repeated Morgan bitterly ; ' and for the last week you have avoided me without disguising your dislike.'

' It was to ask pardon for my behaviour that I called you Oh, you know too well I could never dislike you.'

' How could I otherwise account for your conduct ?'

' I know, caballero ! When you are away I am sad.   I see you, I hear you as if in a dream, and then I love you so well that I could give my life to spare you a grief ! When you are near, my heart seems crushed, tears come in my eyes.   I am so wretched.   I fancy that you laugh at my ignorance ; that I seem to you stupid, foolish ; that you despise me ; and after all perhaps you are right,' continued Wildflower, more and more moved.   ' I have never quitted our woods ; I am so unlike the fine ladies where you were brought up.'

The poor girl stopped ; then in a supplicating tone added :—

' Forgive me, Sir Lewis, I entreat you.   I do not know what is the matter with me, perhaps a sudden illness ; it came on the night we all three talked together, and I have prayed earnestly. However, the most important thing is that you should forgive me.   Oh, if you were killed to-night and died thinking that I did not love you, would be far worse to me than death.   You do forgive me, Lewis ?'

'Yes, I forgive you, dear Jennie,' replied Morgan ; 'that is, I love you.'

'But not as well as the Spanish lady ?' returned she, a dark light shining in her eyes.

'Yes, Jennie, as much as I love her. All my friendship is yours—all my love hers.'

This answer made a strong impression on Wildflower.

'Are there then two ways of loving ? Oh, how I abhor my ignorance ! I ought no doubt be pleased to hear you say that you love me like a sister, but it makes me so unhappy ! Leave me ! I love you very much ; still it makes me wretched to see you.'

Morgan left without answering ; to offer trite consolations to that poor suffering heart would be almost profanation.

'Oh, how I long to see this beautiful Spanish lady !' murmured Wildflower, looking after Morgan.

When the hour for landing was close at hand, Lawrence begged Morgan to go with him into his cabin.

'Comrade,' he said, 'I cannot hide from myself that I am on the eve of committing a great imprudence. Nevertheless I am persuaded that the rashness of our attack renders its success more probable. It is scarcely possible that the Spaniards can dream of a town being attacked by buccaneers that is ninety miles from the sea. I count much on the superstitious terror that our arrival will cause. Still, as we must neglect nothing, I will tell you my plan. We will land in four large boats, each containing twenty men ; ten will stay on board to take care of the vessel. Our first point for making, if we succeed in the first moment of surprise in pillaging the town, will be the large square before the church. Our boats, in charge of two men each, will be lying in the kind of canal close to the deserted quarter of Santa Eugracia, and in case the Spaniards repulse us, they will afford us an easy means of escape. Thanks to Lightfoot's chart, we are all thoroughly acquainted with the localities. And now, mate, a last word, and to me the most important. I have great confidence in your personal courage and coolness in danger ; your eye I know is just, your hand prompt ; but what I want to know is whether I can count on your obedience. From want of unity in command, failures generally arise. Lewis, in the name of your ancestor the greatest of buccaneers, and of the men I command, I require from you a promise of obedience, of passively executing my orders, though you may not be able at the moment to comprehend their intention. On your passive obedience depends in a great measure our success to-night. Sure of being obeyed, I shall know how to command What is your answer ?'

'I answer, mate,' said Morgan, 'that on my word as a gentleman, I engage to obey you blindfold.'

'That is well, dear Lewis. Now I am easy. Grenada is ours !'

CHAPTER XXXI.

THE WOMAN SCORNED.

WHEN he left Morgan, Lawrence knocked at Wildflower's cabin door. The girl was half-reclining on her hammock, so much engrossed in thought she did not hear the knock. Lawrence opened the door, and entered. The buccaneer could not, as said, have been dead to all feeling, for the soft melancholy of the gentle girl had a strong effect on him ; he gazed at her for a few moments in silence.

'Wildflower,' he murmured softly.

'Who is there ?' cried Jennie. 'Oh, you, Lawrence ; what do you want ? is it time to go ?'

'No, Jennie, not quite yet ! some time since I heard you, in case of any fatal accident, take a solemn farewell of Morgan ; and as I also may fall in the fight, I come to see you before we leave.'

This answer caused a certain surprise to the hearer.

'Do you love me, then, Lawrence ?'

'Yes, Jennie, I do.'

'As a brother, or as one loves besides ?'

'As a lover,' said Lawrence passionately.

'A lover !' repeated Jennie slowly, 'and what difference is there between a brother's and a lover's love, Lawrence ?'

At this question, asked in a tone of innocent curiosity, Lawrence hesitated. This man, foremost in the fight, whose very look governed his men, who had turned in disdain from the loveliest, noblest, and most wealthy woman, stood now abashed before a simple child.

'You do not answer ! you also make game of my ignorance, Lawrence,' sighed she.

'I am afraid, lass.'

'Afraid! You, Handsome Lawrence ?—of what are you afraid ?'

'I am afraid, Wildflower, of snatching from your eyes their veil of innocence, and showing you what life really is.'

'I don't understand you.'

'Well, she must know it sooner or later,' reasoned the buccaneer, as if making a compromise with himself. 'You ask me, Jennie, what is the difference between a lover's and a brother's love ?

'Brotherly affection is calm and tranquil, like a river slowly meandering through a smiling valley ; a lover's affection is as wild and resistless as the torrent dashing from the hills, and carrying all things along in its impetuous course. A sister separated from her brother is not unhappy ; she easily consoles herself for his absence, and is pleased to see him again ; that is all. A brother is often tired of his sister's company ; if she needs his help he gives it her willingly ; it is his duty, but there is no warmth, no enthusiasm in his devotion.'

'No more, no more, Lawrence, I cannot bear it ! What, is this the cold, indifferent, careless feeling Sir Lewis Morgan entertains for me when he is near me ; does he wish to be somewhere else ? When he speaks to me, is it with his lips only, not his heart ? Oh, Lawrence, you deceive me ! '

'Wildflower, I have described brotherly affection as my experience teaches is in most instances correct.'

'And the love of a lover—can you tell me what that is like, Lawrence ? '

'Yes, sweet Wildflower, for I feel it now for thee ! '

The buccaneer drew near Jennie, and sitting down beside her, took one of her hands in his, and pursued :—

'My darling, love is a feeling unlike every other ; when it once gains possession of the heart everything seems changed ; nature, the world itself, for you contains only the object of your affection. A smile from the lips you love makes you so happy that you scarcely believe there is any unhappiness in life. Again, an indifferent word, a frown from the one you love makes you miserable. The sun no longer shines, your existence is dark, cheerless, and sad ; a gloom imposed on all creatures between the cradle and the grave. You weep ? '

'Oh, this is true !' murmured Jennie.

'But,' continued Lawrence, ' as the sunshine dispels the clouds, and makes us forget the storm, so the first kind word, or slightest favour from the beloved one, changes darkness into light. You accuse yourself of injustice ; you try to tolerate your fault.'

'It is true ; one is often carried away wrongly by one's feelings.'

'Again,' continued Lawrence, ' love differs from friendship in that any sacrifice to the beloved one is the greatest happiness ; the greater the offering the greater the delight. As for the joys of love, Jennie, they are the greatest that human nature is capable of feeling ; no tongue could describe them ; it raises us above humanity, and gives a bliss of which angels alone are worthy.'

Lawrence spoke earnestly and feelingly, and as he concluded, he bent forward and encircled her slender waist.

'Let me go, Lawrence, let me go !' she cried ; ' why do you look at me so earnestly ? '

'Wildflower,' said Lawrence, drawing the poor girl forcibly to him, and pressing her to his heart, 'I feel for you the passion I have described. If you will love me, I, Lawrence, will be your slave. I will bend my pride to your will; I will pass my life at your feet. My courage shall gain for you all your wishes, be they ever so unreasonable. I will submit even to your caprices. Love me, and I will be all you wish—your property, your slave.'

Lawrence looked mournfully at the wild beauty, who strove to free herself.

'Oh, how I love you!' he murmured, as he pressed his lips fervently on her white forehead.

Wildflower shrank back at his kiss, and with the strength of despair extricated herself from his grasp, and cried out :—

'Help! Sir Lewis, help!'

Her resistance had a sudden effect on Lawrence, who turned pale, and a sad smile passed over his face.

'It is useless, Jennie, to call my mate. You are in no danger from me, and his presence might spur me on to commit a crime. I am calm now. Why should I be angry with you, dear child? You do not love me, therefore you repulse me; nothing more simple. It is my fate to suffer! Fare thee well, sweetest Jennie!'

As soon as Wildflower was alone, she locked her stateroom door, and throwing herself in the hammock, in a flood of tears, she ejaculated :—

'Now I imagine what love is! never, oh never, can I bear the thought that Lewis loves me only like a sister.'

After long weeping, Jennie arose, put on her half-masculine buccaneer costume, and took her rifle. 'May a bullet slay me this night! I want to die, but not before I have seen the beautiful Spaniard whom Lewis loves.'

She dried her tears and went on deck.

Morgan was about to leave in a boat. Jennie followed him close.

The freebooters, screened by the large trees, gained the town without incurring any danger of being discovered. Each was armed with one of those formidable guns so deadly in a familiar hand, a pair of loaded pistols, and a heavy cutlass.

'Friends,' said the leader, 'in two hours you will bring back those large bags you have provided yourselves with full of gold. What is of the utmost importance is your letting no enemy give the alarm. Gag and bind submissive prisoners, kill without pity those that resist! Above all, make no use of your firearms except in the last extremity in the general assault. Your cut-lasses will do the work. I go to facilitate your entrance into the town. Before a quarter of an hour I shall be back. If, as is very improbable, anything should happen to me, my mate, Sir Lewis Morgan, kinsman of him who took Panama at greater odds, will replace me, and lead you on to victory !'

In company with one of the bravest and most expert of the band, he went to the gate of the town.

Soon ' Who goes there ?' was challenged by a sentinel.

'Amigo,' answered Lawrence, in pure Castilian.

'Who are you, and whence do you come ?'

'We are fishermen returned from fishing.'

'Pass !' said the Spanish soldier.

Lawrence and his companion walked quietly on till they were close to the sentinel, when the captain threw himself like a tiger on the man ; a flash like lightning passed, and the soldier lay pierced to the heart.   The pirate continued his way.

Spain possesses many brave men but few good soldiers ; the love of indolence and horror of restraint and discipline will prevent Spaniards ever becoming a truly military nation.

Lawrence well knew the character and habits of the people he came to attack.   He was therefore not surprised to find the ten men who were on guard fast asleep, trusting to the very sentinel slain by the captain's hand.

He then returned to his men, who instantly advanced silently in columns.   The soldiers on guard were gagged and bound, and the freebooters entered the town.

When they reached the square before the church, the troops separated, each party to work on a different path.   The spy had informed them beforehand of the richest churches and the houses of the principal merchants.

Morgan was in strange perplexity, yet he felt a wild delight at the thought that he should so soon see Nativa.   He tried to persuade himself that this was only legitimate warfare, that the Spaniards had a hundred times made a descent on the English colonies, burning and destroying everything.   He hoped Nativa might only consider it as a proof of his love, and the only means he had of approaching her.

The band was not idle.   One of them knocked at the door of the church under pretext of wanting the priest for a dying man ; this was so common an occurrence that the sacristan opened the door without suspicion ; he was immediately gagged and bound.

A light burning before the altar showed the treasures that shone within their grasp.

'Mate,' said Morgan to his friend, 'our companions have several hours' work before them.   My presence here is not necessary.   Our guide told me the house where Nativa lives ; it is close by.   I will go thither.'

'Stop !' said the captain coldly, ' on the contrary, I want you here, as I am going to quit this spot.'

'But consider, Lawrence, at any moment we may be discovered, and forced to beat a precipitate retreat. You understand, I should be in despair to have to leave without seeing Nativa.'

'Lewis, I don't like to have to repeat my orders, and I hate discussions. You promised on your honour to obey me blindfold! I tell you to stop—that is enough.'

Lawrence left at once, followed by two of his men. The unhappy young man was a prey to the greatest impatience. The chief knocked at one of the handsomest houses in the square, and when an old negro asked, 'What is the matter?' he answered :—

'Open, in the name of the king !'

The slave, seeing a stranger armed to the teeth, drew back frightened.

'Not a word,' said Lawrence, laying his hand on his pistols, 'or you die! I am a buccaneer from Tortoise Island. Grenada is in our power. Take me to your mistress straight.'

The sight of a buccaneer always inspired the Spaniards with terror ; and the negroes, more ignorant and superstitious than their masters, saw in them supernatural beings whom no promises or threats could induce them to resist.

'Whilst I am talking to your mistress,' said the pirate, ' you will remain lying down outside the door. I warn you that if you make the least attempt to fly, I will kill you.'

Nativa, though it was now near one, was not gone to bed. Seated in a reclining chair, common in hot climates, Nativa was buried in thought.

The buccaneer gazed on her in silence.

'She is really very beautiful — of a more perfect beauty perhaps than Wildflower's. How is it, then, that she inspires me with no emotion ? My heart remains cold, my mind disdainful.'

Lawrence advanced a step, and said aloud :—

'Nativa, you sent for me—I am here. What do you wish ?'

At this sudden and to her inexplicable appearance, Nativa uttered a cry of astonishment, and tried to rise, but her emotion was so great that she fell back nearly fainting.

'Compose yourself,' continued the intruder dryly. 'You do not dream, Nativa ; it is indeed the villainous pirate Lawrence who stands before you. Do you still love me? Ought I to compliment you on your fidelity, or die of despair at your forgetfulness ?'

At first Nativa was too confused to understand his words. Gradually she recovered, for she was strong-hearted. Her large blue eyes filled with tears as she raised them in gratitude to heaven, and said passionately :—

'Thanks, oh thanks, dear saints; you have granted my prayer!'

There was so much fervour in this exclamation that even the sceptical hearer felt something like remorse.

'Well, Nativa, I repeat my question. You sent for me. I am here. What do you wish?'

'First tell me, Lawrence, if your presence here does not expose you to some risk and danger? How did you manage to come to me?'

'I made me master of Grenada, señorita.'

'You have taken Grenada? What do you mean?'

'That my buccaneers are at this moment busy pillaging the town.'

'Oh, Lawrence! is it thus that you should present yourself before me?'

'Well, señorita, what can you else expect? I did the best I could. Everyone knows that I am no boaster, but I must say that to take a town by assault in order to keep an assignation with a pretty woman, seems to me a very uncommon and gallant action!'

'Then you do love me, Lawrence?' cried Nativa impetuously.

'I?—not in the least! I am polite, that is all. I make it a rule always to obey a lady's commands. You asked me to come; I came: that is all.'

At these words Nativa shuddered, but now again a captivating smile brightened her face.

'Lawrence,' she said, 'why are you so cruel? Am I not sufficiently humiliated? Do you not know how noble, how sincere my love is? I will open my heart to you, dearest! After your cruel, even cutting letter, I tried to drive you from my thoughts! I even urged my father on against the buccaneers, but it was only spite because you did not love me. Now, when I have again returned to these soft climates, the hours that I had spent with you recurred with renewed force to my memory, and I imagined the motive which induced you to treat me so unworthily.'

'And what was my motive, if it so please you, señorita?'

'You wished to test my sincerity; you thought to yourself, that girl has rank, fortune, and influence; she thinks she can command me as if I were her slave. If she loves me, let her prove it by taking the advances which my position forbid my making. Lawrence, this design was worthy of your pride. I can afford to be humble, and forget my fortune. My beloved Lawrence, your presence here teaches me what your intentions are. I know that many obstacles still separate us, but your strong will can surmount them all. I will at once procure you highest rank and greatest dignities.'

'And for the Caballero Luis de Morgan,' interrupted Lawrence, 'eh, lady? It really seems as if you were charged with the delicate commission of recruiting for the Spanish army from the ranks of the buccaneers! Carramba! your eloquence was worthy Sergeant Kite ; and to win over a kinsman of Sir Henry Morgan, the terror of your nation—you deserve promotion ! '

At this unexpected answer, Nativa gave the cry of an outraged lioness, and drawing herself proudly up, rejoined :—

' Caballero, to insult a woman is cowardly ; but when that woman loves you, it is the deed of a villain ! '

At this outburst, an expression of intense ferocity flamed on the buccaneer's face, but recovering himself quickly, he replied :—

' Señorita, you have energetic imagination enough ; but your heart is not true, otherwise you would be perfect. Society has spoilt you. Any man who marries you will repent it bitterly. If you have loved me, it is only because my indifference piqued your pride ; not that you wished to console me for the past. A mere woman of the world, you have no heart. Great ladies have caprices, but know not how to love. The letter I wrote to you expressed what I felt. If I did not care to accept your offer of throwing yourself on my protection, it was only because women tire me.'

The insolent tone in which those words were pronounced added to the sarcasm. Nativa, pale, motionless, and confounded, was a prey to rage bordering on madness. Lawrence only smiled. The unhappy girl uttered a piercing scream, and fell back fainting in her chair.

' Just like the other,' commented the corsair ; ' she also swore she loved me, and fainted if I pretended not to believe her, yet later——but all women are alike—spoilt by hypocrisy and flattery. Poor boys who place your hearts in their keeping, experience will make you old before a wrinkle or a gray hair warns you of the fleeting years.'

Lawrence was about to leave the chamber when hurried footsteps approached, and Morgan rushed into the room.

' Mate,' cried Lawrence severely, ' what brings you here? Who authorized you to leave your post ?'

Without heeding his commander, Sir Lewis looked anxiously round the room.

' Nativa,' he cried, kneeling beside her, and taking one of her small hands in his, ' dearest Nativa, it is I, Lewis, who calls you ! Oh heavens, you are as still as if you were dead. If you die, dearest, I shall slay myself at your feet.'

The voice recalled Nativa's wandering senses. In a few moments she said :—

' You here, Señor Lewis ! Heaven sent you to protect me.'

' Protect you ! ' cried Lewis sharply, ' who dares insult you ?'

'Yon infamous wretch, that villain,' cried Nativa, pointing with sovereign contempt to Handsome Lawrence.

'Ah, then, it was to insult the lady I love that you came here, while you forbade me to leave my post,' said Morgan, with concentrated rage ; 'villain, you shall die !' and drawing out a pistol, he rushed towards the buccaneer.

The latter remained motionless, and answered coldly :—

'Sir, I hurl you back, with greater justice, the words you once spoke to me : "Coward and murderer, I curse you !"'

The extraordinary calmness of the speaker saved his life. Morgan, recalled to himself, threw down his pistol, and said :—

'Man, this time one of us must fall !'

'Fight with you, mate ? never !'

'Would you have me murder you ?'

'You, boy, murder me ? You are too noble for such work. I only chuckle over the blind fury which has enraged you against me. Only a fortnight since you swore eternal friendship and devotion to me ; and now, without cause, only on a woman's word, you menace my life ! Your rage pleases me, for does it not explain and justify the sad experience of my youth ? You. so true and honourable, attempt a murder ! Oh, it proves that love is a madness to be pitied, not condemned.'

CHAPTER XXXII.

THE TWO AGAINST THE TOWN.

THE pirate was still speaking when Jennie entered. She stood for a moment uncertain, then sprung towards Nativa, crying out :—

'Oh, this then is the Spanish lady you love, sir ? How lovely she is ! never have I beheld such dazzling beauty ! What is her name ?'

'She is called Nativa,' answered Lawrence. 'Her father is Earl Monterey, who is rich and powerful ; his son-in-law will be envied by all. Yet, Jennie, I would exchange willingly the daughter and a'l her father's riches and power for a smile from you ! You are in ecstasies, child, at her beauty, but forget your own. Do you not know that you are far more lovely than she is ?'

'Is that true, Lawrence ?' exclaimed Wildflower joyfully. 'Do not deceive me. But if it.is, so, how is it that Sir Lewis loves her as his lady love, and me only as his sister ?

Nativa's pride was roused, and she recovered her self-possession sufficiently to say to her defender :—

'Señor, your presence at Granada proves what new kind of life you have embraced. My father, fortunately, is absent, but his gold is here. Don't let me detain you from spoiling. I wish to be alone ; one of my slaves will show you over the house. Take all it contains ; let not my presence hinder you from exer-cising your "craft."'

'Ah, Nativa,' cried Morgan, moved to burning tears by this tirade, 'how do I deserve such words? You well know that it was no motive of vile lucre that brought me to Grenada. My only aim in joining this rash enterprise was to see you again and speak to you of my love.'

'What, señor,' retorted Nativa ironically ; 'you dare to own such feelings before Lawrence! You forget, then, that villain has repulsed me with disdain, that I have rashly forfeited the honour of my name, and am unworthy the love of an honour-able man!'

'Señorita Sandoval,' said the buccaneer, 'I cannot but admire the perversity of your mind. Your feigned humility is most artful. You wish to excite the passions of the knight and egg him on to murder me!'

'Ah, really, Señor Picaroon,' sneered the creole, 'you think too much of your own importance. Why should I wish for your death? For me you have already ceased to exist. I own that, blinded by my generosity and inexperience, I once loved you. I dreamt of raising you from the mire in which you lived. Was it not natural? I knew nothing of the baseness and infamy of your kind. I had only lived with caballeros, and fondly thought that courage and honour were inseparable. If I have committed a fault in this,' continued Nativa mournfully, 'Sir Lewis Morgan has alone the right to reproach me.'

'I, Nativa?' said the Cornish adventurer.

'Yes, señor, for I led you to trust to a love which I did not feel ; I gave you false hopes. But, alas! I am more to be pitied than blamed. Moved by your noble conduct, grateful for the immense service you rendered my father and myself by saving us from certain death at the risk of your own life, the admira-tion with which you inspired me I mistook for a more tender feeling, and I avoided an explanation which I knew would pain you. Now, señor, you know all, for your esteem is dear to me. Let me not detain you longer. Adios, caballero! I shall take refuge in a convent, and there I will pray for you.'

'Oh, Nativa!' exclaimed Morgan eagerly, 'you go into a convent! You so young and beautiful! Such a sacrifice can never be.'

'It can and will be, sir! Do you think so ill of me as to imagine that I could unite my fate to any honourable man? I who have been rejected by such a dog as Lawrence! No, never should my husband be able to reproach me with the wrongs I have suffered, not done, in my past life.'

'Nativa, all you urge only increases my love for you.   Before
this man, who has so unworthily treated you, I ask you to be
my wife.'

Nativa could not repress a start of pleasure.

'Señor,' she answered with captivating softness, 'I expected
nothing less from your generosity.   Thanks for this mark of
esteem.   You have raised me in my own eyes.   I shall be always
grateful to you.'

'You accept, then, Nativa?'

'No ; I refuse.   Oh, try not to contest my resolution.   I
know that you would keep your promise, with no word of reproach.   I feel that with you I might be happy, but, alas——'

'Nativa, you hesitate ; I entreat you to explain.'

'Alas, Sir knight, you forget that I cannot dispose of myself,
I depend on my father.'

'But why, Nativa, should your father not accept me?   I am
of noble birth, young, with the future before me.   Sustained by
your love, I could accomplish anything.'

'What, señor, do you really think my father would for
one moment tolerate the thought of giving his daughter to a
buccaneer?'

This answer confounded the youth ; knowing Nativa was
right, his present position overwhelmed him with shame and
humiliation.

Wildflower, who during this conversation had remained
silent and cast down, at the sight of Morgan's despair roused
herself.

'Sir Lewis,' she interposed, going towards him, 'why do
you love this lady?   She is not worthy of you.   If she loved,
would she reproach you thus?   Oh, come away!   Forget her!
Come back with me to our beautiful forests.   I will love you,
and do all you wish.'

'Jennie,' replied Morgan, pushing away the girl, 'if you
really loved me like a sister, you would not speak thus.   Yes,
Nativa, you are right ; for a buccaneer to pretend to your hand
would be monstrous ; still let me hope.   If you would but swear
that you will refuse all other offers, you will raise my hopes and
strengthen my resolve.   Be not offended at my importunity.   If
I did not feel wholly devoted to you, I dared not ask so much
of you.'

'My lord,' answered Nativa, 'your generosity touches me.
Before heaven I swear that while you live I will marry no
one else.'

'And I, Nativa, swear to you that while you live never will
I wed another.'

Scarcely had Morgan pronounced these words than Wildflower
uttered a scream, and fell swooning on the floor.

Lewis's first impulse was to rush forward to her assistance, but a look from Nativa stopped him. It was Lawrence who raised Jennie.

'Come with me, señor,' said Nativa, 'my woman shall take care of the young stranger.'

As soon as she had passed the threshold, she hissed in a voice almost stifled with anger—

'That man Lawrence must die! Not in a duel, for he is unworthy of such an honour, but like the robber and murderer he is. Here you can remain in safety until the buccaneers have left. Should you be recognised for an Englishman, the worst that can happen will be that you become a prisoner on parole. In this case I can exert my influence with my father. As for me, my first duty is to save the town from the horrors with which it is menaced. Come!'

'What are you going to do, Nativa?' cried Morgan. 'For you I would willingly sacrifice my life, but I cannot sacrifice my comrade's. Lawrence, however he may have treated you, is my companion in arms, I will never desert him. Hold!' He flung himself between Nativa and the door, but the Spanish girl rushed off in another direction. Soon the loud ringing of a large bell vibrating through the stillness of night roused all Grenada.

'Sir Knight,' cried Nativa, returning, 'as I have acted against your will, you will not have to reproach yourself with the fate of your accomplices. Ah! in less than a minute the whole population will be on foot, not one of the pirates will escape. Follow me, and I will conduct you to a place of safety, where you can remain till all is over.'

'Nativa,' replied Morgan, pale with anger, 'that bell sounds my knell. Do you think me such an abject thing as to desert my companions in the hour of danger? Back, senorita, let me pass and rejoin my mates.'

'You fear for that girl, who wished to take you from me? Ay, go back to her if you like; but do not forget that a solemn oath binds you to *me!*'

There was no time to lose. Already firing was heard on all sides. Sir Lewis rushed back to the chamber where still remained Jennie and Lawrence. The latter showed no surprise at his return; he knew his mate would not desert him at this critical juncture. Jennie still dwelt insensible.

'Lewis,' he said, 'there is not a minute to lose; day breaks, and in a few minutes longer flight will be impossible. Hasten to join the two men I left at the door; you will together be able to reach the Santa Eugracia ward and gain the boats.'

'What, man! do you think I would consent to leave you

when I am the cause of your being here?　No, a thousand times
no.　Where you are, there will I remain.'

'What a foolish thing is unavailing generosity!' sneered the
pirate.　'What good can your staying do me?　Why, you will
only be in my way.'

'But what prevents you from following the advice you give?'

'Wildflower!'

'Oh, leave her with me, and if you join your boat you can
come back some time and deliver us.'

'Leave Jennie here? never!' returned the captain savagely.
'I will never leave her.'

He burst open a window, and, calling to the men placed at
the door below, desired them to escape.

'Now, mate,' he said, coming back, 'we must sell our lives
as dearly as we can.　Whilst you arrange the furniture so as to
enable us to fire from the window without being too much
exposed, I will barricade the door in case the count's servants
should assail us, and then we must trust to our good stars.　I
have been in as great scrapes before, and escaped with honour.
We must try our luck.'

While the freebooter locked and bolted the door, Morgan barri-
caded the windows, and then tried to rouse Jennie, but in vain.

'Poor girl,' thought he, 'how cruel I have been to her!
Before she knew me she was free and happy, and I am like her
murderer.　Oh, Nativa! a dark bandage falls from my eyes.
Sweet Jennie, how hard it is not to be able to say I love you!'

As he uttered the last words unconsciously, the girl opened
her eyes.

'Oh, Sir Lewis, why did you say those cruel words?　But
no, I will not blame you.　Is it your fault if you cannot love
me?'

'Child,' said the Englishman, 'say not I cannot love you.
I do love you as my dearest friend.'

'Oh, what happiness!　Then you will not cast me from you.
You will still let me be your sister.　But let us not stay here, or
we shall fall into the hands of the Spaniards.'

'Are you afraid, sweet Jennie?'

'Afraid, with you! not so; but let us leave this place.'

'We cannot; we are discovered—encompassed.'

The girl raised her eyes to heaven, and murmured, 'At least
I shall die with my own true knight.'

'Mate,' broke in Lawrence, 'I have shut up all the servants,
we need fear no assault from them, but I cannot find Nativa;
however, that matters little.　Oh! Wildflower, how bright you
look!　As you are well enough to go with us, I don't see why we
might not attempt to cut our way out and through these raven-
ous dogs.'

As the buccaneer spoke, two shots from outside broke a marble table that Morgan had placed at the window.

'Since we are discovered,' said Lawrence with indifference, 'let us take our stands, and fire from the windows. Wild-flower can load our pistols.'

Several shots were fired, and as many Spaniards fell.

'Well,' said Lawrence, 'if these people will attack us, they must take the consequences. Ah! there is an officer just within aim, that will make the eighth that has fallen.'

Although the combat had scarcely begun, more than half-a-dozen lay killed or wounded on the *plaza*. The Spaniards, frightened by this loss, and ignorant of the number of their enemies, fled on all sides.

'Brave fellows there!' laughed the captain. 'They are quite capable of making a blockade and reducing us by famine, though.'

'But others are coming on now,' cried Morgan.

'Aim at the officers, mate. Look, there falls a colonel! Down, Jennie, the hidalgos return our fire.'

A shower of balls soon fell over the Monterey mansion, but, fired haphazard, none entered the room.

Lawrence laughed aloud.

'Sdeath!' he cried, 'instead of entering Grenada in the dead of night, I should have stormed it in open day. With my seventy men, we should have put all the garrison to the sword. Not a creature left in the square; no firing in the distance. Our men having shipped their booty, will probably come to our rescue. I shall not be sorry to use my sword, this firing is rather monotonous.'

'Still our position is critical; the enemy will soon learn how few we are, and return to the charge,' Morgan observed.

'Oh, things don't look so black,' answered Lawrence. 'We have a good chance yet.'

'I don't see it,' replied the other.

'First, have we not made a good beginning at routing the enemy? then we have a chance of help from our men; and thirdly —and this I count most upon—is my own skill in taking advantage of any favourable circumstance that may arise; and it is my notion we shall get ourselves out of this hobble.'

Morgan could not but admire the undaunted bravery of a man who, with a whole town against him, did not despair of success.

Lawrence's extraordinary feats in arms are matters of history, and surpass all bounds of probability.

This time chance did not favour the buccaneer; two battalions of militia and three companies of regular troops now came forward. Instead of exposing themselves to the buccaneer's

fire, they took up their position in the opposite houses, while a
cannon was brought into the square.

'This is really too ridiculous,' mocked Lawrence, laughing.
'Who could have thought my joke would so soon be a reality?
Artillery to attack two men and a girl! None but Spaniards
could have had such a bright idea! These people, because they
are so grave, have been misunderstood; there must be a fund of
jollity in their disposition.'

'Well, mate,' asked Sir Lewis anxiously, 'what do you think
of things now?'

'They do look rather black now, and except by miracle I
don't know how we are to clear out of this hornet's nest.'

CHAPTER XXXIII.

THE COPE COVERS MANY SINNERS.

THE houses of the rich merchants were built in a style between
a fortress and a palace, and could at a pinch maintain a siege
against the revolted slaves.

The Grenadians, therefore, in having recourse to cannon had
not deserved sarcasm.

'Mate,' remarked Lawrence, 'entrenched as we are, we need
not trouble about the firing. The cannon alone will harm us.
Once the house door comes down, we must be overcome by
numbers, even if we manage to kill a few more.'

'What is to be done, then?' asked his associate.

'Gain time if possible. Aim at every gunner who comes
forward to fire the cannon. See the fellow who starts hither-
ward, ramrod in hand. There, my ball has hit him right on the
forehead. You fire on the other with the flintstock. Aim at
his body. All right, down he goes! You struck him on the
breast. Really, I did not know you were so good a marksman!
How do you feel?'

'Not too comfortable,' answered Morgan, reloading.

'How people differ! It is long since I have been so heartily
amused.'

'You don't think of the inevitable issue of this strife and
the ignominious death which awaits us?'

'What use is it thinking of the future, when the present is
so entertaining? and as to the ignominious death that awaits us,
the Spaniards will be only too happy to kill us at once to think
of taking us prisoners. A third artilleryman out of cover! He
must have good pluck, so I shall treat him honourably. There,
my lead has struck him on the temple.'

The fall of the three artillerymen caused some wavering

then the Spaniards opened a hot fire from the houses. Morgan's hat and Lawrence's coat were pierced with many spatterings of lead.

'The deuce!' cried the latter, 'those rascals are really taking aim. Come, man, each of our shots must tell now.'

It was a wonderful spectacle to see these two men holding a whole town at defiance. As for Wildflower, sheltered in a corner, she loaded the pistols, while Lawrence and the other fired their rifles, so that a constant discharge was kept up.

For twenty minutes this unequal fight lasted.

Lawrence, who at the beginning of the strife only saw a pleasant pastime, was now intoxicated with the smell of powder. His eyes shone with dark fire, his nostrils distended, his hair in disorder, he longed to rush into the square, cutlass in fist.

The Cornishman, calm, grave, and resolute, only obeyed the voice of duty, for all hope had left him.

For twenty minutes there had been a dead silence; Morgan broke it by saying—

'Mate, I have only two more charges. Give me some of yours.'

'I am at my last grain,' answered the other. 'What have you, Wildflower?'

'My horn is empty, Lawrence.'

'Damnation! but no, so much the better! I have long itched to flesh my cutlass. Come, let us fling open the door and fight our way through.'

He was already rushing towards the door, when Morgan caught his arm, exclaiming eagerly—

'Stop! hark to the trumpet! The Spaniards, despairing of conquering us, want a parley to make terms.'

'The Spaniards consent to terms when we are in their power? Impossible! But yes, there is a sergeant coming forward with a white flag in his hand. He is paler than his flag, but he is a brave fellow; I will throw him my purse.'

'What does he say, mate?' asked the Englishman eagerly.

'He proposes a quarter of an hour's truce, that they may take up their dead; this offer hides a *ruse*. But, after all, what does it matter? We can only gain by it. A few minutes' rest will restore our strength for the last effort. We had better accept.'

'Certainly,' assented Lewis; 'who gains time, gains life.'

'Yet that proverb did not save Saint Lawrence from the gridiron. A delay to us is only a prolongation of misery. Let me answer.' He rushed out on to the balcony.

At sight of the pirate, who with a proud, defiant air, his head thrown back, looked disdainfully upon the soldiers posted in the opposite houses, an involuntary murmur of fear and admiration rose from his enemies. Then fell a dead silence.

'Sergeant,' cried Lawrence, in a clear, vibrating voice, 'the truce you ask for is needless for my companions or myself. Thanks to your want of skill, none of us are even scratched. Still to stop calumny, and prove that we are not such pitiless tigers as we are represented, we consent to the short delay that you implore. I engage by my word and honour—I am Captain Lawrence—not to recommence fighting for one quarter of an hour. Make haste and carry off your dead and wounded, for after that term has expired I warn you that, if you do not throw down your arms, my companions and I will sally out, and slash without pity. It is useless to add that, if you take advantage of the truce to commit some odious treachery, my crew will take fearful vengeance. I have finished.'

The Spaniards, on seeing that it was the notorious Lawrence who commanded the pretended garrison, were dreadfully frightened. The two men who made Spanish America tremble were Morgan the Second and Lawrence his lieutenant.

'In good faith,' said the buccaneer, leaving the balcony, 'if at this moment I had but a fourth of my crew, Grenada would be ours.'

'Lawrence!' cried Morgan with a burst of admiration, 'you are the most extraordinary man I ever heard of! But, not to lose time, what had we better do? Wildflower, what say you?'

'Alas! I can propose nothing,' answered she. 'But, Sir Lewis, I entreat you to grant me one request.'

'Say on, dearest sister,' answered the Cornish knight.

'Lewis, you don't know how wicked these Spaniards are, how cruelly they treat their prisoners. I am not frightened to die by your side, but let me not fall alive into their hands. Swear to me that, when all hope is over, you will kill me yourself.'

At this proposal Morgan turned pale and remained silent.

'Oh,' implored Wildflower anxiously, 'you do not answer me! you would not refuse me; it would be so cruel. I am not afraid to kill myself, only if my hand trembled at the last moment, it would be dreadful. Sir Lewis, let me entreat you.'

'My adorable lassie!' interrupted Lawrence, 'be not alarmed. The same idea had occurred to me, and I resolved that the sad office you entreat Morgan to undertake I myself would fulfil rather than you should fall into the hands of these cruel dogs.'

He took the girl's hand and pressed it to his lips.

'What are you weeping for, Lawrence Hardheart?' cried Jennie with wonder.

A tear had fallen on her hand.

'Yes, girl,' answered the buccaneer tenderly, 'I weep for you—for myself I regret not life.'

'Ah, why does not Sir Lewis love me as you do?' murmured Wildflower. 'Thanks, Laury, I am easy now, though I had rather Señor Lewis had done it; it seems as if I should not have suffered.'

Morgan was not less overcome than his mate; he gazed with inexpressible tenderness at Jennie, and never had the fair girl looked more captivating. Her beautiful hair fell loose over her shoulders, her large dark eyes beamed with mournful tenderness and heavenly resignation.

Fearing perhaps that, by looking longer at her, even his indomitable courage might fail, the captain turned again to the balcony, but he quickly drew back, crying out—

'Wildflower, you are too beautiful to die, you shall not die! For the first time for fifteen years I have prayed, and Heaven's infinite mercy has granted my prayer! A means of safety is at hand.'

His mind was so clear, so inventive and full of resources, and inspired both his allies with such confidence, that they already felt themselves out of danger.

'What is to be done, mate?' cried Morgan. 'Here's my hand in help.'

'Look here! from the window do you see that carriage with two mules harnessed to it? It's a prelate taking the viaticum to a dying grandee. The Spaniards—I must do them justice on that point—are far too devout, while that carriage is in sight, to rise from their knees.'

'But what of that, Lawrence? Time hastens on, and——'

'A little patience; when the right moment comes, I'll seize it, never fear!' cried he. 'Now the carriage stops, the priest comes forth, the soldiers kneel.'

'Yes, the priest goes towards the colonel; he leans towards him to bless and absolve him.'

'True, but too late; the colonel is dead! The priest enters his carriage. Mate,' cried Lawrence, 'the moment is come which must be that of our safety or our death. Come, let us out.'

Lawrence slung his rifle round his neck by its strap, and seizing a pistol in his left hand, he said—

'My beloved Wildflower, trust yourself to my love and courage.'

Then raising her in his arms, he said to Morgan, 'Come, mate, go before us and unbolt the door.'

The Englishman obeyed; the outer door was partially open.

'Do as I do,' said Lawrence, who stood with Jennie in his arms for a few seconds behind the door; then suddenly opening it wide rushed out. The priest's carriage was at that moment close to the house. He sprang in with one bound, and seated himself by the side of the priest. Almost at the same moment Morgan placed himself opposite.

This was done so suddenly that none of the trembling soldiers were yet aware of the profanation, and the buccaneer had time to say to the priest—

'Father, I am Captain Lawrence Hardheart! Take me to Santa Eugracia or you are a dead man.'

The stupefaction and consternation of the crowd were so great that it remained for a moment silent and motionless. Such a thing had never happened before. The soldiers knew not what to do. A minute's delay and the buccaneer would be lost none the less.

'Father, must Captain Lawrence repeat his order?' cried the buccaneer, lifting up his pistol.

The priest trembled from head to foot; still self-preservation made him cry out—

'To Santa Eugracia.'

The carriage turned slowly in that direction; the crowd shuddered, but, not daring to add sacrilege to profanation, remained still. All felt that at the slightest resistance the terrible Lawrence would do what he had threatened.

It was a strange sight to see all the inhabitants of a Spanish town bend the knee before two buccaneers, who a few minutes before were in their power. Lawrence and Morgan, with heads uncovered, sat humbly and quietly; no expression of joy or pride revealed their triumph. In a quarter of an hour they had reached the quarter of the town called Santa Eugracia.

'Mate,' said Morgan joyfully, 'our boats are pulling to the shore; no doubt the men are aware of your absence, and are coming to seek you.'

Almost at the same moment the boats grounded. At sight of their chief dismounting from the priest's carriage, the buccaneers gave a loud shout of exultation and delight.

'Well, lads o' mettle!' cried Lawrence, 'your excitement shall not be wasted, I shall put it to good use presently.'

The freebooters lost no time in estimating that the priest's vestments were valuable, as well as the ornaments on the carriage and horses. In another minute they would have possessed themselves of all, had not Lawrence, cutlass in hand, interfered and cried out imperiously—

'The first who touches anything here dies!'

'Father,' resumed he, bowing to the priest, 'you are free to depart.'

'How good of you, dear Lawrence!' said Wildflower.

The buccaneer reddened with pleasure.

'Decidedly the more I see of you, the more I repent of having disliked you and try to love you.'

'And do you think you may succeed, sweet Wildflower ?'

'It is rather difficult, for whenever I try to think of you, the image of Señor Lewis comes before me.'

Lawrence did not answer, but cast a threatening look towards Morgan.

Of all the persons who rejoiced at their return, none was happier than Allan, who greeted his master cordially.

'Mate,' said the captain, 'an evil thought had nearly got hold of me concerning you. I owe you some recompense. The career of a freebooter is not suitable to you ; I will assure your fortune, so that you can return to Europe.'

'Thanks for your kind intentions,' answered Morgan, 'but you are quite mistaken about my wishing to return to Europe. It is true that pillaging towns is not much to my taste, but I shall submit to the exigencies of the case. And I have lost my taste for European life.'

'But if I win Wildflower ?'

The young knight turned pale, but remained silent.

'Now let us speak of something else,' said Lawrence dryly. 'Yesterday was the first time in my life that I drew back before the enemy ; for we must confess, however glorious our retreat was, still we fled. My intention is to profit by the enthusiasm of my men and the dismay in which the garrison of Grenada has been thrown, to attack the town in broad daylight. I will not listen to any objections, and I tell you my project, not to obtain your assent, but to point out the part I want you to play.

'You conceive that really having taken no part in last night's expedition—for really we wasted our time in chatting with Señorita Nativa instead of acting at the head of our men—so now we must make up for our negligence. If I should be killed, you must take the command of the men and at once return to the ship, for if I fall the ninety men that under my orders are worth an army would be a mere handful of adventurers. Do you agree ?'

'To fight by daylight is much more in my way,' rejoined the Englishman. 'I will do my best, and I hope you will be satisfied.'

'Very modestly expressed,' said Lawrence. 'Now come with me.'

He went to his .men, who were eagerly waiting his signal to put off the boats, and said—

'Brothers of the Coast, I have to blame myself for having too high an opinion of Spanish valour. I made you land by night like robbers, instead of gallantly leading you on to battle in

the eye of the sun. You have seen, nevertheless, how my mate
and I for a whole half-hour kept the garrison of the town at bay.
Grenada is immensely rich. We should be for ever dishonoured
if we were satisfied with the scanty booty we have already
taken. Our brothers would think us beggars. Forward,
friends, let us go back and take Grenada.'

One thing alone in this speech was evident to the buccaneers,
that they might double their booty. In less than five minutes
they formed themselves in ranks and were marching forward in
good order.

Shortly they met two hundred Spanish soldiers.

'Friends,' cried Lawrence, ' you have scarcely more than two
men each to dispose of. I shall take no part, therefore, in the
matter.'

The firing began at once, and in ten minutes the whole troop
was killed or severely wounded. The buccaneers had not lost
a man.

The victors soon reached the cathedral square without meeting any further resistance, the Spaniards flying on all sides.

Their leader laughed heartily.

' Friends,' he said, ' as an excess of precaution, let thirty of
you remain on the watch. Pillaging would be perfectly useless.
I take upon myself to make the fat citizens bring us their gold
and silver of their own accord.'

———

CHAPTER XXXIV.

DOVE AND RAVEN.

Soon afterwards the cathedral bells gave notice with their loudest
clang that the inhabitants should assemble.

Though in exceeding terror, they flocked into the church,
which was soon filled with a mournful, trembling crowd.

Lawrence alone would have had the audacity of assembling
the Grenadians in the church which had only the previous night
been pillaged by his men.

A preacher mounted the pulpit, and told the inhabitants, with
deep emotion, that the buccaneers exacted a sum of five hundred
thousand piasters for the ransom of their town. If this were not
paid, they would burn Grenada and kill all the inhabitants that
fell into their hands. The priest ended by entreating his flock
to submit to this exaction. Lawrence granted a two hours' truce
to receive the money. Though we bear in mind the marvellous
audacity of the freebooters, their indomitable courage, the dread
that their very name inspired, yet it seems almost impossible
nowadays to conceive how a town of 12.000 souls could submit

thus to a handful of desperadoes. But it must be remembered that they were commanded by a noted and redoubtable captain, worth in himself an army.

Wildflower, kneeling behind a pillar in the fane, prayed fervently. Now that her life was no longer in danger, exultation and excitement had been succeeded by a heartrending feeling that amounted almost to despair.

The oath that bound Morgan to Nativa raised a barrier between her and the knight, and she felt that henceforth life had no happiness for her. Never till this moment had she felt how deeply, how entirely, she loved him.

A lady, closely veiled, knelt near Wildflower, and studied her intently.

'Jennie,' said the strange lady, coming nearer, 'you must not give yourself up to grief. Have more courage! Sir Lewis Morgan is not worthy of you.'

At the name Wildflower started.

'Who are you?' she asked. 'How could you guess what was passing in my heart?'

'I am your friend.'

'And do you know the English knight?'

'Yes, I do.'

'And perhaps you love him also?'

'Poor child!' said the veiled lady, in a pitying tone. 'By the eagerness with which you ask this question, I guess how great is your affection, how deep your grief. Let us leave the church, Jennie; this is no subject to speak of within sacred walls.'

'Yes, let us leave,' said Jennie; 'I want to know who you are, and how you can know my friend.'

The stranger drew her mantilla still more closely around, and glided through the crowd. Wildflower followed her. They soon reached a small house of mean appearance, where the veiled lady took a key from under her cloak, and opened the door. She motioned Jennie to go before her, and they both entered the house. The stranger then locked the door behind them, and motioned Jennie to an old arm-chair that stood against the wall of the poorly furnished room.

'Sit down, and let us talk, girl.'

'Will you not take off your veil?' asked Wildflower.

The unknown let fall her mantilla, and Wildflower uttered an exclamation of surprise at finding herself in presence of Nativa.

'What causes this emotion?' asked Nativa; 'are you afraid of me?'

'Yes, I fear you.'

'That proves that you have done me wrong.'

'I done you wrong? indeed, no; if one of us has wronged the other, it is not I. Two hours since I did not even know you, and yet did not the Englishman push me from him to go to you? Has he not taken a solemn oath that while you lived he would marry no one else? And do I not love him far more than you ever loved him? You nearly caused his death, and I would give my life to save his! I am better than you, yet I submit; if one of us has wrong to complain of, it is I, not you.'

The quiet dignity with which these words were spoken, the purity and high feeling that beamed in the speaker's face, together with her great beauty, impressed even Nativa, but a dark look of rage and jealousy gleamed from her eyes.

'Jennie,' she answered, 'listen to me; you are in no position to bandy words with me. The best thing you can do is to submit to my wishes, and I will reward you well. What is your present position? That of a poor thing whom any one can insult with impunity. Well, if you will consent to give up your wandering life, I will make you one of my tire-women. You shall have handsome clothes, rare food, and gold. Later, if your conduct pleases me, and you have learnt your duties, I will take you as my lady's-maid, and marry you to one of my father's upper servants. Of course you accept so advantageous an offer?'

During this insulting offer Wildflower's face burned with indignation; but she waited quietly till Nativa had finished; then, rising proudly, she replied—

'Señorita, you do not know who I am, or you would not have dared to insult me. Know that among all the buccaneers, before whom your cowardly Spaniards tremble, not one is there but would risk his life to please me. Every one loves and respects me. Were I insulted, a hundred hands would be raised to avenge me. You think yourself a great lady because you have gold and slaves. This very night Lawrence told you to your face that you were flattered and sought after for your father's money. And if to-morrow the brave buccaneers set fire to your house and carry off your slaves, what will you be then? My father has no riches. I am loved for myself alone. I am better than you. Your pity and offers I spurn.'

Wildflower looked so divinely beautiful as she spoke, that Nativa could not repress an exclamation of jealous rage.

'Take care,' she said, seizing her by the arm, 'you don't know us Spaniards. Think again! I was wrong to offer you my protection. I will be frank with you. What I want is for you to promise not to return to St. Domingo. For which name your own reward.'

'I disdain all your offers,' answered Jennie. 'Farewell, señorita.' The girl advanced towards the door, but Nativa barred her way.

'You dare then to resist my will?' she hissed; 'so much the worse for you. You compel me to use force. Be it so. Here

Juanito, Pepe, come !' At Nativa's cries, four slaves, armed
with cutlasses, rushed in.

Accustomed to danger, Wildflower had no womanly fears,
and was not intimidated by the armed blacks.

'Nativa, for your sake I would believe that you do not
intend to have me murdered.'·

'If you consent to obey me, you have nothing to fear. If
you resist, I will not stop at any means.'

'Not to commit a crime, Nativa ?'

'Not even that.'

'Oh,' cried Jennie, 'I rejoice that your cruelty, passion, and
treachery have dug an abyss between you and Morgan. My
knight is too good and loyal not to hate you when he learns your
conduct to me.'

'And what care I about the love of your knight ?' returned
Nativa, exasperated ; 'what I want is for you never to return to
St. Domingo, so that Lawrence shall never see you more.'

'I cannot understand you,' said the astonished girl ; 'is it not
to separate me from Sir Lewis that you seek to keep me here ?
What ! is it the handsome Lawrence that you love ?'

'Lawrence !' cried Nativa, giving way to her passion. 'I
hate him with the whole force of my soul. By rejecting my love,
he has humbled me to the ground. It is revenge I seek ; I
would torture him through you.'

'And do you not blush to tell me this before your slaves ? I
am ashamed of you ! Poor Nativa ! send away your slaves.'

'Do you promise, then, not to try to escape ?' asked Nativa.

'No, Nativa ! When my friends embark I must follow them.
But while I talk to you send those men away.'

Nativa waved her hand for the negroes to depart, but remain
in the passage. Since she had so nearly fallen into the trap laid
by her rival, Wildflower kept her station near the door.

'Nativa,' said she, 'if you think that you can make yourself loved by Lawrence by violence, indeed you are mistaken.
He never gives way. But now to speak of Sir Lewis Morgan ;
it is very cruel of you, Nativa, to make him so unhappy. If
your heart was not drawn towards him, why make him believe
that you loved him ? He is unhappy, my kind knight, and it is
your fault. Why deceive him ? Why make him bind himself by
an oath ? Oh, if it had not been for you, perhaps he would have
loved me, who love him so much ! We should have been most
happy.'

'Jennie,' answered Nativa, anxious to detain her rival till
the buccaneers embarked without her, 'all men are monsters, who
know nothing of the pure delights of love ; the only sentiment
they feel is pride. What they desire is not so much to be loved
as for people to think they are so. If a man, rejected by a

woman, is capable of any devotion, any sacrifice to obtain her, it is not because she is necessary to his happiness, but that his conceit cannot brook her disdain, and he cannot endure the idea that she should be insensible to his merits. I showed myself insensible to Morgan ; you threw yourself at his head ; it is only natural that he should follow the one who disdains him. Believe me, to be loved you must never love in return.'

'Oh, don't talk so, Nativa ! your words make me shudder. No, I cannot believe what you say ; men are not so wicked. The knight of Morgan avoid me because I have given him my soul!'

'Child,' rejoined the Spaniard, 'you know nothing of life. Look at Lawrence, who is a proof of what I say. How otherwise explain one so proud and superior to all other men loving you, except that your indifference has wounded his self-esteem ? What are you by the side of him ? Nothing, absolutely nothing ! And yet he solicits your smile, he bends to your will. But to-morrow, if you were conquered by his apparent devotion, from a slave he would become a tyrant.'

'But, Nativa, if you do not believe in love, why try to detain me and be anxious that Lawrence should see me no more ? If all men are, as you say, proud and selfish, why be angry because Lawrence is like the rest ? You do not answer me, Nativa ! Oh, you do not believe what you say ! Perhaps because you are unhappy. You feel for Lawrence what I felt for Sir Lewis. I had only just learnt that he loved you, and I was so unhappy, and was unjust to him, and still I felt how much I loved him. It is thus you love Lawrence, and yet try to think ill of him ; is it not so ?'

'How strange,' murmured Nativa, 'that this child of nature should read the state of my own heart ! Yes, Jennie,' she went on, glad to give way to her long pent-up feelings, 'I do love Lawrence.. I can see the abyss which yawns between us. My reason and my pride revolt against my love. My father would curse me. I should be repulsed and despised by everyone. Yet in spite of all, my greatest grief, and what has embittered my life, is that Lawrence does not love me. Child, if I have made you unhappy, if I have even broken your heart, you are revenged, for I am miserable.'

Overcome with emotion, she hid her face in her hands, and sobbed aloud.

Wildflower came softly towards and bent over her, but Nativa drew back haughtily.

'Do you think that a moment's weakness on my part gives you the right of treating me as an equal ? You, a companion of freebooters, dare you pity me ?'

At this fresh repulse Wildflower merely gave her rival a look of gentle pity, and turned towards the door.

The Spanish girl again barred her passage.

'Señorita,' said Jennie calmly, 'you saw just now how little the appearance of your armed slaves frightened me; therefore why try again to threaten me? If Lawrence were to call to you, saying, 'Nativa, come to me, I love you!' you would fly to him, even if by so doing you risked your life. Well, I know at last that Lewis Morgan will find out that I am more worthy of his love than you are, because I love him. Nothing then shall stop me except death! I am armed, and I know how to use my rifle.'

Instead of answering, Nativa opened the other door. 'Slaves,' she ordered, 'if this buccaneer attempts to escape, kill her, and I will give you your liberty and gold besides!'

A roar of glee, like that a bear makes when it seizes its prey, was the negroes' only answer.

'You hear?' said Nativa, turning towards her prisoner. 'Try now, if you dare, to brave me! Slaves, for their liberty, gold, and *aguardiente* will kill even their own fathers or children.'

'Nativa,' answered Jennie, 'never could I have believed you capable of so vile an action. It is anger that makes you so cruel. A little reflection will, I trust, incline you to mercy. The signal to go on board is not yet given. I can wait.' So saying Wildflower retired to a corner, still holding her rifle, calm and silently ready for whatever might happen.

While her life and liberty were thus threatened, the terrified Spaniards were tranquil.

'Mate,' whispered Lawrence to Morgan, 'our revenge on the enemy is not yet complete. I want something more than money, for which we can signalize ourselves alone.'

'I don't know what you would have; the whole town trembles at your feet.'

'You have just suggested a plan to me. You will join me in it, will you not?'

'Certainly, if it be honourable.'

'Oh, never fear. I am in a virtuous vein; my plan cannot harm us, and will not cost a crown or drop of blood. Last night we were tracked like wild beasts; this morning we were forced to fly. Now that we are conquerors we ought to have indemnification, and certainly deserve the honours of a triumph.'

'I don't understand you yet.'

'Never mind, my idea is capital; that must content you for the present. I shall be back directly.'

On leaving Morgan, Lawrence spoke to one of the noble Spaniards who were kept as hostages till the money was paid. The knight remarked his wonder and astonishment at what the buccaneer said; then the soldiers who were guarding the prisoners opened their ranks, and the same Spaniards passed out and departed quickly.

Shortly after, the sound of military music was heard suddenly in the streets near the square ; this caused general wonder. At the first moment the buccaneers thought of a surprise, and seized their arms.

'Don't trouble, lads,' explained their captain ; ' it is only our good friends the Grenadians, who desire with becoming politeness to recognise the honour of our visit.'

He was still speaking when eight Spaniards, bending under the weight of a magnificent canopy of velvet, bespangled and fringed with gold, under which was a large arm-chair, appeared on the square.

'Mate,' said Lawrence to Morgan, ' you see that as the population of Grenada is so great, and we are so much appreciated and liked, it would be cruel in us to repress the ovation of such good people, and refuse them the pleasure of seeing us near to. Sit down by my side, and let us take a turn round the town ; it will remind you of our first meeting. I am passionately fond of music.'

Although the danger of such temerity was extreme, yet the idea was so droll that Morgan could not forbear laughing as he took his seat beside Lawrence under the canopy.

The trumpets sounded louder than ever as the train began its march.

'You are mad, mate,' whispered the Englishman ; 'it is impossible but that the sight of this spectacle should not awake the pride of the Spaniards, and we shall not come forth from our triumph alive.'

'Oh, I assure you, the Grenadians are delighted with us ! See how happy they look at our condescension. Besides, I have taken the precaution to make them understand that there is nothing in this humiliating to them. Listen, and you will find how humble I am in victory.'

The procession stopped, and a sergeant who preceded it cried out in a loud voice—

'Friends, behold Captain Lawrence, who to give us pleasure takes a turn round our good town of Grenada. Take off your hats !'

Lawrence took a handful of gold pieces from a bag that was placed at his feet, and scattered it among the people. The beggars threw themselves instantly on it, and cried out—

'Long live the great Commander Lawrence !'

'Let us show, in return,' said the buccaneer, 'that I am delighted with the kind feeling of these good people.'

The extraordinary audacity of this proceeding proved such confidence in his own strength, and was besides so entirely out of the common run, that not a single man in Grenada dreamed of taking umbrage. Wherever the procession passed the crowd took off their hats with a feeling of awe, if not respect ; as for the beggars, they applauded heartily.

The triumph was a disgrace to the rich and powerful, that is to say, their masters. That was enough to rejoice the rabble.

The strange show had returned to the square, when Morgan eagerly seized Lawrence's arm, and cried—

'Did you not hear ?'

'The blessings of the people ? Certainly, mate.'

'Don't joke, Lawrence ! I fancied I heard Wildflower calling for help.'

'Wildflower! Oh, what an idea ! But, in fact, not improbable.'

The buccaneer stood up, and extending his hand, cried out— 'Silence,' in a voice that was heard even above the shouting of the crowd. Almost at the same moment the report of a gun was heard from a house close by, followed by a cry of 'Help, Sir Lewis, help me ! '

'By heavens !' ejaculated the Cornishman, 'they are murdering our sister ! '

The youth jumped from his seat, and with superhuman force threw himself against the door of the house whence the cry proceeded. It gave way.

'Death to all murderers ! ' shouted Lawrence, as he followed his mate.

'Oh, I was sure that Heaven would not desert me ! ' cried Jennie, who came forth pale, and her bosom heaving with emotion, holding her smoking rifle in her hand.

'Jennie, my sister,' said Morgan, ' where are the wretches that attacked you ?'

'I unhappily killed but one,' replied she wildly; ' but come away, sir, I want to leave this place. Pray come away.'

'No, Jennie, I must punish the bandits, even if I risk my life to do it.'

'What good will that do ? Besides, had they not a right to attack a foreigner and a buccaneer ? Come, let us fly.'

Not heeding her words, he passed her. At the end of the passage he saw a negro lying dead.

Seeing a staircase he was about to ascend it, when Lawrence called—

'Come, mate, here is the really guilty hand.'

This time Morgan was obliged almost to use violence to join his friend, so great were Wildflower's endeavours to prevent him.

What was the youth's consternation on entering the room where Jennie had been kept prisoner to see Nativa ! Lawrence stood by the Spanish young lady, with an expression of irony that beggared all description.

'Nativa, you here! By what chance?' muttered Morgan, struck by a fatal light, tortured by a horrid doubt.

'Not chance unites the executioner and his victim,' answered the pirate captain.

Although these words only confirmed the Englishman's dreadful suspicions, he still doubted.

'Oh, it is impossible. I am mad! My senses are leaving me,' he moaned, passing his hand convulsively over his forehead. 'But speak, Nativa—what has happened? For heaven's sake explain.'

Señorita Sandoval did not seem even to hear him. She stood gazing at Lawrence, unconscious of all besides.

'Nativa,' appealed Morgan, a prey to the most poignant feelings, and seizing her arm he shook it violently. 'Answer me, I insist on it. Tell me how you came here with Wildflower?'

'Wildflower,' repeated Nativa slowly, 'is a worthless hussy. I ordered my slaves to kill her, because Lawrence loves her and I love him.'

At this answer the Englishman gave a piercing cry, in agony of heart.

'No, Sir Lewis, don't believe Nativa, she loves only you,' cried Jennie.

CHAPTER XXXV.

THE LONG CHASE.

It was more than a minute before De Morgan recovered his scattered senses.

Jennie's tears first proved to him that something dreadful had happened, but perceiving Nativa he conquered his weakness and emotion. He gently pushed back Jennie, who strove to prevent him, and walked towards the Spaniard.

'Nativa,' he said, in a voice like a sob, 'do not fear reproaches or entreaties from me. Heaven is my witness that, had you not attempted Jennie's life, I should have felt against you neither anger nor hatred. Your conduct towards me has been cruel, it is true, but you were the victim of an ardent passion, and despised love makes, I know too well, all hearts cruel and pitiless. In this I only am guilty. I was wrong to confound my hopes with the reality, and believe in your affection when nothing proved it. It seems as if a bandage had fallen from my eyes, and I look at the past not through the prism of my hopes, but with clear eyes. You have never loved me.'

'Nativa,' he continued, after a short pause to steady his voice, 'one word more before I leave you. I have sworn that while you

live I will never marry any one else. A gentleman has but one
word, I shall keep my promise! Farewell, Nativa! you found
me full of enthusiasm, youth, and faith; I leave you with my
heart embittered, saddened, desolate. I do not reproach you,
but if in future, remembering how much I have loved you, in a
caprice you recall me to you, remember I am no longer the
ardent youth you met at Penmark, but a man who has lost
all hope.'

'Lewis,' answered Nativa, 'your generosity is my greatest
punishment. I will not attempt to justify my conduct, but you,
who have so devotedly loved, will understand how a love so cruelly
trampled on can lead to crime. Pity me, then, and if possible
forgive me, and in the convent, where I trust to hide my sorrows and
my faults, I will remember your name in my prayers. Farewell!'

Morgan was too much moved to reply, and only bowed.

'Sir Lewis,' said the sweet voice of Jennie, as with gentle
persuasion she placed her hand on his arm, 'you have been good
and generous to this poor lady, and Heaven will reward you.
When you called me sister it made me sad. Now it will make
me happy! Remember what delightful days we passed in our
forests, how night came on us before we were aware. We will
return to that life, and when you feel unhappy I will mingle
my tears with yours. Oh, it does good to have some one weep with
you. Come away, beloved.'

Wildflower, thus trying to console, was so lovely in her
earnestness and self-devotion, that even Nativa was moved.

'Jennie,' she said, 'you are as good as you are beautiful;
your gentleness even subdues my pride. Forgive me.'

Wildflower looked uneasy. 'Nativa,' she answered, 'you are
so unhappy I should be sorry to pain you, but I cannot tell a
falsehood. I can forgive your insults, your disdain, even your
ordering your slaves to kill me, for your passion had made you
mad. But, Nativa, I cannot forgive the misery you have brought
on Sir Lewis, and your cruelty to him. If knowledge such as is
acquired in towns teaches such deceit, I rejoice at my ignorance.
Nativa, I can only pity you!'

The Spaniard seemed moved with her candour and gentleness, but soon raising her head proudly and turning to Lawrence,
who had stood silent and thoughtful, uttered this farewell—

'Lawrence, I was naturally kind and generous, you have
made me proud and revengeful. Man, I curse you!'

Nativa's energy made the buccaneer shudder, but he quickly
recovered, and answered with a sneer—

'Thanks, señorita, for your charming adieu! so ends our
love. I always had a wish to try the efficacy of curses, you have
now given me the opportunity I desired. Too loving and too
violent Nativa, I am your very humble and *grateful* servant.'

He drew near the door with a radiant face and proud bearing to call his porters, and said to Morgan—

'Let us proceed on our triumphal march.'

'Thanks, Lawrence,' answered Morgan dryly, offering his arm to Wildflower. 'I have no mood for merriment. I will follow you on foot.'

'Be it so,' answered Lawrence with irony, 'it is only just that you should leave me all the glory, as you engross all the love.'

'Alas!' thought the buccaneer, casting an envious look at his comrade and Wildflower, 'here I am again alone in my power. I was wrong to go out of my track. What have I to do with tenderness or friendships? What is the use of trying to resuscitate a dead heart? I was wrong to take Lewis for a companion, wrong to give way to my feelings for Wildflower. Pride, power, riches, diversions, battle, these are all that is fit for me now; they alone can make me forget the past! Still Jennie is sublime in her purity and uprightness! More deception, perhaps! I was deceived in her too. I thought her an angel of truth and innocence, perhaps only because her feelings slept; now that they are awakened and she loves, she may turn out a very woman after all. As to Morgan, when we are no longer mates, he will be to me only an obstacle, and obstacles I crush!'

Handsome Lawrence, when he returned to the square, found that the Spaniards had collected the required sum, and so anxious were they to get rid of their terrible guests, that they offered mules to take the money to the boats.

An hour later, the buccaneers were already on board their vessel on their way down the river.

Two days afterwards, they were in the open sea. Enchanted with the success of their enterprise, and the booty they had secured, they reminded their chief of his promise to go to Jamaica. Lawrence complied.

A great change had lately come over the brave captain. He now always invited the oldest of the buccaneers to dine with him; there was perpetual carousing.

Wines of the costliest kinds flowed *ad libitum.* Music was always heard, and dice rattled continually.

Morgan, almost ever with Jennie and Allan when the service of the ship did not require him, understood nothing of this change; although he blamed Lawrence for giving way to such revelry, still he could not but admire the way in which Lawrence held his own in these orgies.

He sat in an arm-chair, the others on stools. He never allowed any one to keep his hat on in his presence. Glass in hand, he still kept up his dignity as captain, and a frown from him was sufficient to awe even the most inebriated of his boon companions.

The third day after they had left Grenada, Morgan, wrapped in his cloak, was sleeping on deck, when at daybreak the cry of 'A sail!' from the look-out roused him suddenly. Lawrence was by his side.

'What vessels are those, mate?' he asked.

'Two that I know well,' answered Lawrence with a strange smile.

'What makes you smile, mate?'

'Oh, I am not insensible to such good luck.'

'Then are they silver ships? Do you expect them to be an easy prey?'

'On the contrary; they are ships of war. But why trifle with your impatience and curiosity? You wish to distinguish yourself, mate? Here is a capital chance for you.'

'No,' answered the knight mournfully, 'my only wish now is to forget.'

'In other words, you are tired of life? Well, man, death may not be afar. Those two vessels bearing down on us are the finest ships in the Spanish navy, one of them commanded by the admiral in person; each carries sixty guns and a thousand men.'

'And do you think of battling with them?' asked the Englishman quietly.

'Think of resisting?' repeated Lawrence ironically. 'What, do you rate me so much in love that I am no longer the veteran rover? Why, rather than yield I would blow up the ship. But we will talk of that by-and-by, now to our duty.'

He called out through the speaking-trumpet: 'Clear away for action!'

Thanks to the experience, intrepidity, and coolness of his crew, he had established on board a much more perfect discipline than on board men-of-war of that period.

Although the danger was not immediate, all hands set briskly to work, and in a few minutes the bulwarks were surrounded with sacks of sand to act as protection against the enemy's fire; the chests of arms were opened, the hatches were closed, and only a dim light gleamed in the powder magazine on the non-combatants, *i.e.*, the two cooks, the musicians, and stewards, who placed themselves in readiness to supply ammunition and receive the wounded.

The ports were closed, iron boxes full of cartridges placed close to the guns, swabs and rammers were within reach of the gunners; the buckets were filled with water, and, lastly, the surgeon took out his instruments. The preparations completed, Lawrence ordered the vessel to run before the wind, as if flying from the enemy. This command caused some murmuring among the crew.

'Lads,' said the captain, with a gentle affability which he seldom used except before a fight, 'moderate your impatience, and, above all, don't attempt to reason on the orders I give. You are all of proved courage, some have even commanded vessels, but, believe me, not all your experience united is as high as my gifts. Once for all, don't forget that I am *never* mistaken. You desire a fight, and you shall have such a bellyful that even the annals of the old freebooters cannot supply the like !'

At this speech all murmuring ceased ; such proud words were not a vain boast. After a two hours' chase, it was evident that one of the Spanish ships much outstripped her companion, and the distance between them increased every minute.

Towards ten in the morning, the freebooters could distinguish every port of the formidable Spanish galleon, and her size made them look grave, brave though they were.

Walking with Morgan on the quarter-deck, their chief talked on indifferent subjects, as if he had forgotten his terrible enemy. Suddenly raising his voice, he called out to a man on the look-out—

' What sail does she carry ? '

'She is under reefed topsails and foresheet.'

' Good. Sir Lewis, order them to steer for her.'

Morgan gave the command, and Lawrence seemed to trouble himself no more about the enemy.

Half-an-hour later the vessels were scarcely three gunshots apart.

' How goes the *Hidalgo ?* ' inquired the buccaneer.

'She steers to larboard to close on us when she veers to the wind,' answered the Cornishman.

' Is she far off ? '

' Close enough to see under the waterline when she rolls.'

Lawrence stood a few moments silent ; then in a voice which resounded over the whole vessel, summoned :

' All hands amidships ! '

The buccaneers obeyed this order with alacrity.

Their leader gave a rapid glance on his companions. A smile rose to his lips, for the faces of all around him told him that he could rely on them to the death.

' Brothers of the Coast,' he said, ' you have too much experience not to judge the peril we run, and you are too brave to fear it. Here we must hazard everything, and be prepared for everything ; we must attack and defend ourselves at the same time. Valour, cunning, temerity, and despair even must befriend us now. If we fall into the enemy's hands we can only expect the most shameful treatment, cruel torments, and an ignominious death ! Let us do our best to escape such infamy, and to escape it, let us fight.'

'Ay. ay, captain, let us fight,' repeated all the freebooters.

Lawrence waved his hand for silence, and continued :

'Friends, your ardour does not surprise me. I know you of old. If for several hours we have fled before the enemy, it was because, having remarked the different rate of sailing of the two ships, I wished to separate them and pass to windward of the admiral's ship. I have succeeded, and now that we are to windward of the flagship, we are safe from the guns of her consort, so that we shall only have one to fight. Our victory is certain. Nevertheless, if by some mischance that I cannot foresee, fortune declares against us, I wish our defeat to be glorious, our death useful to our brothers. Sharkley, step forward.'

A freebooter, with his skin so bronzed by a tropical sun as to look like a mulatto, and a calm and resolute demeanour, came forward. The man known by the name of Sharkley was one of those men with a form of granite and a heart of bronze, one of those vigorous organizations in a physical point of view, but of low mental powers, so many of whom are found among the knights of the black flag. Governed by an irresistible instinct of destruction, Sharkley's element was in the midst of carnage. Then he was triumphant ; but once the battle over, and the enemy conquered, he became sad, morose, and unhappy. In a word, he was an admirable and powerful machine of war, but he needed an impulse. No freebooter obeyed his chief so willingly as he when the order was to fight.

'Friend,' said Lawrence, 'I wish to give you publicly a proof of my esteem.'

The seaman's face remained impassible.

'During the action you shall hold a match in the powder magazine ; at my signal or, if I die, at the command of Sir Lewis, you will blow up the vessel. You understand ?'

'All clear, sir,' answered Sharkley, with a grim smile.

He slouched off to his post. A shudder ran through the men, but no one thought of raising an objection, for they all approved.

'Now, my lads,' added Lawrence, 'the last word ! Our barkey contains a goodly sum ; putting aside my share, and that of the outfitters, each man may consider himself possessor of some five thousand pounds. To be beaten under such circumstances would not only be cowardice but sheer madness. Defend your gold ! Hurrah for the darkey's head and crossbones !'

'Long live Captain Lawrence !' resounded from all sides, and then each man returned to his post.

'Mate,' said Morgan, who alone remained with the leader, all dissimulation between us is useless Let us

Do you see any means of safety? for I reckon our position is hopeless.'

'It is too true,' answered the buccaneer sadly, 'that our sixteen pieces and eighty odd men are in too fearful a disproportion to the forces cf the enemy to give us grounds for hope. Still, knowing my crew as I do, I do not despair. There is not one of ur gunners who could not hit an orange at two hundred paces. Skill must make up for weight of metal; frankly, I cannot foretell the issue of the fight. And then, between you and me, there is a final hope.'

'What is that, comrade?'

'Do you see a dirty gray cloud ringing a white spot just above the horizon, southward?'

'Yes, now you point it out I see it.'

'That is the storm's eye.'

'Eh?'

'That cloud is an indication of a fierce squall. It is doubtful whether, until it breaks over us, we shall be able to resist the enemy. But not a word more; leave me to my thoughts.'

Lawrence, who, on the appearance of the Spanish vessel, had put on a splendid dress, now mounted watch.

It would have needed a painter to give a faint idea of the handsome appearance and grand demeanour of the corsair captain. Pride and grace were united in him. His crew gazed on him with proud satisfaction. Among these coarse fellows, disdaining all luxury, Lawrence alone could without injuring his popularity allow himself showy attire which became him so well. All knew that under that splendid embroidery and costly lace, beat a heart that feared nothing.

In their rapid course, the Spanish admiral's ship and the clipper of the buccaneers approached each other; they were scarcely a gunshot apart when Morgan saw Wildflower approach.

'You here, sister?' he reproached her; 'your place is below, out of danger of the enemy's shots. I implore you, Jennie, hasten down below; the firing will begin directly.'

'My place is near you, Sir Lewis,' answered Wildflower in a tone which, though gentle, was resolute. 'Quit you in danger?— never.'

'But, girl, your presence here can be of no use to me. On the contrary, it will take from me that coolness that I need so much. I entreat you to go below.'

'Sir Lewis,' answered she, without stirring, 'I am said to bring good fortune! If that is true, I shall save you from the enemy's balls, and if I cannot do so we will die together; I shall be glad to die, Lewis.'

'Mate,' cried Lawrence, with the intent of breaking the con-

versation between Wildflower and Morgan, 'go and see before
the firing opens if the tops are manned, if sufficient grenades
have been taken up, if our best marksmen are at their places in
the crow's-nest, and in the boats to pick out the Spanish officers
and fire at them from under cover. Make haste.'

Morgan left instantly, and Lawrence immediately said to
Jennie—

'Wildflower, go under hatches at once. I will have it so.'

The tone admitted of no reply. Jennie sighed and departed.

'Everyone lie flat on deck till further orders!' cried
Lawrence.

CHAPTER XXXVI.

THE WASP AND THE BULL.

NOTHING is so imposing as two vessels going into action.

A solemn silence, broken only by the captain's orders, weighs
heavy on the bravest hearts.

Each man, even those most accustomed to danger, gives a
melancholy glance over his past life, and asks himself whether he
ought to rejoice or tremble. Allan, crouched at his master's feet,
had never before witnessed a naval engagement, and felt deeply
the awe which precedes strife. One thought supported him.

'In good faith, master,' he whispered, 'I don't understand
why the captain should give battle instead of scuttling away.
Since I know I am the owner of five thousand pounds I am
turned a coward. I, Allan, the possessor of such a sum! It seems
a dream. To think that I am rich enough to buy Penmark out
and out, eat fresh meat all day, have a servant, and yet that perhaps in half-an-hour I shall be cold mutton. It breaks my heart.
Do, master, entreat the captain not to be so swaggering, which is
a sin, but to try and escape.'

'How could you expect, Allan,' answered the knight, 'that
we could escape from a vessel that sails so much faster than we
do, that with shortened sail she has gained on us so greatly?
Come, Allan, take courage ; don't forget that you and I represent
Cornwall, and that we must not dishonour the Duchy of Tin and
Fish.'

'Then, master, it is the Spaniards who force us to fight ?'

'Undoubtedly.'

'By the whiskers of the Pope ! the rascals had better
beware! You wretches! What, not content with having slaugh·
tered so many poor Indians, you want to rob me of my fortune
also, do you ? I long now to grapple with you, I do. I feel like
a hungry wolf.'

Lawrence's voice interrupted the conversation.

‘Lower away. Hand in the top-gallant sails,’ he ordered.

The admiral’s ship, seeing that the buccaneers offered fight under lower sails only, imitated their example. With their port-side to the pirate, the Spanish man-of-war hailed the cruiser, and ordered her colours to be struck.

A smile of immense disdain lit up the buccaneer’s face.

Rushing down from the quarter-deck Lawrence jumped on the bulwarks, and proudly daring, his head high, his breast turned toward the enemy, he roared in a voice that rung clear, like a note from a clarion—

‘I am Captain Lawrence. Now, then, all hands afoot. Fire the broadside !’

A sheet of fire burst from the frigate. The Spanish answer followed quickly, an avalanche of fire rushed on the frigate, which would have swamped her, had not the man-of-war’s guns been too high to rake her hull, and the shots only sundered some of her running lines.

‘Cease firing !’ bawled Lawrence. ‘ Rifles must do the work now. Aloft there ! Shower down your grenades on the enemy’s deck. But don’t hurry, take your time to aim, let every missile tell !’

The order to haul in the great guns was a bold stroke. With his quick and unerring perception, he saw at once that with his eight cannons he could do little against the enemy’s thirty, and the men at the guns might be better employed in the rigging, with their unerring rifles, picking off the enemy. For an hour the small-arms fighting continued with unabated ardour on both sides. The buccaneers, incited by Lawrence, did the work of double their number. The Spaniards, although they had been considerably impressed by finding themselves opposed to the noted captain, confided in their superior powers. They had such immense advantages there over their antagonists, that thinking a defeat impossible, they fought with ardour.

It is needful to remember the marvellous coolness and infallible skill in shooting of the buccaneers to believe the immense damage which during this hour they had done the Spaniards. Two hundred Spaniards had fallen. The gunners, exposed without any defence to the buccaneer’s rifle-shots, were picked off each time they tried to train a piece. Those who had retired behind the bulwarks, amidships, no sooner showed themselves than they were punished for their temerity.

It was indeed a strange sight to see so powerful a ship harassed by so petty a foe which she could have run down at once.

Morgan, rifle in hand, seconded Lawrence in the command, but fought like a simple sailor. Allan’s first surprise past, he had taken his station in the maintop-castle, and showed an intelligence and eagerness that astonished himself.

'Oh, you rascally Spaniards!' he muttered. 'You are going to take my fortune away, are you? You massacred thousands of unoffending Indians, did ye? You shall see if I can't stop your tricks,' and as quick as lightning he reloaded and fired, every time with effect.

The deck of the freebooter, covered with blood, proved that this momentary triumph, or, rather, brave resistance, had cost them dear; twenty had already fallen.

'Mate,' said Morgan, 'would it not be better to attempt boarding than let ourselves be decimated thus? Who knows if a last glorious effort might not save us?'

'I like your impatience, mate, but the responsibility which weighs on me prevents my sharing it. What can fifty or sixty men do against seven or eight hundred?'

'Then we are lost,' said the Englishman in a low tone.

'Yes, if the squall on which I count does not arrive soon.'

'You only expected it in three hours.'

'But the sky has changed since then; if we can only hold out another hour, we will be saved by the tornado.'

'Another hour? impossible! At the next broadside we shall go to the bottom.'

'We may have a few dropping shots, but not a broadside. Our brave fellows cut off the gunners too quickly for that. As for foundering, you forget that Sharkley is in the powder magazine. We shall go up, not down.'

'In truth, then,' cried Morgan, 'I hold for boarding, the more as from the beginning of the fight the Spaniard has always shirked it.'

'That is nothing wonderful,' answered Lawrence. 'They know I am here. If I had that ship with sixty guns and her crew, I should have annihilated a bark like this long ago! Don't talk to me, mate, of such dogs. Pushed on by favour or by chance, they reach important posts; but the genius, the instinct of war is lacking. Not one of our buccaneers, if in command of that ship, but would have already powdered small fry like us to atoms.'

Standing at his post of observation, where he was exposed to fire, and with bullets continually whistling round him, Lawrence spoke as quietly as if in a taproom. Master of his will, he could even resist the excitement of the fight.

'Ha!' he ejaculated a moment after, 'here is the Spaniard on us! She wants to fire her broadside into our stern. Not a bad idea either, mate.'

He was going with his orders when, suddenly, he fell off the skylight on the deck; the fortune that had hitherto protected him had shunned him.

The moment was critical, but Morgan perceived his opportunity. 'Brothers,' he shouted, jumping on the lid from which Lawrence had just fallen, 'a man more or less does not make a defeat. There is no cause for despair. Stand steady, don't let them rake us. Let us spoil their sport by anticipating them.'

'Hurrah for Morgan's descendant!'

Animated by Sir Lewis's energy and boldness, and happy to find a leader in their urgent need, they hastened to obey the command of one whose name had long been a rallying cry.

'The fools!' sneered Morgan, with a look of scorn at the admiral's ship, 'they opened their hand when they held us fast.'

Several buccaneers, when they saw their captain fall, had run to help him.

'Back to your posts, lads,' he shouted; 'there's no harm done! Only a splinter. What bullet could kill me? Ha,' added he, on seeing Morgan in his place. 'Bravo! You lost no time in taking possession of your inheritance.'

A wild delight accompanied these words.

Presently Morgan sprang down from his elevation, and going up to him, whispered—

'I estimated you too highly! You are an extraordinary man, comrade, but you have your weak points like other men.'

At these words Lawrence blushed.

'I understand now,' he said, 'why Wildflower loves you better than me. She judged you rightly. You are a grander man by a thousand times; for never shall I forget your having saved my bark.'

During another hour the combat took even a more serious character than hitherto. There remained only twenty men unwounded, and they, knowing that all hope was lost, no longer hid behind the rigging but with furious cries demanded the hand-to-hand fighting.

Lawrence, ever cool and resolute, examined the sky; the storm that he hoped might serve them still delayed.

If the position of the freebooters was hopeless, their enemies had paid dearly for their victory, for half their men lay dead or wounded.

After the last broadside which the admiral's ship contrived to pour into the poop of the frigate, the issue of the combat was no longer doubtful.

'Mate,' said Lawrence dryly to his friend, 'we must die! Your hand! God help you.'

'Where are you going, Lawrence?'

'To give Sharkley the signal.'

'A captain ought to remain at his post till death takes him. The man will obey me. Stay where you are. Farewell!'

Morgan was departing, when Lawrence rushed after and

stopped him. 'I guess your purpose,' he cried, 'you wish to see Jennie and die beside her. That I will not allow.'

'Who shall prevent me?'

'I! Do you hear—I!'

'What,' returned Morgan angrily, 'a threat?'

'No, a command.'

The companions in arms glared at each other with blind fury, then by mutual consent they lifted their cutlasses.

It was a horrible spectacle to see two men thus give way to their impetuous passions, while the enemy's fire threatened every moment their lives, and a volcano ready to burst under their feet and a tornado on their heads, standing as it were on the very threshold of eternity, they yet thirsted for each other's blood. Yet, cool even in their madness, they defended and attacked with skill. At the first charge neither was wounded, but finding themselves too close to use effectually their cutlasses. they drew back a step, but only to attack each other with more ardour than ever.

Surprised at first by the rapid movements of the buccaneer, Morgan stood on the defensive, but waiting his opportunity, cut his antagonist full across the breast.

'You are wounded!' exclaimed the Englishman, drawing back clear.

'What matters that if I kill you too, and I will do it!' yelled Lawrence. Exasperated at the obstinacy of his foe, Morgan determined to be implacable, but scarcely had they crossed weapons again, before the Cornish knight tottered back against the bulwarks. A Spanish ball had lodged in his thigh.

Lawrence's first impulse was to take advantage of the accident, but recovering himself instantly, he threw down his blade, and rushed to Morgan, clasping his hand with fervour.

'Lewis,' he said, 'you alone made me ashamed of myself! You are right; a captain ought never to abandon his post. You shall see Jennie; a minute suffices to tell a woman you love her. Let Sharkley fire the train.'

Scarcely had Lawrence finished speaking before Wildflower came on deck.

'Oh, he is alive!' cried she with such intense delight that it seemed as if a halo of smiles shone round her head. 'But how pale you are! Oh, heavens, you are wounded!'

'Yes, Jennie, but what does that matter? we shall soon all be dead.'

'Is there then no hope, Lawrence?' she said; 'you are so famous a captain, cannot you save us? Why don't you fly?'

'My sweet child,' he answered, 'if the heaven such angels fall from, sought to snatch us out of the clutches of the Spaniards, it could not do it now.'

'Oh, Lawrence, don't blaspheme. One day I saw an eagle pounce down on a dove, but Leathercap was with me, and he shot the eagle ; the poor dove was saved.'

'And what do you infer from that, child ?—I am no dove.'

'That if a dove can be saved out of an eagle's clutches, we who are not yet in the clutches of the Spaniards may be saved too.　　What, Lawrence, not if a ball went right through the Spanish mainmast ? would not that cripple her, and could not we escape like the dove ?'

'Jennie,' roared the buccaneer, 'heaven has spoken by your. mouth ! How is it so simple a thing never struck me ? Mate, take my place ; never mind Sharkley !'

Rushing into the midst of the remaining crew, the commander chose five men and made them load the Long Tom. Morgan and Wildflower watched his movements with intense anxiety, and prayed that an enemy's ball might not hamper this last effort. They saw Lawrence with his body bent and motionless as a statue, his eye fixed at the sight at the breech of the gun, watching the heavings of the sea. Soon a flash shone. Lawrence had played his last stake. He was so marvellous a marksman even with great guns, that Morgan thought he saw the enemy's mainmast already tremble.

'Load again !' cried Lawrence.

Turning towards Wildflower, he remarked, chuckling : 'The eagle is winged, next time the pinion will be lopped off.'

He made no vain boast : half a minute later a terrible crash, followed by cries of rage and despair from the admiral's ship, showed that the shot had told.

A loud hurrah arose from the freebooters, who had nothing more to fear from the flagship.

'As the coward dared not board us, let him bear the penalty of his cowardice,' cried Lawrence. 'Had I only fifty men, in half-an-hour the admiral's ship should have had her flag ignominiously flying at her bowsprit.'

There were only sixteen available pirates.

'Friends,' cried the captain, 'all now depends on our impudence. The admiral's supporter is coming down hand over hand. To hazard another fight with such fearful odds is not to be thought of. But the boldness of our demeanour is our only safeguard. Let us wait for her, and offer her battle. The condition of the first ship must make her too sick to accept our challenge.'

This prediction was fulfilled : his audacious manœuvre met with complete success, for the Spanish ship sheered off.

'Wildflower,' said Lawrence, with an emotion he could not conceal, 'angelic child, you have not only saved the vessel, but you have converted me. The intervention of Providence

has been so evident that my pride bows in humble thanksgiving
for such a miracle. Mate,' he said, after a brief pause, to Morgan,
'our trials are not yet ended. We have still to wage war with
the fury of the elements. The squall is upon us, and the vessel,
riddled as she is with the enemy's shot, leaks damnably. Let
the man in the magazine be relieved.'

A dreadful roll of thunder burst forth, and the tornado
sweeping over the disabled vessel drove her under the raging
billows. Notwithstanding the blood he had lost from his wounds,
the chief took his speaking-trumpet and gave his orders as
calmly as ever.

CHAPTER XXXVII.

THE TORNADO.

THE rest of the day, and all night, brought much suffering to
the buccaneers.

The tempest raged fearfully most of the time.

There was an appalling sight on board the clipper. The
groans of the wounded and their shrieks of agony were mingled
with the howlings of the wind and the creaking of the lead-
peppered spars.

The sixteen men who were unwounded, overcome with fatigue,
only imperfectly performed their double task of manœuvring
the vessel and working at the pumps. The water gained on
them fast, and Lawrence saw that unless some fresh miracle
saved them, they must founder.

The next daybreak an immense mass of lead-coloured clouds
enveloped them almost in the darkness of night.

About ten the frigate, caught by a wave, rolled on one side.
All gave themselves up for lost in this dreadful position, but
Laurence's voice still rose calm and clearly.

'Courage and silence there,' he cried, 'the ship answers to the
helm yet ; what cause is there to give her up ?'

The frigate, having several times risen to the tops of the
raging waves, only to be engulfed for a moment in the abysses
between, always at last righted herself. Few vessels of other
build would have lived through such a sea.

As it was impossible for the clipper under such circumstances
to sail in the teeth of the wind, Lawrence was obliged to give up
steering for Jamaica and scud away.

As this course left the vessel still exposed to the danger of
being again caught by the Spanish, the buccaneers considered
themselves near their last hour.

'Sir Lewis,' said Wildflower, who, lashed to the bulwarks,

would not, in spite of the danger she was in of being washed
overboard, return to her cabin, 'I feel that it is all over with
us.   Lawrence is a good seaman, but what can he do against the
anger of Heaven ? Nothing. But why do you look so sad, Lewis ;
do you fear death ?'

'My beloved sister,' answered Morgan, with emotion, 'Heaven
is my witness, I do not fear death ! I long for it.   What makes
me sad is that I brought this fate upon you. Had you never
seen me, you would still have been contented in those magnificent forests that you love so well. Your pity for me, lonely
wanderer on the earth, has ruined you.'

'Don't speak so, Sir Lewis,' answered Wildflower in mild
reproach, 'you are indeed mistaken. When you first came to
my father's, I was not as happy as in my childhood. I was often
sad, unhappy, solitude seemed sometimes unsupportable to me,
and then the company of Leathercap, kind as he was to me,
wearied me. It seemed as if far away there was a world where
I might be happy. Don't therefore let my death distress you,
Sir Lewis ! You caused me great misery, but that was not your
fault, and if you knew——.'

Confused and blushing, she stopped short.

'Wildflower,' answered Morgan, 'why by generous falsehoods, which are only greater proofs of your goodness, aug-
ment the pain I already feel, that death will separate us so
soon ?'

'I tell falsehoods ? oh, Lewis, I am not cunning enough for
that !   I repeat, you have no cause to reproach yourself for my
death, for if you knew——' Jennie spoke with a trembling voice,
and Morgan felt his heart beat with rapture in spite of the pain
of his wound, and the precarious state they were all in. He
whispered to her—

'What do you mean by those words, "If you knew"?'

She hesitated.

'Why does my question make you uneasy ?'

'I don't know. Perhaps you would laugh at me ; therefore
I am silent.'

'But if you will not tell me all your thoughts, Jennie, I
shall think you do not like me.'

'Not like you, Sir Lewis ?' ejaculated Wildflower with
innocent indignation. 'How wrong of you to think such a
thing ! I will tell you if you wish it ; only, you will rate me
foolish and perhaps laugh at my ignorance. It seems, Sir
Knight, that before I knew you, my life was a tranquil sleep.
Only since then have I found out I have a heart. Then everything changed : the face of nature, the perfume of flowers, the
song of birds, all seemed to give me a delight and enchantment
which I had never felt before. I felt how happy life might be

You smile, señor,' said Jennie, hanging her head. 'You think me very foolish, do you not?'

'Go on, dear,' murmured the Englishman softly; 'to die listening to such words would only be quitting one heaven for another.'

'My lord,' continued she, as if in spite of herself, and as if her feelings overpowered her will, 'you must not then reproach yourself for my death, because before I saw you I knew not what it was to live. You caused me much pain. Wherefore? I cannot tell, nor you either; perhaps it was the fear of losing you. You must not accuse yourself of making me suffer, for—but you will think me so extravagantly foolish—but my past sufferings are dear to me; the remembrance is sweet. At this moment, it seems that suffering is happiness.'

Wildflower, like all simple, pure natures, had a poetry of expression that harmonized with her soft voice and lovely features, giving her an irresistible charm.

Captivated, enthralled, the Cornish adventurer hesitated how to answer consistently with his honour and her happiness, when two monstrous seas washed over the frigate, and all on board gave themselves up for lost.

In this awful moment, Morgan threw his arms round Jennie, clasped her passionately to his breast, and whispering 'Wildflower, I love you!' imprinted a burning kiss on her lips.

She shut her eyes, a convulsive trembling came over her, a death-like pallor covered her face, and like a lily snapped from the stalk, she drooped her head and swooned outright.

At this instant the vessel, again victorious, rose above the crests, and Lawrence's steady voice gave courage, almost hope, to the fainting crew with these words:

'My lads, you are too brave to fear death, but uncertainty and suspense are dreadful! Choose a part worthy of you. Let us risk in one mighty effort the chances that remain. In five minutes we shall be either safe or gone under!'

He got around outside the rattlins, and mounted the rope ladder. Grave, thoughtful, and with the experience he possessed to so high a degree, he studied the state of the atmosphere, the plans and mysteries of the hurricane.

Soon his face lighted up with boldness and inspiration; a smile of triumph crossed his lips, and through his speaking trumpet he bellowed: 'Down-haul the mizzen-trysail, and the mainstaysail! tack the foresail! and haul all to windward, hard —jam 'em down for your lives, men!'

A dead silence followed this command.

'Well, boys,' cried he with a sneer, 'are you all changed into Spaniards? Fires of Tophet, you skulk in cowardice!'

The buccaneers, ashamed of having for a moment doubted the

infallibility of their captain, made up for their halting by enthusiastic alacrity. The manœuvre was accomplished with a rapidity which, considering the small number of the crew, was incredible. The vessel, already labouring in the trough, yielded to the helm, fell off before the gale, clearing the hill of waters. She righted herself and swam well with the wind on the quarter. Her rapid course neutralized the force of the tempest One danger alone remained imminent, that she could not mount the boisterous waves, but Lawrence ordered a drag-cable to be thrown out of her stern, and by this happy expedient the bark was steadied and her nose kept clean from the water ; she rolled little and lurched no more.

Lawrence now turned to the part of the quarter-deck where stood Morgan. Wildflower was just recovering her senses.

'Where am I ? what has happened ? Oh, I remember ; a monstrous wave was carrying me away ! I felt myself dying. It was you, Sir Lewis, who recalled me to life. Oh, it was wrong of you, death came so sweetly !'

Morgan hung his head and dared not answer.

'Mate,' said Lawrence, 'I find that I cannot for two minutes longer resist the weakness that oppresses me ; I have lost too much blood. I must give in. Take my place. These are my instructions.' He explained briefly but clearly what he wanted done, then quite overcome, fell on the deck.

'I am faint,' he said ; 'throw your cloak over me ; don't pay any attention. The men must think me taking a cat-nap.'

Morgan entreated Jennie to leave him, to return to her cabin. Her presence troubled him ; for he needed to be alone.

'Good-bye, dear Lewis, take care of yourself,' she said in a soft hesitating voice, not daring to look at Morgan. She too felt as if in solitude alone she could collect her thoughts. After she had left, the knight with an uncertain step walked up and down the quarter-deck.

'What a fearful position is mine !' he thought. 'To feel an ardent love and know that it is returned, and yet be forced to support the presence and odious efforts of a rival. And what a rival—one who lets no obstacle baulk him of his will. Fatal oath that binds me ! Oh, why did I not sooner see the false path on which I had entered ? I ought to have perceived that Nativa only embodied the dreams of my solitude and was not a real love. I ought not to have given myself up to her, bound hand and foot. Must I then sacrifice the hopes of my youth, the happiness of my whole life, to a moment's madness ? What prevents my giving back Nativa her promise, and receiving my own freedom ? However, a Morgan cannot forfeit his word. Do your duty, come what may, is the motto. I am a gentleman, I can bear all. Besides,' he added, sighing bitterly, 'my sufferings will be shorter perhaps than I anticipate. What a fool! I am looking forward sadly to the future when perhaps this very hour is our last.' He gave his whole attention to the vessel, and remarked with astonishment that her speed was much lessened though what canvas she could bear was set.

'Come, lads,' he cried, 'steady at the pumps there; work hard.'

The buccaneers ceased work.

'In truth, comrade,' said one, 'as die we must, we don't care to labour in vain. You are a sharp, brave, true officer, but may the devil strangle me if we obey you. How could sixteen men, tired to death as we are, manage a vessel as leaky as this of ours? All nonsense; two hours' hard work would not reduce by an inch less the water in the hold. Bah! the best course is to let things take their turn. Look at Lawrence who sleeps: there is an answer to all you would say. Do like him; we will drink forgetfulness of the present, and future go hang.'

The buccaneers having lost all hope of succour, broached a cask of brandy, and strove by drunkenness to alleviate their despair; their troubled looks and heavy staggering movements proved to Morgan that he must no longer count on their help.

One man alone obeyed his voice: this was Allan, who had not received a scratch in the fight, and now came towards his master with uncertain steps.

'Master,' he said, 'our comrades are fools; I have told them over and over again that Cornishmen never get drowned, and with one aboard they therefore have nothing to fear. But these fellows are regular unbelievers. I will go to the pumps and you shall see.'

Persuaded that he could work the clumsy machine alone, he was astonished at his ineffectual endeavours.

'Well, how odd!' he grumbled, 'it won't do. Oh, I see; it is rusty.'

'Sit down by me, Allan,' said Morgan; 'I will not let an honest fellow like you die in drunkenness.'

Though flattered by being asked to sit down near his master, he could not help casting a longing look at the brandy cask.

Morgan, convinced of the fruitlessness of all remonstrances, threats or entreaties, no longer pleaded with the crew; he owned to himself that they were not altogether wrong to refuse to work when their efforts would do no good.

An hour passed, and the state of the vessel was still more dangerous. The knight calculated that before night she must sink.

'Lawrence,' he called, stooping over the captain, 'I want you.'

'What is the matter, mate?' he asked coolly.

'The matter is that the crew are drunk and refuse to ply longer at the pumps.'

'What can I do?　It was not worth waking me for that, the men are plaguy sensible mutineers.'

'Shall we not at least try to get out the boats?—there is no time to lose.'

'Assuredly, let us try.'

Although Lawrence affected to show neither ill-humour nor weakness, Morgan felt sure that the buccaneer was completely spent, and incapable of further action.

'What I want of you, Lawrence,' he continued, 'is for the crew to hear your voice, I'll manage the rest.　Another word; what shall we do with the wounded that cover the 'tweenships? There are twenty men mortally wounded, how can we take them with us?　Well. we shall see.　What is most essential is to get the long boat out.'

Morgan went down into the cabin; the water was already encroaching upon it.　He called Wildflower.

'Here I am, Lewis,' she replied, coming out of her state-room.

'Were you sleeping, Jennie?　Come quick up on deck, the bark will soon go down; the boats are being got out now.'

CHAPTER XXXVIII.

THE SINKING SHIP.

On his return, the Englishman was much surprised to see his mate, whom he thought entirely prostrate, occupied in stimulating the zeal and activity of the crew.

The buccaneers, under the influence of drink, listened carelessly to the previously all-powerful eloquence of their captain, and seemed little disposed to obey him.

'Lads,' said Lawrence, 'I have still power enough left to save you, but the horrible agony that your cowardice fills me with, forces me to punish you.　I go to set the powder on fire. Good-bye, mutinous dogs.'

These words, spoken solemnly, made a strong impression on the men; two or three rose and sought to stop him.

'Let any man dare to stop me, I will blow his brains out,' cried Lawrence, clapping his hand on his pistols.

He walked on with a steady step.

'Pretend to be afraid, and ask pardon for the men,' he whispered rapidly as he passed Morgan, who, perceiving at once the captain's intention, lent himself to it with great presence of mind.

'Captain,' he cried, rushing after Lawrence, 'I beg of you to wait a little longer. I have not refused to obey you, therefore I do not deserve to share the fate of those cowards. Before you put your desperate resolution in force, give me time to clear away a cutter and save myself.'

Lawrence seemed to hesitate, so Morgan continued more earnestly,—

'Captain, life is too sweet to sacrifice it without a struggle. Who can tell if I may not meet with a friendly vessel?—that a month hence, at the head of a valiant band, I may not capture a rich Spanish galleon? What joy I shall feel then, when, surrounded by gold, women, and slaves, I shall be able to say that I owe all to my own courage. For the last time, captain, I implore you, before you carry out your horrible design, let me take to a boat.'

'Let me go with you, master,' Allan appended.

Lawrence appeared to reflect before he replied,—

'Mate, your request is just; I give you ten minutes to get out one boat.'

Instantly the crew rushed to the boats. Lawrence shrugged his shoulders with disdainful pity.

'Men are children,' he muttered; 'to lead them it is not needful to be superior in strength or intelligence, but only to know their weaknesses, and address yourself to their low passions; stupid brutes who obey me because they are afraid, and their fear prevents them from considering that the powder-room was swamped, and therefore my threat was vain.'

The vessel possessed three boats, a pinnace and two others. The crew first thought of the pinnace, placed between the mainmast and the mizzen; but, alas, scarcely had the pulleys raised it half a foot when it broke in two, completely riddled with the enemy's shot. One of the boats hung a-port had not suffered less, and was utterly useless also.

This discovery confounded the crew. The same men who before refused to make any effort to save themselves, now lamented that they could not escape their doom.

Morgan ran to the other boat, which hung at the stern, and found it uninjured.

In less than five minutes a barrel of water and some provisions were thrown in, and it was lowered into the sea.

Although the fury of the waves made the latter manœuvre very difficult, it was successfully accomplished.

Two men let themselves down by a rope into the boat, shipped the rudder and laid the oars in readiness.

'Come, Wildflower,' said Lawrence, 'time is precious; your knight has made you a cradle-line to help your descent and save you. Make haste.'

Wildflower, before seating herself in the rope-chair rigged
for her, hesitated.

'The wounded,' she inquired piteously.

'Be quiet,' cried Lawrence ; 'don't you see the boat is already
too small for the living ? The fate of war is often dreadful. We
must not think of those poor wretches, but try to persuade ourselves that they died in the fight.'

He seized Jennie, and almost by force put her into the chair.
Morgan trembled violently as the poor girl was several times
nearly carried away by the waves. Pale and with her eyes fixed
on the Englishman, Jennie wore a sweet expression of resignation, for she guessed his agony, and though frightened herself,
experienced a throb of joy.

An hour later, two men alone remained on board, Lawrence
and the Cornishman.

'I fear, mate,' said the former, 'that during the time it will
take us to embark, the vessel will founder and suck the skiff
down with it.'

The embarkation was indeed very difficult, by the state of
the sea, and the precautions it was necessary to take to prevent
the boat from being swamped ; it took ten minutes to get each
man on board.

The two young men, considering their fatigue and wounded
condition, could not be less than half-an-hour getting on board.
There was every likelihood that the vessel would go down before
that time.

'Comrade,' said Morgan, 'in sacrificing ourselves for others,
it is not a crime, but merely duty.'

The young man bent over the side, and collecting all his
strength, called out with a voice that was heard even above the
raging of the storm—

'Boat ahoy ! the ship is going down, shove off at once.'
Wildflower, farewell.'

Turning to Lawrence he subjoined—

'Mate, forgive me if without consulting you I have disposed
of your life ; time pressed.'

'Lewis,' responded the rover, holding out his hand, 'you are
a fine fellow. We shall both die bravely, you sustained by your
virtue, I by my disgust of life.'

While Lawrence was speaking, a touching scene took place
on board the boat.

As soon as the buccaneers heard Morgan, they hastened to
obey his orders, and pushed off at once.

Carried away by the waves, they were already two cables'
length from the vessel, before Wildflower rose and with the
energy of despair spoke as follows :

'My friends, I entreat you to return to the ship. What,

would you be so cruel, so ungrateful as to leave him to die, who has devoted himself for you? It would be a disgrace you could never wash off, and would follow you everywhere. Would you give the Brothers of the Coast the right to point at you and say, yonder are the cowards who abandoned their captain! Courage! back to the ship.'

Wildflower had spoken so eagerly, and standing up in the boat, in danger every moment of being carried away by the waves, she displayed such resolution and courage for a young girl, and she was so beautiful in her enthusiastic devotion, that the buccaneers were moved, and for a moment rested on their oars, but this lasted but a moment.

'Wildflower,' answered one, 'we all love you, and you have seen us often enough under fire not to doubt our courage. If we refuse you now, it is because your request is madness.'

'Brothers of the Coast,' continued she, 'you believe Heaven hearkens to my prayers? If you refuse to obey me, I will entreat Heaven to let us all perish. I will curse you all; not one, I predict, will survive this crime.'

The freebooters, so calm under the enemy's fire, so terrible in an assault, so indomitable always, were nevertheless, like other seamen, very superstitious; therefore Wildflower's speech had a great effect upon them.

'But, Wildfire,' said the one who had already spoken, 'we would willingly save Lawrence and his brave partner, if it were humanly possible. But see, the barque is going down. The best that we can do is to wait till she disappears, and then perhaps we may be able to pick up them as floats.'

This chance of salvage turned the rest of the crew from attending to Jennie's entreaties.

'Oh, you cowards!' she screamed, 'how much time is lost!' She fell fainting on the stern-sheets.

During this scene, which lasted much less time than it has taken to relate, Allan had remained with his head down and his brows bent, but had not backed Jennie's appeals. All in a moment, overturning the man next him, he rose, brandishing a hatchet.

'Look you here,' he cried, 'if you don't go back to the ship I'll capsize every man Jack o' ye !'

The gesture was expressive, and it was easy to understand that one blow of his hatchet would wreck their frail and overladen boat.

In this critical juncture the buccaneers obeyed.

'Come, Sir Knight,' cried Jennie, with passionate eagerness.

The position of the vessel, two-thirds submerged, rendered it easy for Lawrence and Morgan to leap into the boat, which they did in a few minutes.

'Thanks, my lads,' said the captain, who, ignorant of Wildflower's and Allan's intercession, thought he owed his relief to the devotion of his men.

'Wildflower,' said Morgan, holding her hand in both of his, 'my last thought was of you ; but Heaven has not willed we should be separated. In its infinite mercy we are allowed to die together.'

'We are very young to die, Sir Lewis,' observed Jennie, 'why not hope ?'

She was still speaking when a fearful yell arose from the buccaneers—the vessel had gone down with all the wounded and the treasure taken from Grenada.

'Come, take to your oars and pull steadily,' cried Lawrence's impassible voice. 'Who knows, lads, if soon we may not envy the fate of our companions ? All is over with them ; they died without feeling the pangs of hunger and the more frightful suffering of thirst.' Half-an-hour after the vessel had foundered, darkness overshadowed the frail skiff, tossed on the mighty waves of the storm-tracked sea.

Wildflower, with her head leaning on Morgan's shoulder, and her hand in his, felt so calm in her delightful weariness, that she was thankful for her happiness.

———

CHAPTER XXXIX.

THE RESCUE.

THE day that followed was dreadful ; the storm, instead of abating, seemed still to increase ; each moment the boat was in danger of upsetting.

Once used to their position the buccaneers uttered no murmur or complaint. Their constant familiarity with danger, and contempt of life, replaced in them Christian resignation ; they had only the courage of the brute, but they possessed that in a high degree.

As each wave broke over the boat it filled it with water, and covered them all with spray. Wildflower gently pressed the Englishman's hand in hers, a simple action which awoke strong emotion in the bandit's breast, overcome with fatigue and a prey to a violent fever brought on by his wound. He no longer reasoned, but gave himself up to his emotions. It seemed to him that the dark clouds that hung over them dispersed, and an azure sky, studded with stars, over-canopied them ; that the boisterous roaring of the sea was changed into a gentle murmur, and the howlings of the tempest into a soft evening breeze ; but most part of the night, overcome with weakness, he slumbered.

'How strange,' thought Jennie, 'that this peaceful sleep seems to refresh me more than if I slept myself!' Oh, lately I have lived more through the chevalier than in myself. Can he have taken my soul? Oh, never could I survive him! How little have I thought until now.'

The next morning, when a dull windy day succeeded the darkness, the boat contained a strange sight. Wildflower, with blooming complexion, smiling calmly and rested, while the buccaneers around her, strong men used to hardships, looked haggard and overcome.

Towards three in the afternoon the wind somewhat abated, and although the sea ran still very high, yet it was possible to steer the boat.

Suddenly a cry of 'a sail!' made all hearts beat. Every one got up, at the manifest risk of upsetting the boat. About a quarter of a league off, lay a brigantine with all sails set, braving the storm. The height of the waves had prevented the shipwrecked crew from seeing it sooner. At the sight of help, a cry of exultation rose from all, till it was somewhat cooled by an old sailor saying, 'Perhaps she is Spanish.'

'We have our cutlasses, let us board her,' cried Sharkley.

'No fear, lads,' said Lawrence, 'that ship is not Spanish; there is only one man in the world that would crack on with all sails set such weather as this, and that man is Morgan.'

At the name there was a burst of joy.

'Morgan?' echoed Sir Lewis. 'Wildflower, you are our good angel.'

'Don't be too sure,' remarked Lawrence with a constrained smile, 'it is possible he may not spy us; it is too early to whistle till out of the waves.'

The way in which these words were spoken surprised Sir Lewis.

'Truly, mate, it would seem you wished it so.'

'Well, yes,' answered the buccaneer; 'why should I seek to hide it? I would rather perish than have help at his hands. The Island of St. Domingo is too small for Morgan the Second and me. There is but one sun in the heavens, and Morgan or I must suffer eclipse.'

He spoke in a whisper, but had he said it aloud, not one of the crew would have heeded it, for all hearts, all minds, all thoughts were engrossed in the brigantine.

Very soon, from the vessel's change of course it became evident that the boat had been seen, for the brigantine headed directly towards them. Then these men, who, with death staring them in the face, had not uttered a murmur, gave vent to mad transports of joy.

At this moment Morgan was for them the greatest captain in

the world, the prince of buccaneers, a demigod of the sea, Neptune revived. Half-an-hour had not passed since they perceived this vessel before the poor shipwrecked mariners were safely on her deck.

'You, my boy!' cried Morgan, with evident delight, as soon as he saw Lewis. 'Heaven be praised! This happiness makes me forget much trouble; I find I love you even more than I thought.' The old buccaneer's reception of Lawrence was very different; he bowed to him with infinite politeness and then turned away.

'Morgan,' said Lawrence with a sneer, 'own if you had known I was one of the party, you would not have shown so much zeal in coming to our aid. Ha, ha! I cannot help laughing at your disappointment. You, too, have saved me. Your star must be on the wane; your luck must have left you.'

Morgan remained unheedful.

'Captain,' he returned, 'you do me injustice. I thank Heaven that I have saved you all. Don't affect a gaiety that is only skin-deep, and comes not from the heart. Why should I wish you death? Do you think I see in you a rival, an enemy? Your pride blinds you. You have astonishing intrepidity, it is true, unsurpassed coolness and self-possession, infinite resources, every talent in fact that fits you to execute bold enterprises with success, and sustain with glory unequal fights. But beyond that, you are nothing. Your impetuosity and passions prevent your success in a larger field of action. During a fight you are my equal, in common life only an instrument that I make useful. Believe me, put aside all that boasting and parade which are not natural to you, and only degrade you. You know in your soul and conscience that I do not fear you.'

Morgan had expressed himself with the calm authority of conviction. Lawrence tried several times to interrupt him, but the tiger was obliged, in spite of himself, to recognise the superiority of the lion.

'Morgan,' responded he, 'I am surprised that, contrary to your usual prudence, you did not fear to irritate me. Take care. You count upon no strife being possible between us, but you forget what weight my accusation may bear when we are face to face at—you know where. It shall not be said that you have squandered our gold without a voice being raised to call you to account for the unlimited powers with which you have been invested. I warn you that you will find me an implacable enemy.'

'Then you will soon have the opportunity of displaying your eloquence. Thank chance that brought you on board my brigantine, for I am on my way to the Stronghold.'

This answer gave evident satisfaction to the captain.

'Well,' he answered, 'then you see I was right just now to say that your star was on the wane.'

'Foolish fellow,' said the old pirate quietly, 'don't you know that as soon as you thwart me I shall crush you?'

The buccaneer chief bowed again and moved away.

'Yes, it is too true,' said Lawrence, biting his lips; 'this man does not fear me.'

On leaving Lawrence Morgan went into the cabin, where Sir Lewis was lying on a chest of arms, Wildflower kneeling by him. The sight of the sweet girl made the old buccaneer smile.

' Well, boy,' he said to his nephew, 'so you have been baptized in fire. You have had, it seems, a glorious fight, but you have been struck. Let me look at your wound. My pretty Wildflower, go and fetch me a phial from the cuddy. You will find it in the locker.'

While the girl was gone, Morgan examined the young man's wound. An expression of grief, almost of terror, passed over his face, but before Lewis could observe it, he had by a strong effort recovered his usual calm demeanour and voice.

'It will not be much damage,' he said; 'the ball has not touched the bone. A few days' rest will, I trust, set you all right. Do you suffer much pain?'

'Very great.'

'Yes, over-exertion has a little inflamed the wound; you want rest. A good sleep would do you good.'

He took up the youth in his arms, as easily as if he were a child, carried him into his cabin, put him on his bed, and left him; murmuring, 'Poor boy, I much fear his wound is incurable. It seems a hopeless case.'

CHAPTER XL.

THE CAVERN-HARBOUR.

FIVE days had passed since Morgan's brigantine had picked up the shipwrecked sailors. It was near sunset, a favourable wind was bowling them along at six knots an hour. Morgan, reclining on a settle on the poop, was scanning with a careless eye the vast horizon.

A great change had come over the young man; his hollow eyes shone with feverish brilliancy: his cheeks were pale and sunken; all spoke of suffering and weakness. Seated at his feet, Wildflower gazed up at him with sorrowful anxiety, but when the knight looked at her, her forced smile was more distressing than a sob.

With his arms folded and head bent, old Morgan walked with a nervous, irregular step backwards and forwards. Whether the presence of Morgan was hateful to him, or his wounds obliged him to keep quiet, for five days handsome Lawrence had not left his room.

The words 'Land ho !' cried by the man on watch awoke young Morgan from his stupor.

'Wildflower,' he said in a weak voice, 'did I hear aright? Have they just signalled land?'

'Yes, Sir Lewis ; patience a little longer. In a few hours more you will have the rest you need so much, and the care you cannot have on board. Heavens ! how rejoiced I am to return to St. Domingo.' Wildflower ran to the taffrail and looked in the direction designated by the man on watch.

'It is very strange,' she said, 'I don't recognise the distant coast of our island.'

'That proves, Wildflower,' said the captain, who had drawn near, ' that you have a sailor's eye. Our brigantine is not going near Tortoise Island, but towards the Cape south'ard of the Spanish port of St. Domingo.'

Morgan's answer caused great surprise to his hearers ; a cloud came over the Englishman's face.

'Have we mistaken our way?'

'Child,' answered his uncle, 'Morgan never mistakes his course. We are going where I wished to go.'

'Explain yourself, sir ; your words and actions are riddles to me. Why give us up into the power of our enemies?'

'Never fear, Lewis, we are as safe here as if we were at anchor in Tortoise Island ; however, I will explain all later on. The sound of the land currents is already heard ; the vessel needs all my attention now.'

Hardly had he left them, when Morgan and Wildflower were astonished at a singular phenomenon. Although the sea was calm and the wind light, the brigantine without any apparent cause doubled its speed to twelve knots an hour. At the same time a loud, incessant roar was distinctly heard ; it reminded Morgan so strongly of the Friar's Well, that he shut his eyes to complete the delusion.

The youth also observed, and this increased his astonishment, that whilst the brigantine's crew paid no heed to the noise, the men from the lost cruiser showed a surprise as great as his own.

Rising from his seat, Sir Lewis looked over the handrail ; the speed of the brigantine was so great as almost to dazzle him ; they were going at the rate of eighteen knots an hour ; the vessel had certainly entered some irresistible current.

Without the unlimited confidence he felt in his kinsman he would have given the vessel up for lost.

For an hour the swiftness increased rather than diminished,

The vessel was coasting round the cape, and what a coast ! steep cliffs and inaccessible ravines in granite rocks.

Morgan's temerity seemed such an act of folly, so out of all ordinary seamanship, that Lewis thought he must himself be under some painful delusion.

'Well, boy,' said his uncle, 'what do you think of our fashion of nearing land ?'

'Nothing, sir ; only I can hardly believe my own senses, and fancy I must be dreaming.'

'Your wonder will increase presently. Do you see those gigantic rocks which rise like sentinels solitary in the midst of the sea, and seem to lean one against the other at the top ?'

'Perfectly.'

'We are going to run between those two rocks.'

'Oh, impossible ! there is scarcely room for a canoe.'

'The distance deceives you ; they are at least sixty feet apart. Only if the barque fails to answer her helm she would drive to pieces ; therefore, I am going to take the helm myself. No more questions, dear boy ; I require all my attention and coolness.'

Whilst he took the tiller, the roaring in the distance approached with fearful rapidity ; very soon it was impossible to hear one another speak.

The person most alarmed on board was Allan, who knelt down in a corner and prayed to good St. Bride.

'My dear, kind lady,' he implored, 'don't believe, I entreat you, that I have anything to do with this sea-devil's work. If I had been allowed to leave, I should have gone long ago on shore. Only let me be saved by another miracle, and I promise to present your shrine with sterling silver candlesticks ! Only, unless we take another town, I am puzzled where the silver will come from ! Our brigantine is going to throw herself on those enormous rocks ! Oh, we are lost.'

The moment that the vessel glided beneath and between the gigantic rocks was one of those solemn ones which leave a deep trace in a man's life.

The silence of death reigned over everyone, save old Morgan, who smiled.

The manœuvre succeeded perfectly.

Scarcely had the light vessel passed over this fearful bar than it was at the mouth of a very lofty cavern formed in the rocks, either from the constant chafing of the water, or by some volcanic eruption. The sea rushed furiously into this deep cavern, whence issued sulphurous vapours so thick that Morgan, weakened by illness, felt himself fainting.

'Oh, this is the gateway to—ahem ! whew !' sneezed Allan ; ' oh, it's getting hotter ! '

The spectacle of the ship enframed, as it were, in this sublime and terrible, yet fantastic retreat of nature, no pen could describe. Carried forward by the force of the current, the brigantine disappeared in the cavernous gloom ; but soon a bright light shone on the obscurity, and she lay at rest in a deep subterranean lake, light coming from large openings in rocks overhead.

'What do you think of this snuggery, Lewis ?' asked Morgan, 'I don't think even your imagination could conceive what nature at this moment spreads before our eyes.'

'Where are we, sir? Don't abuse my credulity, for my mind is so bewildered that I could receive the greatest absurdities for truth.'

'We are in a chasm, Lewis, which if not often explored is well known, called the Gulf—El Golfo Tristo.'

This inlet, the sides of which are bordered by rapid currents, caused such terror, not only to the Spaniards, but also to the buccaneers that were not familiar, that they dared not approach within miles. Whenever an earthquake was near, such a dreadful moaning proceeded from this abyss that it spread alarm even as far off as Port-au-Prince.

'This place is seven leagues south of the Neiba, one of the principal rivers of the island. The environs belong to the Spaniards, but are not inhabited ; they are very fertile and yield us precious resources, for at our leisure we can here provide ourselves with wood and water, and we can hunt the wild boar and buffalo. Now that your curiosity is half satisfied, let us go on shore. I will tell you, presently when we are alone, the motive that brings me here, and the mysteries that are connected with this Sad Gulf.'

Sailors with torches now entered a boat and took their leader, young Morgan, and Jennie on shore.

'Jennie,' said the captain, showing her a natural excavation formed in the rock, 'here is the Knight's room, ask them to bring from the ship all that he may want. We will return directly.'

He took his nephew in his arms and carried him through the darkness with the sure step of a man well acquainted with the way.

'Sit down on this moss,' he said after a minute's walk, and having lighted a torch which he fixed against the wall so that it shed light all around, and would prevent any one coming on him unawares. 'My dear Lewis,' he continued, 'I have already told you of the mysterious association of which you refused to be a member. Our coming here has to do with that society. Do not forget that you are in honour bound not to reveal any particulars which I shall confide to you. This gulf is to us of the utmost consequence, and an immense aid. Sir Henry named it the Stronghold. Not only does it often enable us to escape from the Spanish cruisers, but it affords us a sure receptacle for our treasures. The Stronghold contains immense riches, nearly all the funds of our association. As a further precaution, I have placed at the entrance of the cave that encloses our wealth, a large quantity of gunpowder, so that if the Spaniards discovered our retreat and dared to follow us, their audacity would be punished with death. Isolated buccaneers wander about the neighbouring cliffs, and an enemy's vessel approaching would be signalled to me at once.

'My presence here proves that we call an extraordinary meeting, in which is to be considered an important expedition which I am going to propose.

'All the sailors in my brigantine are buccaneers, many of my associates are already here. That surprises you ; but this inland gulf extends right up to the mouth of the island. I have only to add that your comrade Lawrence will use every means to make me unpopular and suspected by our brethren. It is possible that his pride and ambition will bring on a catastrophe, therefore, Lewis, I have made my will. Don't interrupt me ; you will vex me by renewing this subject. Good-bye, Lewis ; I leave you to tell my associates of my arrival.'

Morgan went about twenty paces off, and having listened for a few moments, fired a pistol in the air, the report of which resounded with a thousand echoes.

CHAPTER XLI.

THE REVOLT.

In one of the most picturesque chambers of this marvellous grotto, which for many years had served as a place of refuge to the buccaneers, the day after their arrival a strange scene was passing.

The chamber itself, a vast natural cave, was adorned with thousands of stalactites and other crystallisations, which reflecting with inconceivable brilliancy the red glare of the torches, seemed like gigantic blocks of the most dazzling jewels. Several deep and narrow cavities which surrounded this oasis of light and brightness, enframed it in a mysterious shadow. Eighty initiated buccaneers composed this important assembly ; they were armed to the teeth. They stood leaning on their guns, and observed a respectful silence while Morgan was speaking.

'Brothers of the Coast,' he said, 'the time is come when we ought to cease to be obscure adventurers. Until now we have patiently grown in the shade, but it is the hour to declare our power in broad daylight. The part of Skimmers of the Ocean, *pirates*, suits neither our dignity nor our courage ! let us show that we are a nation. Thanks to my efforts, seconded by your intrepidity, we have immense resources at our command. With gold and steel, what obstacle can stop our progress? None.

'Brothers of the Coast, I come from Europe. I have treated with King William of England. I succoured him in his need, and thus have morally bought the authority which will make him our ally. I have obliged him to serve our interests ; soon, in concert with him, we undertake an important expedition, that of besieging—I mean taking Carthagena. Sir Henry had it once—again shall we not hold it? I have stipulated that our forces shall be commanded by one of ourselves, that our chiefs shall rank with those on board the British navy. I have reserved for myself full power.

'Brothers, I have no wish to make you deny your respective countries. We will remain Englishmen, or Frenchmen, or South Americans, but I wish that our submission should be voluntary, and leave us complete independence and freedom. Once masters of Carthagena, and consequently of all that coast of South America, Jamaica will fall naturally into our power. Jamaica being the chief isle of the Antilles, no human force will be able to destroy us, to oppose our progress, or stop our conquests. Before ten years are over, the Spanish possessions in America will belong to us ; a century hence, perhaps, our descendants will bring European civilization into the tropics. My eyes are dazzled with the certain and splendid future which awaits us !

'A last word, brothers. Thanks to deep research and study, thanks also to chance, I have made immense progress in naval tactics. I defy all the powers united to beat us on the sea.

'The empire of Old Ocean is ours. Even my bringing my brigantine into this gulf is a proof of this. Who amongst you, brave as you are, would dare to enter El Golfo Tristo, except in a small boat? Who amongst you will dare to take my brigantine out again into the open sea, in spite of the currents and the rocks? If there is one who can do it let him try, and if he succeeds I will own him as my master.

'Brothers of the Coast, I have said my all. Since I have held Sir Henry's place, I have always enjoyed your confidence and devotion. I require from you passive obedience in this, and I promise in return to give you dominion of the waters, and make you a great nation. Remember, I have never forfeited my word, nor failed in my promises. What I engage to do I do. Can I rely upon you ?'

These words breathed such enthusiasm and perfect self-confidence, that the buccaneers seemed electrified. They answered with immense and continued applause.

The noisy expression of their approbation was still echoing, when a sonorous, ironical voice arose to object. It was that of handsome Lawrence.

The popularity, or rather the reputation of the brilliant buccaneer was so great that there was immediate silence.

'Friends,' cried he, 'I shall not imitate Morgan the Second. I will not address you with a long-meditated and prepared speech. Few words suffice me. Brothers of the Coast, let us beware ! Morgan wants to engage us in a course which is neither suited to our instincts nor our tastes. What are we ? Dare-devil and devil-may-care adventurers. What do we want ? Fighting, gold, wine, and women. For what do we risk our lives ? For luxuries and enjoyment. What is the future to me ? What do I care to be the founder of a problematical power—a future nation ? What I want is a short life and a merry one. Morgan, I admire you ! What, because you are ambitious and dream of glory, do you propose to sacrifice us to your personal advancement ? Do you, in the height of your pride, dare to say to us :—"Friends, become the passive instruments of my fame. I consent to make use of you to transmit my name to posterity !" Really, this is carrying effrontery rather too far. And what do you offer us in return for the sacrifices which you require at our hands ? In exchange of our precious liberty, you offer us hateful slavery—to become your subjects. You despise us, undoubtedly ! '

Lawrence made a short pause ; then, assuming a solemn tone, he continued : ' Not only do I reject with all the pride of my independence the vile slavery that you offer us, but I go still further ; I accuse you loudly, in the face of all, of having abused our confidence and sacrificed our interests to your personal ambition ! It is in our memory that your namesake ran away with more than his share of spoil and with it bought a title of King Charles the Second ! Brag of him no more ! You may try to drape yourself in your own greatness, your hypocrisy does not blind me ; I will tear the mask from your face. Morgan, this is the end you have in view. Banished from England for having conspired against the royal authority with the exiled James, you would give us up bound hand and foot to the British crown, in order to get back your confiscated estates. I know well what you did in your late voyage to England ; you have made away with our gold, given thousands to the Dutchman. What did it matter to you ? The money you squandered was not yours, it came out of the common stock ; by ruining us, you might recover your fortune. Brothers of the Coast, you have heard my accusation ; nothing prevents Morgan from justifying himself, but I defy him to prove his innocence.'

Lawrence's attack was made with consummate skill ; by appealing to their gross and dissolute instincts, to their cupidity and love of independence, he had produced a strong effect.

Before so popular, old Morgan was now looked upon as a traitor and an enemy.

'Brothers of the Coast,' he rejoined at once, 'I am far from concealing that I did give thousands to the King of England. This even is a glory to us, and besides excellent policy. The taking of Carthagena will furnish us five times the sum.'

'The expedition to Carthagena will not take place,' returned Lawrence vehemently. 'Although I do not squander immense sums in bribery, I also have news from London. I received the formal assurance that Lord Russell had declared himself adverse to this enterprise. Brothers of the Coast, let us rejoice that, though we do lose some money, our beloved chief will be restored to his rank and estates. Hail to Sir Randolph Morgan !'

At this ironical exclamation, threatening howls and cries of 'Death to the traitor !' resounded from all sides. A sadly disdainful smile that played on Morgan's lips showed that this ingratitude and injustice of his associates, unexpected though they were, did not surprise him.

His head high and his arms folded, he waited till the storm raised against him by Lawrence's perfidy and hate had somewhat subsided ; then the word 'Silence !' pronounced with imposing authority, overcame the tumult. The buccaneers, expecting another accusation against their chief, held their peace.

A man, who had hitherto been hidden in the dark recesses of the grotto, advanced into the midst of the crowd. At the apparition of the new-comer a strong feeling of curiosity mingled with wonder and respect was manifest among the freebooters.

'The governor of the island !' muttered Lawrence.

Although royal authority did not weigh directly on the freebooters, still the power of Louis the Fourteenth in the seventeenth century was considered by the French almost divine. All the freebooters were also aware that the liberty which the French king allowed them he might at any time take away, so they always showed particular respect to the governor.

Marquis Ducasse especially, who had acquired an immense fortune as a freebooter himself before he was made Governor of St. Domingo, enjoyed considerable credit among his former comrades.

Everyone did justice to the loyalty and firmness of his character ; he was known to be merciful and tolerant as well as just.

'Gentlemen,' said the nobleman, 'do not consider in me the

Governor of St. Domingo, but your old partner. I have come
here to recall the most brilliant part of my life. If ever Morgan
the Second tried to free himself from the respect he owes his
king, I would send in my resignation or challenge him in single
combat. So might he me if I turned my coat against my
sovereign. But that only regards my conscience. Brothers of
the Coast, just now your extreme injustice and ingratitude
affected me deeply. What do we care for France or England,
Louis, James, or William, till after we have thought of ourselves? Morgan as a buccaneer is worthy of the respect of all.
The half-a-million which he is accused of having squandered is
not lost: William cannot go from his word, and I engage my
honour that the expedition to Carthagena will take place in
less than a year. Spain is equally the hatred of France as of
England.'

'Even against royal authority, if his Majesty objects?' asked
Lawrence.

'Yes, Monsieur Lawrence, even against our or Morgan's
king's will. A simple signature will make me free again, and my
buccaneer's rifle is not so rusty but that I long occasionally to
use it.'

The words spoken by Ducasse in that cool, resolute tone
which always makes an impression on the multitude, changed
suddenly and completely the feelings of the rovers, who all
hastened personally to assure Admiral Morgan of their devotion.

'Thanks, old comrade,' said Randolph half-an-hour later to
Ducasse, 'I did not expect less from you. But don't you think
you have made a very serious engagement? Suppose King Louis
should turn against you, and William not keep his word to me?'

'Then, mate, I shall write to the king thus : "Sire, you have
slain a faithful subject," and I should blow my brains out.'

'How French you are! How much more profitable to waste
the bullet on a Spaniard!'

'In any case we are agreed. King or no king, we will take
Carthagena.'

Morgan, when he returned to Sir Lewis, found him in a high
fever. Near him was a surgeon, attached to the Brethren.

'Well,' asked the visitor anxiously, 'what do you think of
your patient?'

'Gangrene has set in,' answered the doctor, 'and amputation
is a question of life or death.'

Wildflower uttered a piercing scream, and interposed between
the surgeon and the wounded knight. 'No one shall touch my
friend.' Then falling on her knees, she added in a voice broken
by sobs, 'Heavenly powers, save him or let me die with him!

CHAPTER XLII.

THE CRITICAL MOMENT.

Two days after the assembly of the buccaneers, Sir Lewis, Wildflower, and Allan were together on board the admiral's vessel. The latter, near the hammock where lay the unfortunate chevalier, looked anxiously on his pale, thin face. In vain the buccaneer chief tried to deceive himself, he saw death too plainly written on the poor wasted features to entertain any hope of his recovery.

'Poor Lewis!' he sighed, 'why did I snatch you from your solitary, peaceful life? I could so easily have ensured him a handsome fortune, an honourable independence. I was prompted by selfishness. I wanted a heart to love me, an arm on which I might lean. Brother, do not curse me. Willingly would I sacrifice my life to save him. I bring misfortune on all connected with me—all become victims of my fatal influence, while I alone invulnerably pass through the greatest dangers, and death does not even touch me with its wing. If my past life is stained with blood, it has been bravely shed. Terrible in the fight, I have been clement after the victory. Yes, my life has been that of a soldier, but my thoughts have not been those of a Christian. I have been animated by the spirit of vengeance, not justice, and to see a Spaniard dying at my feet has given me joy. My brother's memory makes me implacable. I always hear his dying groans. I know that I ought to renounce my hatred, but I cannot; no, I cannot. But perhaps Lewis's death is a warning from heaven that I have let the guilty remain too long unpunished.'

It was Naife-under-the-Bluff whither the vessel was bound, and though the distance was above 300 miles, thanks to Morgan's clever sailing and favourable winds, they accomplished the distance in three days. But that time had sufficed to make a sad change for the worse in the poor invalid; it was only with the greatest precaution that he could be brought on shore. At the Cape Morgan had a splendid mansion, and thither he caused his nephew to be brought and installed in his own room, where were instantly summoned the three surgeons of the settlement. Many surgeons without practice, knowing how much the buccaneers needed their assistance, emigrated, even in those days.

The consultation resulted in a unanimous decision that the limb must be amputated, and even then they would not answer for saving the patient's life.

'Is there no means of saving his leg?' urged Randolph, to whose active mind the idea of his nephew being forced to linger out a long life of inactivity seemed almost worse than death.

"I will give the half of my fortune to either of you who can avoid crippling him.'

All three gave it up as hopeless.

'Then, gentlemen, if it must be, the sooner it is done the better,' said Morgan, with a violent effort to repress his emotion. 'Who will inform the patient of his fate ?'

The surgeons all rose to do so, but Wildflower, who had been a silent witness of the consultation, cried out—

'Stop ! the chevalier is my adopted brother, I alone have the right to warn him.'

'My good Jennie,' said the pirate affectionately, 'I fear this effort will be too much for your strength. You have already watched night and day by his side. Let the surgeons tell him.'

'No, never !' cried Jennie, 'I will tell him, and alone.'

'But what is your hope ?'

'Don't you understand, captain,' responded Wildflower in a whisper, 'that, if the chevalier is afraid, no one must see his weakness ?'

'Strange child,' mused the buccaneer, 'who could have expected such a thought from you ?'

'You do not know me, captain. I am no longer the ignorant savage. Since I have won Lewis, a change has come over me ; I am stronger than you think. Trust to me, and let me tell the knight the truth.'

'May heaven help you, my dear girl !' proceeded Randolph, with emotion. 'Yes, you are right ; Lewis will bear the sad news better from you than from a stranger. Go, Jennie, we will await you here.'

When she entered Morgan's room, the young man lay asleep.

Approaching the bed gently, and leaning over him, she murmured softly—

'Sir Lewis, it is I, Jennie ; will you not speak to me ?'

Morgan opened his eyes, and a soft smile played upon his lips.

'I was dreaming of you, sister.'

She felt her tears overpower her, but, suppressing them, she continued : 'I have sad news to tell you. I have deceived you ; and I was wrong. Since the shipwreck you have always seen me smile, but despair was in my heart. My poor beloved, how can I tell you all the truth ?'

'Speak, and fear not, Wildflower,' said Sir Lewis sadly. 'I am not a spoiled child of fortune that cannot bear suffering. My life has been too little happy for me to dread the worst. What is this bad news that you have to tell me ?'

'It concerns your wound.'

Morgan smiled. 'I know it is mortal,' he said.

'And you did not tell me,' reproached Jennie, sobbing.

'Of what use was it to make you more sad, my sweet Wild-flower? There is time enough to say farewell. Don't weep so, your sobs make me miserable.'

'We were deceiving each other, Lewis.'

'Because we loved, Wildflower; and wished to spare each other sorrow. Do the surgeons think there is no hope? How long do they give me to live?'

'No, dear knight, the doctors do not despair; only if you knew——'

'I guess what you mean; but it is enough already, Wild-flower, that I should lie helpless here, I will not consent to an operation which will probably be useless. I have a right to prefer death to being a helpless cripple all my days.'

Whilst he answered Jennie seemed plunged in thought.

'Sir Lewis,' she said, 'will you promise me on your honour that, whatever Morgan says, you will not yield to his prayers or entreaties?'

'Willingly, girl, but what is the meaning of this?'

'I cannot tell you now. Time is precious. You shall know all by-and-by. Secure in your promise, I leave you. God help you, darling.' Jennie, with a radiant smile, then left her lover wondering at her strange conduct.

———

CHAPTER XLIIL

THE REMEDY.

It was midnight. A heavy atmosphere hung over the colony. The evening breeze had not as usual refreshed the air. Old Morgan, reclining in an arm-chair, watched by his nephew's side, when a violent thunderclap roused them both.

'How do you feel, boy? do you want anything?'

'I am comfortable,' answered the other, 'I only want one thing : would you go and lie down? For four days and nights you have not left my bedside ; you must be tired.'

'You forget, child, that my body is never tired, though my heart aches for you. Why will you so persistently refuse the only means of saving your life? It is not that you fear the suffering— no, Lewis, it is that you are tired of existence.'

'And if so, have I not suffered?' answered Morgan with feverish petulance. 'My love has been betrayed, the only man who called himself my friend and mate, Lawrence, became my rival and your foe.'

'Wildflower,' said the admiral softly, trying to turn the young man's thoughts from such gloomy retrospection.

'Wildflower was the sunbeam that only showed me more

clearly the darkness of all around ; but she too has left me—
left me when my hours are numbered——'

'Dear boy,' said his uncle tenderly, 'I own that Jennie's
absence is extraordinary, but I would stake my life on her devotion. I have faith in that girl, Lewis, and you know I have no
cause to think too well of mankind.'

An hour passed away in silence. Lewis strove hard against
the depressing thoughts that overwhelmed him ; at every slight
noise he turned his languid eyes towards the door. A few claps
of thunder alone broke the stillness of the air.

'Uncle,' murmured he at last in a voice so feeble as to be
almost inaudible, 'give me air, I am stifling.'

The buccaneer opened all the doors and windows.

'A little patience, dear Lewis. This storm is only the heel of
the tempest ; very shortly rain will cool the air and refresh you.'

'Raise me a little, and turn my head towards the window. I
long to breathe the fresh, cool breeze.'

Almost at the same moment the early drops of a tropical
shower fell, which were quickly followed by torrents of rain.

'Do you remember, captain,' said Lewis, revived by the
cool drops, 'that I first saw Nativa in a terrific storm? A true
emblem of my great love—tumultuous, terrible. The voice of
nature seemed then to curse our meeting, and has not fate done
so since?'

'My dear boy,' said the buccaneer, 'instead of recurring to
such sad remembrances, do try to sleep a little. Let me give you
this cooling drink.'

The buccaneer raised the young man and put the cup to his
lips.

Lewis uttered a piercing cry and sank back on his bed.

The captain turned quickly, and saw at the threshold of the
window Jennie, her clothes drenched and her lovely hair hanging
dishevelled over her shoulders, but her face radiant.

'Sir Lewis,' she cried, turning to him, 'I have been long
away, but I made all the haste I could ; don't be angry with me.'

Lewis could only welcome her with his eyes.

'Wildflower,' he murmured at last, pressing her hand to his
lips, 'now I have seen you, I can die happy.'

'Die ! impossible !' cried Jennie. 'Do you think anything but
the hope of saving your life could have kept me four days from
your side? Call your servants, let them make a large fire ; I
want some boiling water at once. Make haste, man !'

'Sir Lewis,' continued Wildflower, taking the captain's place,
'listen to me ; you can hear me, can you not?'

'Since I have you again beside me, dearest, I seem to have
recovered strength. Speak, speak, it is heaven to hear your
voice again.'

' I come from Saline, near the Massacre River, where lives an old Spanish woman, to whose son I rendered a great service a year since. He was condemned to be shot, and I saved him—but you shall hear all that another time. This old hag is noted for her skill in plants and the dangerous wounds she has cured. I went to her, her son knew me again. She embraced me with tears in her eyes. I told her what had happened, and described the symptoms of your illness. "My dear child," she answered, "if this man is not a Frenchman, I would stake my soul I could save him, but the French have killed my husband and my son." "He is not French," I answered. "Then I will do what you wish." You can imagine, dear Lewis, what joy I felt when I held the precious plants in my hand. I set off directly, and here I am.'

As Jennie finished speaking, Morgan returned.

' The water is ready.'

' Then take this handful of leaves and steep them in a tumbler of boiling water. I cannot leave my charge.'

' Wildflower,' said Lewis, with tears of gratitude in his eyes, ' I don't wish to pain you with my doubts, but don't put too much faith in the old witch's prescription ; and then, whatever virtue there may be in the plants, my wound is very serious. Rather accustom yourself to the idea of a separation.'

' Oh, I don't fear being separated,' cried Wildflower, ' I should not survive you.'

When the captain returned with the infusion he found his nephew and Jennie engaged in an animated conversation. Imagination has so strong an effect on the sick, and moral influence has such weight, that since her return Lewis was quite revived.

Wildflower seized the cup, and presented it to Lewis ; then, drawing back, she said, ' Let me see whether it is properly prepared,' and drank.

' This medicine is too hot,' she said, ' we must wait.'

After the lapse of a quarter of an hour, with a delicious smile, she presented the cup to Morgan. ' There is no danger now,' she said.

' Wildflower,' said Randolph, who had observed her attentively, ' what do you mean about there being no danger now ?'

' Why need you ask such questions ?' answered Jennie, pouting.

' What are you talking about ?' asked Lewis, who had emptied the cup.

' Only,' said his uncle quietly, ' that I have found out Wildflower ; she feared there might be poison in the herbs, so she risked her life for yours.'

' Jennie,' cried the patient, with unspeakable emotion, ' if the devotion of a life——'

'Stop, Sir Lewis, stop !' said she quickly. 'You forget, brother, that you are already bound.'

'That is indeed too true,' cried the young gentleman, his head falling back hopelessly on his pillow.

For a week Wildflower scarcely left his bedside, and it was only by the most urgent entreaties that old Morgan could prevail on her to take a few hours' rest.

Lewis's health improved gradually, and in a week's time the doctors, much to their surprise, acknowledged him out of danger.

A month later Morgan, in company with Wildflower, went out for the first time.

'Jennie,' he said to her mournfully, 'how can I ever repay what I owe you? You have saved my life, and I, unhappy wretch! have not the right to offer you my name and consecrate my whole life to you. My future no longer belongs to myself.'

'Sir Lewis,' answered she pensively, 'why regret the past? Let us enjoy the happiness before us.'

'But, Jennie, that fatal oath that binds me !'

'And what does that oath bind you to do? Only not to marry. Well, are we not very happy as we are ? Do we not live under the same roof, and spend our days together? Really, Nativa has not done much harm. I at first was quite contented, thinking that your oath would keep you from me. But are we not together still ?'

Morgan only answered with a sigh.

CHAPTER XLIV

WILDFLOWER'S DEPARTURE.

In another month the Cornishman was quite recovered. Jennie still fancied he needed her care, and remained his companion.

The colony, which a few years later became the richest and most luxurious town in Saint Domingo, was at this period the abode of many European families, who came there to seek their fortunes.

It was to enjoy their society that old Morgan had fixed one of his residences there. The buccaneer between the intervals of strife liked to rest where the refined manners of the Old World formed a contrast to the rude, savage life of the rovers.

Moreover the correspondence which these ofttimes noble exiles kept up with their fatherland enabled him to gain information of what was passing in Europe.

Among the young gentlemen Wildflower had created quite a sensation ; dazzled by her beauty, and little judging from her anomalous position the purity and innocence of her heart, they vied with one another to attract her notice.

Morgan's presence, who always accompanied Wildflower, had hitherto prevented the manifestation of their admiration, but one day, when her gentle tenderness caused the young man too much regretful anguish for him to conceal his emotion, he had left her suddenly, and she was accosted by one of her new admirers, a man of about five-and-twenty, of agreeable appearance, but silly and frivolous, and impudent in proportion.

Surprised by a language heard for the first time, and not understanding the high-flown compliments he paid her, Jennie only answered by a few monosyllables, and tried to quit him. He held her back, saying with a sneer—

'Come, my angel, don't be so cruel! What is the use of so much pretended modesty, when everyone sees you parading the English chevalier? A penniless adventurer, who cannot be generous! I have an estate which my agent tells me is worth five hundred thousand francs! Will you help me get rid of it?'

This proposition seemed so absurd to Wildflower, that she smiled.

'Come, I see you are much less cruel and keener witted than I thought you,' continued the coxcomb. 'You accept? That is a bargain! Well, frankly, on the score of interest in your lover, you are right to leave him. You cannot think how injurious it was to Sir Lewis Morgan always to be tied to your apron-string. How ridiculous it made him look. He really seems to have no sense of propriety. Not one of us would have consented to bear him company.'

Of all this, Wildflower understood but one thing, that her being continually with Morgan was prejudicial to him, and this she fancied explained the gentleman's occasional sadness when he was with her.

This discovery caused her exquisite pain, and had it not been for the presence of a stranger, she would have burst into tears.

'How unhappy I have unconsciously made Sir Lewis! How good he has been to me! Too patiently he has borne with me. How was it that I did not sooner perceive that the society of a girl like me did not suit his rank and talents? How my ignorance must have humiliated him! Ah, I will find courage, I will sacrifice myself to his happiness. It will be my death, but at least he will be happy.'

Jennie then ran away, leaving her admirer dumbfoundered.

Wildflower sought a solitary walk, and gave free course to her tears. For a long time she remained in a state of grief bordering on distraction; then, taking a long lingering look toward Morgan's villa, she bent her course towards the river.

At night Morgan, uneasy at Jennie's prolonged absence, went out to look for her. In vain he traversed the environs of the town and the places they usually walked to. He then fancied

that she must have by this time returned, and that he should find
her there. Passing the harbour, he mechanically cast his eyes
towards the sea, and saw a little coasting boat putting out.
Morgan started ; a sad presentiment seized him.

'Jennie, my sister,' he shouted with all his strength, 'is that
you?' Some moments passed before he had any answer ; then
the evening breeze brought to his ears, 'Farewell for ever.'
Doubt was no longer possible, it was Wildflower's voice. At the
same moment the tiny vessel spread its sail to the wind, and was
quickly wafted from the shore.

Morgan ran down to the beach, but no boat was within reach.
For a moment he had the desperate thought of throwing himself into the sea and swimming after the boat.

Sad and depressed, he watched the little vessel till it was out
of sight, then returned to his uncle's residence.

'Oh, what a fool I have been,' he said to himself, 'to trust to
any woman's affection ! There is no happiness in this world.
But for Wildflower to treat me thus coldly seems impossible.
I must be in a dreadful dream.'

When he reached his uncle's, where old Morgan was waiting
supper for him, he exclaimed anxiously—

'What is the matter, my boy? you are quite pale and un-
strung. You must have committed some crime, or met some
great grief.'

'You are mistaken, nothing particular has happened.'

'Where, then, is Wildflower?' asked the host.

'I think she has departed,' answered the gentleman, affecting an indifference which he did not feel. 'You know, sir, she
could not stay here for ever, she was tired. Perhaps she has
gone to rejoin handsome Lawrence !'

'Yes, you are right, I dare say it is so,' answered Morgan
dryly.

'Wildflower rejoin Lawrence? What shameful credulity in
you. You do her injustice,' cried Lewis, who had attacked
Jennie in hopes that the old buccaneer would have taken her
part. 'Wildflower is an angel of beauty, piety, and devotion.
She return to Lawrence! The dove would as soon seek the company of the hawk, the gazelle that of the tiger ! It is blasphemy
even to dream of such a thing !'

'Poor Lewis !' observed the rover, 'you are wretched ; but
take courage, boy, Wildflower is worthy of your love. Why
she has left I do not know, but, whatever her reason may be, I
rejoice that for the future no cowardly love will mar the high
destiny which is before you. Never would I have tried to estrange
you and Wildflower, for do not you owe your life to her? but I am
pleased she has left. An energetic nature like yours requires
action. You think me ambitious. Perhaps I am so, but mine

is a noble ambition, that of founding an empire, and, by bringing commerce and industry to these shores, making thousands happy. Believe me, Lewis, a man is only happy when by talent and industry he carves out his own path in life, and improves to the utmost the parts Heaven has granted him. You are too noble-minded to devote your youth to sentiment and romance. Be a man ! Shake off this sadness, share my projects, labours, and dangers, and then alone you will know what life is.'

Enthusiasm is contagious. Morgan, proud of his uncle's good opinion, touched by his kindness to himself, and more than all seeking in exertion some alleviation of his misery, responded—

'I am willing to listen to your advice ; what is it ? '

'The first thing I should advise,' answered his uncle, ' is your not seeing Wildflower again.'

'Not see Wildflower again ! You require too much, sir ! Why not ask my life at once ? '

'My poor boy, the wound is deeper than I feared ; but I spoke in the interest of your ambition. But would you lower yourself by entreating for that affection that has been withdrawn ? If Jennie wishes to forget you, would you seek her out and ask her pity, if you could not gain her love ? '

'No, as long as Wildflower, whatever be her reason, estranges herself willingly from me, I will never claim her love or her pity, but should she ever ask me again for my affection, I feel that my heart will be hers more than ever.'

Weeks passed away, and no news came from Jennie. Young Morgan hid his sufferings as well as he could, and tried to interest himself in his uncle's projects. Randolph respected his nephew's grief, and never afterwards referred to Wildflower. It was nearly two months since she had left, when Sir Lewis one daybreak heard a violent knocking at his door, and Greybeard entered his room.

Morgan felt a thrill of joy when he saw Jennie's father. 'Sir Lewis,' said the old buccaneer, in that drawling voice which was habitual to him, 'I have come to tell you that Wildflower is dying.'

His hearer uttered a loud cry, and threw himself from his bed.

'Speak, speak ! ' he cried, seizing the old man's arm ; 'what is the matter ? What has happened ? '

'Nothing has happened,' replied Greybeard, with his usual tranquility, 'except that Wildflower has made herself very unhappy about you, and now she has fallen ill, and gets worse and worse, spite of all we can do.'

It would be impossible to describe Morgan's feelings—a delirious joy mingled with his anguish.

'Will you come ? ' asked the buccaneer quietly.

'At once,' answered the youth, hurrying on his clothes.

Greybeard stopped him. 'I am tired and hungry,' he said, 'I must rest first and have some breakfast before we set out.'

The buccaneer had a sincere but most matter-of-fact affection for his daughter; as long as he saw health upon her cheek and a smile on her lips he was satisfied. He never troubled himself about her thoughts, her wishes, or her feelings. If she was well, he took it for granted she was happy. Jennie had never mentioned Morgan to her father, but with the instinct of jealousy Leathercap first guessed the secret of Jennie's illness, and communicated his suspicions to her father.

'Old man,' said he to Greybeard, 'if that fellow with the fine clothes were here, Wildflower would soon recover her gaiety and good looks.'

This notion, confirmed by Jennie's blushing, was a ray of light to the old man. He cleaned his gun, embraced his daughter, and whistling his dogs set off for Captain Morgan's abode.

As his daughter was ill because she was separated from the Englishman, what more natural, he thought, than for him to fetch the knight, that his daughter might be well again?

Accustomed as he was to conceal his feelings, Randolph could scarcely hide his vexation at the arrival of his old friend when he learnt the motive of his visit. Several times during break-fast he entreated his nephew not to accompany Greybeard, but the youth was determined, while the old buccaneer was apparently solely occupied in satisfying his appetite, and took no part in the conversation; only as they were setting out he said, 'I am delighted, my boy, that you did not listen to the captain, for it saves me the trouble of blowing your brains out! You need not look so astonished; your making Wildflower unhappy is reason enough for me to have challenged you. Had I killed you, Jennie, having lost all hope of seeing you again, would have been consoled at last. However, I much prefer having you alive, Jennie will sooner recover her health and spirits.'

As they were taking leave of old Morgan, Allan presented himself, dressed for the journey, gun in hand; he looked delighted.

'I shall have some more steak of my own providing,' he remarked, smacking his lips; 'it's amazing how much sweeter the meat is that one kills himself!'

Morgan, on parting, made his nephew a present of a splen-did rifle, and, embracing him, said—

'We shall soon meet again. You will either come to ask me for active service, or I shall go to you for an especial purpose.'

CHAPTER XLV.

WILD MEN AND WILD CATTLE.

GREYBEARD's habitation was nearly a hundred and fifty miles distant by land, and to the hardy foot traveller who undertook the journey there were not only considerable obstacles to be surmounted, but great danger to be incurred.

The obstacles, without counting the difficulty of finding one's way through a wild, deserted country, were hunger and thirst, and the meeting with parties of Spanish troops.

After a short day's march the three companions reached a place called Pleasure-cup, where Greybeard determined that they should pass the night; it was a fertile country, and the village contained a tolerable sprinkling of inhabitants.

Greybeard entered the largest cabin. At this time hospitality was a sacred right in Saint Domingo. Their host was a north countryman who had shipped or emigrated, and in course of years had become a rich man. The planters, or farmers, at this era stood in considerable awe of the buccaneers; therefore Greybeard and his companions were received with much distinction, and from his host Morgan learnt some curious details of a planter's life.

At daybreak next morning the buccaneer, Morgan, and Allan, pursued their journey. After Atalaze, a village which the travellers reached that same evening and where they slept, they entered the uncultivated *savannahs*.

No one who has not seen it can conceive the solemn desolation of these immense prairies of tall grass, reaching as far as the eye can see, and rippled by the wind like the waves of an inland sea. Knots of trees here and there rise like small islands, and over all reigns a silence that may be felt.

'Is not this a solemn, tranquil scene?' said Greybeard to Morgan. 'Would you not fancy the Spirit of Peace reigned here? And yet there is not any part of the whole island which has been so often the scene of bloodshed. This savannah, which divides the Spanish possessions from the French part of the island, has been the arena of the most furious battles between the two nations, and even now fearful contests often take place, and horrible murders are committed, while the English and men of no country attack either or both, when perchance in union.'

The travellers had already walked for five hours through this wilderness, when the first stopped and listened.

'What is the matter?' asked Morgan, joining him.

'Two shots have just been fired,' answered the old buccaneer.

'And what does that mean?'

'Nothing yet, only we are not alone in the grass-swamp, and

must be on our guard. Of all animals here, man is the most cruel and sanguinary.'

The buccaneer continued his way as calm as usual, but a flush of excitement rose on his weather-beaten cheek, and his hunter's instinct returned, at the prospect of an encounter with his old enemies, the Spaniards.

Shots were heard more distinctly, and, therefore, nearer than the others.

'What now, friend?' inquired Morgan, already priming the rifle his uncle had given him.

'Well, happily they are friends,' answered Greybeard with a sigh.

'Friends! how do you know?' asked the other.

'Do you think it is possible not to recognise the voice of the heavy rifle we alone use?'

Half-an-hour later the travellers reached a boucan or hut, erected by the side of the river Artibonite. Morgan, who had never seen such a house, examined with curiosity the rough construction, covered with palm-leaves, whence issued large volumes of smoke and a most unpleasant odour.

Greybeard at once entered the hovel, and Morgan followed him. All round the shanty hung slices of boar's flesh on sticks placed crossways, which were being smoked by a circular fire lighted on the ground, and fed with the bones and skin of the animals. It sent up such suffocating fumes that Morgan was obliged to leave almost immediately.

'Why don't your people use wood for their fire?' asked he of the buccaneer veteran.

'Because the reek from the skin and bones gives a fine flavour to the meat; in good faith, I am not sorry to have met with our fellows. Nothing rests you so well after a long march as a steak of boar's flesh boucaned. Shall I tell the smokers to serve us some at once?'

'Smokers?' ejaculated Morgan, 'whom do you mean?'

'The men who were in the boucan.'

'Were there men there? I did not see one. How could the poor creatures breathe in that smoke?'

'A man with a firm will may nerve himself to anything,' answered Greybeard. 'We have a knack of bringing up our assistants so as to mould them to every kind of hardship.'

Half-an-hour after the arrival of our travellers the hunters returned from their sport, and welcomed their old friend Greybeard very heartily.

'How long have you been in these parts?' asked he.

'For the last fortnight. Ten of us gathered together to explore the woods bordering the river, and so far we have had good luck. We have shot some two hundred buffaloes, and nearly as many boars. To-morrow evening we shall pull up stakes and strike further into the savannahs. Have you come to join us?'

'No; I am on my way home.'

'What, alone?' cried the other buccaneers, with surprise.

'No, these two young men are with me.'

'To cross the savannah with only two in company is really too risky. Take my advice, Greybeard, and remain with us until the day after to-morrow. There is a band of Spaniards, with no good design, not far off. The day after to-morrow we shall be going into your neighbourhood, and thus you will escape danger.'

The other buccaneers so strongly advised the same course that Greybeard gave in ; he knew the Brothers of the Coast were not men easily frightened, aud that 'danger' with them meaut almost certain death.

Morgan, vexed at the delay, tried to make him alter his mind, but Greybeard's only answer was—

'Jennie's health too much depends upon you for me to let you be killed. As I took the trouble to go for you, I shall keep you alive, if possible.'

The chevalier, finding remonstrance was useless, made the best of what he could not change, and turned his attention to observe the buccaneers. These intrepid and indefatigable sportsmen were like those who had come on board Morgan's vessel on her first arrival at Tortoise Island. Great cordiality and extreme frankness reigned among them. There was also something grave and serious in their demeanour which surprised the young observer, and it seemed to him that in point of morality the buccaneers were far superior to sea rovers. Before supper the buccaneers stretched all the skins they had taken that day ou the ground, hair downwards, and fastened them with pegs to dry.

This done, they all proceeded to the agreeable occupation of supper. Out of a large boiler, the only cooking utensil the buccaneers take on their expeditions, with the aid of a sugar-cane a large piece of buffalo was taken, which had been stewing since morning, the greasy liquor from which was poured into a large calabash, the juice of several lemons and some spice added. This was called a ' pimentado,' or ' spiced mess.'

The buccaneers sat in a circle on the ground, and each with his knife and a piece of corn cake attacked this huge joint with wondrous appetite. When they had done ample justice to the boiled beef, they finished with some smoked boar's flesh.

Allan, at sight of this meat and the savoury smell, uttered an exclamation of delight ; and, in fact, it is really a delicious dish. When supper was over, the buccaneers lighted their pipes, and smoked quietly while their ' hands ' regaled. Then they made a target and amused themselves with shooting at a mark. Morgan was astonished at their marvellous skill, and no longer wondered at the dread the Spaniards had of them.

At night each buccaneer retired to a tent covered with skins, which the assistants had put up while their masters were shooting.

The servants and dogs slept at the entrance of the tents; sentinels, relieved every two hours, kept guard through the night.

The next morning at break of day all were on foot, and prepared for the day's sport. They were to have a last hunt in the woods near the river. Morgan, highly interested in the proceeding, by Greybeard's advice joined himself to a buccaneer named Homfrey, who was considered a model sportsman. He had six assistants and a pack of twenty-five dogs.

As soon as they reached the entrance of the wood, he advanced, rifle in hand, ready to fire. His servants, holding the dogs by leather leashes, followed him in a file. The pointer, the only dog who was loose, ran in all directions hunting for a buffalo. Soon the intelligent creature, somewhat in advance of the huntsmen, gave a sharp bark, at which the other dogs became outrageous to be let loose.

'Loose the pack!' ordered Homfrey.

The men did so, then tightening the girdles round their waists, they rushed after the dogs.

Morgan had scarcely gone a hundred yards before he saw the buffalo coming towards him.

'Hide behind a tree,' cried one of the assistants.

Turning every now and then to fight the pack which barked at his heels, the buffalo, although he apparently tried to avoid the huntsmen, seemed rather angry than frightened. His long and pointed horns, his massive forehead and short, thick neck, showed that he was no mean adversary, and that he would not be overcome without danger.

Homfrey followed the animal's movements with the greatest coolness; several times Morgan saw him raise his rifle to take aim, but as one of his servants or dogs was always in the way, he waited.

After having endured for a few minutes the persecution of his enemies, the buffalo assumed the offensive.

The helpers and dogs, not daring to fly in Homfrey's sight, as he would have made them pay dearly for their cowardice, displayed extraordinary agility in avoiding the buffalo's charges.

'Why does not that man fire and bring down the creature?' asked Morgan of one of the assistants, pointing to one only a few feet from the animal.

At this question the assistant looked surprised.

'Fire before the master?' he answered, 'what can you be thinking of, sir?'

'But it seems more natural to me to be wanting in respect to the master, than to let one's self be goaded by the buffalo.'

'Oh, no, sir, a butt from a horn does not always cause death, whereas a bullet in the head is mortal.'

'What, would Master Homfrey murder one of his people for shooting before him?'

'He would punish him, sir, that is certain.'

'And is his manner of punishing then to blow a man's brains out?'

'Yes, it is the custom here.'

The assistant was still speaking when the buffalo rushed towards Morgan, who did not hesitate to fire.

The terrible bovine pitched forward, and for an instant stood still; then its fury being increased by the agony of its wound, with a loud bellow and foaming mouth it rushed after the Cornishman.

Ignorant of the first rules in buffalo hunting, he fled instead of turning round the tree which was his shelter; the consequence was he soon found himself entangled in the creeping plants which his enemy crushed beneath his weight. The buffalo gained on him, and already he felt its hot breath upon him, when a louder bellow than before, and the fall of a heavy body caused him to turn round. The buffalo lay lifeless at his feet.

'No use running any farther,' remarked Homfrey, 'the trick is done!'

'Thanks,' cried Morgan, 'I shall never forget that I owe my life to you.'

'It is not worth speaking of,' answered Homfrey. 'I mean the service, not the life. I do the same thing every day to save one of the dogs.'

'How did you manage to bring the creature down? He fell as if struck by lightning.'

'Very simply. I first hamstrung him, and when he was on the ground I finished him with a thrust of my bayonet in the head; out of a hundred buffaloes that I kill, I don't make use of my rifle ten times. I prefer using steel, as it economizes powder and does not injure the animal's skin.'

The hunter did not vaunt in saying this. His mark on the kins was known and prized, even in the European markets.

Now that the buffalo was dead, one of the assistants ripped up the carcase, took out the shin bones, and presented them to the chief, who kept two for himself and offered the other two to Morgan, who, not understanding such huntsmen's politeness drew back, rather disgusted.

'That's the effect of living in towns, young man,' said the

other, smiling ; ' one grows old, and never learns what is good.'

The buccaneer cracked the bones, and ate the marrow with great relish.   The sport then began again.

Every time the buccaneer brought down a buffalo the assistants skinned it dexterously, and folded the skin in a small compass, that it might not catch to the trees.   One of them laid it on his shoulders, and with this burden, which weighed at least a hundredweight, followed his master as before.   About five in the afternoon, each assistant having his load, Homfrey returned to the encampment.

The next morning all the buccaneers set forward to seek other hunting fields.   As they were not a strong party they determined to go across the great Zuava savannah, as far as the Spanish territory.   This expedition, as Greybeard told Morgan, was extremely hazardous.   For five years no one except Greybeard himself had dared to traverse this desert in a straight line.

The little caravan, for with the assistants it comprised some sixty men, had been on the march since five in the morning, when it came to a little wood in the midst of the savannah.   As the heat was overpowering, the buccaneers called a halt there.

Several of them, while the helpers put up the tents, resolved to explore the wood to see if they could find some paths through it.   Morgan followed them in company with Greybeard, who, since that gentleman's adventure with the buffalo, chose to keep him always in sight.

The buccaneer who headed the little party had scarcely gone a hundred yards into the wood before he uttered an exclamation of surprise.

' Friends,' he exclaimed, ' here are traces of men ! '

They all examined the footmarks, and then called on Greybeard for his opinion, whose judgment in these matters was considered infallible.

' Brothers,' he pronounced, ' I see here the foot-prints of a man, followed by a pack of hounds and two boars.   But the fact is it is so extraordinary that I don't pretend to understand it.'   It seemed equally inexplicable to all the rest, how a human being with a pack of hounds and two boars could possibly live in a wood situated in the midst of a waste savannah.

' Old fellow,' cried Homfrey, ' if you are not joking you must lead us on these tracks ; no one can follow a trail better than you.'

' I always speak in earnest, mate.'

' Then come on.   One word more ; do you think these footmarks are recent or have been made several days ?

' Very recent, not more than an hour ago.'

As Greybeard was a man of few words, he took the lead, his

eyes fixed on the ground. The old huntsman was so used to life in the woods, that though the traces were barely visible he followed them rapidly and without hesitation. From time to time the ground, covered with thick grass, afforded no trace. The trailer stopped a few seconds and looked carefully round in a circle, and seizing a new indication, whether a broken branch or tuft of grass out of its place, went on with a confidence which showed he had no fear of going wrong. After half-an-hour's walk, he turned round to his companions and said with a smile :

'Here at least is one of the boars.'

'That is true,' remarked Homfrey, ' but finding a boar does not prove that there is a wild man here with a pack of dogs ; a boar rooting about a forest is not such an unusual thing.'

'But if you look at the creature, man, you will see that this is not an ordinary wild boar.'

'That is true, there is something strange about it ; perhaps it is bewitched. I happen to have a silver button upon me that will do the business.'

The buccaneers, like other ignorant people, were extremely superstitious. Homfrey loaded his piece and fired ; the boar uttered a plaintive grunt and bounded into the wood.

A moment afterwards a piercing cry was heard ; the buccaneers stopped short, for courageous as they were in real dangers, they had a mortal fear of anything bordering on the supernatural. However, they had little time for conjecture. A man, armed with a knotted club and followed by the wounded boar, rushed out of the wood. The man was only covered with a few rags, and his face was almost hidden by his hair and long beard.

This apparition was so startling that all the buccaneers drew back, except Greybeard, who was taking aim at the man when Morgan seized his hand, already on the trigger, and interposed.

'Stop, we are too strong to have anything to fear. You will commit a needless crime.'

'Right you are,' returned Greybeard quietly, ' perhaps the creature is a human being.'

The wild man at first bounded away with an agility that left his pursuers in the lurch, but changing his mind he returned and laid himself down by the wounded boar.

In half a minute he was surrounded by the buccaneers, and Greybeard cried out :

'Who are you, and how did you come here ?'

At this question the savage with the club opened his eyes very wide, and said in a rough voice :

'I was a hunter's help. Why did you wound my mate Jim ? He never did you any harm.'

'This man is a deserter ; we must shoot him,' uttered Homfrey.

This threat seemed to have little effect on the poor wretch, who was too much occupied with his dumb friend to heed what was said. Soon tears coursed down his cheeks, and a deep sob told that his "friend Jim" was dead. St. Anthony could not have loved his porcine familiar more sincerely.

The curiosity of the buccaneers was so strongly excited that they paid no attention to the severe proposition. All were anxious to know the history of the deserter.

Greybeard first questioned him.

'What is your name, and how long have you lived in the savannah?'

'My name I don't remember; oh, yes, it was Toby Perring. But how can I know how long I have been here?'

At this answer one of the buccaneers looked at him very attentively.

'This man tells the truth,' said he, 'he is an old assistant of mine; I remember him now. He left me three years since.'

'I knew he was a deserter,' said Homfrey joyfully.

Toby's former master hesitated, and Greybeard, who remarked his embarrassment, said sternly

'Friend, you know that to deceive our brothers is considered a crime among us. Is it true that Perring is a runaway?'

'No,' answered the buccaneer. 'Perring, finding himself at St. Domingo without money, consented to become my assistant. Unfortunately unable to support a hunter's life, he tried my patience, and I took a dislike to him. One day, when he had only been in my service three weeks, I gave him two buffalo hides to carry. He tried, but in ten minutes he fell down, and declared he could not go a step farther. Exasperated at this and determined to make him get up, I gave him a blow on the head with the butt end of my rifle : he uttered one groan and remained still. I put my hand on his heart and found it did not beat. I thought I had killed him, and went away, taking his weapons with me.'

'Now, man,' said Greybeard to the fugitive, who was still absorbed in grief for the loss of his swinish partner, 'tell us what happened after your fainting.'

'When I came to myself,' answered Toby, speaking with hesitation, and as if he found it difficult to remember language, 'and found myself alone and abandoned, I was very distressed. I passed the night in a kind of delirium. The next morning, though weak with the loss of blood, I managed to get up, and tried to find my master. Then I first perceived that one of the dogs had stayed with me—the faithful creature licked my hands, and seemed to invite me to follow him. I trusted to his instinct, and walked as far as my strength would permit. Night came, and with it the agony of hunger. Luckily, my master had left me a piece of buffalo meat, that I was carrying for his evening meal. I divided it with the dog.

'The next day I managed to climb the tallest tree in the vicinity. I spied the sea. Knowing that my master was going to ship off his hides, I hoped to find him if I could manage to reach the shore.

' I listened as well as I could, but I had hardly taken ten steps before I perceived how useless would be my endeavours; it was impossible for me, in this mass of verdure, to find my way. Several times meeting with the footmarks of buffaloes and wild boars, I was deceived with the hope of getting out of the forest. I followed these traces, which only led me further astray.'

Morgan, surprised at the good language that Perring made use of, interrupted him by saying :

'May I ask you, my friend, why you left Europe, and what was your position there ?'

'I was a professor of music in Plymouth,' said Perring, ' and an unfortunate love affair obliged me to leave my country.'

This answer, by informing Morgan that this was a man of some education, and that he was not a convict in exile, increased the interest the young gentleman felt for him.

' The third day after my master left me,' continued Perring, ' my dog, pressed by hunger, began to hunt for game ; he came upon a litter of young pigs, and killed two of them. I tried to light a fire with two sticks, like the Indians, but I could not succeed ; so I was forced to eat my meat raw. The horrible disgust I first felt at this gradually decreased, and I got used to the savage life I have led ever since. Associating my intelligence with the instinct of my only companion, I began to study the habits of the wild boars ; I learnt the pastures they frequented, the plants they liked best, where they slept, and what was the best time to attack them.

' From that moment I no longer feared to die of hunger ; I was sure of being able to procure myself abundant food. I had led this kind of life for three or four months, as far as I can remember, when my dog brought me two little pigs alive. I determined to bring them up and make them my companions. Success crowned my endeavours. Poor Jim, which you killed, was one of them. We liked each other so much; his faithfulness was extraordinary, as well as his intelligence.'

He turned a mournful glance at the dead boar.

'One day I found a litter of wild dogs ; those I brought up, too, and, surrounded by so many faithful friends, I was happy ; for I was no longer alone. I got used to my new life, and from continual exercise I became so hardened to fatigue and so swift of foot that I could run down a deer quite easily. Now you know my history.'

His simple tale greatly interested the buccaneers, except
Homfrey, who said :

'Comrades, we have nothing to do with feeling ; it is necessary that our rules should not be broken.   I don't admit that
Toby could not in three years rejoin our encampments.   Our
duty is to consider him a deserter, and fire on him.'

Morgan expected to see this proposal rejected with indignation, but it was not so.   Tradition was sacred among buccaneers,
for it constituted their strength.

'Friends,' said Greybeard, 'I don't agree with our companero.   I maintain that it might be impossible for Perring,
lost in the savannah, to find his way out.   There are too many
instances of new hands being lost in this way, and dying of
hunger, even close to habitations.   I propose that we put it to
the vote.   Let the majority decide.'

This was unanimously agreed to.

'Come, friend,' said the old buccaneer to Toby, 'whistle your
dogs and follow us.'

'I don't refuse to follow you, but I won't whistle my dogs
until poor Jim is buried.   I won't give his brother the pain of
seeing him dead.   And then if you intend to shoot me, why
reveal where my friends are hidden ?'

When the buccaneers returned to their camping-ground they
held a council ; their deliberation was short, and Toby was,
by a majority of voices, declared innocent.

'Now, friends,' said Greybeard, 'one formality is to be complied with.   You know that every assistant after three years'
novitiate can claim his freedom as a buccaneer.   Since he has
been voted not a deserter, Toby has fulfilled his time ; his master
owes him a rifle, three pounds of powder, six of shot, a new
suit, two pairs of shoes, and three dogs.'

To this there was no answer, and the master who had so
cruelly used Perring was obliged to submit.

The next morning, Morgan, his pilot, and Allan, separated
from the buccaneers ; the most dangerous part of the savannah
was passed, and four days later they reached Greybeard's habitation safely.

CHAPTER XLVI.

WILDFLOWER AT HOME.

GREYBEARD'S dwelling was much handsomer than the rough
houses of the planters ; constructed with much care, it resembled
a Swiss châlet.   Morgan in two bounds mounted the stairs, and
came to a half-opened door which led to Wildflower's chamber.

There he stopped short, for he felt he ought to restrain his emotion, not to give too great a shock to the invalid.

'Sir Lewis,' called a sweet, low voice, whose plaintive accents went to his heart, 'why do you hesitate to come in ? I have so longed to see you !

Morgan, overcome with emotion, forgetting all prudence, rushed in.

Jennie, dressed in white, and with her luxuriant tresses hanging loose, lay in a hammock. Illness and suffering seemed only to have idealized her beauty, not to have lessened it ; she looked like an angel ready to take flight to heaven.

Unable to speak, the new arrival took her hand, and covered it with tears and kisses.

'Oh, why are you unhappy, my lord ?' said Jennie, with a heavenly smile. 'If you knew how happy I am you would not pity me. How kind of you to come and see me once again ! how very good !'

The gentleman's emotion was still too great to allow him to peak.

'You cannot think how impatiently I watched for your coming. Since you set out, my spirit has been with you through the savannah. Perhaps you doubt my words ; but indeed I speak the truth. I felt as it were in a trance, yet I was awake, and knew what was going on around me. Still I watched you all the time, and just now I saw you mount the stairs and stand for a moment at my door, with your hands on your heart. But speak, Lewis ; I long to hear your voice, I have heard it so often lately of a night.'

'Jennie, my dearest Jennie !' said Morgan passionately, 'if you die, I cannot survive you ! Your love—your friendship, if you prefer it—alone attaches me to life. You in heaven—oh, what could I do on earth ? My adored, live, if you would not drive me to despair. Never can I tell you how dear you are to me ! my soul clings to you as its greatest blessing.'

'Sir Lewis,' murmured the girl, with sweet surprise, 'do you really love me at last ? I thought you were ashamed of me, and only pitied me. Are you sure you love me ? the thought is too bright, too beautiful, to be true. It is impossible.'

Wildflower paused a moment, then added with gentle resignation : 'Oh, you are so kind ! You are sorry to see me ill, and that makes you think you love me. But if I should recover, and you no longer feared for my life, I should be again to you the ignorant simpleton who is only a trouble to you. To avoid making you ridiculous in the eyes of your acquaintances, the people in town, I shall be obliged to fly as I did before, and, perhaps, now I should not have the strength to do so. So, dear

chevalier, it is perhaps better for both that I should die.   I am
so happy ; I have no fear of death.'

Whilst Wildflower spoke, Morgan, unable to restrain his feelings, sobbed aloud.

'Jennie,' he cried, as soon as he could speak, 'you pierce my
heart by talking of pity.   I swear to you, I love you with a
passion that is killing me.   I love you with all the strength of
my being.   Your image is never out of my thoughts.   Is that
pity ?   I love you so much that the thought of your loving anyone else would be agony, and I feel I must kill him, even if by
doing so I should break your heart.   Is that pity ?   Oh, Jennie,
you will never know what I suffered when you left us ! the bitter
jealousy, the agony that crept into my heart !   I was mad, for I
doubted your love.   Oh, Jennie, it is wicked to say that I only
feel pity.   Forgive me !   I hardly know what I say !   I am beside
myself with love and despair.'

Whilst Morgan thus gave way to his feelings, which he had
so long tried to suppress, his hearer was overcome with emotion.
Her face beamed with a heavenly expression of purity and
love.

'Forgive you, Lewis !' she murmured, 'what have I to forgive ?
If you knew how happy, how blessed your words make me !   Oh,
never could I believe my happiness so great as to be loved by
you.   How good of you to come to tell me that you love me—for
you do love me, I feel sure of it now.   How can I thank you for
making me so happy ?'

'By living, Jennie dearest,' answered he.

'Living ?   Am I, then, in danger ?   I am so happy, I could
die with joy.   But no, Lewis, I could not leave you.   No—
never !'

Wildflower was much moved, and turned pale.

'But if I were to die, what would you do ?'

'Jennie, you have pronounced our doom yourself.   We must
not part.   I should follow you.'

'Yes, Lewis, to meet in heaven.   We shall not be parted,
even in death.'

As she finished speaking, Greybeard entered.

'Good day, girl,' he said, kissing her.   'I hope you will get
well directly, now that you have your knight with you.'

'But why, father, should I get well because the chevalier is
here ?'

'Why, because it was his absence that made you ill.'

'Oh, if I suffered for you, Sir Lewis, I am untroubled now.
It is so sweet to love and feel one's self beloved.'

Greybeard shrugged his shoulders.

'How little even father and daughter are alike !' he said.   'I
never loved like that.   Come, child, you have talked long

enough. You must try and sleep a little. Good-bye for the present. I will send the knight to you when you wake. My daughter already looks much better,' remarked Greybeard. 'I should not wonder if we had her well again in a fortnight. What a good thought it was of mine to fetch you, for I was afraid we should have lost her. What strange things young girls are ! there is no accounting for their whims. Now there is Leather-cap, as proper a man as you would see anywhere—six feet and over in his bare feet—a capital shot, can lodge a ball in the bull's-eye at a hundred paces, and never was there such a hand at making a *boucan* and smoking boar's flesh ; what would the girl have more, I wonder? and yet, forsooth, she could not fall in love with him. Well, they are all alike. Impossible ever to under-stand a woman's caprices, so it is useless trying,' added the old buccaneer philosophically.

During the first week after Morgan's arrival, Jennie's con-valescence progressed rapidly, and by the end of a fortnight she could, with the aid of the gentleman's arm, walk in the garden. This really miraculous cure only proved to Sir Lewis how deeply he was beloved, and enhanced, if possible, his devotion for the sweet girl while it increased his poignant regret that honour forbade him to offer her his hand. Yet to know that he entirely engrossed all her affection was happiness of itself.

The time passed quickly for the lovers ; they were so engrossed in each other that the outer world seemed as nothing to them.

Being much engaged out of doors, the host and Leathercap left them to spend their time in delicious chats.

One day, when Wildflower had quite recovered her strength, she said :

'Sir Lewis, I could not sleep last night for thinking of my beloved forests. How many weeks have passed since I have seen them ! I so long to sit under their delicious shades ; to breathe the sweet-scented air ; this idle life in the house makes me weary. Come, take your rifle, and let us go to the forests.'

'I will call Allan, and follow you,' said Morgan.

'Oh, why need Allan come?—we are so much happier alone,' said Jennie, and so she and Morgan set forth.

<hr>

CHAPTER XLVII.

THE SPUR TO THE WAR-HORSE.

For the first few hours Jennie gave herself up to the pleasures of the chase and rambling in her beloved forests ; she clapped her hands joyfully, and led the way to their favourite haunts.

Never had the bloom of health mantled her cheek with such

brilliancy, never had her step been so buoyant, her smile so dazzling, the ring of her laughter so joyous.

Morgan's eye followed her every movement, and he forgot his sport in admiration akin to rapture.

When the sun had risen high, and the heat became oppressive, Jennie threw herself on the velvet sward and proposed to Morgan to rest.

'But you forget, Wildflower,' he answered, 'I have not yet shot anything ; you rest there while I try to make up for lost time.'

'But, sir, at this sultry hour, all animals are in repose,' answered Jennie ; 'come and sit down by me ; it would be useless to look for game now.'

After a moment's hesitation Lewis placed himself by her side. Nature seemed wrapped in silence ; not a breath of air moved a leaf, the flowers hung down their heads with faintness, a solemn grandeur pervaded all things.

Jennie rose, and gathering a plantain leaf, seated herself again by Morgan and fanned herself ; then giving the leaf to him, took off her hat and let her luxuriant hair float over her shoulders.

'The heat is overpowering,' she said presently, laying her head on Morgan's knee ; she looked up.

'Have you gone to sleep, Lewis ?' she asked.

'No ! Let us go home, Jennie,' said the Englishman abruptly. 'I cannot stay here ; I am too unhappy. I am a miserable scoundrel,' he said, 'not to be able to bear what I have brought on myself, and I am ungrateful to Heaven who has given me so great a blessing in your affection.'

Morgan shouldered his rifle and walked quickly away.

Jennie called the dogs and followed him in silence. During the remainder of the journey she was pensive ; all her glee and light-heartedness had fled.

In the evening on their return, the first person who met them was old Morgan, whom Lewis saw with pain.

'Perhaps you have already forgotten me, Lewis ?' said the pirate admiral, with an accent of slight reproach ; 'after all, why complain of your indifference when you are in love ?'

'Indeed, captain,' answered the youth, 'I have often thought of you, but seeing you so suddenly it surprised me.'

'And annoyed you too, my lad, I am afraid ! However, we will talk more about it after supper. Greybeard is waiting for us to sit down to table.'

Perfectly determined that he would not yield to Morgan's advice, prayers, or even commands, Lewis felt little uneasiness at his arrival, so sitting down to table, he merely said :

'Uncle, having come to look after me, are you about to engage in a new expedition ?'

‘Yes, boy, an expedition which will, I hope, one day hold a glorious place in the annals of America. I have been for the last fortnight going round the country beating up recruits. I have now finished preliminaries, and we shall start to-morrow.’

‘What do you mean by us, uncle?’

‘You and I.’

‘You then make sure of me without doubting my obedience?’

‘Assuredly, dear Lewis.’

‘Well, you are wrong, for I shall not go with you.’

‘We know what youth is,’ said old Morgan, smiling, ‘they decide upon a thing without even knowing what they are talking about. I assure you, you will accompany me to-morrow without hesitation. Would you pass your life in this idleness?’

‘Certainly, uncle; warfare has not been so favourable to me as yet, that I should seek fresh adventures. I still have a little money which I brought from Europe—enough to buy a patch of ground.’

‘A very honourable way, truly, of mending your fortunes and maintaining your name.’

‘My name,’ said Lewis bitterly, ‘is that of a buccaneer, a rover, a pi——who remembers my name?’

‘Lewis,’ said the captain gravely, ‘your name you inherited from your father, and to support it properly is a duty you owe to your murdered father. We are on the eve of a great event; faithful to his promise, William III. has sent a fleet to our aid, and the taking of Carthagena is a fixed fact. What Sir Henry Morgan did, Sir Lewis Morgan may well try to repeat!

‘You know, boy, the glorious part reserved for us in this attack. Commanded by chiefs whom we have chosen ourselves, we shall fight under our own flag. The greatest equality will be established between the king’s officers and our own, our power will be on a par with theirs. King William treats us like allies, not subjects. The king, I know, attaches great political importance to our success, and his gratitude will be commensurate with the service we shall render him. Lead the storming party, Lewis, and thy forefather’s memory will be done justice to. If you fall, what matters? you will have done your duty. Answer, last of the Morgans, do you still refuse to follow me?’

Morgan hesitated, when Wildflower, who while the freebooter was speaking kept her eyes fixed upon him, interposed in a decided tone:

‘Sir Lewis, you must accept this offer.’

This intervention surprised the young Englishman, but did not make him give way.

‘No, Jennie, I will not accept. I comprehend your generous sacrifice, and thank you for it. You fear to injure my prospects

in life. You are mistaken, girl. I am so entirely cured of
ambition, and see so plainly the hollowness of all glory and
wealth, that I renounce these offers.'

At these words, spoken earnestly, the buccaneer curled his
lip, and said :

'I should have wished my boy to have obeyed the voice of
glory, not of duty only ; but as his heart is cold to the glory of
the strife, and he prefers changing his father's sword for a plough-
share, I must tell him as an incitement what I would otherwise
have kept for a reward. Know then that the new Governor of
Carthagena is the man who caused your father's cruel death,
because he could not—would not have dared face Sir Henry
in mortal combat !'

At these words Morgan uttered a cry of rage and clapped his
hand to his sword.

'Say no more, man !' he cried ; 'I fly to avenge my
father !'

Too much excited to eat, the youth sat down by a window
and gave himself up to his boiling thoughts. Wildflower interrupted them.

'My brave knight,' she said softly, 'you know that Morgan is
as prompt in action as in words. I should not be surprised if he
sets off to-night. Promise me not to leave without seeing me
again.'

The resignation which Jennie displayed at so sudden a separation filled her lover with mournful surprise.

'Jennie,' he said, 'I love you too well to wish to hide from
you my thoughts. With you my heart, not my lips, communes.
I will own that it was a painful surprise to hear you advise me
to join the corsair. You did not then know that I owed a sacred
duty to my father's memory. Has my presence then become
wearisome to you ?'

'Oh, Sir Lewis, I love you better than ever. I depend on
your promise not to go without seeing me again, but I must leave
you now ;' on which the girl left the room to give vent to her tears.

The next morning at daybreak Randolph left his room.

'What, you here, Wildflower ?' he cried, seeing the girl in
the garden. 'You must have risen betimes this morning.'

'I have been walking here all night,' answered Jennie carelessly ; 'but tell me, captain, do you know what has become of
Nativa ?'

'Yes, child, I know,' answered he, smiling.

'And where is she ?'

'I cannot satisfy your curiosity, Jennie. An indiscretion on
your part might thwart my plans.'

'I promise, sir, I will never tell anyone your secret. Oh, I
entreat you, let me know where Nativa is !'

‘Poor child,’ rejoined Morgan gently, ‘I will do what you wish, for I trust you, Jennie ; but my answer will only grieve you.　Nativa is now in Carthagena.’

Jennie turned so pale that Morgan thought she would have fainted, but recovering herself with a violent effort, she said :

‘Captain, will you save my life ?’

‘Your life, child ? who threatens your life ?’

‘Grief, sir.　Don't smile, I speak seriously.　If you do not grant my request, grief will kill me !’

‘Well, what do you want me to do, child ?’

‘Go to my father and induce him to join you in this expedition to Carthagena.　I may accompany him.　Don’t refuse me ; he will be sure to go if you ask him.’

‘Your father is not an easy person to lead, pretty one, but as he is one of our best marksmen, I’ll try my best.　Ah, I think I know a way ; so, little Jennie, I’ll do your request.’

‘How good you are, captain !’ cried Wildflower, seizing the buccaneer’s hand and drawing him into her father’s room.

CHAPTER XLVIII.

EVERY MAN HAS HIS PRICE.

WHEN they entered Greybeard’s chamber, they found the old buccaneer already dressed.

‘Grizzly,’ said the captain, ‘I want to have some serious talk with you.’

‘Speak away ! I am listening,’ answered the other laconically.

‘Old friend,’ continued the freebooter, ‘with men like us, long-winded speeches are useless.　I want you to join the expedition to Carthagena.’

‘What good will that do ?’ said Greybeard after a moment’s reflection ; ‘what advantages should I get by putting myself so much out of the way ?’

‘Why, you would realize more in a month than a whole year’s fatigue here would gain for you.　Carthagena is extremely wealthy, our booty will be immense.’

‘Of what good is money to me ?’ answered the hunter indifferently ; ‘hunting brings me in enough to supply all my wants ;　and why exchange independence for servitude ?　The discipline of a camp would not suit my taste at all.　I refuse.

‘This haste to refuse before you have heard a man out is not in accordance with your usual good sense and judgment.’

‘You offered me gold, and because I did not want it, I refused to sacrifice my liberty to obtain it.’

If you had not interrupted me, old friend, I would have explained that far higher considerations than mere pecuniary advantages induced me to make you this offer. All of us have in our hearts some hidden wish, some desire to gratify. King William of England has invested Commander Bloxam with full power to give titles. If this admiral, for example, granted you those titles of nobility that you have coveted so long, the king would be certain to confirm them.'

'Do you think so, Morgan?' asked the hunter, with greater animation than he usually displayed.

'I speak with certainty. Now suppose, for instance, that taking advantage of the influence you have over the buccaneers in these parts you were to induce them to join you, and then putting yourself at the head of this party of picked marksmen you went, not to offer your services, but to make a bargain with the admiral for a regiment, do you think he would refuse you? No, my good friend, he would at once accept your conditions for the sharpshooters.'

'Morgan,' answered Greybeard proudly, 'I don't seek for benefits, I only ask for justice. I have a right to the name of Buckingham, and that I will maintain before the whole world!'

'But the justice, old friend, that depends on the powerful is called a favour,' replied Morgan; 'I don't advise you to ask for a title of nobility, but permission to claim your inheritance. If you decide on joining us, I will answer on my word of honour that the admiral will grant your desire. Time presses, I must leave you; answer yes or no?'

'Your word is enough for me, captain. To-day I will get together ten men at least, and by the end of the week I don't fear but that I shall be at the head of a hundred. Where is the place of meeting?'

'The same where we always meet, on the Little Zuava.'

'All right! then farewell!' Without more ado the old buccaneer shouldered his rifle and left the house.

'Thanks, captain,' cried Wildflower joyfully, 'if my brother Lewis is going to see Nativa she will make him unhappy! I must be there to console him.'

Half-an-hour later, Captain Morgan, his nephew, and Allan set out and took the road to Seogane, where the governor Du Casse was then staying.

Knowing that he should soon see Wildflower again, Lewis felt little grief at parting, but every now and then dark thoughts came over him; he remembered that he was about to avenge his father. And thoughts of vengeance were greatly at variance with this bright vision of sweet Wildflower.

As Morgan, Lewis, and Allan proceeded on their way, the captain met a buccaneer whom he knew, leaning against a tree.

'Good day, friend,' he said ; 'are you out hunting already?'

'Yes, I am hunting,' said the stranger gloomily.

'How oddly you speak ; you look as if something had gone contrary.'

'Nonsense ; nothing is the matter with me.'

'Well, mate, I am beating up for recruits to join the fleet. You had better come with us ; and whether you do or no, I would advise you not to come here with any friend if you wish to keep your secret.'

'What secrets ? I have no secrets! '

'Oh, you know best,' continued Morgan II. ; 'but I have heard sad rumours lately about you and your wife ; and are you sure that under that newly-made green hillock at your feet which you are gazing on so intently does not lie a human corpse ?'

At this strange question, the buccaneer's eye glared with vindictive fury.

'And if it were so ?' he returned in a suppressed growl ; whose fault is it ? An honest buccaneer must obey the law, and it is his duty to punish the guilty.'

'Then it is as I surmised ?'

'Let the dead rest in their graves,' replied the stranger savagely. 'I only exercised my right, Morgan. I will join you to-morrow,' and without further adieu he plunged into the forest.

'What !' cried Lewis indignantly, on seeing Morgan quietly proceeding on his way. 'Shall we let such a crime pass unpunished ? Shall we not seize the murderer and deliver him up to justice ?'

'Your indignation is quite natural, Lewis, but it is useless here,' answered the captain ; 'the man has only conformed to a law very general among buccaneers, who are little scrupulous about the past life of the degraded convict women that the French Government sends over here. If they take their fancy, they marry them, whatever their antecedents may have been, but if after marriage the wives fall guilty, their husbands are implacable ! Death is the punishment of every unfaithful wife. Indeed, a buccaneer who failed thus to revenge himself would be despised by his companions, be admitted to no expedition, and be treated as a pariah.'

When the party reached Seogane, they saw the royal squadron at anchor in the roadstead.

At sight of these warlike preparations, Sir Lewis Morgan felt a glow of enthusiasm.

'At last,' he said, 'I shall fight under the royal flag, and for the glory of England ! '

'Boy,' answered Morgan, 'your heart rejoices because you see men dressed in fine uniforms, who at their master's signal will fight any enemy, however unjust the quarrel. These men that the world calls heroes draw their swords often at the caprice of a tyrant, or even of his mistress. When we pirates fight, it is against an enemy who has injured us, and whom we hate with all the strength of our souls. We fight for vengeance and liberty, therefore nothing but death stops us. I vow, Lewis, you will see the glorious contrasts between the courage that is bought and that which is inspired. But as you seem to have a fondness for the king's uniform, come with me and I will present you to Bloxam. His rooms, no doubt, are crowded with officers.'

Giving their horses to Allan to mind, Morgan took his nephew's arm and led him into Government House.

Scarcely had Sir Lewis crossed the threshold than he was surprised to see handsome Lawrence, magnificently dressed and decorated with the order of St. Louis, surrounded by a crowd of officers.

CHAPTER XLIX.

THE SEA-EAGLES ASSEMBLE.

MANNERS are so changed, that it would be difficult now to understand the importance that in the days of Louis XIV. was attached to the order of St. Louis, then to Europeans what that of the Garter is to Englishmen. A noble, who, after forty years of hard military service, was made as his sole reward simple knight of this order, saw all his hopes realized, all his ambition gratified.

This distinction, which he had paid for at the price of twenty wounds and the greater part of his patrimony wasted in camps, gave him immense consideration in his province, and obtained for him an honourable old age.

Sir Lewis, who at least had no feeble opinion of the value of gentility, felt deep astonishment, therefore, at seeing his former mate so decorated ; it bordered on stupefaction ; while Randolph, who was surprised at nothing, uttered an exclamation of wonder. As for the naval officers who surrounded Lawrence, it was easy to guess by their puzzled looks that the fact that the cross of commander of the order should be worn by a sea-rover was to them as marvellous as inexplicable.

'Pardy! mate, you come in the nick of time,' hailed Lawrence, advancing to the Cornishman, ' I was just talking of you to these gentlemen.'

'What were you saying of me, mate ?'

'I was publishing your good qualities, for, would you believe it, these gentlemen had formed a most awful opinion of us buccaneers. They fancied we were drunkards, and swore, blasphemed, and fought without intermission.   That we were, in fact, a kind of cross-breed between a brutal sailor and a Carib Indian.   I must do these gentlemen the justice to admit that they have slightly changed their opinion.   What I want to prove to them now is that the Indies contain all sorts of persons ; some worthy from their wit, birth, and courage to compete with the most noted at European courts.   I was citing you as a model of delicacy and consistency in love.'

These words made Morgan redden.

'There, now, you are going to be angry.   Why the deuce, mate, you know I always joke ; but come, give me your arm, I want to speak to you.'

Handsome Lawrence bowed with great politeness to the French officers, and went off with the Englishman.

'Lewis,' said Lawrence, as soon as the two young men were alone, ' my long silence has perhaps appeared strange to you. As your mate I ought to have interested myself about you, informed you from time to time of my proceedings, and proposed to you to engage in the short and successful expeditions I have made lately.   Nevertheless, comrade, I had your interest in view in not doing so.   It was clear to me when we parted that you cherished an ardent and sincere love for Wildflower.   You are aware of the impression that sweet girl had made on my heart. On seeing you wounded, perhaps dying, a generous feeling came over me, I thought I could renounce Wildflower.   That is the reason you did not hear from me."

'And what is your intention now, Lawrence ? '

'Now, mate, I feel sure virtue, generosity—all that kind of thing—is out of my line ; for the more I tried to forget Wild-flower, the more her beauty, gentleness, and purity, captivated my imagination, and sank into my heart.   Had it not been for the arrival of the double squadron, I should certainly have sought her out.   What an absurd thing love is !   But when you believe in nothing, and would avoid the cowardice of suicide, there is nothing left for you to do but to gratify your heart's desire, cost what it may.   All consideration for others is all weakness ; if you want happiness you must take it by assault.'

'Lawrence,' answered Morgan gravely, 'my frankness shall equal yours.   I love Wildflower passionately ; she is to me the universe, to live near her is my only dream, my one desire. Should the day come when I shall be forced to renounce the happiness of seeing her, my mind will lose all elasticity, my body all strength.   I shall become a living corpse.   After this confession, it is useless to add that I shall use every means to thwart your intention.   A proud mind like yours, Lawrence, disdains falsehood.   I adjure you to promise me that you will use no un-fair means to gain Wildflower's consent.   If you do I own frankly that I would not expose Jennie's honour to the uncertainty of a duel, I would slay you straight!'

'You are the same as ever, mate.' answered Lawrence placidly, 'honestly violent, furiously virtuous! Your energy is not original, and borders on monotony ; still, it is so young, so fresh, it pleases me. As you know me too well to think that fear of your dagger influences me, I promise you only by fair means to gain Wild-flower's consent to my suit. Will that satisfy you ? That I shall succeed at last I have not the slightest doubt, for I have faith in my star if in nothing else.'

Morgan and Lawrence's conversation was here interrupted by the sounds of drums which announced the governor's return to his house, in company of the English admiral, as they called Bloxam, as head of the English fleet.

'Shall we go and show ourselves at the reception ?' hinted Lawrence. 'I own I shall not be sorry to show off my cross and diamonds before the officers. This way of putting down their impudence is, I find, more efficacious than the one I first adopted.'

'And what was that ?' asked Morgan.

'Oh, a most vulgar one : I fought half-a-dozen duels, and left four officers for dead, and two badly wounded. Come, shall we go to the presence-chamber ?'

'If you please ; but I wish while we are still alone you would tell me how you came by that commander's cross you wear ? I know enough of the French Court to be aware that the greatest nobles, generals, and marshals of France vie for so great an honour, and you are too young, and, allow me to say so, too wild to have been made knight of that order.'

'The cross which sparkles on my breast,' answered Lawrence, 'was placed by the king's own hand on my cradle. Louis XIV. was, it seems, on good terms with my parents ; but you will oblige me by not asking more questions about it, as I must decline answering any.'

'You relieve me. I feared that there was some hand of the Jacobite court at St. Germain's which had pressed Versailles into decorating you.'

Handsome Lawrence's entrance caused a great sensation in Government House. The Marquis Du Casse, at sight of the commander's cross, grew pale. He feared it all a joke, and that such profanation reported at Versailles would compromise the future of the Island of St. Domingo, as well as injure him and his former comrades.

The governor's embarrassment increased two-fold when the English admiral, pointing to Lawrence, asked who that distinguished man was.

'You would not remember him, Bloxam. He is later than of our old cruising days. But he is the most popular of our freebooters, after Morgan ; he is known as Le Beau Laurent. It was he who lately maintained that incredible and glorious fight, the renown of which must thrill even Europe, in which, with a vessel of sixteen guns and sixty men, Lawrence put to flight the Spanish admiral and his ships, which had two hundred guns and two thousand men.'

'That was truly a glorious deed,' answered Bloxam ; 'but I wish to know how it is a freebooter wears the grandest order of France.'

'In good sooth, I know not,' answered DuCasse, 'I have never heard of his wearing it before to-day.'

'Don't you think, Governor, an explanation is necessary ? for both the French and English regular officers are not eager to embrace the brothers of the black flag.'

'Certainly, I think so. I will seek it out'

Du Casse then went towards Lawrence, and said in a low voice,—

'Will you give me a few minutes' conversation ?'

'Certainly, my dear Du Casse, with the greatest pleasure.'

'Then come with me into my private room with Commander Bloxam.'

The Marquis and Lawrence's departure with the British admiral was remarked by every one and produced a great sensation. The most contradictory comments were made upon it.

The naval officers, exasperated by the buccaneer's insolence who had dared thus to profane the order of St. Louis, loudly expressed their indignation. Lawrence's brothers in arms applauded not less energetically Lawrence's conduct.

'After all,' cried one of them called Pierre Salée, 'if it pleases handsome Lawrence to wear a red ribbon, why should he not ? Who among those who wear it have deserved it better than he ? Who knows if Lawrence has not donned it to show that our navy deserves the same esteem as any king's navy ? Lawrence is a dare-devil. We are worth our weight,' added Pierre, raising his voice. 'Thunder and flames, gentlemen, speak with more respect of Lawrence, or curse me, if you continue to insult him cutlasses and pistols will come into play.'

Salt Peter's words found an echo in the hearts of all the freebooters who were present ; cutlasses were drawn, pistols cocked. The French admiral, the Count de Pointis, who had been warned by Du Casse and Bloxam of the angry susceptibility of his allies, hastened to interpose his authority.

'It is not we who have made you admiral,' cried Peter, 'and we will only obey chiefs of our own choosing ! Don't meddle with what does not concern you ! Come, let us see who dares speak ill of Brother Larry ! Curse me if I don't blow his brains out.'

The naval officers, restrained by their admiral's presence, happily did not answer this defiance.

Almost at the same moment the door of the private room opened. All eyes were turned on Du Casse and Lawrence.

Du Casse, hat in hand, made way for Lawrence to pass, and Bloxam appeared behind them with amazement on his countenance.

'You forget, Governor Du Casse.' said Lawrence, 'that on the threshold of this door I am only Lawrence the Buccaneer.'

The opinion that everyone had of Du Casse's loyalty, power, and abilities was so high, that no one for a moment supposed he had been made a dupe.

'Gentlemen,' said Du Casse, with that confidence which carried with it conviction, 'I declare publicly here on my honour that Monsieur Laurent is really and duly Commander of the Order of St. Louis. He has deigned to explain to us, on our promise of inviolable secrecy, the motive which has hitherto prevented his assuming his rights. I quite agree with him, and in his place would have done the same.'

Whilst the Governor spoke all eyes were of course turned on the French buccaneer, who stood, with his head erect, and an ironical and disdainful smile on his lips; he seemed neither annoyed nor pleased with the attention he had excited; he looked like a man who had been too long accustomed to awaken general curiosity and receive homage to care for it. Scarcely had Du Casse finished speaking when with a sarcastic smile Lawrence observed :

'Gentlemen, I wished to prove to you that among pirates and bandits, whom in your ignorance you treated with disdain, were men superior to you in rank and birth! I hope I have succeeded! Now I carry my pride still higher. Chains may be gold, but still they are chains. Fetters, however glorious in the eyes of the world, are still fetters. This cross of which you dare not even covet possession, I lay it aside now and for ever! Livery does not suit men of my temper; the harness of domestic animals will not bind a lion or tiger. What I want is a dress that leaves me free, and the sight of which recalls no ideas of subjection and servitude. The sea rover's dress is my choice.'

At this answer a burst of applause rose from the buccaneers.

'Burn me, but that's fine!' shouted Morgan, with generous warmth.

Lawrence went towards Captain Pierre Salée and said :

'Will you change coats with me ?'

'But, Laurent,' said the surprised buccaneer, 'your dress is splendid enough for a saint in St. Peter's, it is worth at least fifteen thousand francs, whilst mine are of the coarsest cloth! You would be too great a loser.'

'Your clothes have seen hard service and been baptized with the enemy's fire. Your hat is pierced with the enemy's shot, therefore I gain in the exchange ; I trade worthless jewels and you give me glory and renown.'

Lawrence then took off his magnificent coat and put on Pierre's rough, battle-stained garment.

Still louder bursts of applause from the buccaneers showed how highly they all appreciated these sentiments, and without paying the slightest attention to the presence óf the admiral they filled the air with cries of ' Long live Larry !   Vive à jamais le Beau Laurent ! '

' Well, Morgan,' said his nephew in a whisper, ' you do not join in the applause.   Has Laurent's triumph been too great to please you ? '

' I applauded just now, Lewis,' answered Morgan, ' because Laurent's pride was genuine : he spoke from his heart.   Now he does not think what he says ; he is playing a part with the design of captivating his audience.   I allow it shows immense tact and cleverness.   He could not have chosen any one better than Captain Pierre, at this moment the poorest of our brothers. Yes, it was very "deep!"   And after all, why should I be uneasy ?   What has just happened teaches me nothing new ; I always knew Lawrence was very keen, especially in small things. But his tooth can never do more than bite my heel.'

' But if the tooth is venomous the poison will find its way to the heart.'

' Ay, if the heel before it is bitten does not crush the serpent's head.'

After having been presented by Morgan II. to the Governor, Sir Lewis amused himself with rambling about the town.   He was soon accosted by some of the naval officers, who, judging from his appearance that he was a gentleman, were anxious to get into conversation with him to learn something of the buccaneers.

De Morgan received their advances cordially, and before the end of the day he was on good terms with his new acquaintances.

' Really, chevalier,' said a young officer named De Rolard, ' you cannot think how greatly we have been astonished since our arrival here.   We were so far from expecting to meet among the freebooters men of distinguished rank and talent such as we come across continually.   Until now we always put down as fairy tales the extraordinary exploits related of the Brothers of the Coast.   Now, frankly among ourselves—and this question need not offend you, as you have told us that only for the present affair you have joined the buccaneers—do your companions fight as well as they are said to do ?'

' I have only yet been in two engagements ; one on land, the other on the sea,' answered Morgan; 'but the intrepidity which I have witnessed gives me the highest opinion of their valour.'

'At what engagements were you present, chevalier ?'

'The taking of Grenada, effected in one night with a force of a hundred and twenty men, and a sea fight waged successfully by a frigate of sixteen guns and ninety men against two Spanish ships of a hundred guns each and two thousand men.'

'What, were you in that affair ?'

'Yes, I was Lawrence's mate,' answered Morgan in a modest tone which still further enhanced the consideration with which his new friends now treated him.

'In faith, chevalier,' cried De Rolard, 'I see that to maintain the honour of the royal navy there remains but one chance to us, that is, to get ourselves killed to the last man !'

De Rolard little thought that speaking thus he prophesied his own doom. A month after he was wounded in the thigh while performing prodigies of valour, and died two days afterwards from the effects of amputation.

When the dinner hour arrived the officers begged Sir Lewis to join them on board their ship, but Admiral Morgan came hurriedly to them.

'Sir Lewis,' he said, 'I was looking for you. Bloxam receives all the buccaneer captains to dinner to-day. Du Casse, who was requested to give the invitations, asked me twice not to forget you.'

Morgan took leave of the officers and accompanied his uncle, and an hour later was seated at the admiral's table. This dinner. which he had planned to make acquaintance with his allies and enable him to study their characters, presented a strange spectacle.

One's wonder was the more intensified at the remembrance that, though for the time being French, English and independent sea-rovers and hunters were in friendship, each party had been the other's foe, and that now only the common enmity against the Spanish united them and caused the goblets to be loving-cups.

The freebooters sat as much at their ease at the admiral's table as if they had been on the deck of their own vessel ; they presented a strange variety of dress. The gold. silk and jewels of those who had not yet had time to get rid of their last booty contrasted oddly enough with the worn leather. coarse cloth and rough garments of those who had been less fortunate. But whatever the brilliancy or dulness of their present appearance they all treated each other on a perfect equality. Lawrence, proudly dressed in Pierre's worn-out coat, was seated on the admiral's left hand, Morgan II. was in the place of honour on his right, next to De Pointis. Du Casse occupied the other end of the table.

Accustomed to give themselves licence, the buccaners did

full justice to their host's wine, and in consequence an hour had
hardly elapsed before conversation was carried on in a high tone
and everyone frankly gave his opinion.

The Count de Pointis, a man of considerable intelligence,
listened to his guests' conversation with an attention which
proved how anxious he was to form an opinion about them.

'Brothers of the Coast,' cried a pirate captain, 'I propose
Lawrence's health ; long live Lawrence.'

This toast was received with great applause.

Lawrence rose, and bowing with peculiar grace, said, looking
triumphantly at Captain Morgan :

'To the health of the Brothers of the Coast and to the hope
of rich booty.'

Morgan sprang to his feet, and added :

'I drink to our present independence and future glory.'

This toast, which did not awaken the avarice or violent
passions of the freebooters, was passed over in silence ; the captain
sat down with a smile on his face, but rage in his breast.

In a moment a voice from the other end of the table made
him start ; it was Morgan's, who now rose glass in hand.

'Gentlemen,' he said, 'I drink to the health of King William
and to his royal navy.'

This was greeted warmly, as well as its logical rider, a toast
to the French monarch.

'Who is that young man ?' asked Bloxam, in a whisper to
Morgan.

'The only son of the last of my line, Sir Lewis Morgan; his
father's lands were confiscated and he died miserably in exile,'
answered Randolph, with emotion.

After dinner, Bloxam went up to Sir Lewis Morgan, and
drawing him into the embrasure of a window and taking his
hand, warmly said,—

'Captain, will you allow me to give you a piece of advice
which if it caused your death would really grieve me, but when
we reach Carthagena, try every means to distinguish yourself, and
believe that you will always find in me a true friend. Your
uncle will tell you Ned Bloxam knows what true friendship is.'

Having said these words the admiral left Morgan abruptly,
without giving him time to reply.

Four days after the admiral's dinner, that is to say on the
30th of March, 1697, the forces which had been so long ready
under Morgan's superintendence to help in the siege of
Carthagena, were all assembled on the Little Zuava River, the
usual meeting place when any large expedition was contemplated
by the buccaneers.

It was necessary to name the captains of the different vessels,
and this was to be decided by vote.

The freebooters who offered themselves for these posts were without exception members of the mysterious and formidable association of which Morgan was at the head.

Furnished by royal letters with supreme command, he resolved, in order to keep his movements perfectly free, to serve as a volunteer on board the Sceptre, the flag-ship.

The ships which Morgan brought to strengthen the royal squadron, were thirteen in number. Eight were manned with Brothers of the Coast alone, three by buccaneers, and two by negroes.

Lawrence was elected to the Serpent, Pierre Salée to the Kite, Truculent Tom to the Pembroke, and so on.

In the election of first officers, Sir Lewis Morgan, already respected by the freebooters for his gallant conduct in the action with the two Spanish ships, was chosen Lawrence's second.

Du Casse, as had been agreed to beforehand, was to take the command of the buccaneer fleets with the title of Admiral.

A native of St. Domingo, Sieur Pitty, was appointed chief of the negro auxiliaries, in consequence of his great experience among them, and the influence he had acquired. The French fell under the orders of De Pointis.

The forces of the adventurers were 1,650 strong ; those of the royal squadron 2,638 and 3,400, and together they made a fleet of 29 sails with a reserve at St. Domingo. Faithful to his promise, Greybeard arrived on the 25th of March, with his party of a hundred buccaneers. Presented to Bloxam by Morgan, he clearly and briefly explained that he brought this force only on condition that justice should be done him, and that his right to the name of Buckingham should be acknowledged by the king and lords. The Admiral, duly appreciating the immense service that the buccaneers might render him, accepted this condition. It is useless to say that Wildflower accompanied her father. The naval officers, warned by the captains of the freebooters of the superstitious reverence that Jennie inspired, confined their admiration within the limits of all proper respect.

On the morning of the 1st of April, the triple fleet set sail.

CHAPTER L.

THE COUNCIL OF WAR.

HAVING met with contrary winds, the fleet took five days to reach Cape Tuburon, but at last on the 12th of April anchored before Carthagena. The north of the town, defended by rocks and quicksands, was inaccessible.

The St. Louis, which led the van, approached nearly within

gunshot and fired. The broadside had no effect. Seeing the uselessness of firing at that distance Captain Levi tried to approach nearer, but was obliged to wear as quickly as possible ; his ship not having sufficient draught of water had nearly gone on the sands, and the captain considered himself very fortunate to clear her off.

'Mate,' said Lawrence to Sir Lewis, 'don't you think this would be a good opportunity to give a lesson to the officers of the navy ? '

'What do you mean, Lawrence ?

'Why, to accomplish what Captain Levi has tried to do and failed. I know these shores perfectly. I take upon myself to run the Serpent in among those formidable rocks ; she draws much less water than the St. Louis or Sceptre ; we could get within gunshot of the town.'

'Take care what you are about, Lawrence. You know the independent minds you have to deal with. It is not unlikely the men will murmur at this manœuvre, which is as dangerous as useless. The same fellows who will run head foremost at a battery when they see some chance of success, may rebel when you risk their lives for a whim of your own. This would not have been the first time they have deposed a captain. Take my advice and don't put your popularity to such a risk.'

'It is just a trial of my popularity I want to make ; I long to learn exactly what influence I have over them.'

'Still, Lawrence, reflect.'

'Nonsense ! I never do reflect ; but come, jump on the quarter deck and go halves with me in the glory of the enterprise.'

This proposal was too agreeable for Morgan not to accept at once ; he took his station by Lawrence's side and said,—

One last word, mate ; don't you think it would be prudent to tell the crew what you think of doing and so make them a party to your dangerous scheme.'

'Not bad advice ; I'll follow it.'

'Brothers of the Coast,' began Lawrence, 'we all have the same end in view and all desire the same result, still our devotion to the common cause is not so great as to prevent our seizing with joy any opportunities that may offer to show our superiority over the regular sailor. You have all just witnessed the discomfiture of the St. Louis. Are you willing that in sight of the whole fleet we should attempt what she has failed to accomplish ? I don't deny it may cost us a little bloodshed. But what pleasure it will be to give these gentlemen a lesson and show them what sea-rovers can do. As regards the ship, fear nothing ! I would answer with my head for her safety. I know these shores thoroughly. Time presses ; say whether we shall crow over the bluejackets or not.'

' Yes, let us humble them,' shouted all the pirates with one voice. Not to let their zeal cool he ordered the ship instantly to be put about, which was done with a rapidity and unanimity that argued well for success.

The Serpent, gracefully gliding from its place in the squadron, bore down upon the town.

Morgan, busy with helping his mate in working the ship, had not remarked that Wildflower, who had been present at their conversation, had followed him upon the quarter-deck.

' You here, Jennie ?' he exclaimed in a tone of soft reproach ; ' go below, dear sister, I implore you.'

' It is useless to ask me, Sir Lewis,' answered she resolutely. ' The buccaneers are cheered by my presence, and it is my duty to be with you in this act of folly.' Then drawing nearer to him she added : ' Between us two, brother, there is not room for a cannon ball.'

The course of the Serpent was watched with intense interest by all on board the united fleet.

The stillness on board was only broken by the rippling of the water at her forefoot.

' Top men, to your posts, gunners stand to your guns, all others flat on deck,' shouted out Lawrence. ' The music will soon begin to play ! '

In this moment a cry of alarm rose from the whole fleet. The Serpent, tacking as she was steered towards shore, ran right upon the rocks. It really appeared like the premeditated suicide of all on board.

The Spaniards, from the top of their ramparts, looked in bewilderment, almost stupefaction, at the extraordinary behaviour of the Serpent. They could not comprehend such fatal rashness.

But while the Serpent was still in the midst of the rocks and quicksands, and was scarcely a gunshot from the town, the gunners, throwing off their torpor, stood with lighted matches at their guns, and half a minute afterwards a torrent of fire fell with a dreadful noise upon the ih-fated vessel, and enveloped her in a cloud of thick smoke.

The few moments that followed seemed like hours to the eager spectators, which was followed by one cry of joy and triumph as the wind having cleared off the smoke, the Serpent was seen unhurt, and Jennie's scarf still waving from the quarter-deck.

' Now, men, give them a broadside,' ordered Lawrence.

The broadside burst forth as from the crater of a volcano The freebooters returned with interest the hot reception the Spaniards had given them.

Either from chance or from the skill of the gunners, the volley was fatal to the Spaniards, who had two cannons dismounted, and many men killed.

Lawrence, taking advantage of the temporary confusion of the enemy, ordered about his ship, and coasting the quicksands with equal courage and good fortune brought his ship off safe and sound from her perilous enterprise. This departure was a triumph, and taking off his hat and bowing to the town, Lawrence called out 'Soon again, Senores.'

The words repeated from ship to ship caused a tremendous sensation, and were followed by loud and repeated cheers.

The naval officers now began to understand the fabulous successes that had been achieved by the freebooters.

Admiral de Pointis, anxious to distinguish himself, had the squadron anchored out of reach of the cannon opposite Carthagena, and commanded the bomb-ketch, under one Captain Monts, to begin the bombardment of the town.

This bombardment continued all night without intermission, but was so far off as to cause more alarm than damage to the Spaniards; it was the first time mortars were used in the West Indies.

The 13th was passed in arranging the plan of attack. From time to time the ketch let off a few bombs to keep up the terror of the inhabitants.

On the 14th, the combined squadrons coasted along the nine miles of threatening cliffs from the town to the roadstead, and anchored off the port of Boca-chica (Little Mouth), which derived its name from the narrowness of its entrance, which only allowed one vessel to pass at a time. To keep this fort was therefore of the utmost consequence to the Spaniards, it being the key of Carthagena.

Boca-chica had four strong bastions on the west; it was defended by the sea, which washed the foot of its ramparts and on the three other sides by a deep ditch. The ramparts, were celebrated throughout the West Indies for their solidity and impenetrable thickness; they defied even bombs, and its walls were equally impervious to cannon balls. A thirty-six pounder ball fired at them within pistol range did no injury. This fort had thirty-three great guns. The two flagships, supported by the ketch and the other ships, began the attack.

Atthe same time, by Du Casse's order the freebooters took to their boats and, protected by the fire of the vessels which prevented the Spaniards from attempting a sally, they coasted round and landed. They directly formed in order of battle and advanced three-quarters of a mile inland to protect the regular troops from being surprised while coming on shore.

A little before nightfall four thousand men with their arms, were landed on the Spanish coast, and the officers assembled to deliberate.

'Gentlemen,' said Admiral de Pointis, 'our arrival being

known, we cannot hope to find our enemy unprepared ; still I
am of opinion that we may turn to advantage the terror with
which we have inspired them.   My advice is not to give the
Spaniards time to recover, but to march straight on the fort.   I
know that this cannot be done without loss, but still this will
be better than the time it will take to invest Boca-chica.'

'I approve,' said the English commander.

The proposition was about to be applauded, when Du Casse
and Morgan both rose to speak.

Du Casse smiled and said to his old friend, ' Morgan, I yield
to your experience, and beforehand subscribe to your opinion.'

' Governor Du Casse,' answered the English adventurer, respectfully, 'you are in command here.   Speak ! it is most likely
our plans are the same.'

'Gentlemen,' said Du Casse, ' Admirals Bloxam and Pointis
forget that they have sea-rovers for allies.   With such help
the same policy is not required as for regular troops alone.   To
openly attack Boca-chica from the sea where its fortifications are
strongest, is exposing the regiment that tries to do so mad
thing to certain destruction.   It is no reason because the freebooters have a hundred times vanquished the Spaniards that we
should undervalue the courage of our enemies.'

' I have known them for many years,' observed Morgan, 'and
I promise you that the garrison of Boca-chica, which you are
pleased to think much alarmed, would give us a very hot
reception and make us pay dearly for our temerity.'

'Conclude, if you please, sir,' interrupted the Count de
Pointis, drily ; ' we are losing precious time.'

'Admiral de Pointis,' answered Du Casse proudly, ' some
minutes spent in avoiding a disgraceful defeat and bloody
catastrophe cannot be called losing time.   The only reasonable
way of attacking Boca-chica is by passing through the virgin
forests that surround it, and taking it on its side.'

'Pass through the virgin forests ! Can you dream of such a
thing ?' interrupted the French admiral, though Bloxam smiled
approval.   'These   forests   are   impassable ;   it would require
months to cut a road.'

'You are mistaken there,' answered Du Casse ; 'wherever
the sun penetrates, there buccaneers can pass.   Your soldiers,
having no longer to fear ambuscades or other obstacles, can
follow them.'

Du Casse spoke with so much certainty that his words made
a strong impression on the council of war, and when put to
the vote his plan was adopted unanimously.

CHAPTER LI.

THE INCONVENIENCES OF SHORT SIGHT IN GENERALS.

GOVERNOR Du Casse, in spite of the high rank he now held, was much attached to his ancient reputation. It was always with renewed pleasure and very pardonable pride he related the adventures of his youth, when poor and without resources and protectors, trusting to his own perseverance and courage, he had entered that life of adventure which had brought him honour and riches.

When made by the king Governor of St. Domingo, which had been the theatre of his early trials, he did not, blinded by success, deny the past. He still took part in spirit with the enterprises of his old companions and gloried in their success. Therefore he had greatly at heart the issue of the expedition which he had advised. He did not like the free-booters to be found less capable than he had boasted of their being, when saying that where the sun penetrates they could do the same.

'Morgan, he said, drawing his old partner aside, 'I fear I went too far in mentioning that the Brothers of the Coast could in one night cut their way through this forest. Do me a great service and go yourself at their head.'

'In fact, Du Casse,' answered the Englishman, 'I much fear it cannot be accomplished in so short a time. Nevertheless the French must not get this advantage over you. By all that is sacred, here comes Greybeard; heaven sends him to our aid. He alone is able to take us out of this scrape. Barbe-grise,' called he, 'do you come from the forest?'

'Yes, this very moment.'

'What is your opinion of making a path through it?'

'It always gives me pain,' said Greybeard, 'to see trees cut down which fifty years could hardly replace. That mania for destroying without motive God's work seems to me sacrilege. What is the use, Du Casse, of turning hunters into lumberers?'

'It is absolutely necessary, cost what it may, that the troops' should cross the forest, to get possession of the fort of Boca-chica.'

'How now! are men less intelligent than wild boars? Do they want a road cut for them to pass where animals run freely? Order your woodcutters to put away their axes, and I'll take upon myself to lead our men where you want them sent.'

'Are you very sure you can do so?' asked Du Casse eagerly.

'I am always sure of what I advance.'

'But,' asked the governor, 'in what way?'

'Very simply : an hour since I struck a path, and I followed it.'

'A path in the thicket!' cried Du Casse, fearful such good news could not be true.

'Certainly. The path is not wide as a church door, only one man can pass abreast. You understand that wild hogs don't amuse themselves with making *plazas.*'

'But if the Spaniards, who must know of this path, have already lined it with troops ?'

'We can pass over their bodies.'

'If the forest is full of ambuscades ?'

'So much the worse for them—we shall cut them to pieces.'

It was still in his usual slow, deliberate manner that Greybeard gave these energetic answers which delighted Du Casse. He said :

'Follow Morgan, old man. I trust entirely to your experience.'

The old buccaneer with the greatest indifference followed the freebooter. Du Casse, relieved from great anxiety, went towards the shore where the regular troops were encamped.

'Oh, it is you, my young friend,' he said, perceiving Sir Lewis walking mournfully in front of the lines. 'How dull you look! has anything happened to distress you ?'

'Not at all, governor ; I was only meditating.'

'Your meditations were not pleasant, I see! Some love affair does not prosper, I suppose? Well, that is natural at your age.'

'You are mistaken, sir.'

'What was their subject, then ?'

'Oblige me by not asking. My respect for your excellency keeps me silent.'

'Oh, then, if it concerns me, you show me more obedience than respect. Pray explain.'

'Well, your excellency, as you wish it, I was thinking that belonging to the nobility, and worthy therefore to serve the king, I am enrolled in an irregular band of men whom I cannot esteem, with whom I feel humiliated.'

'Morgan,' answered Du Casse, 'I can understand your feelings, and they are natural to your age and rank ; but you are unjust to freebooters. They are not now, I own, what they once were ; formerly they fought for the love of devilry, then for glory, now more often for mere wealth. You see I am frank with you. Still there are amongst them noble hearts, brave spirits, and lofty minds. Your kinsman, for instance ! But to return to what concerns you, I only know one way to satisfy your wish. Will you be my aide-de-camp ?'

Morgan flushed with pleasure.

'A hundred thanks ! I accept gratefully, and will do my best not to give you reason to repent your choice."

'Then that is settled,' said the governor ; 'let us return to the camp. I fancy that my fellow-countryman wishes for my presence ; he has to take his revenge of me, and he is not a man to leave such debts unpaid. You know I am rather freebooter than French.'

Du Casse was not deceived ; as soon as the French admiral saw him, he eagerly advanced to meet him.

'Governor,' said the count, 'though I always yield to public opinion if it is against me, still I am extremely obstinate when I feel myself right. The council decided that it would be better to attack Boca-chica in the rear ; but as I still think it may be necessary to return to my plan, I imagine it may be useful to explore the environs, so that if we have to renew it we may be prepared. Will you accompany me on this excursion ?'

'With pleasure.'

'Captain Levi will also be of the party.'

'And I take with me my aide-de-camp, the Knight of Morgan, whom I beg to introduce to you, and who will represent Commander Bloxam on this reconnoitring affair.'

The moon being at the full inundated the whole prospect with its clear silver light, rendering doubly hazardous this venture, which even on a dark night would have been dangerous. Du Casse, suspecting that the admiral's intention was to carry this reconnaissance as far as possible, in order to revenge himself on the governor, resolved not to give him the opportunity. After half an hour's silent walk along the shore, Du Casse drew nearer to the admiral. In less than a minute a flash of fire was followed by a cannon ball, which fell only ten paces from them.

'It seems the Spaniards are on the alert,' remarked De Pointis curtly.

Scarcely had he uttered the words before another ball fell almost at their feet, covering them with sand as it struck the ground.

'At all events, they are not bad marksmen,' commented De Pointis.

'They do their best,' answered Du Casse, 'and then it must be owned we are rather far off them. Shall we give them a better chance ?'

'I was going to propose it.'

Five minutes later the officers were so near that muskets also were fired at them.

Their position was no longer tenable ; to persevere would have been certain death.

'Governor,' said De Pointis, whose coolness and Captain

Levi's remained as steadfast as Morgan's and the governor's, 'don't you think we have learnt enough of the enemy's position?'

'Excuse me, Admiral, I am so dreadfully short-sighted, I cannot even see the fort! pray let us step a little nearer.'

The admiral followed Du Casse a hundred yards farther; had it not been for a rock that screened, death would have been inevitable.

'Ah, really,' cried Du Casse, 'we are getting warmer. I think I can discern a corner of the fortress! Oh, no, I mistake, it's a rock. We are going wrong; pray, my lord, let us turn nearer the sea, or our sight will be obstructed by that stone.'

Admiral De Pointis seized Du Casse by the arm. 'How far do you intend going?'

'Oh, only to the moat; my dreadful ophthalmia makes me a perfect St. Thomas. I must touch a thing or I can never believe it is there.'

'To go beyond those rocks that shelter us would be certain death. Governor, the lives of both of us are too necessary to this expedition to run such tremendous risk. It is a general's duty to keep himself as much out of danger as he can.'

'Well, my lord, the moment I saw you, an admiral, adventure your life like a simple scout, without the slightest precaution, why, I thought you must have a peculiar method of making war, and confiding in your experience I followed you blindly. Now I am of opinion that as we have gone so far out of our duty we had better go on. Who knows if the Spaniards, overwhelmed with fear, as you hinted, might not let us four take Boca-chica by assault? It would really be a glorious feat of arms, and would remind me of the time when I was a buccaneer. Believe me, Admiral, we had better go on.'

The count, who perfectly understood Du Casse's raillery, was on the point of accepting this challenge, but duty carried the day, and he turned back.

The return of the little party was luckily effected without injury. Morgan, who walked behind Du Casse to screen him as much as possible, received a ball in his hat, however.

After they were beyond the reach of the cannon, and therefore out of danger, Du Casse lingered behind the admiral and said to Morgan, rubbing his hands joyfully,—

'Chevalier, the admiral has not got his revenge yet; we must do all we can not to give him the chance.'

Though the Count de Pointis's rugged features displayed no ill-humour, yet rage gnawed his heart.

'Ah, Du Casse,' he said to himself, 'you reckon you have gained a great advantage over me in the sight of my captain and your cursedly cool Englishman, but if you knew what are my

instructions, and what fate is reserved for you, you would not be
so triumphant.   As for these skimmers of the sea, who dare to
put themselves on a par with the royal navy, and have even
dared to insult me, they are doomed !   The blow that reaches
Du Casse will be fatal to the crew of them, English, or French, or
mongrel.'

The rest of the night passed without adventure.   The troops
had retired behind earthworks, but no attack troubled their
sleep.

At day-break, a messenger sent by Greybeard announced the
arrival of the freebooters under the fort by the way of the forest.
The army at once followed them, and by mid-day four thousand
men were within cannon shot.

Everyone was now busy preparing for the assault, when a
report of firearms was heard in front of the foremost lines. Soon
the scouts brought in two prisoners, a monk and an Indian, who
had been seized while they were trying to pass through the woods
to get to Carthagena to ask for help.

'Who knows,' said the Count de Pointis, 'if the Spaniards
will not yield ? We must send them the monk to parley.'

'As it won't shackle us, let us send the monk.   Only, I warn
you, admiral, that Spaniards are extremely proud, and will not
lay down their arms before they have fought well, or have found
a pretext for capitulating without dishonour'

The monk, preceded by a drum and trumpet, set forth ; he
was only desired to tell the Governor of Boca-chica that if he did
not yield, the allies would put all his garrison to the sword.

The monk returned half an hour afterwards, accompanied by
a Spanish drummer sent by the governor.

'The answer of my master,' said the drummer, when taken
into the presence of the three admirals, 'is that he does not
understand your arrogant message. He begs you to attack him
with all the valour and impetuosity you can summon up, and he
promises to give you a good lesson.'

CHAPTER LII.

TAKING THE FORT.

THE immediate attack of Boca-chica was resolved upon, and
caused a feverish excitement in the besiegers' camp.

Accustomed to clearing land, the negroes under the command
of Pitty in less than an hour felled the trees which protected the
fort ; levelled the soil, and prepared it for the batteries, which
were quickly mounted under the superintendence of Vice-Admiral
Coëtlogen for the French, and Captain Bacon for the English
guns.

Firing began at once. The buccaneers, disseminated round the fort, by their admirably directed firing protected the gunners and dreadfully harassed the Spaniards. Any one who showed himself on the fort was instantly killed.

Du Casse, accompanied by young Morgan, moved about the buccaneers' lines, but took no part in the artillery duel.

The batteries, though admirably worked, produced little effect on the bomb-proof walls of Boca-chica.

' If this siege goes on in this way,' said Du Casse to Sir Lewis, ' it is likely to outlast that of Troy ! I really cannot conceive how the count, who is a military man and not a sailor like Bloxam, can act thus. I can only explain his tactics by his fear of seeing us play an important part here which might lessen the glory of victory. He is in the wrong. The deuce take me if I interfere without I am asked. The aid of my buccaneers is at least worth that much honour. When these navy gentlemen find they want us, we will march, not before. Only, as this might happen any moment, let us be ready.'

The firing on the fort had lasted two hours without any successi ; ill-defended by the earth mounds that had been hastily raised, the gunners had suffered immense losses for so short a space of time, the battery was covered with blood, and twenty men had fallen.

Admiral de Pointis, angry and impatient, owned to himself that he had been blamably hasty, and tried to repair his error.

As for Admiral Bloxam, he affected with the tact of a gentleman not to make the French admiral feel the greatness of his fault. Only, every time an English gunner fell, he frowned, and under pretext of giving his opinion of the Spanish, uttered volleys of oaths.

Aware that such a state of things continuing might compromise the expedition, the French admiral decided upon acting otherwise, if only to keep the English in good temper.

An order was given to the battalions of grenadiers, commanded by Monsieur de la Cherau, to prepare for the assault with a troop of the English marines.

One slight difficulty presented itself to carrying on this operation—to mount an assault a breach in the walls is necessary, and the fort had not lost one stone.

' What a stupid thing is self-love !' murmured Du Casse, on seeing the mixed column advance on the fort ; ' these brave men are marching to certain death, when it would be so easy tospare them if he would only have recourse to my freebooters. The unlucky part is that these poor devils will pay for their chiefs, and bear the punishment of their folly. But is it not always so ? I can't change the usages of war.'

For a moment De Pointis thought that his temerity would

succeed. Just as the grenadiers rushed out of the entrenchment, the fire of the Spaniards ceased.

Alas ! the admiral's delusion was of short duration ; scarcely were the troops a hundred paces from the fort when a dreadful discharge of grape-shot stopped the scaling party ; forty of their number fell dead, and sixty more were wounded, whose bodies delayed the Englishmen.

'Close the ranks, and forward !' cried their captain.

The grenadiers re-formed and went forward boldly in obedience to their commander, though aware that destruction faced them.

'Brave men !' cried Du Casse, almost wild with emotion ; ' but if they did not know our eyes were on them, I fear they might have given way.'

Another fall of grape and ball caught them in full column ; a hundred men now fell dead, more English than French this time, as the two parties had changed their order of precedence.

'Close the ranks and forward,' cried their leaders again.

But it was useless ; the grenadiers turned on their heel and fled, and the British, seeing themselves so few in number, sensibly retired also.

Admiral de Pointis, a prey to an emotion that he could hardly suppress, bit his lips till they bled, and seemed undecided how to proceed ; but suddenly making up his mind, he rushed towards Bloxam and said, 'God forgive me, admiral !' Then, seeing Du Casse, he seized his hand, and said,—

'The thought that the French alone might have the glory of victory dazzled me and has made me commit a great crime. Now that the honour of France is compromised, let all the reward be yours ; it matters not. All I want is to repair at any cost the check we have received, raise again the spirits of my army, and not let the Spaniards have cause to vaunt that they have put the regulars to flight. Bring your freebooters forward.'

Du Casse was touched with this frank appeal and answered,—

'Admiral, your notion that the Spaniards were terrified by us to a great degree justifies your rashness. You now own that our buccaneers can help you, and I will do my best to confirm you in this opinion.'

'What do you think would be best to do ? Would it not be better for us to understand each other on this point ?'

'Admiral,' answered Du Casse drily, 'I kept on one side while you and Bloxam did as you liked. I ask from you the same concession. The wars in Europe and in the West Indies differ completely. There everything is calculated with mathematical precision ; here everything is accomplished by surprise. Once before Carthagena, had we to sit down coolly to besiege the place, I would listen with attention to your experience. At this moment it is a question only of sudden daring : a bold stroke must do the business.'

'Governor,' answered Pointis, annoyed, 'a frank avowal does not constitute weakness or dependence. I have no intention of finding fault with your plans, but it is only natural that I should wish to know what they are.'

'If you take it on that score, admiral, I will frankly own that my plan is very simple. I shall go to the freebooters and say to them, "Shipmates, we want to get into Boca-chica before we go on to Carthagena, and we depend on you. It is now four o'clock, by six you must be masters of the place." You see, admiral, my plan cannot be more simple !'

'What ! will you not lead them yourself ? '

'Why should I ? Have they not already taken a hundred Spanish towns without me ? You may believe me, admiral, they won't make much ado about Boca-chica.'

Commander Bloxam grinned and nodded.

'Then, according to you, governor, two hours hence the fort will be ours ? '

Du Casse looked at his watch. 'It is half-past four,' he said ; 'by a quarter to seven at the latest you will see floating on that citadel the black flag of the buccaneers ! You may plant the white one of France where you like then.'

Du Casse hastened to the freebooters. On his way he met Morgan.

'Mate,' he said, 'I have just broken a lance with the French admiral, for the honour of the buccaneers.' He related what had passed between his countryman and himself.

'Now, Morgan,' he went on, 'I count upon you ; you must arrange the attack and take the command of our forces. I will go with you as a simple volunteer. It will really be a treat to me. Let it be a brilliant feat and try to keep me a place close beside you. It makes me a young man again to follow the raw head and bloody bones ! '

'Nothing is easier than to get possession of Boca-chica, answered Morgan quietly ; 'my preparations are already made, but as to heading the attack, I refuse.'

'Oh, you refuse, you old glutton,' returned the governor smiling. 'I suppose it is too small a morsel for your capacious maw.'

'Not at all,' answered the Englishman, 'I refuse to take part in the attack simply because I don't chose to expose myself to being killed.' This answer was given too truthfully for Du Casse to doubt it, yet his surprise was great.

'Is it possible, friend,' he said after a short pause, 'that you are afraid to storm such a paltry place ? I can hardly believe my senses.'

'Friend,' answered old Morgan gently, 'you misunderstand me. I did not say I was afraid, but that I did not choose to expose myself to being killed. Do not look so wonderstruck, it is a fact.'

'Explain yourself.'

'You know my past life and the debt of vengeance I owe to my brother's murderer. This man is now in Carthagena. On the eve of avenging my brother's death have I the right to risk my life for king or country? No, certainly not! This is the reason I refuse your request.'

'Poor mate,' answered Du Casse, 'I know how much the sacrifice costs you, but you are right. I will head the attack, then, myself.'

The freebooters, on hearing that Admiral de Pointis had been forced to ask their help and that Du Casse was going to lead them, were overjoyed. To have regular soldiers witnesses of their success where those soldiers had failed, exalted to heroism men who were at all times indifferent to danger.

Their arrangements were quickly made. They resolved instead of moving forward in close bodies to divide into parties of five or six men and to try to scale the walls at twenty places at once. For supposing even the Spaniards should succeed in repulsing nineteen parties, they well knew that if only a dozen freebooters got a footing on the fort, Boca-chica would be theirs.

At a signal from Du Casse, the Brothers of the Coast, carrying with them ladders and planks to serve as flying bridges, rushed towards the fort. This time the Spaniards did not wait till they came near, for more frightened at the sight of the freebooters than of the French and English, they fired all their cannons. A fruitless effort. The besiegers, laughing and cheering, advanced as to a mere game at play, which in fact it was to them. If one fell, his place was instantly taken up by another; their gaiety continued as if they were invulnerable. In a moment a cry of rage and despair burst from them, for Du Casse, struck by grape-shot, fell.

'Friends,' cried Sir Lewis Morgan, 'let our cry be vengeance!'

At sight of their bleeding chief and the sound of the young man's voice, they rushed furiously on. In a minute's time they had reached the foot of the walls. Twenty planks thrown at once over the ditches supported the scaling ladders, the men, overturning each other in their haste to be first, mounted to the assault.

'Vengeance!' was their cry.

Soon a loud exclamation of joy burst from the lookers-on. All saw a black flag with white crossbones waving in the air. At the foot of the flagstaff, his graceful form and bold features cut clearly against the blue sky, stood the descendant of Sir Henry Morgan, where, perhaps, his famous ancestor had also stood in victory.

CHAPTER LIII.

THE AVENGER.

The capture of Boca-chica opened to the combined squadrons the entrance of the bay and consequently the roadstead of Carthagena. The ships, with sufficient men on board to work their guns, attacked under Lawrence the fort of Santa Croz, and after having taken possession of it bombarded the town.

The troops, put on shore about three miles from Carthagena had hard work to do. Before they could begin the siege of the town they had to make their way through dreadful roads and take two forts by assault, those of Our Lady, a large convent admirably fortified, and of St. Lazarus.

Numerous parties of Indians whom the Spaniards had called to their aid harassed incessantly the assailants and rendered their task still more difficult.

Still the emulation that had sprung up between the troops and the freebooters was so strong that nothing could stop their progress ; each day was marked by a new fight, and each fight by heroic deeds.

Admiral de Pointis, cured of his folly in wishing to do without his wild allies, in concert with Bloxam, Du Casse having been severely wounded in the leg, directed the operations. The count becoming himself again, showed remarkable military skill together with great activity and indomitable coolness, so that he inspired his forces with great confidence. Bloxam more particularly distinguished himself on the sea.

It was after taking the fort of St. Lazarus that on the twenty-first of April the siege of Carthagena began, or rather that of Gezemania, Carthagena being divided into two towns by a deep ditch over which was thrown a drawbridge.

The Admiral de Pointis in advancing too fearlessly, as was his custom, to reconnoitre the position of the enemy, was struck by a ball which took the flesh completely off his chest. This event caused much consternation in the army, but Admiral Bloxam took the command at once over the allies.

From the twenty-first to the twenty-ninth the besiegers kept up a vigorous firing, and on the morning of the thirteenth of April it was announced to the admiral that the breach in the walls was large enough for two men to enter abreast.

The baron immediately got up and had himself dressed in full uniform.

At two the assault was to take place. The solemn moment arrived, the troops moved forward. The first attacking column was headed by Du Casse, who in spite of the pain of his wound walked as nimbly as a young man ; near him was young Morgan who, publicly complimented by the admiral after the taking of Boca-chica, where he had signalized himself so greatly, had shown equal intrepidity in his subsequent conduct.

After Du Casse came the bluejackets under Bloxam in person.

When the troops had come out of the intrenchment they were exposed to the fire of a bastion named St. Catherine, which poured grape-shot upon them, and caused immense losses though they still remained firm. It was only after the third discharge, and when the ground was covered with dead and wounded, that some hesitation became apparent among the attacking troops.

Then occurred a deed which is without precedent in the annals of war. All the officers with mutual agreement quitted their separate posts and formed themselves into an heroic band.

The Count of Coëtlogen, who was at the head of it, received just as it set forth a musket-shot in the shoulder.

'It is nothing,' he said with a smile, and still boldly advanced. It was necessary to raise the soldiers' courage. Three days after the vice-admiral died from his wound.

The example given by their officers excited the soldiers to enthusiasm ; they rushed impetuously to the assault.

The freebooters were not a whit behind ; they clung tooth and nail to the least projection of stone and let themselves be trans-fixed by the Spanish lances, rather than give way or flinch to escape death. After a quarter of an hour's unexampled courage the enemy hung a white flag over the battlements ; they wanted a short truce.

'I give you a quarter of an hour to surrender at discretion,' answered Admiral Bloxam ; 'that delay expired, I shall be implacable.'

Although the firing ceased, not one of the freebooters or soldiers quitted his place ; all hung as it were round the walls. But scarcely had ten minutes passed when a fearful report was heard. The Spaniards, unfaithful to their oath and the inviolability of a truce, treacherously fired on their too confiding enemy.

The roar of 'vengeance' rose spontaneously from two thousand men. It was too full of hatred and rage to leave the issue of the fight long doubtful, and it was quickly followed by a shout of victory. A few minutes more and the treacherous flag of truce was replaced by the three standards of the allies. Terrible as had been the treachery, equally implacable was the vengeance. Two hundred Spaniards who had taken refuge in a church were pitilessly put to the sword. The town of Gezemania was one vast field of carnage ; wounded there were none, all had been pitilessly killed.

The first of May, they summoned the governor of the upper town, Señor Don Sancho Ximenes, to yield. He answered that he wished to hold a conference with the commanders.

Du Casse left the camp under the safeguard of a truce, for Carthagena ; Morgan, disguised as a drummer, went with him.

They returned towards evening, Senor Ximenes having rejected every proposal. This refusal was anticipated, for the town of Carthagena itself, defended by a deep, wide ditch, guarded by eighty cannon, and provisioned for six months, was in a good state of defence.

'My dear Lewis,' said Morgan, 'to-morrow we shall enter Carthagena, and the hour of vengeance will at last be ours. I have to-day seen my brother's murderer. This man, entrusted with greater authority than Ximenes, is the real governor of Carthagena.'

'How can we enter Carthagena to-morrow ?' asked Morgan. 'We ought to think ourselves very lucky if we take the town after a long and bloody siege.'

'What, boy, do you doubt my words ? Remember, I never state a fact until I am sure of it ; and also that for two years I have been preparing for this expedition, and that all my measures have been taken. To-morrow, I repeat, our hour of vengeance will sound.'

Without further discussion he left his nephew and went to seek Bloxam.

'Old comrade,' said he, 'it is nonsense for us to be preparing to take Carthagena in the usual way by a regular siege. Order some of our vessels to cannonade the town vigorously to-morrow, and by night the town will be ours.'

The admiral looked astounded, but knowing the speaker's eminent sagacity and deep knowledge of warfare, the only conclusion he could come to was that he had lost his reason.

'Admiral,' answered the old pirate smiling, 'your bewildered air proves what little account you make of my words. Why do you think it so astonishing that I on my side have been working for the success of this expedition ? It is true that I have taken no active part with the troops. I knew they would sooner or later take Gezemania, that was enough for me. But, after all, what harm will it do to bombard and cannonade the town to-morrow ? Even should this measure be unavailing, it will at least keep up the spirit of the shipmen.'

'Let it be as you wish, brother,' answered the admiral ; 'but the plague take me if I understand a word you say.'

The next day the *Sceptre*, the *Vermandois*, and the bomb-ketch opened fire on the town, among others, with long guns.

At three o'clock two flags of truce waved from the ramparts; the governor of the besieged town asked for another interview; only this time he wanted to see the English admiral himself.

'Send your conditions to Don Ximenes, and don't trouble to go,' suggested old Morgan.

Greatly surprised that his companion's prediction so soon seemed likely to be realized, Bloxam followed his advice.

'Above all,' added the pirate, 'make Don Ximenes perfectly understand that if he refuses the treaty you are so good as to offer him, you will act towards the upper town as you have with the lower, and every soldier will be put to the sword.'

The following morning, being the third of May, Ximenes accepted and signed the capitulation.

The stringent articles having been agreed to on both sides, Du Casse sent a detachment of freebooters to occupy one side of the bastion of St. Catherine, and one of the gates of the town.

The French grenadiers took possession of the ramparts, and the English guarded all the approaches of the town.

'Well, admiral,' said Morgan, who could not recover from his surprise and delight at this unexpected surrender, 'was I deceived? But I don't wish to mystify you any longer. The taking of Carthagena costs me ten thousand pounds, which I have spent among men condemned to the galleys, who have been incorporated in the Spanish army These brave men, anxious to avoid falling into our hands, executed with zeal an order I gave them to foment a sedition. Threatened by us from without, and his own soldiers from within, the governor had no choice left but to surrender.'

The fourth of May, at daybreak, the Spanish governor left the town at the head of seven hundred men.

Old Morgan looked at all the men, as they filed out, with great attention.

'Well,' he said to himself, 'my order has been obeyed; the murderer remains in my power!'

Immediately after the departure of the garrison, the victors entered Carthagena The first act of the French was to go to the cathedral, and have a prayer offered up, and a *Te Deum* sung for the king of France. We regret to say the English merely broached some rum in honour of their sovereign, 'Black Willie.'

Whilst the cathedral resounded with songs of praise, Morgan at the head of a dozen freebooters, and accompanied by Sir Lewis, knocked at the door of one of the handsomest houses in the town.

'Where are you taking us, uncle?' asked the knight.

'In this house is your father's murderer,' answered his uncle.

At these words Lewis turned pale; an expression of ferocity inflamed his features; he rushed towards the door, and tried to break it open.

'Beat in this door, friends,' said the buccaneer to his men; 'we are not the sort to be kept waiting.'

Though Admiral Bloxam had given strict charge, and threatened with death any soldier or freebooter who should make a forcible entry into any private house, the men did not hesitate to obey Morgan, certain that he would bear them out in what they did by his order.

'Stop, Lewis!' cried the captain, laying forcible hold of the young man's arm as he was rushing in, 'let me go first.'

Scarcely had he passed the threshold, when a Spaniard, a servant by his dress, rushed out, a pistol in each hand, and fired at him.

The captain uncovered his breast, and showing a bullet-proof cuirass under his coat, said:

'My revenge was too dear to let it escape me for want of precaution!' He threw himself on the Count of Monterey, whom he had recognised under the disguise, and cried:

'This man, Lewis Morgan, is your father's murderer.'

The young man stood for a moment thunderstruck; he recognised the features of Nativa's father.

The Spanish grandee had little heeded the words, and thought he had only to do with common freebooters.

The first thought that presented itself to his mind was, that they wanted his wealth.

Still his hatred towards the English was so great that he could not bring down his pride to speak civilly to them.

'The capitulation signed yesterday,' he said, ' ought to have saved me from this violence; but as you have force on your side, and have no notions of honour, tell me at once what you want for my ransom.'

'I cannot answer you here,' said Morgan. 'Friends, bind this wretch hand and foot, and follow me with him.'

His followers executed his order with such good will and dexterity as showed that they were used to such things.

At the head of the party the captain passed through the hall to a large court beyond it.

The Count de Monterey, pale with rage, could hardly restrain his fury.

'Do you want ten thousand piasters?' he asked.

The freebooter smiled in so sinister a manner that the count shuddered.

'Well, we'll say fifteen thousand,' he went on, anxious to conceal his fear, 'I wish to be rid of you.'

'What think you, Lewis?' sneered the freebooter, 'would
that sum pay for your father's death?'

'What I want,' cried Lewis, 'is his heart's blood! all the sufferings he caused my poor father must be atoned for.'

'Take care!' cried Monterey, 'you will lose an excellent opportunity of gaining money.   Fifteen thousand piasters for a
few drops of blood!   I pay rather dear for them.'

Lewis was about to answer, when Morgan stopped him, and
placing himself before Monterey, said:

'Sandoval, you are grossly mistaken in taking us for thieves.
We are your creditors, and come simply to claim a sacred debt
you owe us.   Look at me, and see if you know me?'

'I never saw you before in my life.'

'And this youngster—do you know who he is?'

'Not at all,' answered Sandoval.

'Well, since your memory is so bad, I must jog it.   This
young man is the Knight of Morgan, who threw himself into
the sea to save you after your shipwreck off Penmark.'

'Then,' interrupted the count joyfully, 'I have nothing to
fear; but as it is beneath the dignity of a grandee of Spain to
make terms with his preserver, I will say thirty thousand
piasters.'

'Good heavens! how you deceive yourself,' cried Morgan.
'You offer money to men who have millions, and insult gentlemen of as high rank as yourself.   Aye, an English noble is peer
of all Spain.   But to return to what concerns me; you don't
know me, you say.   Perhaps I have much changed, for I have
suffered much.   I am called Morgan the Second.'

'Morgan!' repeated the count, staring eagerly at the man he
had hated so long.   'Then it was not the hope of gain that
brought you here.   You have some secret design.'

'My designs you will know all in good time; but before I
gained the name which I bear now, do you know who I was?'

'What matters that to me?   Proceed.'

'But it matters greatly to me.   Morgan the Victorious, as I
am called, Morgan the dread of all Spaniards, and whose head
would be worth a large sum to the King of Spain, was once *the
slave* of El Conde del Monterey!'

'What do you say? that you have been my slave?'   •

'Yes, twenty years ago! does not the date recall something
to your mind?'

'Nothing,' answered the count, whose face became livid.

Morgan fancied Lewis's feelings were too intense to give him
even the relief of tears.

'Twenty years since,' said Randolph, controlling his emotions,
'your mansion was the scene of a fearful tragedy, the remembrance of which is as vivid in my mind as if it had occurred

yesterday. Your wife, an angel in beauty, a demon in spirit, had a lover—you know whom I mean ?'

'You lie,' interrupted Monterey, 'like a coward and villain as you are !'

'Gag that man,' said Morgan, an order instantly obeyed.

'Surprised one night in her shame, your wife to conceal her partner accused one of your slaves of having laid a snare for her. This was odious ; still, the woman to save herself was forced to lay the blame on some one ; but you, who knew the contrary, who knew the innocence of the unhappy slave so unjustly accused, you affected to believe this lying accusation. The unhappy man, seized and pinioned, was brought before you ; and when he tried to defend himself, you had him gagged. The scene is much the same as at this moment ; only you are the prisoner instead of the tyrant.'

Morgan's emotion forced him to pause.

'Sandoval,' he resumed, ' this slave whom, deaf to all cries of justice and mercy, you put to a most horrid death, left a son and brother. His son is that young man, the Knight of Morgan ; I am his brother. You must now be aware what fate awaits you. Lewis, pronounce his sentence ; it is just that a son should decide the fate of his father's murderer.'

Young Morgan had sank on his knees ; he now rose and rejoined : 'Sandoval, God is my witness that had you killed my father in war or a duel, your life should now be sacred to me. But, savage monster as you are, let the blood you have spilled so unjustly, so cruelly, fall on your own head. You are unworthy of pity. To pardon you would be to make myself an accomplice in your crimes. Murderer, you shall die by the same death that you inflicted on my father.'

The freebooters instantly stuck four bayonets into the ground, and fastened Monterey's arms and legs to them with strong cords.

'Friends,' said Captain Morgan to them, ' this man is not worthy to die by your hands ; call in his slaves.'

Six slaves soon stood ready to begin their brutal work.

'Strike !' said the pirate.

The whip-lashes whistled in the air and fell on Monterey's naked body, leaving marks of blood.

'I heard my brother's shrieks, I will hear thine !' cried Morgan fiendishly, tearing the handkerchief off Monterey's mouth.

The agony of the wretch lasted long. After it was over, Morgan took his nephew by the arm, who, pale as death, had stood all the time at a little distance.

'Come, my dear son,' he said, 'let us try in the excitement of business to forget the fearful duty we have accomplished.'

The young gentleman followed his kinsman in silence to the

great square of the town, when a voice whose sweet accents
thrilled through him, though now it sounded sad, said :

'Sir Lewis, pray come with me! I am going to my father
who is dying.'

'Your father dying, Jennie ?'

'Yes, he was wounded at the attack of Gezemania ; and
little hopes are given of his recovery.'

Wildflower, followed by the two Englishmen, entered the
governor's palace, fitted up temporarily for a hospital.

Greybeard, lying on a mattress on the point of death, still
retained consciousness.

'Oh, you have come back, girl,' he moaned ; 'I have impatiently counted the minutes and seconds since you have been
gone.   Well, will he come ?'

'Yes, father, in an hour, he promised me.'

'But in an hour it will be too late. I shall be dead,' said the
buccaneer. 'Go to him again ; say I want him at once.'

'Of whom are you speaking, my poor friend ?' asked old
Morgan.

'Of Admiral Bloxam.   He has, as you told me, full powers
from the king. I wish before I die that he should recognise me
as a Buckingham.'

'I will do your commission,' answered the pirate leader.

'Then make haste ; if I had not expected the admiral I should
have been already dead. I cling to life till I have seen him ; but
there is no time to lose.'

Before the buccaneer had finished speaking, Morgan had departed ; ten minutes later, he returned with the admiral, who,
leaning over the dying man, said, 'Ralph Buckingham, in the
name of his Majesty King William Third, I pronounce you noble,
and that you belong by lineal descent to the ancient family of
the first Dukes of Buckingham, and are permitted to use their arms.

As the admiral was speaking the pale cheeks of the dying
man recovered for a few moments their colour ; his features
grew animated.

'Then,' he said joyfully, 'I die a Buckingham ; Jennie, kiss
me !   I am sorry to leave you, child, but the knight will make
you happy. Have a stone put on my grave and on it write,
''Here lies a Buckingham of the old family.''' He had raised himself up while the admiral was speaking ; he fell back and died.

'Oh, father !' cried Wildflower, throwing herself on the body
sobbing ; oh, father, leave me not alone in the world !'

'You forget you have a brother, dear Jennie,' said Sir Lewis
softly.

CHAPTER LIV.

THE JACOBITE PLOT.

SINCE the entrance of the fleet into the roadstead of Carthagena, Jennie had lived on board the *Serpent,* commanded by Lawrence. The crew and buccaneers treated her with the greatest consideration. After the troops had landed, Wildflower, separated from her father, remained under the care of Allan, who had become almost her slave and followed her everywhere. If Jennie spoke to him in the Cornish tongue, or sang a familiar song, Allan would go into ecstasies and cry like a child.

'My sweet lady,' he said sometimes, 'you are so modest and so good that your beauty, for you are very pretty, does not frighten me. I look at you without being timid just as if you were a man.'

Her father being dead, Lewis did not like Jennie to return on board the *Serpent,* fearing that everything would remind her of her father.

'My dear sister,' he said, drawing her away from the hospital, 'come with me ; we will try to find some Spanish family who will receive you for a day or two.'

Wildflower, absorbed in her grief, followed him in silence. They had not gone far when they met Morgan, to whom Lewis stated his difficulty.

'Not to lose sight of Bloxam,' said the captain, 'I have taken up my quarters at the palace. It has only one room, but let us take Jennie there. You and I can walk the streets all night ; for there will be plenty of work to do.'

'My duty calls me to Governor Du Casse.'

'Never mind, Du Casse or me, it is all the same ; besides, I want you.'

When Jennie was established in the room, and Allan appointed to remain with her and await her orders, Morgan and his uncle went out together.

'My dear Lewis,' said the elder, 'my presentiments are rarely wrong ; for some days my mind has been troubled. I feel sure that I am on the eve of some great event. I am pleased to have you with me, for I want to open my breast to you. Have you remarked the great coolness, without any apparent cause, that has sprung up between Admiral Bloxam and Lawrence ?'

'Yes, this coolness did strike me.'

'Well, do you know it makes me uneasy.'

'But why ?'

'Because Lawrence is not a man to bear from any one in the world airs of superiority and command. Now the way in which

De Pointis treats him is almost insulting.   If Lawrence gives his opinion in council, the admiral turns away and speaks to some one else as if he disdained to answer him.   It is true handsome Lawrence gnaws his moustache and plays with his sword-knot; but he does not go beyond such inoffensive pantomime. Believe me, Lewis, between your mate and the admiral there is some secret connivance.   They work together for the same end, and have some interest in common.   The thing must be serious; it really makes me uneasy.'

'Your hatred for Lawrence and your dislike of the French mislead you, uncle.'

'I hate Lawrence! how little you understand me.   I know men too well either to hate or love them.   I study them to make use of their good or bad qualities, that is all.'

'But supposing your conjecture is right, what can be the mutual interest that unites the two Frenchmen?'

'In good faith, I don't know.   If I knew their designs I should no longer fear them.   But as I am in a confidential humour I will confess one thing, that notwithstanding my contempt of the human race and the little consequence I attach to the world's judgment, in my last voyage to France I was so stupid as to give way to an impulse of self-love, which perhaps may cost me dear.   You had no acquaintance with the secret springs of the Court at Kensington.   I had.   It is honeycombed with treason. Honestly I fear that the succour of the French fleet has been accorded us for some other aim than helping King William. What if Lord Russell, suspected of being a Jacobite, has only let Bloxam come out here for the same end as maybe that of the Frenchman, to help the cause of the Stuarts?   I know that I offended Mr. Barstairs; may he not have given Bloxam—who has been changed by his official position from the frank bluff seaman of our early days,—some secret instructions? A plot between the admirals is a grave matter.   Not that I fear even that; for after all, attacking me is not conquering me.   Our party possess sufficient vitality to bear a pretty good shock without being destroyed. If I am attacked treacherously I will raise the banner of independence and fight it out openly.   But Lawrence alone makes me uneasy; he is a man fertile in petty expedients, and has a mind as deceitful as bold.   His jealousy of me is likely to urge him on to some daring and deceitful act against me.   Oh, if I were only sure of his neutrality, I should be easy about the others.'

Whilst Morgan had been thus conversing with his nephew, night had come on and heavy clouds hung over Carthagena.

At every step the buccaneer met patrols sent out to watch the inhabitants, and prevent any attempt at revolt; the two friends gave the password and proceeded unmolested on their way.

'Is it not time that we returned to the palace?' asked Lewis.
'perhaps Wildflower will be uneasy at my being away, or may
require me.'

'Let us return then,' said the other. 'The town is quiet
enough; the inhabitants seem resigned to their fate, and this
walk in the fresh air has done me good.'

Morgan had been in Carthagena before besides, when a boy
with his namesake, and knew it well. He led his nephew
through some back streets, and they were soon in sight of the
house they sought.

Almost at the same moment two men came from opposite
directions, before the general's quarters.

Morgan seized his companion's arm, and whispered,—

'Silence, and observe!'

The new comers having approached within ten paces of the
admiral's quarters, exchanged a few words in a low voice, and
separated; one came forward and entered the palace.

'Who goes there?' cried the sentinel.

'A friend!' answered a voice which the Morgans at once recognised as De Pointis's.

As for the man who had just quitted him, his agile yet firm
step and graceful figure left no doubt of his being handsome
Lawrence.

'Well, Lewis, what do you think of that?' asked Morgan as
soon as they were alone. 'Now will you accuse me of being
actuated by hatred for Lawrence? Do you think the meeting of
those two men was accidental? I repeat, Lewis, I am on the
eve of some great event. In a short time either my power will
be unbounded or I shall be no more. Good-bye, boy, go and see
Wildflower. Who knows? perhaps happiness only exists in good
and tender feelings. Perhaps in mixing you up with my ambitious projects, I might have made you less happy. Let fate decide. No, it may perhaps declare against me, and I would not
drag my dear Lewis down with me.'

'Uncle, I cannot forget,' answered the Cornishman, 'that you
are my father's brother. I refused, it is true, to join you in your
ambitious projects, but nothing shall prevent my sharing your
dangers. When the hour of peril comes call on me to obey
you.'

'Thank you,' answered the captain with emotion, 'I did not
expect less from you. I will think over it. To-morrow we will
talk over this again. Wildflower expects you. Farewell.'

He pressed his nephew's hand and left him.

As soon as the heavy door bad closed upon the youth, Morgan returned, and stationing himself in the dark angle of a wall
where he had seen De Pointis and Lawrence, he remained on the
watch. For two hours no sound was heard but the measured tread

of the sentinel, then the same figure returned creeping by the side of the wall.

'Who goes there?' cried the soldier. It could be no other than Lawrence's voice which answered.

'Well,' murmured the old rover to himself, 'now I am certain of the fact, and it is assuming too serious a character for me to go feeling about in the dark. I must go straight to the end and without a doubt being left on my mind.'

As soon as Lawrence had entered the governor's quarters, an aide-de-camp seemed to be expecting him, for he took him at once into the admiral's presence. As soon as he entered, the Frenchman rose from a table covered with papers and advanced to meet him, spite of his wound.

'I did not expect less promptitude from you, sir,' he said. 'A man accustomed to board ships must know how to take a negotiation by assault.'

'Thanks for the compliment, admiral,' answered Lawrence drily, 'but in future I shall be obliged by your putting compliments aside. I am so far above any price you can give me that it would be mere waste of time. We serve each other because we need each other. Now our position being settled, let us come to facts. I am returned, as was agreed between us, from sounding the feelings of five or six captains, and I don't deny that I found them very favourable to Old Morgan. If this man had only in his favour the immense services he has rendered the freebooters, we might overturn him easily; ingratitude is found everywhere. Unluckily the Brothers of the Coast believe that Morgan alone can give them wealth, and maintain our power. They love him through interest. Therefore we must give up our first project, and wait for a more favourable season.'

'I am astonished, Captain Lawrence,' answered the count, evidently vexed, 'that a bold, clever man like you should give a thing up at the first brush, and lay down your arms without a struggle. However I may regret not having your help, still my orders are too stringent to allow me to be lukewarm in the matter, or to consent to a delay.

'It is his Majesty's decided wish to destroy the strength of the freebooters in the West Indies. The power of these adventurers, which is daily on the increase, and threatens to become colossal, naturally makes the king uneasy, who fears that this irregular naval power may become a dangerous instrument in the hands of the king's enemies. People of the reformed religion have already thought of spreading their heresies over this land of liberty, and forming for themselves an inviolable refuge. What England has done in Massachusetts, she may attempt on the Spanish main.

'I shall not draw back from any sacrifice of men or money to carry out the king's wishes. As for you, though I am ignorant of your past life, and do not even know your name, still the grand order that you wore proves clearly to me that under a humble disguise you conceal an illustrious name. Pardon me the expression, but is it not disgraceful for you to be dependent on obscure adventurers—men of straw? Reflect a little upon the change of your position if our plans succeed. Possessing immense riches, disposing of forces that the king will no longer allow to remain in the West Indies, a vast future is open to you. The Pacific Ocean becomes your prey. Your dreams may even carry you forward to founding a kingdom—an empire. Such a prospect in view is surely worth some efforts. Do not any means occur to you to replace the plan which the attachment of the freebooters to Morgan obliges us to abandon?'

Whilst the admiral was speaking, Lawrence seemed lost in thought, still, as soon as he had ended, he responded:

'Admiral, the part that I and you are playing at this moment is not one to give us much confidence in each other. You betray Du Casse and I Morgan. It is true that I am engaged by oath only to serve our party, and that its ruin being decided on at Versailles, it might be only saving it to throw it into other quarters. Nevertheless, our present conduct has a black side.'

'Monsieur Laurent,' cried the count, 'these reproaches prove to me——'

'That I don't fear to call things by their right name, that I don't rush forward blindly without knowing where I am going, and consequently you can count upon me : this proves my frankness. I repeat that your treason towards Du Casse, not to say the English admiral too, prevents my having entire confidence in you, and I own this is a pity, for could I depend on your word, I could show you an infallible means of destroying the entire society of freebooters.'

The admiral knew already too well Lawrence's passionate character to be offended with his bold language ; he thought only of one thing that he had said, which was that Lawrence could fulfil the French king's great wish, the destruction of the pirates. The thought of the high favour in which he would be placed at court if he could only accomplish this delicate and difficult task surmounted all minor considerations, and almost humbly he said :

'Captain Lawrence, I am ready to submit to the precautions you may judge necessary to assure yourself of my good faith. Speak ! what do you require from me?'

The day was breaking and Admiral de Pointis and handsome Lawrence were still together. By the baron's delighted air it might be guessed that he had been able at last to gain the freebooter's confidence, and that the plans he had suggested were to his mind.

'Admiral,' said Lawrence, 'day is breaking, and I must leave you. Thus everything is arranged and settled between us. Don't for a moment forget the line of conduct I have laid down for you ; the least imprudence on your part will compromise the whole affair. Don't forget that our sailors are very distrustful, and extreme precautions are necessary to hoodwink them. As for me, now I am assured of the loyalty of your intentions, and as you are in my power, I will second you to the best of my means.'

'Captain Lawrence, rest assured that your zeal in this matter shall be fully laid before the king, and his Majesty, I do not doubt, will feel greatly beholden to you, and will reward you as you deserve.'

Lawrence shrugged his shoulders with disdain.

'Now, my lord,' he returned, 'are you going to treat me like a poor Judas, a traitor in the second degree—something equally stupid as base ?'

'You deceive yourself greatly ! I serve Louis XIV. Pray whom do you take me for ?'

'My interests for the moment run parallel with those of your master, nothing more natural that we should make a temporary alliance. The king recompense me, indeed ! I beg to tell you that Louis XIV. could not, in spite of all his influence, raise me to so high a station as the one which I have voluntarily given up.'

Towards the middle of the day, Sir Lewis, who had passed the morning with Wildflower, determined to see the governor. He found the two old friends in very animated conversation.

'Good morning, sir,' said Du Casse ; 'you have no doubt been round the town ? What news do you bring ? Have you seen any violence committed by our men or the royal troops ?'

'Governor,' answered Morgan, blushing, 'I have only now left the house, and know no news ; but is it true that a sailor has been shot ? What crime had he committed ?'

'That of forcing open the door of a public-house and obliging the people to give him some drink.'

'Is that all that he has done ?'

'All ?' cried Du Casse quickly. 'Don't you perceive that if the very first day we get possession of Carthagena the men commit violence, before a week is out the town will be on fire ? If we don't wish our glorious feat of arms to be changed into an odious act of piracy, we must maintain strict discipline, punish faults as crimes, and strike the least guilty with a hand of iron.'

You are right, governor

'For the rest,' continued Du Casse, 'I count much on Admiral de Pointis's firmness. His character as a martinet is well known, he well knows how to keep his troops in order. Morgan and I take charge of the freebooters, and Bloxam's men are miracles of steadiness now that they have had their fill of rum.'

Du Casse had scarcely finished when piercing cries were heard. A dozen tipsy soldiers had got hold of two girls whom they were pulling about.

'The wretches,' cried Du Casse, 'let us go to their aid.'

The three rushed out with drawn swords, and snatched away the two girls.

The governor's intervention did not produce the effect it should have done on the revellers, who seemed not in the least awed by his presence. Indeed, one of them, a Frenchman, said insolently :

'Why do you meddle with us ? we are not under your orders, our conduct does not matter to you. Another time mind your own business and not spoil our sport. Any way you are more of a buccaneer than a Frenchman.'

'I shan't spoil your sport any more,' said Du Casse drily, 'for you are going to die. On your knees, and say your prayers,' he added, drawing a pistol from his girdle and pointing it at the man, 'you have only a minute to live.'

'Mercy, mercy,' cried the soldier.

'Never will I pardon an act of insubordination ; all violence against the inhabitants of the town was to be punished with death ; you know you must die.'

Du Casse fired, and the man fell dead.

'As for you,' said the governor to the others, 'your admiral shall decide on your fate ; follow me !'

The grenadiers, awed by Du Casse's tone of authority, made no resistance, and ten minutes afterwards were brought pale and trembling into the admiral's presence.

Du Casse explained briefly what had happened.

'In good faith, my dear comrade,' answered De Pointis, 'I don't share your severe principles. I think, in fact, that the treachery of the Spaniards at Gezemania deserves reprisals from our men. It is only justice that our brave soldiers, after their labour and fatigue, should amuse themselves a little. As to the man who insulted you, you were perfectly right, and I applaud you for your prompt punishment. Go, soldiers,' he said to the men, 'and when the service gives you time, amuse yourselves as you like.'

The soldiers joyfully hastened away.

Du Casse, pale with anger, cried, 'Admiral, now that officers are alone present, I demand from you an explanation of your conduct. Even had those wretches been innocent, at my word you should have condemned them ; but in releasing them from all authority you have committed a base and dishonourable action, you have rendered discipline impossible, and given up to pillage and murder the inhabitants of a town which had yielded trusting to the honour of France and England. The whole French army is dishonoured by you. As for the compliment you pass upon me, I reject it with disdain. I am your equal in every point and you have nothing to do with my conduct. One more word, Admiral, if you attribute my harsh language to passion, you are wrong ; every word I have said I am willing and ready to maintain it with my sword, and I am at your orders.'

Admiral de Pointis with violent effort mastered his wrath sufficiently not to take up the gauntlet so plainly laid down.

'Governor,' he answered, 'it is certain that under other circumstances I should not leave such conduct unnoticed, but now I do not belong to myself ; the fate of the army depends on me. I own I was wrong to speak of your conduct, but it was only done in kindness and sympathy for you. I am willing to recognise your independence ; I must be ; you will leave me mine. I consider it necessary to give the soldiers some licence to animate their zeal. Don't forget what you once judiciously observed yourself, that war in America was very different to war in Europe. In making this an exception to my usual severity, I am only following your good advice. A last word, Governor Du Casse, above our authority is that of the Minister of the Navy, and it will be for Lord Pontchartrain to decide which of us two has best understood his commission, and done his duty.'

The artful moderation of the admiral's speech made Du Casse reflect. He saw the trap laid for him, and determined to avoid it.

'I take account, admiral,' he answered, 'of your explanations. If, as I foresee, your injudicious tolerance produces bad effects and compromises this expedition, I shall not hesitate to accuse you before any one whatever.'

'I am not accustomed to deny my words. You may count upon my repeating to M. de Ponchartrain the explanations I have given you.'

'Then, admiral, it is agreed from this time that we shall act each as we think best, and separate our forces.'

'Certainly, in all that does not compromise the safety of the army.'

'Then I promise you my freebooters shall keep good discipline.'

'That is your affair, governor.'

To vaunt often brings ill-fortune ; scarcely had Du Casse nished speaking before circumstances gave him the lie.

A man with his hair and clothes in disorder, and bleeding,

rushed into the chamber, and falling on his knees cried out, 'Justice ! protection !'

'Who are you, and what do you want?'

'I am one of the canons of the cathedral,' cried the new comer, 'and I entreat you to stop the odious scandal that is going on within its cells. The robbers—pardon, I mean the freebooters—have broken open the cathedral doors, they are pillaging everything there, the altars turned into counters for selling wine increases their hideous fury. I cannot tell you the horrors they are committing. Oh, admiral, not in the name of justice alone, but of common humanity, I implore your aid.'

The poor canon, who had spoken in very bad French, but with great energy, dragged himself to the admiral's feet, and embraced his knees.

'' Come, come,' he cried, 'every minute some new crime is committed.'

'I regret, reverend sir,' answered the admiral, 'that I cannot do what you wish ; the freebooters are not under my command, their conduct does not concern me. Yonder is their chief ; address yourself to him.'

The count pointed to Du Casse.

'Get up, father,' said the latter ; 'when you speak in the name of justice you should not humble yourself before any human power. Follow me.'

'Count de Pointis,' said Morgan, who had remained a silent spectator of all that had passed, 'will you give me a minute's private conversation?'

'Oh, certainly, with pleasure, my dear captain. I am at your command. Gentlemen,' added the nobleman to his aides-de-camp, 'have the goodness to see that we are not interrupted.'

Du Casse, accompanied by Sir Lewis and the canon, hastened to the cathedral.

The priest had hardly done justice to the awful scene which now met their view ; it was like one vast orgie of madmen. For a moment Du Casse stood aghast. To stop such a scene alone would have been to sacrifice himself without avail.

'Governor,' said Morgan, whose heart revolted at the acts of brutality that were being committed, 'here is Lawrence, and if he will join his efforts to yours, he is capable of stopping these horrors.'

Moments were precious. Du Casse instantly approached the French buccaneer

'You here, governor,' cried he? 'delighted to see you ! You have come, no doubt, to enjoy our little carouse. See how our men are amusing themselves. What spirits they are in !'

'Is it you, Laurence, who dare to speak thus, whose illustrious birth'—,

'Your pardon, governor,' answered Lawrence ; 'but I cannot let you finish your speech.   I only confided my secret to you after I had received your word of honour not to divulge it.   In my mind, therefore, to throw my name to the winds will be a great infringement of the law of honour—which I merely state the fact, not utter a threat, for I know you incapable of fear—that I swear to punish instantly by blowing out your brains.   But let us talk of something pleasanter.   What do you think of the treat our brothers are giving themselves ?'

'I think,' answered Du Casse gravely, 'that if you do not second me in the efforts I shall make to restore order I shall no longer feel friendship or esteem for you, for I shall consider you an accomplice of these ruffians.'

'Then, governor, I must resign myself to bear your displeasure,' replied Lawrence calmly, 'for really the sight of this little debauch, of which our enemies the Spaniards bear the expense, gives me too much gratification for me to consent to put a stop to it.   On the contrary.   Oh !   I know morality is outraged, but freebooters are no cenobites.   I am sure, governor, that at this moment you are under the pious Morgan's influence, whose nephew perhaps bore you his orders, and that it was at his instigation you came here.   The devil take Morgan, who worries us !   It is no reason because he has taken it into his head to play the king that we are all to give up our privileges—indeed, all fun—and from lions turn into fawning lap-dogs.'

Lawrence's answer left Du Casse no hope of his help to quell the disorder, and the governor feeling it would be useless to attempt to do so alone, and that he would only compromise his own authority, turned away from the dreadful scene.

CHAPTER LV.

THE FIRST BLOW.

While Du Casse and Lawrence were having their fruitless argument, Morgan and De Pointis came to an understanding.

'Admiral,' said the former, 'not to compromise military discipline, I kept silence before your officers ; now that we are alone I will explain myself freely.   I will not tell you, as Du Casse did just now, that we are equals—we are not equals, and it is a command I am about to lay upon you.'

'Go on, sir,' said the admiral coldly ; 'I am listening to your insolence with the contempt it deserves.'

'Before I go on, admiral, I will show you my authority,' said the captain, then drawing a piece of parchment from his pocket sealed with a large stamp on wax.

'Useless, sir ; I know its contents.'

'And what does it contain ?'

'A decree of his Majesty Louis XIV., who grants you absolute and unlimited power during the course of the expedition to Carthagena.'

This answer seemed to surprise Morgan, but after a moment's pause he continued—

'Well, admiral, it is in the name of this authority that I command you to make the army observe strict discipline and repect the stipulation that has been signed. The king no doubt, in authorizing and aiding the expedition of Carthagena, could not be swayed by the prospect of a little vile booty, but no doubt desired to open vast commercial enterprises to the French nation, therefore it is most desirable that the inhabitants of Carthagena should be conciliated, not outraged. Therefore, I beg that from this moment by watchfulness and severity you will atone for the culpable weakness of which you have been guilty.'

'My answer, sir,' said the count, 'shall be as open and frank as your request. I refuse in the most peremptory manner to recognise your authority.'

'Take care, baron ; you are not now speaking to Morgan, the pirate, but to a man to whom your king has given full powers, as the king of England has accorded on his side.'

'Which king of England ? James or William ? Both ! Ah, but this is quite an error of yours, my dear sir ! You remain still the freebooter. Pray take notice of *this* paper ! Mine is dated after yours, and therefore has greater weight. You will see here that King Louis revokes the powers he granted you to give them to me. I am really very sorry to have thus to wound your self-love, but you have only yourself to blame for it. Without your persistence I should have left you in the pleasant delusion of the absolute power you fancied confided to you.'

At these words, pronounced with ironical gentleness which made them still more bitter, Morgan turned pale.

'Let me look at this paper, admiral.'

'You of course don't wish to insult me by doubting my words,' answered the admiral smiling ; 'here is the document. You may perceive that his Majesty's signature in mine is rather firmer than in yours.'

'Oh, kings, kings !' cried Morgan bitterly, 'they are all alike ; easy tools to courtiers who flatter their detestable vanity ; shameful ingrates to those who would add to their power and glory. But why should I be surprised at this treason ? Monarchs never forgive a service rendered, it wounds their pride. In helping Louis in his distress by the influence of Montbars *Sans-merci*, my dear old comrade, I acted like a madman or a child ! It is but right that I should bear the punishment of my folly.'

'Now,' said the admiral, 'I can understand your vexation, but I warn you if ever you let fall any expression disrespectful to my king I should consider it my duty to put you under arrest.'

The admiral tried to carry his triumph too far.

At this threat the Englishman started and stood for a moment trying to conquer his indignation.

The baron mistook his motive for remaining silent, and thinking by one bold stroke to complete his victory added:

'You will now immediately return on board the *Sceptre* and remain under arrest until I shall allow you to come on shore. On your docility and good conduct will depend the length of your punishment.'

'Death and fury!' cried the pirate, 'have I fallen so low by my too great trust in a Frenchman and a king! This is too much! Do you forget I have the English on my side, who mock at Louis as at James—and my pirates? Bah! Scoundrel, who have dared to outrage me in my liberty and my power,' proceeded the buccaneer, advancing slowly on De Pointis, 'down *on your knees* and ask my pardon! Servant of a perjured king, kneel before the rover—or die!'

The count was brave, but there was something in the speaker's rage so fearful, so more than human, that he was cowed by it.

'Sir,' he stammered, trying to keep up appearances, 'don't aggravate your position by an irreparable fault.'

'I said on your knees! When I speak I will be obeyed.'

Seizing the admiral by the arm he threw him to the other end of the room, then rushing to the door, he double-locked it.

'De Pointis, nothing but your submission can save you from my anger.'

'I have my sword,' said the admiral, getting up.

'A courtier's sword is a mere plaything,' returned Morgan in extreme disdain. 'If you dare to draw yours, I will break it over your face!'

De Pointis rushed on him with blind fury.

The buccaneer did not take his out of his scabbard, but unbuckling it, he parried the admiral's sword, which fell from his hand ; the victor seized upon it and breaking it in two across his knee, he threw the pieces in the count's face.

'Well, varlet, do you begin to understand that what I say I do?'

'I know you to be a bully!'

The pirate laughed aloud.

'In good faith, I admire your impudence! It is really treating my scabbard too harshly. Now I have repaid your insults, I don't want to bandy words with you. I will give you the choice of two things ; if you accept my conditions you shall have your liberty, if not I kill you. My conditions are that you

shall tear up that treacherous paper that you had from your
king, then you shall declare in presence of your staff that I
have shown you a paper from the king recognising me as your
superior in command, and that every one is to obey *me*.   As for
your projects of vengeance, I leave you at full liberty to
prosecute them.   I shall always have a sheathed sword to oppose
to your naked steel.   Answer, which do you choose, death or
dishonour ? '

The position of the admiral was critical, but one hope
remained to him

'Before answering, let me make one or two observations.   I
don't belong to myself, my life belongs to the army.   But what
would you gain by my death?   Only certain vengeance ; all the
French would rise.'

'Then we should have a battle,' answered Morgan coolly ;
'with my fifteen thousand freebooters I should soon beat the
royal troops, throwing out of the lists my countrymen under
Bloxam, who, however, would hardly let their old enemy, France,
attack their kinsmen ; your fleet would be the reward of my
victory.'

'I admit that might be, but then——'

'Then, when the servant was punished, I would attack the
master !   You are astonished ?   Born to servitude, you cannot
understand liberty.   What can Louis XIV do against me?
Europe torn to pieces engages his attention and gives him
enough to do without sending his fleets over the seas, and even
if he did send one against the freebooters, who could answer that
we, the first sailors in the world, should not beat those ships ?
Your death, admiral, will be of no consequence to me.   But we
are wasting words ; decide.'

He drew a pistol from his belt.

The admiral perceived that longer hesitation would be fatal.
He suppressed a sigh and offered the paper to Morgan.

'Did I not say that you were to tear it ?   I never retract, I
never forget ; obey.'

The admiral, trembling with rage, tore the paper up.

'Now, own me as your superior before your staff,' cried the
English desperado, opening the door while the count arranged
his dress and hid his broken sword.

'Gentlemen,' said the admiral when he returned to the
council, 'Captain Morgan has shown me papers from his Majesty,
giving full power into his hands, power unlimited and superior
to mine.   You will therefore obey the commands of Captain
Morgan.'

This declaration did not astonish the officers so greatly as
the admiral's death-like pallor ; but they attributed his emotion
to annoyance at being thus superseded.

'Am I still to go on board the *Sceptre ?*' asked Morgan

ironically, as he took leave of the count, who bit his lips in silence.

De Pointis murmured as soon as his conqueror had departed, 'You shall pay dear for your ephemeral triumph, I would not have humbled myself before you, had I not hoped to have my revenge.'

Morgan hastened to repress everywhere the licence of the royal troops and the freebooters. Unluckily his authority was little recognised ; their brutal passions having been once excited it was next to impossible to bring them under control.

In several instances he was inclined to punish severely, but was stopped by the consideration that it would be of no avail. The undermining influence of the treacherous Lawrence thwarted all his efforts.

In a month the soldiers' excesses and brutality had changed the flourishing town of Carthagena into a fearful desolation. For the first few days some order was kept and the poor inhabitants who hastened to take their wealth to the treasury were treated with something like respect. The soldiers and freebooters, delighted at sight of such treasures, were in a happy mood, but when they could no longer satisfy the cupidity of their conquerors, the latter had recourse to the most cruel means to extort more from them ; pillage and incendiarism were carried on to so great an extent that the once handsome town was little more than a heap of ruins.

Slaves or servants were rewarded with a tenth of the spoil for denouncing their masters, and revenge and treachery had full scope. Many rich merchants being accused of having kept back part of their wealth were put to the torture and died in agonies.

In vain Morgan and Du Casse tried to stop these horrors ; the freebooters, drunk with carnage, were deaf to the voice of their once respected leaders. Lawrence, who encouraged them to pillage, increased in popularity every day.

All the wives and daughters of the rich and noble families had left the town at the approach of the enemy, but those of the poorer classes that remained were subject to the most cruel usage.

A terrible epidemic, engendered by the want of fresh provisions and the fatal emanations from the unburied bodies that lay about, caused fearful havoc among the victors and the wretched Spaniards. It was resolved to abandon the town.

Before leaving it, Lawrence proposed to have a hunt round the environs in search of the fugitives who, when the town had capitulated, had secretly carried off their treasures.

This proposal was acceded to at once, and three detachments of freebooters, each five hundred strong, set forth in different directions, their object being to search for the fugitives, and pillage all the villages and towns on their way.

The booty they had already obtained came to nearly ten millions of dollars. The day after these detachments had left, Morgan, accompanied by his nephew, was strolling sadly on the shore, when he was startled by an extraordinary sight. The French squadron was hoisting sail.

'What can that mean?' he exclaimed. 'Does the admiral wish to employ his men to prevent their coming on shore? his precaution is rather of the latest. But look, Lewis, it is odd that not one of the French soldiers remain on shore. This looks very suspicious. Let us get into a boat, and go on board Bloxam's flagship. If this is an innocent naval manœuvre, he will be in concord with De Pointis.'

But Commander Bloxam, irritated at some of his best men having gone on shore and joined the buccaneers, answered curtly. He knew nothing, and cared less, what the French fleet did. The town was reduced, and the force was too large. For the turning of a feather, he would sail away to St. Kitts for a change himself.

'We shall learn nothing here,' observed Morgan to his nephew, 'let us go beard De Pointis.'

In a few moments they were rowed to the *Sceptre*.

'What is the meaning of this pretence of departure, admiral?' cried the captain, when they were on board.

'It is no pretence, it is a reality, sir. Our task is completed here. I have deigned to tell you so much; but you are aware an admiral is not bound to answer questions.'

'But an ally has a right to information concerning an enterprise that has been undertaken in common.'

'True; but I do not see the gist of your observation. If you mean the help which the freebooters have given to the royal troops, Du Casse and myself will settle that. But if you refer to the part of the booty that comes to your share, I have orders to pay every freebooter in the same proportion as the sailors.'

At this answer Morgan could hardly restrain his indignation. He now saw the trap into which he had fallen, but how could he ever suspect an admiral of such an abuse of confidence, such an impudent theft? He knew that De Pointis, on board his own ship, surrounded by his own men, wished to be insulted, that he might have a pretext for harsh measures towards himself; therefore in as calm a voice as he could assume, he said:

'Thanks, admiral, for answering my questions. May I ask where the Brothers of the Coast will receive the wages due to them?'

'At the entrance of Boca-chica, where the squadron will remain two or three days to take in water.'

As soon as they had quitted the admiral's ship, Morgan gave full vent to his anger.

'Can you conceive, Lewis,' he cried, 'greater infamy! It is the death of our society. Half a million the French rob us of! And I counted on that large sum, and more on the immense advantages we might have derived from Carthagena. I repeat, it is death to us. But, by heavens, we'll see yet if we cannot retrieve the loss!'

He went straight to the English flagship again. But after a secret conference with Bloxam, he returned to Lewis in the boat, and whispered :

'It is a deep-laid plot. Bloxam is a traitor to his king as well as to his old comrades. He will not lift a finger to detain the Frenchmen, and I fear, too, he will not pay over our share of the spoils. It is enough to make one never trust man more! But, at least, he will not defend De Pointis—that is, he knows his men would not defend the French. The contrary winds will not allow them to get into open sea yet. No cause for despair! So De Pointis wants action, does he?'

'What are your intentions, uncle?'

'Simply to attack the French squadron ; it will be a fine battle. Death and fury! our freebooters' coats cover as bold hearts as beat under the royal uniform. Come, Lewis, pull hard ; minutes are worth years now.'

Before the boat touched land Morgan jumped on shore.

'To arms, friends,' he cried, 'to arms,' as he saw a group of freebooters watching the manœuvres of the departing ships.

In a few words he explained the admiral's treachery, and the robbery of which the freebooters were the victims. The rage of these men, who worshipped gold, was unbounded.

'Curses!' cried one of them, 'and our brothers away! What is to be done?'

Morgan then remembered that fifteen hundred had gone out to pillage the environs.

'Ah!' cried he, 'with what infernal art this plot has been contrived ; but, friends, we must still hope to right ourselves. There are nearly two hundred of us, that will make a fine crew. Go and tell your comrades that we shall sail in an hour.'

Scarcely had that time passed when the *Serpent* hoisted her sails and followed the squadron, leaving the inhabitants of Carthagena wonderstruck and overjoyed at the unhoped-for departure of the bulk of their conquerors.

As soon as the *Serpent* was within gunshot of the fleet, Morgan cried out, 'Up hammocks! clear for action.'

The two formidable rows of guns on board the *Sceptre* alone rather cooled the anger of the freebooters, and Morgan's order was executed with ill-will.

Captain Pierre Salée was the first to give expression to the general dissatisfaction.

'Old mate,' he said, 'after the innumerable proofs of obedience and devotion which we have given you, you cannot doubt our trust in you ; don't take in bad part, therefore, what I am going to say. Man is not infallible ; not withstanding your great experience and superior mind, you may make a mistake sometimes ; now it is my opinion that you are committing a great imprudence in this matter, and can never hope to come out of it clean. If yon vessel were Spanish, well and good ! I'd say nothing against our attacking ; but they are protected by the English vessels. How the devil can two hundred hope to succeed against three thousand ? and if we fail we shall certainly all be hung at the yard-arm ! Now I don't mind more than another a bullet in the head or a thrust from a sword, or even an axe does not frighten me, but I must own I have a strong objection to being hung. It is my opinion it would be sheer folly to attack the French in such force.'

The murmur of applause produced by this speech showed Morgan too plainly that by persisting in his intention he should not have the concurrence of his crew ; still he tried to rouse them.

The Brothers of the Coast remained unmoved.

'Facts speak too plainly,' said Captain Pierre, 'for you to be any longer in doubt. We admire your undaunted courage, but we cannot share your hopes.'

'Then it is open mutiny,' said Morgan, frowning.

'Not at all,' answered Pierre in a respectful tone ; 'it is only an appeal to our laws. You know we have a right to change our captain if during an expedition his conduct seems to us against our interest. In spite of the admiration that I feel for your great talents, if you persist in your determination, I shall consider it my duty to advise the crew to take from you the command. And if the majority declare in your favour, that is, agree to your proposal of attacking the *Sceptre*, I will obey you as I have done before. Brothers of the Coast, do you agree that we put this to the vote ?'

A general assent was the answer.

A tear of grief and anger fell from the old pirate.

'Oh, cowards and ingrates,' he said, ' to repay me thus for the devotion of my life !' But quickly recovering his resolution for which he was remarkable, he repressed all sign of emotion and spoke thus :

'Brothers of the Coast, in the name of the services I have been so happy to render you, grant me one favour. It is the first time that word has passed my lips. Will you hear me ?'

'Speak !' cried all.

'Friends,' said he, ' I give up the hope of leading you on to fight, but I wish if possible to get back your money. All I ask of you is, while I am away, that you will show an appearance of

resistance.   If you doubt me, or fancy I would draw you into a
snare, uncharge your guns, and throw powder and shot into the
sea.   You need not blush, brothers, I do not say this to humili-
ate you.'

The crew, remembering the marvellous exploits of their chief,
and roused moreover by a hope, however faint, of recovering
their gold, promised to do as required.

'Let a boat be lowered! I am going on board the admiral's
ship.   Lewis, come with me ; I will make you rich.'

'You shall not leave me,' cried Wildflower, laying her hand
on Morgan's arm ; 'you are no freebooter! you do not care for
gold.'

'I am in haste, Lewis,' said Morgan impatiently.

'Wildflower has answered for me,' said the youth ; 'thanks
for your interest, but I would rather remain poor all my life than
join your schemes.'

'This blow I did not expect, Lewis, from you! you abandon
me too ?'

'You are unjust, Morgan ; if danger threatens you, I will
follow you willingly.'

'One Englishman facing five hundred Frenchmen is not in
danger ! but still I want you,' said Morgan with arrogance.

Lewis pressed Wildflower's hand, and followed his uncle.

Before entering the boat, the latter took Pierre on one side
and whispered a few words, which the other answered by a nod.

As the wind was contrary, the squadron made little way, and
six stout rowers soon brought Morgan's boat alongside the
Sceptre.   The appearance of the freebooter on board created
some surprise, and an officer asked him curtly what he desired.

'To speak with the admiral,' was the answer.

De Pointis came forward almost immediately.

'You here, sir !' he said angrily, ' you surely must count much
on my patience and leisure.   People of my rank don't choose to
be troubled with impunity.   What do you want with me ? Do
you come to ask again for your wages ? You shall be paid when
the rest are paid.   Still, if you are personally in want of
money——'

'Admiral,' answered Morgan, 'I have no need to throw
myself on your generosity.   I am come to warn you of a great
danger that threatens you and the fleet.   If you refuse to hear
me, let the responsibility be on your own head ; I shall have
done my duty.'

The admiral looked alarmed.

'But cannot you tell me the danger here ?'

'Impossible, admiral.'

'What, you wish us to be alone ?'

'Alone, as you say.'

The count hesitated; he remembered his former contest; but considering it his duty, he assented, and only stipulated that Sir Lewis should be present.

All three went down into the cabin.

'Admiral,' said the pirate, placing himself before the door, 'I cannot conceive how, with so much duplicity as you have yourself, you can let yourself be so easily taken in. You are in my power, you know me to be a resolute man, and if you call for help my pistol will answer you, and my aim is sure. Now one of two things you must choose, either to order your fleet to return to Carthagena, and I shall be by your side to see you do so, or I take your life.'

'Captain,' answered the admiral, 'you presume on the weakness I showed when you took me before at advantage, but the same reasons do not now exist which compelled me to yield then. I refuse to do your bidding. The fleet shall not return to Carthagena.'

'Is your resolution final, my lord?'

'Irrevocable.'

'Then mine is the same!'

He drew a pistol and pointed at De Pointis.

CHAPTER LVI.

THE SECOND BLOW.

Sir Lewis had hitherto remained a silent spectator of what passed, but seeing the admiral's danger, just as the captain was about to fire he rushed between them.

At this unexpected intervention the pirate's eyes flashed fire.

'Back, boy, you are playing at the wrong game!'

'I am doing my duty. I will be no accomplice in such a crime.'

'Once again, back!' cried Morgan with violence. 'Lewis, I break all who oppose my will! Take care, boy! I am master of myself now, but in a few moments it will be too late.'

'Sir,' cried the youth, 'you shall not in my presence commit such a crime. I know the admiral has behaved shamefully, disgracefully, vilely taken your property, and betrayed your trust, yet defenceless as he is you shall not murder him.'

'Then, boy, take this other pistol and defend yourself.'

'No, you may deny your name, but I cannot forget that the tie of kindred unites us; never will I raise my hand on you.'

Morgan was moved; he pressed his nephew's hand, and said,—

'Lewis, you are a noble fellow; I am proud of you.'

'Chevalier,' said De Pointis, 'I thank you for my life; you have nobly done your duty.   Your hand.'

The Cornishman drew back.

'I cannot take your lordship's hand ; you are unworthy to be my friend.'

The admiral looked astounded.

'Do you dare to accuse me, sir ? '

'I repeat that I cannot be friends with a man who has robbed the freebooters, and kept faith neither with friends nor enemies, as you have done.   As admiral I pay you respect ; as a man I despise you.'

The Count De Pointis reddened at the taunt, but recovering himself, said,—

'Chevalier, you have a loyal heart, but you should reflect before you thus speak to an old man, and a gentleman ; but the difference of our ages and positions makes me willing to excuse you.   For myself, I have only acted by the king's commands.'

The buccaneers then left the *Sceptre* and were soon rowed back to their own ship.

As soon as they mounted the deck of the *Serpent*, Morgan was surrounded by the crew, anxious to hear what had passed.

'Well, my friends,' he said with an ironical smile, 'I might have seized the treasures of the *Sceptre*, but I should have risked the lives of a few of our men, and so, knowing your present pacific notions, I thought you could not pardon me such a sacrifice, so I forbore.'

The freebooters hung down their heads in shame ; had Morgan persisted in his first plan, they would have fought by his side.

The *Serpent*, after her short and useless expedition, remained at anchor near Boca-chica.   It would have been useless with so small a number of men to return to Carthagena, and lie under the English guns.

For a fortnight all the French ships held much the same position. The sight of the squadron, kept back by contrary winds, aggravated still more the freebooters, who could not think with patience of the robbery committed at their expense.

The admiral, this once faithful to his word, offered them fifty piasters each, the proportion of booty accorded to his own sailors, but this had been indignantly refused.

As for Du Casse, by late dispatches placed under the admiral's control, he had been sent off on some trifling mission.

Tempted by the splendid opportunity, the freebooters had sent out scouts in all directions to find the expedition under Lawrence, which did not return, and, what was still more extraordinary, the scouts could obtain no information about the direction taken by the three parties.

They even began to fear that they had fallen into some ambuscades, and been cut to pieces by the Spaniards.

Morgan passed his time mostly alone ; it was evident he was revolving some new plan in his mind.

'Dear Lewis,' he said one evening to Morgan, whom he met walking on the shore with Wildflower, 'I owe you a debt of gratitude for not letting me complete my revenge. It has given a new and healthy tone to my mind, I have formed new plans, and I foresee a splendid horizon for my future efforts.'

On the twentieth day after leaving Carthagena, the French squadron set sail, followed by the curses of all the freebooters.

The same evening Lawrence returned to Boca-chica with the three companies of freebooters. To the questions asked him, he only answered that in consequence of strong ambuscades of the Spaniards, they had been forced to camp in the woods.

It would be impossible to describe the rage of the freebooters when they learnt the Frenchman's base conduct. With one accord they wanted to embark and give chase to the royal squadron, or fall upon the Englishmen in port for not having stopped the traitors.

'Friends,' said Lawrence, 'I feel as indignant as you do, and would give ten years of my life to be within reach of them. But, alas ! it is not to be thought of ; innumerable obstacles are in the way. Who can assure us that our vessels left at Carthagena have not been taken by the Spaniards? And then, supposing we do find them all right, think of the time it will take to get them to sea, and what a march the royal ships will have stolen upon us. No, I repeat, strength won't avail us now. Then we are without a chief, Du Casse is out of the way. Friends,' continued Lawrence, after a moment's thought, ' will you confide to me the heavy task of being your chief ? I pawn my honour that I will find means to give you riches, at least as great as what you have been robbed of.'

At these words, spoken with energy and conviction, the freebooters shouted enthusiastically. Lawrence was at once voted chief.

Morgan, who, engaged with his own plans, had kept somewhat aloof from his old companions, was still startled at having Lawrence preferred before him ; such a blow he had not expected.

'Uncle,' said Morgan, 'who knows but that this ingratitude is a happy thing for you? It shows you what little dependence could be placed on mean wretches, whom the promise of a little dross makes ingrates to you, to whom they owe everything. Morgan, your dream may be shattered, but the reality of life remains. You are rich, still young ; what should prevent you from assuming your own name and title in England ? The king

would find honourable employment for your powerful mind.
Put away your past life—begin a new existence at home.'

'Lewis,' said Morgan, almost crushing his nephew's hand in his,
'you know nothing of the human heart.   I have hugged ambition
to my bosom for twenty years, and you ask me to throw it off in
a moment as if that were as easy as casting aside a worn-out
garment.   Well, the trial of strength between Lawrence and me
will soon come to an issue; you know the proverb, "Fools hurry
events, wise men wait and use them."'

CHAPTER LVII.

NATIVA REAPPEARS.

HANDSOME Lawrence, once invested with the power of chief, lost
no time in making his companions acquainted with his plans.

'Brothers of the Coast,' he said, 'I have pledged myself to
give you back wealth equal to what you have been deprived of,
nothing is easier than to keep my promise.   My plan is simple—
the repetition of the one I adopted so successfully at Grenada—
it is only to retake Carthagena, and force from its inhabitants
another ransom.'

'You forget, Lawrence,' cried a freebooter, 'that Carthagena
has already been pillaged completely, and that there is not left in
it an ounce of gold, or a single precious stone.   Your project
won't do.'

'Your remark only proves,' answered Lawrence, 'that the
interests of our society are better placed in my hands than in
yours.   Let me explain what I mean.   When we took possession
of Carthagena, in conjunction with the Royal troops—cursed be
our allies—the principal inhabitants had already fled and carried
off the greater part of their wealth, and this is what I covet.
To obtain this, all that is necessary will be to take to our ships
for a fortnight, and pretend to leave.   The fugitives will return
to the town with their treasures.   Then in one night we cross
the roadstead and at daybreak pounce like eagles upon our prey.
This plan is as infallible as it is simple, nothing can prevent its
success.   Brothers of the Coast, I already see our ships loaded
with ingots.   Then another delight, I think I hear the thanks
of the pretty señoritas whom their parents carried off from our
homage, and who will bless our unexpected return.   Gold and
ladies both in abundance.   It will be an orgie unprecedented in
the annals of our order, an orgie which, in one fortnight, will
give us ten years of enjoyment.'

Lawrence pronounced the last words with such zest that he
took his auditors by storm.   They fancied themselves already at

the junket. Everything played into their hands. The English vessels in their turn departed, and left the coast free for any misdeed.

'Popularity founded on Lawrence's principles cannot be lasting,' said Morgan. 'What tears and blood will be shed! God grant that it bring not on the ruin of our party.'

The freebooters re-entered Carthagena, took possession of their vessels, which the Spaniards, happy to see such terrible guests depart, helped them to refit; then weighing anchor, they sailed round the coast for a fortnight, then fell again on the luck-less town, scarcely recovered from its last terrible disaster. It would be impossible to describe the consternation of the inhabi-tants at this new infliction; grief and despair reigned every-where.

Lawrence's surmises were but too correct. The fugitives had returned with their treasures, and, taken unawares, became a rich prey to the freebooters.

Lawrence called together the principal Spaniards in the cathedral, not this time to force them to sing an hypocritical *Te Deum*, but to give them his orders. He exacted from them twenty millions more.

The unfortunate people objected. Lawrence ordered twenty to be shot on the spot.

'Spaniards,' he said, 'if in one hour you don't accept my con-ditions, I will have forty of you shot. Each hour the number of victims shall be doubled. Your reluctance and ill-will must give way at last, for I am resolute. Now you are warned, your blood will be on your own heads. I wash my hands of it.'

Three-quarters of an hour later a deputation of merchants waited humbly on Lawrence, and brought him the assurance of implicit obedience. Only they asked for a delay of two weeks in order to get together so considerable a sum.

'You have done right,' answered Lawrence, 'to throw your-selves on our generosity. I grant you the delay you ask, and am glad you repent of your contumacy.'

As they left the church, Morgan, whose indignation had now become excessive, drew Lawrence towards him, and whis-pered, 'Two words with you.'

'Four, if you like,' answered the chief; 'only I fear you will lose your time. I know by heart the sermon you are going to preach.'

'Your words prove, Lawrence, that your conscience still speaks; that only aggravates your crime.'

'There is the beginning of the sermon; I was right. Mate, as I am in a hurry, put off the remainder till a more convenient season.'

'You granted me four words, Lawrence, three will serve my turn: I despise you!'

'I know that well enough,' answered the other, without showing the slightest emotion. 'What do I care? Am I to make myself unhappy because you are too narrow-minded to understand me. You are mistaken, my friend. I have something else to do than to play at foils with you. Good-bye, mate.'

'I your mate after what has passed? never!' cried the gentleman indignantly. Lawrence, who had gone a few paces, turned back.

'Chevalier,' he said gravely, 'have you well considered your last words? Do you seriously break the tie which bound us to each other?'

'Yes, gladly, and with pride I renounce our fellowship. My lips express feebly what is passing in my heart.'

'Well, be it so,' answered Lawrence. 'This breaking off only favours my projects. Perhaps —— but that is hardly probable. I might have been restrained in carrying out my designs by a feeling of false and absurd generosity. Now I am free ; *au revoir*, Chevalier Morgan.'

'God grant we may never meet,' cried Morgan energetically, for he fancied he could discern in his ex-mate's words an allusion to his passion for Wildflower.

Lawrence departed without answering this defiance, but his sinister smile showed plainly that he counted on revenge.

Scarcely had Lawrence left him when Morgan was accosted by Jennie. Since the horrible execution of the twenty merchants the poor girl had been a prey to the greatest indignation.

'Oh, Chevalier Lewis,' she said, taking the young man's arm, 'how I long to leave this accursed place. I never can be happy again. Oh, why did I quit our forests, and bring my poor father into danger. Oh, I feel that his death was my work.'

Wildflower paused for a few minutes, then added slowly,—

'Oh, I wish I did not love you so much ; but what am I saying? I am mad ; not to love you would be death.'

Jennie, at the idea of loving Morgan, clung to his arm instinctively.

Morgan's heart thrilled within him.

'Cruel girl,' he murmured, ' you are my only joy in life. Fatal oath that binds me. Jennie, I would give my whole life to have a right to call you mine. To die pressing a kiss on your lips would be to mount at once to heaven.'

Jennie's heart beat violently. She was overwhelmed with a joy that was at once ecstatic and painful. Tears trembled on her downcast eyelids, while a heavenly smile played around her lips. Suddenly she shuddered and cried out,—

'Oh, chevalier, do you not hear a woman's cries? Some poor creature is being ill-treated. Let us go and defend her.'

Scarcely twenty paces off was a crowd of freebooters round a woman, who was uttering piercing cries.

The youth, disengaging himself from Wildflower, was soon in the midst of the party.

'Rascals,' he said, with happy inspiration, 'don't you see that by thus insulting the woman before you get the Spanish gold you will only exasperate the people, who will refuse you their treasures ? Wait to give way to your passions till your vessels are filled with booty. For the common good I take this woman under my protection. Woe to him who dares lay hands on her. I will denounce him to our brothers as a traitor.'

To speak thus was the only means to obtain the freebooters' attention.

Had Morgan threatened them with his sword he would have been lost. As it was, the freebooters, unconscious that he was no longer Lawrence's mate, which gave him immense importance among them, gave way and let Morgan approach their victim.

At this moment Jennie joined him, and both uttered a cry of surprise as they recognised Nativa.

'In good troth, brother,' cried one of the fellows, tapping Morgan on the shoulder, 'you don't seem half pleased with your bargain. We shan't accuse you of wishing to engross the young lady to yourself. Though she is devilish handsome, quite a dainty morsel for a king,—still, duty before love—gold before everything. The ducats once on board, we will have our revenge.'

The freebooters then departed, leaving Morgan and Wildflower alone with Nativa.

The latter was the first to break silence.

'Señor,' she said, 'I thank God who has sent to my rescue the bravest and most generous man I know. Near you I have nothing to fear. How can I express to you my gratitude ? I owe you more than life. You have saved me from a crime, for I could not have lived dishonoured, and suicide would have been my only refuge.'

Nativa's gratitude, and it seemed sincere, caused Morgan pain. His conscience told him that he had no right to accept thanks from the Count of Monterey's daughter.

As for Wildflower, it was easy to guess, by the way she stamped her little foot, by her cold glance, and the contraction of her beautiful eyebrows, how unpleasant to her was this unexpected meeting.

'Nativa,' she said, 'you owe no gratitude to the Count de Morgan. You have made us both suffer too much for us to love you. We came to your aid because you were in distress. Now that you are safe, we will leave you. Farewell.'

Wildflower put her arm in Morgan's, and tried to draw him way but at Nativa's entreating glance she stopped.

'What do you wish for now?' she said more gently, for she repented already her first impulse of impatience. 'Do you want to bind the chevalier by another oath? Do you want him to promise never to see me again? Oh, he would not obey you, would you, Chevalier Lewis? It is best for us to separate. Adieu, Nativa.'

'But, Wildflower,' pleaded Nativa, for the greatness of the danger she had been in had conquered all her pride, 'don't you know that to leave me here would be only to expose me to the insults of the first wretches I meet? Oh, you already repent having saved me. You wish my death.'

'Oh, Nativa, how can you say anything so dreadful! It is true that in my haste to depart I had forgotten the danger you were in. Chevalier Lewis, we must save Nativa.'

'I am at your orders, señorita,' said Morgan, in a broken voice. 'Where do you wish me to take you?'

Nativa cast on the Englishman a mournful glance.

'Caballero,' she answered, 'some infernal wretches have murdered my father in his own house while the French army occupied the town. Now that it is in the power of the freebooters there is no place of safety in Carthagena.'

'Chevalier Lewis,' said Wildflower, 'a thought has struck me. Let the lady put on a man's dress, and we will take her on board the *Serpent*, where I can share my cabin with her; no one will go to look for her there.'

'Thanks, Wildflower,' said Nativa. 'I accept. You are a noble girl; forgive my past conduct. I knew not how good you were.'

Morgan, Nativa, and Wildflower were already in search of a dress to disguise Nativa, when Jennie said abruptly,—

'Chevalier, my project is impracticable. Let Nativa die rather than you should incur such a risk. You know that any freebooter who takes a woman on board is punished with death. On this point the Brothers of the Coast are inexorable; they would even sacrifice handsome Lawrence if he did such a thing.'

At Wildflower's words a deathly pallor came over Nativa's features.

'Be not uneasy, senorita,' said Morgan, 'this danger shall not prevent my doing my duty. Jennie,' said the young man, taking Wildflower's hands in his, 'when one can no longer esteem a man one ceases to love him. You would despise me if I could leave the senorita in this cowardly manner. Do you wish then to lose all friendship, all affection for me?'

'I despise you, sir! impossible,' cried Jennie.

'You could not do otherwise if I were to act thus, Wildflower.'

'Then let it be as you wish,' replied Jennie gravely.

An hour later Nativa, dressed as a servant, took possession Jennie's cabin on board the *Serpent*.

CHAPTER LVIII.

TAKEN UNAWARES.

WILDFLOWER'S artifice for getting Nativa on board succeeded the more easily as the freebooters had most of them left the vessel to wander about the town, leaving only a few assistants on board.

Every day Jennie went to procure food for Nativa, and returning remained with her till the following day.

Jennie's solicitude for her welfare was the more meritorious as the sight even of her rival gave her great pain. She could not forget that Nativa formed the only barrier between the chevalier and herself. And dazzled as she could not help feeling by the great beauty and accomplishments of her Spanish visitor, she occasionally felt a vague dread that Morgan might again be captivated by her, and fall again under her influence.

Nativa's language was not calculated to allay her fears, for never did the two girls talk of the chevalier without a blush suffusing Nativa's cheek, and a softer cadence became perceptible in her voice.

Poor Wildflower's experience in such matters was not great, but she was a woman, and jealous ; these symptoms were not lost on her.

'Nativa,' said Jennie to her one day, 'it seems to me impossible that any one so beautiful as you are should not be good also. Perhaps it is only your town education that has perverted you, and your heart is still open to good and generous impulses. Well, Nativa, without intending it you have caused me great sorrow. Will you swear to me by the Holy Virgin that you will not try to take advantage of my inexperience, but answer from your heart the questions I wish to put to you ?'

'Speak without fear, Wildflower. I promise you, on my salvation, that I will only tell you the exact truth.'

'Thanks, Nativa, now I can trust you.' Jennie paused a moment, then, with her eyes cast down, added,—

'Nativa, did you once, some time since, love the Chevalier de Morgan ?'

'No ; I only esteemed him then.'

'And now, Nativa, do not forget your promise.'

'To-day I love him,' answered Nativa in a low tone.

'Oh, you love him !' cried Jennie, putting her hand to her heart. 'Oh, why were you so cruel as to tell me this ?'

'Did I not swear to tell you the truth.'

'Oh, yes, you are right. I know not what I say. Then you

do love my Chevalier Lewis? I do not wish to grieve you,
Nativa, but think of the folly of your love. To what can it lead?
Never to happiness. You are proud, you could ill brook to find
your love disdained, rejected ; and the chevalier would reject it,
be assured. Believe me, Nativa, renounce this fatal love. Do
not expose yourself to certain shame. You are so rich, so
beautiful, many Spanish noblemen would be honoured by your
hand. Marry one of your own countrymen. Indeed, it would
be best for you.'

'It seems to me, Wildflower,' interrupted Nativa, with a
proud air, 'that from questions you are going on to advice. I promised you truth, but not obedience. Do you think, child, that
your troubled features, your suppressed and trembling voice, do
not plainly indicate the passion and jealousy which govern you?
It is not my interest that you plead for, but your own. Now
listen to me. After our meeting at Grenada I wished, finding
how little Lawrence was worthy of my esteem or affection, to
retire from the world. In spite of my father's entreaties I came
to Carthagena, where one of my relations was abbess in a convent, and took the white veil. It was then first in solitude I
became aware what a deep impression the Count de Morgan had
made on my heart. I remembered his devotion, his generosity,
his valour, his nobility of mind. By degrees his image entirely
engrossed my thoughts. I ended by bitterly regretting the ingratitude I had shown him. To-day that I am free ; that the
death of my honoured and lamented father obliges me to seek a
protector ; to-day that an extraordinary and providential circumstance had brought us again together, you may easily conceive,
Jennie, what my wishes and my hopes are.'

' But the Chevalier Lewis no longer loves you,' cried Jennie,
with the frankness of despair.

'Oh,' answered Nativa, softly shaking her head with an air
of assurance and triumph that increased Jennie's uneasiness, 'I
don't fear his indifference. His heart was once too entirely mine
for him to be able to resist my repentance. His pride was hurt,
and for that I only esteem him the more, but his heart remains
the same.'

' But I love him,' sobbed Jennie. ' I feel I love him better
than any one does. What will become of me ?'

This outburst of grief was so violent, even Nativa was moved
by it.

' My poor Wildflower,' she answered gently, 'you will feel
some comfort from the thought that your chevalier is happy, not
only by me, but also because his position in the world will be
brilliant. I am very rich. The name I bear, one of the most
illustrious in Spain, will give him interest at court. The Count
de Morgan will be able to aspire to the greatest honours. the

greatest dignities. Jennie, be calm, be reasonable. Nothing is yet done. Let us talk it over coolly. Let me explain things to you. If the count married you, what would be the result? A fearful awakening from a bright dream on your part, eternal regrets on his. After six months, a year if you will, want and misery will sit at the threshold. Nobility and poverty are the two things which, if united, form the most wretched position. What would the count do? He is proud and independent ; he would work. Poor Wildflower, your chevalier out of generosity might try to conceal from you his annoyance, his humiliation, his regret, but by the sound of his voice, by the sadness of his brow, you would guess but too quickly his cares and griefs. Then, knowing yourself to be the cause of his misfortunes, your life would be embittered with remorse. Your nights would be sleepless, your days spent in tears. My sweet Jennie, I don't wish to deceive you ; remember my promise. Now I assure you, that if I foresaw any happiness could result from your union with the Count de Morgan I would give him back his freedom, I would not prevent your marriage. Let me yet add a few words. You think now perhaps that death alone could banish his image from your heart. You are mistaken. You loved the count because he was the first who took notice of you. In a year you will be astonished to find how little you care for him. The wealth that I will give you, a new admirer——'

'Silence, Nativa,' cried Wildflower, interrupting her, ' I could bear your pride, your insults, but never will I listen to such blasphemy. I forget the chevalier? Never ! Your words are daggers in my heart, but I know that they are false. My heart tells me that my chevalier could never be happy without me, that I could never be happy away from him——'

'Your chevalier is a fool,' said a vibrating, sneering voice, which made Nativa and Jennie both tremble.

The door of the cabin opened and Lawrence entered.

At the unexpected sight of the freebooter Nativa shuddered.

'Be quite at your ease, señorita,' said Lawrence, with a smile and a low bow, ' I do not come here as your enemy but as your friend. I am still grateful for the good opinion you once had of me, in spite of my indifference in not gladly seizing the opportunity of making myself agreeable to you. If you will have the kindness to accompany me to Carthagena, I will give you a safe conduct which will make any house which you choose to inhabit a safe asylum. As for the chevalier, I am sorry to say that duty will compel me to punish him. Poor young fellow, he was endowed—I speak of him as if he was no more, as he will be shot within an hour—he was endowed with a credulity and blindness that would have made him a capital husband.'

'What do you say, Lawrence?' cried Wildflower, turning pale, 'you speak of shooting my lover! You are joking, of course!'

'Alas! my dear Wildflower, I am in earnest. You know as well as any one the laws of the freebooters. You know how severe and implacable they are. Now it is an undoubted fact that the chevalier has brought a lady on board dressed in man's clothes. I received full information about it. The presence of the señorita, as charming as ever under her new costume, is proof positive against the chevalier. He is a dead man.'

Wildflower wished to answer, but emotion choked her voice. Nativa was almost as much moved as her rival.

'Unhappy wretch that I am,' she cried, 'after I have so tortured Morgan's noble heart, must I now be the cause of his death? No; he shall not suffer for his generosity; my presence here alone condemns him, I will save him.'

Nativa rose, and eagerly pushing aside Lawrence, who stood at the door, she rushed with a firm yet rapid step towards one of the open portholes in the cuddy into which the cabin opened.

For a moment taken by surprise, the freebooter soon guessed Nativa's intention, and in one spring had reached and seized her; a moment later and Nativa would have thrown herself into the sea, and Morgan would have been saved.

'Pardy, señorita,' cried Lawrence, 'what splendid devotion! quite worthy of the days of chivalry. Drown one's self to leave one's lover to a rival; it is superb. But perhaps you did not give yourself time to reflect and to think that once you would have probably done the same for me. How happy are your lovers! You have the same affection for them. But here I am talking instead of acting. I must get witnesses to prove the unhappy chevalier's crime. I will be back directly.'

Lawrence pretended to leave, when Jennie, recalled to her senses by the imminent danger of the chevalier, stopped him.

'Lawrence,' she said, 'it is impossible you can speak of putting your threat into execution; a monster alone would be capable of such infamy.'

'Then perhaps I am a monster,' answered Lawrence, turning away.

Wildflower clung to him. 'Is there no way of saving the chevalier? Come, coward, tell me the truth; you know I would rather die than let him suffer.'

'Yes, Jennie, there is one way of saving the chevalier.'

'Then tell me, tell me how to do so!' cried Jennie, almost beside herself.

Lawrence, who believed in nothing; who, bold, independent and unshackled, laughed to scorn all that was sacred; the unscrupulous pirate who never stopped at crime to gratify his

passions, remained for a moment confused and disconcerted at
Jennie's question.

But his hesitation was short, very soon he regained his audacity,
his eyes recovered their look of proud disdain, his lips their
cynical smile, and drawing Jennie towards him he said,—

'Jennie, I love you! consent to be mine and the chevalier is
safe.'

CHAPTER LIX.

NATIVA'S REVENGE.

At this proposal Wildflower drew back with horror.

Lawrence smiled with an air of disdainful pity.

'Child,' he said, 'the aversion you show is only another
attraction to me. Your heart in revolt pleases my audacity. To
make you love me will be not only a happiness but a triumph to
me. Wildflower, every second which passes brings your chevalier
a year nearer his grave. I give you one minute to make up your
mind; do not forget that your refusal will be his death warrant.'

The poor girl's state of mind was fearful; she knew Lawrence
well enough to be sure that he would carry out his threat, that
he would be without pity. The image of Morgan falling under
the fire of the freebooters presented itself to her mind with all
the horrors of reality. She shuddered at the dreadful picture.

'I am waiting,' said Lawrence, who gazed unmoved on her
agony and despair.

Jennie at last, in a voice so low that it was almost inaudible,
said, 'My sweetheart Lewis shall not die. Lawrence, I will do as
you wish.'

At these words the freebooter started violently, a gleam of
light shone from his dark eyes, but soon recovering his coolness
he said, 'Very well, come, follow me!'

Wildflower remained motionless.

'Lawrence,' she said, after a pause, 'a man capable of committing such a crime as you wish to commit does not deserve to be
believed on his word. As long as Nativa remains on board
the life of the Englishman is in danger. What assurance have
I that the men left here will not accomplish your hateful purpose? I will only follow you when Nativa has left the vessel and
Sir Lewis is no longer in danger from your treachery.'

'Be it so; at nightfall I will come back for you and the
senorita. But I warn you that all attempts to escape will be fruitless, I shall have the vessel guarded. Good-bye then, Wildflower.'

Lawrence tried to take her hand, but she flung it from her
with disdain.

'I am not yet yours, slave! leave me.'

This insult seemed to increase Lawrence's satisfaction, who, with a smile on his lips, left them. After his departure a long silence reigned in Jennie's cabin. Nativa was the first to speak.

'Jennie,' she said, approaching the poor girl,' who, pale and motionless, her head bending forward and her arms hanging listlessly by her side, and vacant gaze, seemed almost unconscious of every thing ? 'Jennie, you are a noble creature ; God will reward your devotion. His justice, superior to human prejudices, will reward your sublime sacrifice.'

The sound of Nativa's voice roused Jennie, a bright colour returned to her cheeks.

'Oh, be silent,' she cried, 'and do not by hypocritical pity add to the misery which is your work ; you were right just now when you said misfortunes follow your footsteps. Twice you have stood in my path, and each time I have suffered bitterly. Do not pretend to pity me, Nativa, I read too well what is passing in your mind. You rejoice in my fate, because it will place an inseparable abyss between the chevalier and me. You are wrong ; do you think I would betray my chevalier's love ? Never. To gain time I was forced to deceive Lawrence, and I promised what he wished, but when he has once placed you in safety and there is no longer any proof against the chevalier, I will kill myself before Lawrence shall call me his. Poor Lewis, my death will leave him exposed to your artifices.'

Wildflower had surmised the truth. If Nativa did not rejoice at her rival's fate, yet a wild hope sprang up in her bosom, which she dared scarcely own to herself. At Jennie's accusation she hung her head.

'Nativa,' said Jennie, after a pause, 'a bad action always bears bitter fruits ; be for once kind and generous. Do not return my kindness with ingratitude, for it was in saving you that I have lost myself. Help me now, advise me ; what can we do ? How leave here ? Let us set fire to the vessel ; in the hurry and confusion we might escape. There are several barrels of brandy on board ; it is a dangerous plan, but my position is so hopeless I would risk anything. Will you help me, Nativa ? '

At the thought that Jennie delivered from Lawrence would again become a formidable rival in Morgan's affections, Nativa felt an impulse of rage which stifled every generous emotion.

'Good heavens, Jennie !' she answered, 'one would really believe that Lawrence's love is the greatest misfortune. Lawrence has many good qualities ; he is rich, he will make you happy.'

Wildflower, occupied with her own thoughts, paid no attention to Nativa's words.

'Nativa,' she said at last, 'do you remember the offer you made me at Grenada of giving me a place among your women ? I refused it then, I will accept it now ; I will do more, I will be your slave if you will help me to save myself ! '

Wildflower was so urgent in her entreaty, so willing to sacrifice her liberty and pride to escape from Lawrence, that Nativa's anger was kindled ; and it was in a proud disdainful tone she answered :

'Jennie, all this overstrained delicacy is absurd in a girl of your station ; give it over at once.'

'I don't exactly understand you, Nativa ; but do you refuse me ?'

'Yes, a thousand times I do. Do you think I am going to set fire to a vessel, to lower a boat ? I don't understand such work. I am not a freebooter.'

'Then you refuse to help me ?'

'Certainly I refuse, Wildflower.'

'I pity you, Nativa ! I shall try alone !'

'No, indeed, I shall prevent your doing so. I don't choose to be the victim of your imprudence.'

'You will have to stop me by force, for nothing shall make me renounce my resolution.'

'Yes, I will employ force if necessary to save my life,' she answered.

'Now, indeed, you speak like a freebooter,' said Jennie sadly. 'Nativa,' she added, 'you have signed your own death warrant. Attempt to move and I fire ! Nativa, you will not help me to escape the dreadful fate that awaits me ; you wish to place an insuperable barrier between me and the Englishman, but you little know the abyss that is between you and him ; even were he deeply in love with you, duty would oblige him to shun your presence.'

'I don't understand you, Jennie.'

'Would you take for your husband your father's murderer ?'

At these words Nativa cried out,—

'It is false ! it is false ! You wish to deceive me, make me hate Sir Lewis, but you will not succeed. My father perished by a dreadful death inflicted by robbers——'

'By order of Sir Lewis,' interrupted Jennie. 'Years ago, your father inflicted the same horrible death on his father. Lewis avenged the innocent and punished the guilty. The death of the Count de Monterey was not a crime, it was just retribution.'

Wildflower might have gone on speaking ; Nativa was too much overcome to interrupt her. A long pause followed.

'Nativa,' said Jennie at last, 'since we both live without hope, let us make common cause. Let our mutual misfortune unite us. I say again, help me to save myself and I will become your slave. We shall perhaps be less unhappy if we are together, for we can speak of him before each other without being ashamed of our tears.'

Native was too wretched now to care much what became of her, she was reckless what happened.

'Do as you will, Jennie, I have no courage to oppose you.'

Familiarized from her childhood with danger, Jennie set about her project ; she took a lantern, and carefully avoiding being seen she got down into the hold of the vessel. In a few minutes volumes of smoke and jets of flame issued from it.

'Now, Nativa, we shall need all our presence of mind ; see, twenty boats are already rowing towards us, the ship will be towed out to a distance that she may not set fire to the rest. Let us mingle with the crowd, no one will notice us, now we shall get safe on shore.'

'And once on land, will you go with me, Jennie ? you promised that we should never part.'

'I will go wherever you take me, Nativa.'

'I have faith in your word, Jennie. I swear to you that we will never part, not even in the grave.'

Nativa pronounced these words with strong emotion.

'Yes,' she murmured to herself as she followed Jennie on deck, 'thus my father will be avenged, and Jennie will never again see the murderer whom my cowardly heart still loves.'

The event exactly realized Wildflower's hope. In the midst of the confusion consequent on the *Serpent* being on fire the two young girls reached shore easily, as they were scarcely two cables off.

'Let us hasten, Jennie,' said Nativa, as soon as their feet touched land; 'we must not be seen by Morgan or Lawrence.'

In half an hour the fugitives had safely crossed the town, and had reached a solitary part of the country.

CHAPTER LX.

IN THE COILS.

A luxuriant vegetation that had hitherto bid defiance to cultivation reached nearly to the city gates and made the outskirts almost deserted.

At sight of the thick foliage, which reminded her of her own beloved forests, Jennie heaved a deep sigh.

'What ! does your resolution fail you already,' cried Nativa ; 'you who feared not to set a ship on fire, to mingle in the most desperate schemes of robbers; you who make use of firearms as if they were playthings ; you, only at the thought of leaving your sweetheart, show all the weakness of our sex ! Return to Carthagena. I no longer keep you. Physical courage, which is the mere force of habit is all that you possess. Greatness of soul, of strength, and will are wanting. Go, the Spanish girl can no longer feel jealous of you.'

If Wildflower had not been absorbed by her own feelings she must have perceived a strange want of harmony in Nativa's words and her looks, and a dark fire in her eyes that boded evil. Wildflower only perceived in her words an unjust reproach.

'You do wrong to accuse me,' she answered gently. 'I promised not to leave you and to become your slave. The future will prove that I can keep my promise. The sacrifice is so very great to me that I must bewail it. Still regret is not forfeiting my word. Fear not, Nativa ! I will follow you if you desire it to the end of the world. Where are we going? Into some distant village where we can remain hidden until the freebooters leave ?'

'Forgive my suspicions and reproaches, dear Jennie,' cried Nativa joyfully. 'I judged you wrongly. The idea that you were going to abandon me made me unjust. Do not speak of being my slave. You shall henceforth be my sister. We will never part, even in the grave we will be together.'

Nativa, who had uttered the last words with energy, continued in her natural voice : 'Although we are only just outside the town we have finished our journey, for we are going to the Convent of Nostra Señora.'

'To the Convent of Nostra Señora !' repeated Jennie in astonishment ; 'only a mile out of the town. Lawrence will be sure to find me.'

'Be not uneasy, I answer for your safety. This convent after it was abandoned by the ruffians was the refuge of most of the ladies of the town. I remained here nearly a month and know every part, even the most secret.'

'Is it possible, Nativa ? What, while the regular troops and Brothers of the Coast scoured the villages round ?'

'The nuns and the riches that they sought were close at hand. We left the woods to hide in this convent, persuaded that our enemies would never seek for us so near them. Our conjecture proved correct. Besides, this nunnery possesses such hiding places that Lawrence even if he knew we were here could never find us out.'

'But, Nativa, if the Brothers stay another week here we shall have to go out often for food ; shall we not risk being seen, and followed ?'

'We can do without provisions.'

A sinister smile passed over Nativa's face, but she added, 'The ladies who were here before brought more provisions than they needed, there is plenty left for us. We shall have abundance of biscuits and dried fruits. I will arrange all that.'

This answer satisfied Jennie. The convent was situated on the north-west of the town on a steep hill ; a narrow path cut in the rock led up to it.

Thick brambles that hung from the rocks helped the foot traveller to mount this rough path and offered him a chance of safety if his foot slipped.

'Why did you bring us this way, Nativa,' asked Jennie, 'instead of entering by the gates ? I speak only on your account, for this path must be very irksome to you only accustomed to soft carpets and smooth roads.'

'No more reflections, I desire,' answered Nativa drily. 'I have made up my mind, I have good reasons for coming this way.'

Soon Nativa stopped and said, 'We are at our journey's end.'

Wildflower looked around her but could see nothing on one side but the precipice and the high wall of the convent.

'You see,'said Nativa, with a smile,'there is not much danger of our being discovered, as you cannot even see an entrance.'

Nativa then showed her companion an entrance that looked like a loophole about two feet square in the solid wall.

Nativa made a slight pause before she boldly entered the loophole. Wildflower followed her. The sweet girl was unusually courageous,yet she had scarcely descended two feet before a sudden faintness came over her and she had nearly fallen. Was it alone the sudden change from the genial warmth of the sun to an atmosphere oppressive with dank humidity, or was it a presentiment of evil that warned Wildflower of approaching danger? The stairs ended in a narrow passage, which the young girls reached without hindrance.

'Where are we, Nativa?' asked Jennie, who had become uneasy.

'Behind the altar in the chapel—look.'

Nativa pressed her finger on a spring, a panel slided back and the dark passage was suddenly lighted by a golden ray of light. Wildflower had scarcely time to see the devastated chapel before all was again dark.

'Oh, how delightful is sunshine,' she murmured with a sigh.

She heard a door creak on its hinges and a feeble light shone down on them.

'Here is a refuge where the robbers will not think of looking for us,' said Nativa. 'Here you need not fear Lawrence's persecution.'

Wildflower hesitated. 'I am afraid,' she said, trembling. 'What is this place?'

'An *in pace* or prison of the convent. To avoid the outrages of your friends the buccaneers, whom I call robbers and murderers, I was forced to hide myself in this dull place for a month,' answered Nativa. 'I am familiar with these mournful places. Shall I set you the example and show you the way, brave buccaneer as you are?'

'If you will, Nativa. I know not why, but I am much frightened. Pass first.'

If Jennie had only seen the cruel smile upon her companion's face, she would have refused to follow.

'What a dreadful place,' cried Wildflower as they entered the narrow *in pace;* 'these dank walls seem like a load of ice on me. I can fancy I hear the cries and groans of the unhappy creatures who years ago died in all the tortures of a slow, lingering death. Heavens! how delightful freedom is. Nativa, let us leave this place—let us fly from here! I know forest life well. I could provide for our wants. We should have sun and air. You do not know how lovely is nature. The sweet odours of the flowers, the joyful warbling of birds, oh! we should be as merry as the day is long, we should forget the world! Oh no, we could not forget the past, but at night, when all nature sinks to sweet repose, we would talk of him. Oh! there would be sweetness even in the tears we might shed.'

'Your words prove, Jennie,' answered Nativa, 'that handsome Lawrence does not seem so terrible to you as he did. Wildflower, it is not well to sacrifice the chevalier's deep love for a caprice of the handsome buccaneer. Poor Lewis, he little thinks that I take his part. Jennie, I will not let you leave this place.'

Nativa double-locked the door and took away the key.

'Nativa,' said Jennie, weeping, 'why do you thus insult my grief? Why torture me thus? You know that I would prefer death a hundred times to being Lawrence's wife. If I proposed that we should stay in the forest it was because I knew Lawrence was too busy now to think of following me. But if you prefer this prison to the free life of the forest I must submit. Did I not promise to obey you?'

Wildflower now began to look round her as well as the dim light would permit. Thick walls shut them in on all sides, on one of which was an aperture of about half a foot, through which entered light and air.

'There is no fear that Lawrence should come through there,' said Nativa, who with the same cruel smile was watching her companion's movements. 'That aperture is situated above a deep precipice, and is not visible from the outside. Oh! we are perfectly secure here. No one will think of looking for us here.'

A long silence followed. Wildflower, leaning against a wall, gave herself up to sad thoughts.

'Jennie, said Nativa, 'I want to ask you a question, and as I have given up all hopes of the chevalier's love it would be useless now to try to deceive me, so you must tell me the truth, Jennie!'

Wildflower hung down her head in silence.

'Well, now you distrust me. That is not well, Jennie. You deceived me, did you not? You were jealous and wanted to place an eternal barrier between me and the chevalier, so you accused him of a dreadful crime of which he was not guilty. Tell me the truth, was not Monsieur de Morgan innocent, Jennie?'

'I never tell falsehoods,' answered Wildflower in a low voice. 'My lord Lewis avenged his father; he was not guilty in doing what he did.'

'If Señor Morgan avenged his father then all is explained,' answered Nativa with strange gaiety. 'Come now, my pretty one, shall we talk of the future? Of your free, happy life in the woods when we get out of this dull place?'

'Oh, Nativa, do not speak in that tone, you frighten me. It seems as if it were like the hissing of a serpent.'

'Jennie,' cried Nativa, with a laugh that was almost a scream your instinct did not deceive you. Foolish girl, why did you not take warning by your first impression? Now nothing can save you. You belong to me. I have sealed your fate. Jennie, you have only a few days to live, and those in agony. Your future, Jennie, is to die of hunger and thirst in this dungeon. Look, Jennie, the key I let fall from my hand you can hear resounding against the rocks, *it* is the key of our prison, and all hope goes with it. I told you truly that we should never quit each other, not even in the grave. Jennie, I am revenged.'

Jennie uttered a cry and fainted.

CHAPTER LXI.

THE RESCUE.

Whilst the fire that Wildflower had kindled destroyed the *Serpent*, Sir Lewis Morgan, ignorant of the shameful conduct of his late mate, and also of Jennie's dreadful situation, was having a serious conversation with his uncle, who looked sad and careworn, almost hopeless.

'Lewis,' he said, 'you are utterly mistaken in regard to Lawrence.   In his election you see only an isolated fact, the effect of chance, whilst I can perceive in it a deeply concerted plan.'

'Indeed, you exaggerate matters, uncle.   I do not doubt that your self-love being wounded, causes you to view things on their dark side.   The Brothers of the Coast, in choosing Lawrence for their chief, only give way to a blind infatuation.   Lawrence is the idol of the moment.   He is admired and applauded.   In a week he will cease to be so.   You alone possess their confidence, your power over them is too firmly fixed to be moved by any caprice.   What can you wish for more ?'

'How young and inexperienced you are in the world, Lewis ! You see everything through the prism of your own loyal, generous feelings.   Incapable of committing evil yourself, you shut your eyes to its existence.   I envy you your ignorance ; you at least can be happy.'

'I happy,' cried Morgan with a sigh.

'Oh, I know your love affair does not prosper.   A great misfortune truly.   I wish I could love.   But ambition has been my only mistress, and she has proved fickle at last.   Lewis, I have not acted by you perhaps as kindly as I might ; engrossed with my own schemes, I have not taken into consideration that your hopes and wishes were not the same as mine, but you will find, my boy, that I have done what I could to render your future life independent and prosperous ; we know not what may happen.'

'Don't speak thus, sir !   An energetic mind like yours must not give up so soon.'

'I do not give up, child.   I am only far-sighted, that is all. Lawrence's triumph will not last, I know ; but it may cost me dear.'

One of the assistants entered and said,—

'Master, a man wishes to speak to you directly on urgent business.'

'Who is he ?' asked Morgan, 'a brother or a Spaniard ?'

'A Brother of the Coast ; he speaks too good English for a Spaniard, but he was too much muffled up for me to see his face.'

'Let him come in,' said Morgan.

This mysterious visitor seemed so singular a coincident with his apprehension, that Sir Lewis, in alarm, threw himself between his uncle and the door.

'Thanks, Lewis,' he said, ' for your intention ; but there is no danger.   No one—even Lawrence—would dare to attack me openly.   The Spaniards have given up sending people to murder me.   I divine treachery as quickly as my hand punishes it.'

He was still speaking when the unknown visitor entered.

At sight of young Morgan he hesitated.

'Captain,' said the buccaneer, 'this is my relation, a second self.   Speak as freely before him as if we were alone.'

‘You call me captain. Do you know me ?’

‘Certainly, Salt Peter.’

The newcomer unfastened his cloak, and sat down opposite the speaker.

‘Brother,’ he said, ‘as you answer for the gentleman’s discretion, I believe it, for you are never wrong ; still, before I begin, I must have your promise that not a word I say shall go beyond these walls.’

‘If such a promise does not hamper my freedom of action I make it.’

‘Not in the least. It is about Lawrence.’

‘Speak on, brother.’

‘Morgan,’ said Pierre, ‘you were harsh to me the other day when I opposed your wish to attack the French squadron. Your reproaches at first made me angry, afterwards sorry. I discovered that in thwarting you I had done wrong, and compromised the welfare of our band. But Lawrence dazzled me. This morning, fancying he could make sure of me, he did not fear to disclose his infamous projects.’

‘Ah, then you know Lawrence’s projects,’ cried Morgan with intense curiosity. ‘What are they ?’

‘ He wants to get possession of the treasures of the association, he says they are badly placed in your hands, and to transport our association into the Southern Seas. I won’t repeat all the specious reasonings he made use of, or all the promises he made me to induce me to favour his scheme.’

‘What was your answer, Pierre ?’

‘ At first start to treat the rascal as he deserved ; but on second thoughts I considered that to publicly denounce Lawrence, and reject his offers with contempt, would only expose me to be called a backbiter, and would put him on his guard ; so I preferred letting him think that I was on his side, and coming to tell you of the plot. God grant, Morgan, it may not be too late to stop it.’

‘What do you think of this, Lewis ? Were my suspicions so groundless ? But go on, captain.’

‘Morgan,’ continued Pierre, ‘I own I am a desperate gambler, extravagant, and reckless, but I am true to my flag, and to save it there is nothing I would not do. Command ; I will obey you.’

‘Yes, Peter, I know I can count upon you, but what say the rest of the brethren ? will they follow your loyal example, and repulse Lawrence’s endeavours ?’

‘ Alas, captain, I must confess that most of them have yielded. Few could withstand the prospect of sharing the immense riches which are in your keeping. Ah ! our order is not what it was ; it has degenerated very much since the brave leaders of old.’

'Then,' said Morgan thoughtfully, ' you believe it is Lawrence's intention to take possession of the wealth concealed in the Stronghold ? In truth such a plan would be worthy of his audacity ; it would be a masterstroke. I wonder so simple an idea never struck me before. I had too good an opinion of our brothers.'

'Lawrence,' continued Pierre, 'spoke of his plan as about to be carried out very soon. I should not wonder at his leaving Carthagena at any moment, and setting sail for the Stronghold. The danger is imminent ; moments are precious. What are your intentions ? How do you hope to thwart this traitor's design ?'

'Captain Pierre,' answered Morgan, 'I don't like to be questioned ; but in consideration of the great service you have rendered our order, I don't mind telling you that there is but one means to save it, that is, to kill the traitor. His death will make a great commotion, I am aware,—for just now he is very popular.'

'Yes, you are right ; there is nothing else to be done. There are still brave and loyal fellows amongst us, who, if the brothers wish to avenge Lawrence, will rally round you and defend you. I had not expected less from your energy and decision, Morgan ; but since you answered me one question, would you allow me another. When do you think of punishing the guilty ?'

'Right away,' answered Morgan, coolly, going towards the door.

'Oh, think a little, uncle,' cried Lewis, stopping him. 'Have you well considered your resolution ?'

Do I look angry, Lewis ? never have I felt more calm.'

'It's your calmness frightens me.'

'My calmness, Lewis, after such monstrous ingratitude as the brothers have shown, arises solely from my disdain of human nature. I sacrificed twenty years of my life to make our association what it is. I employed my whole strength, perseverance, and mind to this end, and yet the first comer is preferred before me. Yet I feel neither hatred nor anger, only sorrow.'

Morgan was leaving when an associate came in and said :

' Master, a violent fire has broken out on board the *Serpent ;* the whole fleet is in danger.'

Morgan's thoughts instantly recurred to Wildflower. He rushed out of the house and hastened down to the shore. How much would his anxiety have been increased had he known poor Wildflower's present position in the convent.

The *Serpent* having been towed clear of the rest, a search was made for all on board ; no one had perished. Morgan visited every quarter of the town to find Wildflower. He thought that perhaps both the young girls had gone to his rooms in the town, but Allan had seen nothing of them. His mind a prey to fearful presentiments, he again searched the town in every part, and learnt that Wildflower had been seen in company of a young man, whom, from the description given, he could not doubt was Nativa.

This reassured him a little ; he thought that Jennie, anxious for Nativa's safety, had gone a little out of the town, and that she would return at night. Easier about Wildflower, Sir Lewis again thought of Lawrence and Morgan's severe resolution, and he hastened back to his uncle.

Morgan was absent. Sir Lewis, a prey to deep anxiety, waited for him till nightfall. Every instant he fancied he heard furious cries and firing announcing that the Brothers of the Coast were in arms against each other.

At last Morgan arrived.

'Well?' cried Lewis, rushing to meet him.

'Well,' answered the freebooter, 'I have nowhere been able to find Lawrence ; I fear it is too late ! I have also observed the absence of many of the brothers in whom I have the least confidence. I should not be surprised if Lawrence had left. Pierre has also gone to look for him ; I expect him now. I doubt if he has been more fortunate.

A confused sound of voices was now heard in the street. Morgan opened the window and looked out.

'What is it?' he asked.

'A wounded man brought on a litter.'

'Curses,' said Morgan, 'perhaps it is Pierre !'

A few moments later and a hand-barrow carried was brought into the room where the buccaneers were.

'Pierre, poor Pierre !' cried Morgan, shaking his hand kindly, 'you met Lawrence? I am the cause of your death.'

'Yes, it was Lawrence who killed me,' said the dying man, 'but you were not the cause of my death. I die for the league. I met Lawrence in a boat at the entrance of the bay. He was preparing to embark. He cried out, 'You have betrayed me !' and fired. It seems Lawrence has spies, so beware. If you don't meet with him in two days, you set sail too. You will be sure to meet him at the Stronghold. I would rather have died from a Spanish bullet, but when I am dead what will it matter what is said of Captain Pierre? Give me a glass of brandy, I am faint. Farewell.'

Seeing that Pierre's condition was hopeless, and that medical treatment would only prolong his sufferings a few minutes, Morgan gave him the drink.

The wounded man took a little, said 'Not bad,' and died,

Four days had passed since the death of Captain Pierre, and Morgan, notwithstanding all his researches, had not met with Lawrence.

Wildflower's continued absence made him so uneasy that he knew not what to do. With feverish impatience he had continued his researches until there remained not a house in the whole town that he had not visited.

Allan, almost as wretched as his master, for he was greatly attached to Jennie, had meanwhile explored the environs of the town. Still tenacious and obstinate, he was not discouraged. He came back to the same places again ; he made the air re-echo with cries of ' Wildflower.'

Alas, their anxiety was only too well founded. A distressing scene was passing in the horrible cell of the convent.

Jennie was no longer recognisable. Seated on the damp ground of the prison, her back resting against the wall, the poor girl presented an image of hopeless resignation.

The transparent pallor of her complexion showed how much she had suffered, her large blue eyes half veiled by their heavy lids seemed ready to close in the sleep of death. From time to time a low sigh escaped her tortured lips, as she was seized by a devouring thirst, but no word of anger or despair accompanied this sign of grief. Jennie bore her sufferings meekly, like an angel waiting to take her flight to heaven.

Nativa's behaviour was very different. Broken, not conquered by her sufferings, she strove violently against the approaches of death. Her nervous twitchings, her impatient movements, her eyes that glared with a dark fire, all showed the mortal strife that only increased her agony.

' Jennie,' she cried, suddenly seizing her companion by the arm, ' how can you sleep thus ? You shall suffer as much as I do. Awake ! '

Wildflower raised her heavy eyelids, and answered in a soft voice : ' I am not asleep, Nativa, I am thinking.'

' About Morgan, my father's murderer ! ' cried Nativa. ' Oh the wretch, would I could have made him suffer too.'

' Don't speak so, Nativa ! ' cried Jennie, with an energy that surprised her companion. ' My sweetheart has the noblest heart in the world. If you only knew the beautiful things he used to tell me. To him I owe that I can, that I do not fear to die. One thing alone makes me sad ; it is to witness your sufferings. Nativa, we have both sorrowed on earth, let us try to think of the joys of heaven. Oh, Nativa, I wish I were not so ignorant, that I could describe to you the beautiful horizon that is opening around. Courage, Nativa, our sufferings will soon be past.' Jennie took her companion's hands and pressed them gently.

Nativa shuddered at her touch ; her pale face recovered for a moment its colour ; a ray of fury darted from her dark eyes.

‘You always have the advantage of me, even in death,’ she hissed. ‘I reject your generosity, your consolation. Oh, heavens, how I suffer ! Jennie, throw aside your torpor, don’t be so cowardly. I am the cause of your death—why don’t you curse me ?’

‘I pity you,’ answered Wildflower, overcome with the effort she had made to defend Morgan. ‘Why should I blame you.?’ she added, after a pause, ‘perhaps your feelings were natural. I crossed and thwarted you, though unintentionally, and you voluntarily share my fate ; there is something noble in your revenge. I understand your feelings towards me ; forgive me, Nativa, the pain I have caused you.’

The tone of humility, the enchanting gentleness of this entreaty had an extraordinary effect on Nativa.

‘You have conquered, Jennie,’ she said, throwing her arms round Jennie’s neck and kissing her ; ‘may God forgive my crime ! How could I. know and not love you.? Jennie, I owe you the peace of my last minutes ; my tears are sweet. I suffer no more ; my sister, I love you.’

A long silence followed ; the two girls, clasped in each other’s arms, seemed in a tranquil sleep.

Jennie was the first to awaken.

‘Nativa,’ she said, ‘why do you restrain your moans ?. Do not fear to grieve me. I know now that if your body suffers, your mind is peaceful. You do not answer ; Nativa, speak to me ! ’

Jennie raised herself with difficulty, and drew back the tresses of silver hair that covered Nativa’s face.

‘How pale you are,’ she said, ‘but how beautiful ! Do you suffer still, dear ? ’

‘God help you, dear Jennie,’ murmured Nativa, ‘I love you ! Farewell.’ Wildflower felt a light sigh pass over her face.

‘Nativa, awake ; let us leave this place ! Let us go back to the forests where I hear the voice of my darling calling us. I am here. Sir Lewis. Lewis. I am here ! ’

Jennie, in a fever of delirium, wished to rise, but her weakness was too great, and she fell fainting over the pale corpse of her companion. Still her stronger nature battled with death, but her mind wandered. She thought she was with her beloved in Cornwall, and she began to sing some of those ballads which had so often delighted Morgan, and brought tears into Allan’s eyes.

Her voice, at first low and trembling, grew gradually more animated ; it was the bright gleam of the expiring lamp.

As Jennie's voice sank into silence, another voice continued the air.

Wildflower listened to the sounds in ecstacy.

'Nativa!' she cried, 'did you not hear a voice singing the same air that I began? all hope is not gone. Perhaps we shall be saved yet.'

Jennie leant over Nativa and screamed out, 'Dead! she is dead!'

This discovery was too much for the poor girl's weakness; again she fainted.

Whilst Jennie lay insensible on the damp floor of the *in pace*, Morgan and his nephew were together in animated conversation.

'But are you sure that this is true, Morgan?' asked Sir Lewis.

'Certainly; why should I doubt it? It is on board the brigantine, the *Flying Stag*, that Lawrence and his accomplices have embarked. I shall rejoin him, but not a moment must be lost. Lewis, you know as well as I do how things stand. I shall be alone in a party of robbers. I dare not ask you to accompany me. Here is a sealed paper which I leave with you; if I am not back in a week, open it. Embrace me, Lewis; who knows if we shall ever meet again?'

Lewis, greatly moved, knew not what to do.

'Uncle,' he said, 'if it were not for the unaccountable absence of Wildflower I would join you at once and share your danger; but I cannot leave her here, exposed to insult and danger.'

'Reassure yourself, Lewis,' said the buccaneer in a bitter tone, 'Jennie has probably accompanied Nativa. You will soon hear of her. But I must not linger; once again, boy, good-bye, though ambition may have hardened my heart, I feel I love you.'

'I will not let you go alone; you are quite right, Jennie may not want me now.'

In his turn Morgan hesitated, which was indeed extraordinary in him.

'Thanks for your devotion, Lewis,' he said after a moment's pause; 'the game I play is too hazardous, it would be a crime to make you run so great a risk. You forget I go to certain death!'

'That answer points out my duty at once,' cried the Englishman; whether you will or no, I will go with you.'

He took up his arms and was going out, when the door was pushed violently open and Allan rushed in, pale, his clothes in disorder, his face haggard, and threw himself into a chair.

'What is the matter, Allan? is Wildflower dead?'

'Yes, she is dead, and I have heard her soul,' cried Allan in a hollow voice.

At Allan's first words Morgan leant against the wall to support himself. but his last gave him hope again.

'Explaiu,' he cried ; 'speak, WHAT has happened ?'

'Just now,' answered Allan, 'as I was goiug up the convent hill, I heard Wildflower's voice, I mean her soul, siug ; indeed, master, it was Wildflower's voice.'

'What did you do ? What did you say ? Speak !'

'I wished to go on with the song, and just began a few notes ; but it is sacrilege to sing with the dead, so I ran back as quick as I could.'

'Jennie is not dead, let us seek her ! Come, Allan, come !'

He seized the servant's arm and hurried him away.

'Who can trust in friendship ?' murmured old Morgan with a sigh, 'Lewis is brave, generous, loyal, he says he loves me, and he knows that I am eugaged in a deadly struggle—yet the thought of a pretty maid of sixteen being in danger makes him leave me at once ! But what right have I to complain ? I ave sacrificed all to ambition, and who knows but ambiticn may be a pale smoke iu comparison with burning love ?'

Guided by Allau, the lover had in teu minutes climb ed the hill. He was so excited that he hardly knew what Allan said. The only thing that seemed clear to his mind was, that Wildflower was alive, that he should soon see her, and this thought exalted all his ardour and energy.

'Come, Allan,' he cried, 'try to remember exactly where you heard her voice.'

'Iudeed, master, it was her soul that I heard ; but let me consider. It was not here,' said Allan, ' it was on the other side. Take care, master, or you will fall. Ah ! now I remember. I was sitting on that large stone when I first heard her voice.'

'It is impossible—you must be mistaken, Allan,' cried the Englishman, looking round ; 'there is nothing within sight but the path we have just mounted, and the precipice beyond.'

'Well, the voice seemed to come from the precipice,' said Allan.

'You will drive me mad ! How could Wildflower descend such an abyss ?'

'Have not souls wings ? Ah, this is the consequence of keeping company with buccaneers—one ceases to believe in anything.'

'Allan,' said Lewis, ' in the name of all you hold sacred are you quite sure that Jennie's voice came from that direction ?'

'Oh. yes, master ! I swear it.'

'Well, Wildflower's absence is so unaccountable that nothing would astonish me now. Yes ; I must venture,'

'What are you going to do, master?' cried the servant, as he saw Morgau take off his coat and sword, unfasten his sash and throw that and his pistols on the ground.

'I am going over the precipice,' answered the youth calmly.

'My good sir,' cried Allan, 'you will break your neck! indeed you will; and what good can you do by going after a spirit? Oh, master, don't you remember the carpenter who followed a pixy?'

'Be silent, Allan; if it chances, as it is not unlikely, that I fall I forbid you to try to save me. If I fall, you would be certain to do the same. Your following me could do me no good, and would be death to you. If I am wounded, go and fetch a dozen Brothers of the Coast, and use what means you can to get me out.'

Morgan went towards the precipice, and after a rapid glance around began his descent, supporting himself by the brambles that clung to the sides. Allan uttered a sharp cry, and shut his eyes.

Some minutes that seemed hours passed before the servant ventured to look down. There were ten chances to one that with all Morgan's activity he must fall.

Morgan had reached the bottom of the precipice in safety.

As soon as he was for the moment out of danger, he reflected on his folly in imagining it possible that Wildflower could be there alive; then, pondering on Jennie's extraordinary disappearance, it occured to him that she might be a prisoner in the cells of the nunnery. His greatest anxiety was to climb up the precipice again, and seek her there. The rain filtered through the rocks made a pool where he now stood, and he stooped to wash his bleeding hands which had been scratched by the brambles and sharp corners of rock; at his feet lay a key. It could not have been long there, it was still bright. He seized it with a presentiment that it would lead to something; he felt that he was on the eve of a great discovery, and his only anxiety was to resume his search, but how to get up the precipice was the difficulty; he sighed as he said to himself, 'Never can I mount that! my reason tells me it is folly to try, but my heart, my love still urges me forward. I will listen to them.' He uttered a short prayer and began his perilous ascent, catching hold of the brambles which tore his hands, and supporting himself on the slightest ledges of rock; every moment he found some new obstacle to impede his progress, some new danger to surmount. Overcome with fatigue, he had nearly missed his hold and fallen when he perceived an iron bar across a loophole; this he seized with eagerness and held himself up, but his strength was nearly exhausted; he felt that in a few moments he must lose his hold and fall back into the precipice.

‘God have pity on you, Wildflower,’ he said. ‘I cannot save you, and I shall never see you more. My last thoughts are with thee.’

His tired fingers were already leaving go of the bar, when a voice cried,

‘Come, Sir Lewis, come and save me.’

For an instant Morgan thought it was a delusion, but when Jennie called to him again, all his strength returned ; he cried out in ecstasy,—

‘Where are you, Wildflower ? How can I get to you ? It is your lover who is come to save you.’

‘I am in one of the dungeons of the convent. In the chapel, behind the altar, there is a picture—but I am dying ; farewell, Lewis ! ’

The poor girl’s voice was so feeble that Morgan could scarcely catch her last words.

Then with increased energy Morgan again descended the precipice and with strenuous efforts mounted it on the other side.

Allan uttered a cry of joy when he saw his master once more in safety, but without an instant’s delay Morgan rushed towards the convent.

In his haste to save her, Morgan had asked Jennie no particulars about how he was to get to her. ‘ In the chapel behind the altar is a picture,’ was all she had told him, still this was sufficient.

He entered the chapel, and behind the altar found a picture painted on wood ; no doubt it was a panel opening by a spring— but how to discover it. He sent Allan for hatchets, and in a quarter of an hour they had effected an entrance. Morgan, followed by the trembling Allan, forced his way into the narrow passage leading to the cell. Though blinded at first by the gloom, Morgan began his search, feeling with his hands over the damp walls, and calling Wildflower's name in piercing accents.

Soon a low moan was heard. He listened ; it was repeated. Allan trembled violently and fear alone prevented his running away.

Guided by the moans, and his sight becoming accustomed to the gloom, the knight soon found the door and bethought him of the key ; it fitted the lock and the door opened

By the wan light that entered the dungeon Morgan saw Nativa and Jennie lying side by side on the damp floor, to all appearance lifeless.

Stunned for a moment, he threw himself down by Jennie, and taking her in his arms, cried out in a voice broken by sobs,—

'My darling, don't you know me? I am your lover, Lewis. Oh, I am come too late!' he moaned in accents of despair, she is dead. 'Wildflower, if I could not save you, at least I will follow you. Let this last kiss be our betrothal. We shall meet in heaven.'

With one arm round Wildflower, he pressed her in anguish to his bosom and covered her pale face with kisses.

At this frantic embrace, a slight colour came back to Jennie's pale cheeks; it seemed as if the course of life already extinguished had been rekindled by love.

Allan had in the meantime raised up Nativa's head.

'Quite dead and cold,' he said, as he laid her down again.

'She breathes. she is coming to herself!' cried Morgan, almost mad with joy. 'Allan, we must take her into the air.'

Bearing his precious burden tenderly, Morgan cautiously returned into the chapel and left the convent.

'Oh, heavens, how pale you are, my beloved,' he said, laying her gently on the grass; 'you are in pain! what has happened?'

'It is my idea,' said Allan, doubling his fist into his eyes to keep back his tears, 'that the young lady has not had enough to eat—that she is dying of hunger and thirst.'

Allan's sensible answer made Morgan shudder; it explained the extraordinary change that had come over Wildflower.

'Hasten, Allan, get food and water! bring a litter! make haste.'

Allan was already gone. The youth, kneeling by Wildflower, raised her head and looked at her with unutterable tenderness.

Jennie half opened her eyes, and said in a low dreamy voice:

'My lord Lewis, you must not leave me again. I am too unhappy; and while you were away Nativa tortured me. She is very pretty, but she is not good. She would not make you happy; there is no one on earth who loves you as well as I do. Oh, my dearest, let us return to our forests, we will be so happy far, far away from all this misery and bloodshed. The dungeon was so dark, it was horrible! Nativa fell asleep, and I tried to waken her. It was so dreadful to be alone in that fearful place! but she would not wake. Happy Nativa, to sleep and not feel the pangs I do! Oh, I suffered so much.'

This delirium. which revealed to Morgan all Jennie must have suffered, wrung his heart with anguish. The moments seemed hours until Allan returned.

He brought with him two or three Brothers of the Coast, and having administered a cordial to Wildflower, which only partially revived her, they carried her more dead than living to Morgan's quarters in Carthagena.

For two days her life was despaired of, and she remained

almost unconscious of what was going on around her ; she was attended assiduously by one of the ship doctors, and Morgan seldom left her side.

On the third day she was so much better after a long refreshing sleep that the doctor considered the worst symptoms had left her, and, to Morgan's inexpressible delight, consciousness had returned—she knew him. Such joy may be imagined, but cannot be described ; language is too poor to express the feelings of the heart.

In a few days Jennie was well enough to sit up, and she then related all that had happened.

'Oh, my beloved Jennie,' he cried, in a tone of soft reproach, 'why did you not trust to me ? why not confide yourself to my love and honour ?'

'It was your life that was threatened, Lewis, and that not by Lawrence alone, but by the laws of the freebooters, which you had broken, and then a promise once given you know is sacred ; and how could I even expose you to Lawrence's revenge ?'

'You forget, my sweet girl,' answered Morgan, 'that Lawrence and I have fought before now and he bled, not I—but we will talk no more of such things. Lawrence will one day have to account to me for his infamous conduct.'

CHAPTER LXII.

FALLEN FROM HIS HIGH ESTATE !

Whilst our hero was watching over Jennie's recovery, great confusion reigned among the freebooters, who held possession of the town of Carthagena.

Decimated by the epidemic which increased daily in violence, discouraged by the inconceivable and inexplicable absence of Lawrence and thirty of the most influential of their party, the freebooters began to think of retiring.

Lawrence, before so popular, was now accused of treason, and had he returned he would have been in danger of his life.

Along with these disasters came the news brought by a buccaneer ship that a Spanish fleet of forty sail was bearing down towards the town to deliver it, after having daunted the English and French fleets, separated so foolishly.

To stay there longer was impossible. The freebooters assembled in tumult, and resolved to leave the place.

This resolution was no sooner taken than acted upon.

The embarkation was so hasty that they had hardly time to

get provisions on board, and the men were soon reduced to half-rations.

'Heaven grant that we reach St. Domingo in safety,' cried Morgan ; ' and never again, dear Wildflower, will I join the freebooters. Gold watered with tears and stained with blood is too dearly purchased.'

Scarcely had their small fleet left the roads when it was assailed by a dreadful tempest, which lasted three days. The crews, much lessened by illness, were no longer sufficient to work the vessels. Several were seriously injured. The negro ship off the *Cape* foundered, two others were dismasted.

While in this terrible plight the Spanish fleet hove in sight.

'Oh,' cried Morgan, 'if only my uncle were here, there would still be hope.'

In the meantime the chief of the freebooters was in greater danger than he had ever been in before.

Delayed by contrary winds and storms, the brigantine *Kite*, on which were Lawrence and his confederates, reached Hispaniola only after a twelve days' voyage.

At this moment the Frenchman and his thirty followers had safely penetrated without hindrance into the stronghold.

'Brothers of the Coast,' said Lawrence, 'we have not a moment to lose. Let our energy be equal to our circumstances. Morgan may have followed us. At any hour he may attack us at the head of a party of slaves. When once the treasures are on board the *Kite*, his anger need not trouble us. We shall have our hands free to fight him. Brothers of the Coast, you know my intentions. We shall fight for our independence. As long as Morgan had only in view the welfare of our society, we obeyed him blindly, but now that he wishes to use, for his own ambitious purposes, the resources which our toil and blood have gained, we should be base cowards if we gave way to his tyranny. The Southern Seas have not been explored. The Spanish side, which is bathed by the Pacific Ocean, is covered with flourishing towns rich in gold. The prospect that opens before us is immense. With our treasure which we shall seize at the stronghold, and the brave companions which we can easily recruit at the Antilles, Jamaica, and Cuba, we shall soon be at the head of a formidable fleet and army. Our society, threatened for a moment by the signal treason and culpable ambition of Morgan, will soon become more distinguished than ever. Brothers of the Coast, hurrah for gold and liberty ! To the treasury.'

Lawrence's accomplices answered this speech with shouts of applause, and waving the torches they all carried in their hands, they repeated, 'To the treasury.'

The place chosen by the initiated wherein to deposit the

funds of the society was situated nearly a mile from the entrance
of the grotto.   To reach it, it was necessary to traverse inextric-
able passages, narrow paths, and cross deep precipices.   It was
nearly an hour before the freebooters reached the treasury.   At
last a shout of delight announced their arrival.

'Friends,' cried Lawrence, 'you shall have the honour of
going first.   I will go last to inaugurate the perfect equality
which will henceforth reign among us.   Let the locks be broken
open.'

A thick iron door strongly fastened to the rock closed the
entrance of the passage leading to the vast excavation under
ground which contained the reserved funds of the society.

'It will take a long time to break the locks,' said one of the
men; 'let us have recourse to the mine.   A petard well directed
would do the business for us.'

'No,' cried Lawrence, 'the explosion might cause mischief!
Give me a hatchet.   Thanks.'   Lawrence raised his arm and
gave one blow on the lock.   To the surprise of all the door gave
way.

'This is a good augury,' cried the freebooter. 'To the booty,
friends, to the booty.'

The Brothers of the Coast, excited by that magic word, rushed
in.   Handsome Lawrence stood against the wall to let them pass,
with a sardonic smile playing round his thin lips.

'Now I have them,' he said, 'they are mine !   Fill yourselves
with gold, you stupid, ferocious beasts !   Roll yourselves to your
hearts' content over piles of onzes, moidores and piasters !   Make
good use of the last quarter of an hour's liberty that I allow you,
of that equality so sweet in your eyes that you think you will
ever enjoy !   You will soon know with whom you have to deal.
Those fools my equals indeed !   If Morgan had not been so loyal,
foolish and weak, I ought to say, not one of them would have
dared to have betrayed him !   But how silent they are !
Damnation, can Morgan have guessed ?   Can he have taken
precautions beforehand ? taken the treasure away ?'

Agitated by an evil presentiment, in his turn, he entered
the vast cavern known by the name of the Treasury Chamber.
The sight that met his gaze was enough even to confound such
a man.   Morgan, with his head proudly erect, and his arms
folded by his commanding presence, alone had stopped the
freebooters.

'Brothers of the Coast,' he said, 'many years of glory and
devotion alone could efface this moment of error and crime !
You are silent, you blush at your shameful treachery and hideous
ingratitude.   I see that you recognise the enormity of your fault
and that every feeling of loyalty is not dead within you.   Per-

haps if your repentance is sincere, I may forgive you. Bring me the traitor who has made you forget your oath! Let Lawrence be arrested!'

At the bold authoritative tone in which Morgan pronounced these words the freebooters hesitated, struck with terror at his sudden and most unexpected appearance. They were about to obey him when Lawrence called out,—

'Fall on your knees before your master! Perhaps he may forgive you. Oh, too happy slaves, cover his hands with tears, embrace his feet. Yes, an example is wanted. Death to the tyrant, death to Morgan!'

Setting them the example, sword in hand, Lawrence attacked Morgan.

His accomplices, rendered more ferocious still by the weakness they had just shown, imitated him, uttering fearful cries.

Then took place one of those scenes of violence which the pen could not describe, and the most clever brush could only feebly paint.

By a movement as rapid as thought, Morgan drew his broad cutlass and attacked the whole array. For two minutes there continued a horrible massacre. Most of the torches were thrown down and almost perfect darkness prevented the buccaneers from aiming their blows, and they neutralised each other's efforts.

From time to time a vibrating metallic voice resounded through the chamber; that voice was Morgan's.

'Cowards, robbers, murderers!' he said, and at each stroke of his cutlass a man fell.

This extraordinary combat could not last long; but a most commonplace accident took place brought it to an end. Morgan's cutlass snapped short off near the handle, and he fell forward over one of the dead. He was instantly seized and bound.

Not one of the freebooters dared strike their heroic enemy, whom an accident alone had conquered. The bandits, notwithstanding the excitement of the combat, were ashamed of their victory. The torches being relighted, they saw, almost with a feeling of admiration, that fifteen of them lay dead or wounded on the ground.

A solemn silence reigned in the chamber. Morgan was the first to speak.

'Ah, if my cutlass had not broken,' he cried in an angry tone, 'not one of you wretches would have survived your crime! A lion hunted to the death by a pack of hounds. It is Heaven's will! Come, make an end of it, I am tired of my life. Are you afraid to strike me? See, I am bound and cannot defend myself! you need not fear! what prevents you from murdering me?'

Lawrence advanced and placed himself between them.

'It is in vain,' he said, 'that you try to anger us to make us commit a crime. Nothing shall make us swerve from our duty. We are your judges ; listen to the accusation made against you, and defend yourself if you can, and dare.'

'I defend myself ? you my judges ?' repeated Morgan with an expression of sovereign contempt. 'Come, Lawrence, what do you take me for ? Cease this farce unworthy of us both. Do not blush at your triumph. Yes, I can conceive that, anxious to snatch my inheritance, you affect to respect in me the authority with which you will soon be invested. Hoping to succeed me you would not accustom your future subjects to murder their chiefs. It would in truth be a bad precedent, a deplorable example. But what astonishes me is that you should think me vile and stupid enough as to lend myself to your deception. My life every one knows. For twenty years I have made the Spaniards tremble, and increased the power and wealth of our society.'

In spite of his rare audacity and spirit, Lawrence perceived by the doubtful looks of many of his accomplices, that there would be considerable danger to himself in letting their leader speak longer ; therefore, he resolved to put an end to the scene.

'Morgan,' he said, 'if after your explanation we are convinced of your innocence, and give you your freedom, what will you do ?'

'This is probably a new snare you lay for me, Lawrence, and it would be easy to avoid it ; but fear not, I will not even now descend to falsehood. If you are too cowardly to complete your crime, and let me go free, I will use my interest with the true Brothers of the Coast to have you traitors all punished as you deserve. Therefore, you see, it is your interest to get rid of me.'

At this bold speech a murmur of applause arose from the freebooters.

Lawrence bit his lips with rage.

'Friends,' he cried, 'you take for greatness of mind what is in fact only spite. Morgan, exasperated at seeing the mask with which he had covered his ambition, torn from him, and in despair at falling again into the obscurity from which your favour had raised him, prefers death to dishonour. Must we then at the moment when we find ourselves possessed of immense riches, and a splendid future opens before us, sacrifice all to the disappointed ambition of one man ? Knowing that it would be impossible to explain his conduct and the sacrifice of the millions which he squandered at the European courts purely from personal motives, Morgan maintains a dignified silence ; so much the worse for him. We have offered him a trial. He refuses it. We will now proceed without it. In the name of the power with

which you temporarily invested me, and which I shall be happy
to resign when you need me no longer, I declare Morgan a traitor
to our society, and as such condemn him to death. Let him
expiate his own treachery and that of Sir Henry Morgan, who also
ran away with his brothers' hoard.'

At this iniquitous sentence the captive smiled, and said
calmly :

'But at least I shall not die unrevenged.'

These words were spoken with such thorough conviction that
all put their hands on their swords, under the impression that
the speaker was about to renew the struggle.

CHAPTER LXIII.

WHICH WAS THE GRANDER ?

THE old buccaneer smiled again, and said :

'Reassure yourselves, brave companions of Lawrence ! your
leathern straps are fastened strongly ; they enter my flesh. My
revenge is not what you think. I do not need my liberty to
accomplish it. It is only needful to remain silent and my
death will cost you those millions.'

These words produced a magic effect on the freebooters.

'What millions do you mean, captain ?' asked one of them.

'The treasure of which I alone know the existence, but which
my death will leave in the bowels of the earth.'

'Ten millions of which you have robbed the society,' cried
Lawrence. 'I swear by heaven and hell that in spite of you we
will have this gold. Listen, man, instead of being shot—if you
refuse to give up this gold that you have stolen, we will put you
to torture, and hang you like a criminal.'

'To hang me ! impossible !' cried Morgan with emotion.
'My friends, believe me as guilty as you please, yet I am still
the man who for twenty years led you on to victory.'

'Then speak,' cried one of the men, who now there was a
chance of getting millions, no longer felt any pity for their
ancient chief.

'If I am silent you will put your threat in execution ?'

'Rather !'

'I was wrong to speak,' said Morgan ; 'but now I must pay
the penalty. Brothers of the Coast, this is my last concession.
You know me well enough to mark that my resolution is stead

fast. If I do reveal where the ten millions are, it shall be to
Lawrence alone.   I have too great a contempt for you to enter
into explanations with you.   Retire.   Oh, you have nothing to
fear ; I am strongly tied.   And you, Lawrence, if you are afraid
of remaining alone with me, speak.'

‘ My friends,’ cried Lawrence, ‘ for the last time obey Morgan.
Leave us.’

Soon Lawrence and Morgan were left alone. The first looked
uneasy, while over the latter's face passed, for a moment, a smile
of triumph.

Morgan was the first to speak.

‘ Lawrence,’ he said, ‘ were a stranger to see us now, from
your trembling lips and troubled glance, he would take you for a
criminal before his judge, and not a conqueror in the presence of
his victim.’

‘ Since we are alone, Morgan,’ answered the other, ‘ of what
use is deception ? Yes, you are right.   I who have never known
remorse ; who have not hesitated to trample under my feet every
obstacle that stood in my way,—yes, I feel ill at ease at your
defeat.   May this homage rendered to your magnanimity soften
the agony of your last hour.   Had you been an ordinary enemy,
I would have fought you loyally on equal ground.   It was the
consciousness of my inferiority alone that induced me to have
recourse to deceit and treachery.   This avowal proves to you
how pitiless I am ; that you have nothing to expect from me.
Do not uselessly prolong your own sufferings.   Where are the
ten millions which are to save you from being hung ? ’

‘ Lawrence,’ answered Morgan, ‘ thanks for your confession.
I think the better of you for it, and it gives me hope that you
will replace me with honour, that the glory of our society will
not be lessened in your hands. Now you smile with pity. Every
man has his weaknesses. The power of these same freebooters,
who so cowardly murder me to-day, has been the dream of my
life, the end of my labours.   It is sweet to me to think that my
beloved task will not suffer after my death.’

‘ I am sorry to deprive you of your last illusion,’ interrupted
Lawrence, ‘ but you are sadly deceived in regard to me.   I only
see in our society a stepping-stone to my ambition ; nothing else.
The monstrous ingratitude that these fellows show towards you,
to whom they owe so much, is not likely to inspire me with
disinterested devotion to their cause. Rather, Morgan, rejoice
at the contempt I feel for them.   It ensures you revenge.   But
let us end this useless discussion. Where are the ten millions ? ’

‘ These ten millions are within reach of your hand.’

‘ Where ? speak quickly,’ cried Lawrence anxiously.

‘ Take away that pile of silver bricks that lie close to the side of the rock.   That is right ; now pass your arm into that narrow excavation. You hesitate ! Do you fear a trap ? No, pride supports you ! Press upon a knob of metal that you will feel on the polished rock. Right. A door opens and gives us entrance—oh ! a little patience ! that is not all. What, ten millions deserve the few precautions that I have taken ? Enter that passage. It leads to the room where the doubloons shine.'

Lawrence stood still.

'Morgan,' he said, 'your position is so hopeless, the means I was obliged to take to overcome you authorize any retaliation from you, so that I cannot be too prudent or circumspect. A presentiment warns me that you have vengeance in view. One must be a brute or a fool to think that such a man as you would meet death like a victim resigned to his fate. I don't care to venture first into this cave, which is concealed from all eyes with such art and care.'

At these words Morgan laughed scornfully.

'Yes, Lawrence, you are right,' he cried ; 'I longed for revenge, and, thank Heaven, I have my wish ! Call back your accomplices ; let them see their new chief pale and trembling before the old lion, muzzled and powerless. You would be dishonoured, and who knows if, repentant at sight of your cowardice, they might not acknowledge their crime, and ask my forgiveness. How happens it, Lawrence, that with the intoxication of greatness you, once so bold, should now have become a coward ? Well, I forgive it ; your baseness pleases me. Brothers of the Coast,' shouted Morgan, raising his voice, 'come back and reassure your trembling chief ! Oh, Lawrence, what a pitiful figure you cut now. Come, brothers, bring brandy, your chief is *fainting !*'

Lawrence rushed to Morgan and clapped his hand over his mouth. 'Be silent, and I will follow you, only show me the way.'

'Poor Lawrence, you are not recovered yet,' sneered the buccaneer ; 'your limbs tremble still, lean on me. How frightened you must have been.'

Lawrence put his hand on his dagger, but the thought of the ten millions stopped him ; to kill Morgan before he knew his secret—his companions would never have forgiven it.

He took a rapid glance at his enemy to see if he were still pinioned. 'Pass first,' he said harshly.

Morgan rose and staggered into the passage.

There was such complete darkness in the small way which the buccaneer chiefs now entered, that Lawrence, notwithstanding he held a lighted torch in his hand, was blinded for a moment with the intense gloom,

'In truth,' said Morgan, 'I am not sorry to die. I am getting old. That last fight nearly knocked me up. I shall rest here ; so, Lawrence, you will be still more at your ease.'

The speaker threw himself on the ground and rested his back against the rock.

'There, now it is done,' he said joyfully. 'Now, my valiant conqueror, we can talk comfortably.'

Lawrence thought he heard the sharp thrilling sound of a cord snapping violently, and Morgan cried out :

'One step, one movement, and you are a dead man !'

There was such an accent of truth in these words, that Lawrence shivered.

'Fool,' cried the old pirate, 'you had me in your power, yet let me live, and that not from any generosity on your part, but only from a love of gold. Now, Lawrence, the time is come to show yourself in your true colours. The ground on which we stand covers ten thousand pounds of powder. Put your torch towards me, and you will see that I hold a small wire ; it is fastened to a loaded pistol close to the powder ; the smallest movement, and you and I would meet our deaths in the upward swirl of a volcano.'

Lawrence remained for a moment confounded ; then uttered in a tolerably calm voice :

'Well, captain, it is a scheme worthy of you! I shall at least have the honour of dying by your side.'

'Don't affect a calmness you do not feel,' said Morgan. 'If you would be great, be natural. Own that you are afraid, yet do not ask for mercy.'

'Yes,' cried Lawrence, ' I do fear this obscure death which is inevitable, against which my energy and courage are of no avail. Ah, to fall as a soldier on the field of battle, or as a captain on the quarter-deck, that is glorious. But to lose one's life in a furnace, leaving not a vestige of humanity, it is dreadful. But you judged me right, Morgan, in thinking that I should never ask your mercy.'

Lawrence, in violent agitation, walked up and down the narrow passage.

Morgan studied his every movement.

'Well,' cried the Frenchman at last, folding his arms, ' I am waiting ! what prevents you executing your threat ?'

'Respect for myself,' answered the veteran buccaneer coldly. 'You, who pretend to despise the human race, are yet a slave to the world's applause, but I am not like you. With me, my own esteem is the first consideration ; that is the reason we are both still alive. I wish to accomplish calmly the sacrifice your treason has made necessary, and turn my thoughts towards my Creator.'

Lawrence was silent for a few minutes, then said :

'Yes, Morgan, I own that you are greater than I am ! I regret that I began strife between us. But regret is too late now, is it not ?'

'If only the least among our brothers were here, Lawrence, you would threaten and defy me,' answered Morgan, 'instead of speaking thus humbly. You French must have an audience to act well.'

'Captain,' said Lawrence, 'before you put your threat in execution, will you listen to me ?'

'Speak,' answered the other grimly.

'Though you have good reason to think ill of me, can you believe what I say now on my oath ?'

'Yes, Lawrence.'

'Then I swear that what I now tell you is truth. Until to-day I have never known fear. Deeply disgusted with the world, I have sought in battle to release myself from the load of existence. My name, not that of Lawrence, but one illustrious in history, might have procured me a glorious future. I renounced it voluntarily, and therefore you may judge how much I suffered to force such a resolve upon me. My heart had received one of those wounds which is never cured. At twenty-five I had lost all faith and hope. But to-day my heart revolts against death. Gratified ambition gives me the wish to live. If you knew who I am, Morgan, you would not wonder at what I am going to say.'

'Continue.'

'What I long for is to found a large and flourishing empire. You smile ? I know that was your idea also, and you are a simple gentleman.'

'Ah,' cried Morgan, 'why hope that two ambitions like ours should ever agree ? It is impossible that one or other of us, tempted by the opportunity, should not throw his rival over the gunnel.'

'Let me go on, sir ; the check which you have suffered shows how little freebooters are to be trusted, and must have somewhat altered your views. But, frankly, I consider that a good rather than an evil for one noble and bold as you in battle, but not yet fit for a king. Why not be what you have never ceased to be—a brave, noble-hearted gentleman ? You possess a large fortune of your own ; I will add to it any sum you like to name ! Why should you not return to your country, and enjoy the honours and dignities you so well deserve ? Will you agree to this arrangement ? I swear to you that rather than fail in my word I would die. For in case of any opposition from the brothers I swear to stand by you. This is my proposal. I await your answer.'

‘Lawrence, there is only one way in which you can save your life. You are mistaken in what you considered my aim. My dream was not a crown for myself, but glorious independence for the society, which might redound to the honour and glory of England. Now, if you will promise to second me in these views, but always to remain in a position subordinate to myself, I will forget all the past, and place perfect confidence in you ; but remember, I should exact from you implicit obedience, and you would have a right to renounce my authority when you renounced your country. Can you accept these conditions ? ’

‘No, let us both die,’ answered the Frenchman.

‘But what think you of my proposition ? ’

‘Don’t let us speak of it ! Excuse me, Morgan, for offering you wealth as my ransom. I now perceive that any compact between us is out of the question. The Americans themselves could not satisfy the twofold ambition.’

‘You pronounce the sentence of death on us both.’

‘ Yes, Morgan, our death warrant ! You can pray.’

‘Cannot you, Lawrence ? ’

‘I would wish to pray, but it is useless.’

‘ Unless you would die happier.’

They both remained for many minutes silent and thoughtful.

‘Are you ready, Lawrence ? I await your signal.’

‘Comrade,’ said Lawrence, ‘ a few moments only. I cannot help in this last hour expressing my admiration and esteem for you. Shall we die at once friends and rivals ? Will you shake hands with your old *companero ?* ’

Lawrence approached Morgan, but the latter exclaimed :

‘Lawrence, your foot is already in the grave, yet you meditate treachery.’

‘No, you do me wrong,’ said Lawrence meekly. ‘I swear that having let go your hand I would have returned at once to my place, but you have cause to suspect me. See, I will throw aside my arms.’

Lawrence was unbuckling his sword, when the other tottered towards him and held out his bound hands.

‘Lawrence,’ he said, ‘ I will take you at your word. Oh, why were we not born brothers ? we two could together have changed the face of the world.’

Lawrence took Morgan’s hands in both his and pressed them.

‘ Farewell, old partner ! the more I appreciate your noble character the more your death is necessary to me, for I should at length become your slave. Farewell ! ’

‘ May we meet again somewhere, Larry,’ cried the Englishman, ‘ and may God pardon us.’

He had again the fatal wire in his hand, when a great tumult

was heard.   The Brothers of the Coast, impatient at the delay in
taking possession of the millions, had returned.

‘Ha!’ cried Morgan, ‘why should we involve those poor
wretches in our fate? Go, Lawrence, and warn them of what
is about to happen, perhaps one day they will repent, and die
less unchristian than we.’

‘Thanks for this mark of your confidence, Morgan, I will
return quickly.’

Lawrence went out to meet his companions, who overwhelmed
him with questions. Had Morgan kept his word and given up
the money?

‘Morgan,’ answered the Frenchman, ‘holds all our lives in
his hand. We have shamefully misconstrued and suspected him!
his vengeance will be terrible ; not one of us if he chose it would
leave this cave alive. He sits on an immense powder magazine
—torch in hand.’

In a few words Lawrence explained how matters stood and
the freebooters, frightened and confounded, maintained a sullen
silence.

‘You need not tremble thus,’ said Lawrence, ‘Morgan himself
sent me to warn you.   Now leave us.’

They were about to depart quickly when one of the men said :

‘Who knows, friends, whether Lawrence himself is not trying
to deceive us, for him and Morgan to share the treasure between
them? for if this yarn be true old Morgan would never suffer
Lawrence to leave him.’

‘I promised on my honour to return.’

‘Then, Lawrence, as your case is desperate, listen to me.
Keep up a sharp discussion with the fellows here, and I will
quietly creep up to the captain and knock him over the head.’

‘Take care of yourself, Morgan!’ shouted Lawrence, who
instantly drew his cutlass. ‘Come, depart at once,’ added he.
‘I give you one half-hour to get safe away.’

‘Thanks, brother,’ cried Morgan, when he returned ; ‘by help
of an echo in these walls I heard every word that was spoken.
Thanks, brother, I did not doubt your loyalty. You have a
noble soul, which, once redeemed from evil, disdains to sully itself
again with crime.’

At this praise Lawrence reddened with pleasure. No victory
over the Spaniards had ever given him equal satisfaction.

‘Comrade,’ said he, ‘I feel my courage oozing away, my
agony begins! I might have spared this confession, for my
pride would still have sufficed me to hide my sufferings. But
why dissemble to the last? I have too long worn the cloak of
deceit. I will throw it from me. Our companions must be now
in safety. What prevents our launching into eternity?’

'Lawrence, I promised to await your signal. I am ready.'

Lawrence remained silent a few moments.

'Morgan, I little thought how poor and weak my nature was,' sighed Lawrence. 'Face to face with eternity, all our thoughts and feelings seem so mean. No one will ever know the mystery of our last moments! Who will inquire whether I died scorning death, or like a coward prostrate before the dread spectre? yet I can fancy these caverns peopled with an immense crowd watching how the redoubtable beau Lawrence met his doom. Even now I should like to die triumphantly! You pity me, do you not, old mate?'

'No, brother, I only grieve that your splendid talents, your love of glory, and the precious qualities of your mind should all have been tarnished by a misplaced pride. You have in you the makings of a great man——'

'And the great man would only have been a miserable adventurer under the same event. But will you grant me one last favour? pity my foible I had just now, and let me die triumphantly.'

'I can refuse you nothing, brother; what do you wish?'

'That you will let me fire the mine! it will soften my last moments to think that I die unconquered, and fall from my own will.'

'You shall have your wish, Lawrence.'

At this answer Lawrence stamped vexedly.

'Even to the last you remain my superior! Both our deaths are voluntary, but yours is calm, grand, and sublime, whilst I tremble and shudder. Morgan, once more farewell!'

Lawrence advanced towards his enemy, and threw his arms round him.

Their hearts beat in unison in that last embrace. No word was spoken.

Lawrence took the wire in his hand and looked towards Morgan.

Absorbed in thought, the latter seemed hardly to notice his movements; a quiet smile rested on his face, but suddenly his eyes flashed as at the approach of battle, and in a loud sonorous voice, he cried, 'Fire!'

Words must fail to describe the explosion that followed.

The pillars of rocks that supported the caverns were rent asunder; a shower of stones darkened the sky for a mile round.

The stronghold was a heap of ruins—chaos itself!

CHAPTER LXIV.

THE END.

WHEN this fearful event, which was attributed by most persons to an earthquake, took place, the squadron of the Brothers of the Coast, laden with the spoils of Carthagena, fell in with the formidable Spanish fleet, of which we have already spoken.

The glory of the freebooters was departed.

Two pirates alone, the *Graceful* and the *Tornado,* succeeded in escaping their terrible foe.

Morgan, who had been chosen captain to the first of these vessels, rather than fall into the power of the Spanish, braved the tempest with all sails standing.

On the twelfth day the *Graceful* sighted the south of the Island of St. Domingo.

A splendid sunset lit up the horizon. Morgan, seated on the quarterdeck with Wildflower, looked at the girl with an expression of unspeakable tenderness.

Though her eyes were on the ground, Jennie felt his long and passionate gaze ; her embarrassment and her blushes bespoke her emotion ; never had she felt so happy.

A man on the look-out cried out, ' A sail to windward !' and awoke the commander from his reverie. He took a glass and raked the horizon.

' Oh, thank Heaven,' he cried, ' I recognise the vessel. It is the *Kite ;* we shall have news of my uncle.'

Wildflower murmured apprehensively the name of Lawrence.

' Be not uneasy, my beloved,' said Morgan ; ' our happiness is the gift of Heaven ; nothing can disturb it. The crew know Lawrence's treachery, and is devoted to me. I shall hope to take signal vengeance of the traitor. In the meantime be easy, dearest ; you are guarded by my love and my word.'

' If you knew, Lewis, how I long for peace and quiet you would not speak thus. Always bloodshed and violence. Oh, it is dreadful. I implore you, let us make sail and get out of Lawrence's way.'

' Fly before Lawrence. Never !' cried the young gentleman fiercely. ' Forgive my disobedience, Wildflower,' he continued, pressing her hand. ' I would make any sacrifice to satisfy even your caprices, but to forbear from punishing him who dared to insult you is beyond my strength. Do not ask it, it is impossible.'

Two hours later, the *Graceful,* with all her sails set, and prepared for combat, sent a ball at the *Kite,* and made a signal for her to heave to.

The other obeyed, and a boat put off from her and came along-side the *Graceful*.

The astonishment of Morgan and his crew was very great at sight of the five men who came on board. Their pale faces and haggard eyes showed that they were under the influence of a great terror.

The first question that the young captain asked was in two words, ' Morgan ? Lawrence ? '

' Dead,' was the answer ; ' both of them.'

' Dead ! ' cried Morgan with deep emotion.

At this unexpected news an unearthly silence reigned on deck. All the freebooters understood instinctively that the fall of these two great captains was the ruin of the association. The Brothers of the Coast, whom Morgan's magnanimity had saved, related what had happened at the stronghold. They told of Lawrence's treachery and the heroic resistance of the great captain ; then of the dreadful catastrophe which had ended all.

Sir Lewis could not restrain his tears. Wildflower was as pale as death.

'Oh, Lewis,' she cried, shuddering, ' to think that if you had not stayed behind to save me, you would have shared Morgan's fate.'

Allan was the only one who felt but little regret for the pirate's death. The Penmarkian was extremely matter-of-fact.

' Well,' he said, ' my master will inherit all his money ! how rich we shall be now ! We have suffered enough for it. What a lot I shall eat and drink. I can hardly contain myself for joy at the thought, after we have been half starved on board. I shall ask master to give me a negro to wait on me.'

Allan was not mistaken ; Morgan, on opening the paper which his uncle had given him, found it was a will duly made, signed and witnessed, in which his kinsman bequeathed to him his magnificent mansion at the Cape, and a quarter of a million pounds placed in different European banks.

A few affectionate and touching lines which accompanied this splendid bequest proved that had the hero of the freebooters been willing to exchange his ambitious views for the enjoyments of a tranquil life, his heart could have appreciated them fully.

This proof of his uncle's affection increased Morgan's pain at his death, but Wildflower was by to console him.

An hour later the *Graceful* put into the French side of St. Domingo.

In vain Morgan proposed to the fifteen men on board the *Kite* to accompany him ; they refused.

' We will not set foot on shore,' they said, ' until we have taken our revenge out of the Spanish ! '

'Your day of glory and renown is past,' said Morgan to them; 'the world called you buccaneers and freebooters, but now it will despise you as pirates.'

This was true. With Morgan the Second freebooting died out. A few adventurers tried in vain from time to time to galvanise it; their efforts only ended in useless crimes, and the skimmers of the ocean were treated by all nations as pirates, persecuted unceasingly, and when caught hung without mercy at the yardarm.

It is scarcely fifty years since these pale imitators of the prowess of the ancient freebooters still infested the seas of the Antilles, to the great detriment of commerce. But since the invention of steam, those seas have been in safety. Still the name of Morgan has lost nothing of its prestige. Not a negro of the colony, or a sailor on board the coasting vessels who, on hearing that single name, does not begin wonderful, and often fabulous stories, of the heroes of the ocean; in lapse of time the two of the name being blended in one, Morgan has become a legend.

A few words will bring our tale to a close.

After a few days Sir Lewis reached the Cape. As soon as he landed, an aide-de-camp from the Governor invited him to proceed at once to Government House. He did so, accompanied by Wildflower.

Du Casse greeted him warmly.

'Sir Lewis Morgan,' he said, more seriously than usual, 'this paper Admiral Bloxam charged me to give you, and I beg to add that this act gives me sincere satisfaction.'

Scarcely had Morgan ran his eye over the paper presented him than he uttered an exclamation of delight.

'My patent as captain of a frigate!' he cried; 'it is too much happiness. God bless King William!'

A sigh from Wildflower caught his ear, and turning towards her he saw her face bathed in tears.

'Wildflower, my beloved, why this emotion? What mean these tears?' he cried tenderly. 'What prevents you sharing my delight. I am captain of a royal frigate! do you hear? My glory will be yours, a brilliant future is before us. But speak, answer me, Wildflower, what is the cause of your grief?'

'Oh, my darling Lewis,' cried Jennie, in a voice stifled by sobs, and holding down her head, 'I am jealous.'

'Jealous? What, you, Wildflower!'

'Alas, yes, jealous of your glory! oh, do not laugh at my ignorance. This time I know I am right. I feel the truth of what I say. The love of glory leads to ambition! remember your uncle! and ambition makes happiness so difficult.'

At this answer, spoken in a sweet supplicating tone, a shade of sadness passed over Morgan's face.

For a few minutes he remained thoughtful and uneasy ; then, as if he had taken a final resolution which had cost him an effort, he said, returning to Du Casse the royal commission :

'Will you have the kindness to ask your friend Bloxam to be the interpreter of my deep gratitude to the king, and say that I cannot accept the honour his Majesty would confer on me ?'

'Are you mad, Morgan ?' cried Du Casse. 'What, refuse the command of a frigate ! Consider !'

'My resolution, governor, agreeable to the wishes of the Lady Morgan, is final.'

'Oh, what did you say, my dearest ?' interrupted Wildflower with emotion ; 'you called me by your name. Oh, that is too much happiness.'

Wildflower, with a sudden impulse, checked at once by her modesty, turned to her hero as if she would have thrown herself into his arms.

She was so beautiful in her bashfulness and her delight that Morgan, forgetful of Du Casse's presence, clasped the dear girl to his heart. The hearty, though rough voice of the ex-buccaneer recalled Morgan to himself.

'Perhaps you are right, sir. Any way, you and your lady will be gladly welcomed as residents here before all, for you will remind me ever of my best and bravest partner ! Oh, what have we lost in losing old Morgan.'

Nearly a century ago, when the revolt of the negroes took place at St. Domingo, the memory of Lord and Lady Morgan was still so venerated and popular that it saved the lives of their great grandchildren.

THE END.

LONDON : J. & R. MAXWELL, 35, ST. BRIDE STREET, E.C.

Ri 230   5/86   W 66

www.ingramcontent.com/pod-product-compliance
Lightning Source LLC
Chambersburg PA
CBHW021543110726
47902CB00004B/997